T0064432

ON A **BAD** BOY NOTE

DON'T CURSE ME

May you live in interesting times...
A Chinese Curse

ON A BAD BOY NOTE
DON'T CURSE ME

Ansh Seth

PARTRIDGE

A Penguin Random House Company

Copyright © 2015 by Ansh Seth.

ISBN: Softcover   978-1-4828-4922-6
              eBook   978-1-4828-4921-9

All rights reserved. No part of this book may be used or reproduced by any means, graphic, electronic, or mechanical, including photocopying, recording, taping or by any information storage retrieval system without the written permission of the author except in the case of brief quotations embodied in critical articles and reviews.

Because of the dynamic nature of the Internet, any web addresses or links contained in this book may have changed since publication and may no longer be valid. The views expressed in this work are solely those of the author and do not necessarily reflect the views of the publisher, and the publisher hereby disclaims any responsibility for them.

Print information available on the last page.

To order additional copies of this book, contact
Partridge India
000 800 10062 62
orders.india@partridgepublishing.com

www.partridgepublishing.com/india

CONTENTS

Dedicated to all the loving parents who barely know what their progenies might turn into,
To a sister who is the purest source of affection on this entire planet,
To love lost and found in the walks of life...

For Boys; it might help you find the one within you.
And for the Pretty Ladies; it might help you find the 'Bad Boy', you once fell in love with...

For Psychadellica,
Still Waiting For You...

Some promises are made to be fulfilled....

The best way to taste the words is to hear them as you read!

A MILLION THANKS

A million stars twinkle,
Bright or dim... through the night,
Are they for real,
Or just a distant pleasant sight...
But here in the memory lanes of time,
I wandered again and found your rhymes,
Thanks a lot... As for you I wrote,
Some with my heart and few with a rose...

But what if...?
One day I wake up and find no memory lane,
Maybe a failure, or insufficient fame.
Then I got it,
When I realised the cost...!
Without you all in my life,
I will just be...,
So bloody lost...

The 'time' I had lived,
Is the only time I had...
As We survived together,
Through crazy laps...
Of life gone by,
Which might never return,
How hard you try...?
'Time' seldom turns...

A million thanks,
That in the walks of life,
We crossed each other's paths,
And remained in 'time' gone by...

Those who care,
Don't hesitate to dare!
And those who matter,
Expect no flatter...!

A million thanks to all of you,
Who care to read by,
And still a million thanks...,
To a few of you,
Who didn't even try.

My gratitude shall follow, for we crossed paths,
In the lanes of time, or through calendar charts...!
Cheer up my friends, for we shall meet again,
Either living through hell,
Or dead in holy Heavens...

On A Bad Boy Note,
For you I wrote,
The Million Stars,
Written in gratitude...
With all my heart,
"So much... Thank You!"

The way good things come to an end, so does this long night which lasted for 24 plus months. And as they say, "It is the darkest before dawn", I thus write here the most important pages of this book. From the inception to the outcome, it took a lot of hope, smiles and tears to get these words out on pages.

With my head low and respect to its epitome, I would like to thank the **God of Love: Lord Shiva, Mother Nature** and their children. Also to the suns, moons, planets and the stars of this endless Universe.

The Prime People

When I started penning my thoughts, the Universe sent a friend to fight along and that's why my deepest gratitude to *Aditi Katare* for unconditionally supporting my crazy endeavors. A million thanks for standing by my side through thick and thin, and most of all, for the encouragement for my dwindling belief system. Also, for reading the first draft of my manuscript, so many times... And protecting me from all the cosmic shit and black magic that could possibly happen.

God has different ways of blessing menial humans and thus blessed me with a brilliant younger sister. To *Akriti Seth;* my lucky charm... For the few words from your little intellect which made a lot of difference to this book, and to my life. A million thanks for enlightening me with the way you see the manuscript and the world. Also, for all the crazy tiny dreams we dreamt together – they gave me a lot of strength to get up again, whenever I had fallen.

Also, probably when I needed the last push to deliver the dream which I was impregnated with for such a long time, I bumped into *Rashi Mahindra.* Editing a book is way more difficult than writing, especially when you are dealing with a hundred thousand plus words; and you my friend never hesitated to read this manuscript one more time! I know, you might not acknowledge, but it was your belief as an editor that, "This book has all the potential to be a bestseller", really helped me finish. I am very glad to find a friend like you. Also a million thanks for feeding, encouraging, supporting and helping me fight my last battle.

"The reel and real often conflict in the journey of creative manifestations." A million thanks to *Geeta Sadanandan* for teaching me what I needed to know, how to survive in my job, from versioning to formatting to friendship. Heart felt gratitude for teaching me humility, for genuine advices and for being a great listener. Also, for always being cheerful, even through tough times.

If passion inspired people then *Amit Saraf* definitely inspired me. Heart felt respect for your sincerity, creativity and professionalism. A million thanks for designing the mind blowing *On A Bad Boy Note* cover page and promo templates. Sitting alongside with you and watching you work was truly inspiring. I thoroughly enjoyed the funny moments, rumors and obstructions we incurred while making the cover. Thank you for the 'Grunge'!

The next generation is designed to supersede the previous. And so did *Rishabh Sahai Verma,* when he exceeded expectations with his brilliant and supersonic response for the first creative promo. A million thanks for being a loyal friend.

Well, everybody has a boss, but God was kind enough to give me an elder brother in disguise. A million thanks to *Vijay Nair* for living up to the genuine advices, proverbs and stories which he narrates. Thank you for unconditionally supporting, guiding and protecting me. Also for the many lessons I learnt, out of which my favorite is, "Sometimes the one who pours shit on you doesn't have bad intentions. It's just to keep you warm or rather safe!"

A little encouragement can do wonders. A million thanks to *Sugato Basu* for giving me a chance in technology marketing. I thought I would end my career on this subject, but I guess... I begin here. In spite of being the super boss, your pleasant mood and humor kept me going. The continuous challenge which you provided, did help sharpen many minds at our workplace. Many thanks for all the motivation and encouragement with my career and this book.

A little alcohol and unconditional friendship is the trademark of *Vikas Pilania.* Your drunk inspiration and the habit of 'breaking limits' did keep me going. For the "Bad Boy" you are and the way you make such friends. A million thanks for always being super positive and a brilliant dreamer. To the *"Jai-Veeru"* bond which we always shared.

Some friends graduate from mere friends to blood brothers. Many thanks to *Vineet Singh* for staying with me through never ending conversations. For the belief you always had in my word and friendship. Also for the humor, advices and unconditional support. A million thanks for the awesome memories, and believing in me when seldom did.

If anyone who could give the biggest advice in the most humble way, it has to be *Ajay Mishra.* A million thanks for being my friend, brother and well-wisher through good and bad times. Thank you for your impeccable sense of humor and unmatchable goodwill, and being a partner in the umpteen mischiefs which together we did. Indeed a brother from another mother!

Prasad Satpute: For being a great old friend who survived the test of 'time'. A million thanks for also lending a hand in the social media promotions of this book.

Vibhor Mehta: For the hilarious rounds of editing and the super funny conversations. A million thanks for your patient and energetic company. Also for the 'Beardswag'.

Nilesh Rajput: For lending your 'Bad ass' face for the cover. A million thanks for holding on to my idea. May you fulfil all your dreams!

Amit Shah and folks at Algonation: For designing and creating an awesome website for *On A Bad Boy Note.* I am really impressed with your responsiveness and professionalism.

Vaibhav Pani & all the other artists: For the kick ass background score of the *On A Bad Boy Note* promo video. The ones who understand music are really blessed people.

Vaibhav Narula: For caring and protecting my family. Also, for your unique and brilliant entrepreneurial ideas.

Brijesh Singh: For the parties, alcohol and the 'ego trip'. A million thanks for being the elder brother I often needed.

Vajinder Singh: If this book does make it "Big", then remember you were one of the first few people to say it. And even if it doesn't, still a million thanks for the encouragement.

A million thanks to my "Godfather" of entrepreneurship, *Mr. Digvijay Singh:* The Baddest of all Boys. Many thanks for teaching me how to handle rejections, shedding off pride and maintaining consistent self-belief. Also, for the very interesting trainings and conversations, which I always hoped wouldn't end. It was because of you that I crossed many limitations in my own head. Thank you *Bhai...*

No man can make it "Big" by himself. And after thanking the prime people I really want to thank the silent supporters. A million thanks to *Anubhav Bhatia, Mandeep Sharma, Ganesh Kohinkar, Sheetal and Ashish Bacchal, and Rishiraj Mishra* for supporting me in your silent yet very profound ways.

A million thanks to the *'Bhatia'* Family; for giving me a 'home' away from home. *Mr. and Mrs. Bhatia (Sr.)* for the unconditional encouragement and moral support. *Bhavana Bhatia;* for being a friend and critique and for "The butterfly effect" (pun intended). Also, for standing by my side, unbiased and ever so supportive and cheerful.

Saket Agrawal, Aditya Bhalla, Umita Di, Sunil Bhavnani, Nitin Prakash, Riyaz Bhai, Neha Jain, Gagan, Karan Jain, Abhinay Bakshi, Nabin, Kavita, Parul Agarwal, Jitu Bhai, Doctor Mayank, Bhawna Singh, Akshay Sukhwal, Siddharth Shandelya, Rama Sanyal, Sandhya Dushyant, Bebo and each one of you... Friends in need are friends indeed. A million thanks for the continuous unbiased encouragement to follow my dream. After all, we are friends with a certain dream.

And thousand others with whom I learnt the 3 magical words: "Get up Again". My sharing: "It really works!"

The Banana-Graffiti Days

(You were the folks with whom I started... And this book started with you. Keep the artist alive in each one of you!)

Archit Tyagi – for the unconditional encouragement and loyal friendship. Also for your intense love for *Ghaziabad.* A million thanks for cooking at midnights. *Ajay Mishra* – for your experiments with music, mimicry or plain sound. A million thanks for being a partner in whatever I did. *Mallu (Ajay Padattil)* – for your kind heart and humble ways of enlightening minds. Also for your skills at the guitar, keyboards... even a piece of tin! You are one hell of a rockstar I met in my life. *Vini (Vineeth Perumandla)* for the abundance of food, wine and friendship. Also, for your rampant humour, rare anger and apologies. *Pupun (Pritam Pattnaik)* for being the croco dilo. *Simon Varghese* for your enthusiasm, loyalty and super encouraging friendship. *Tom Sahu (Om Sahu)* – for your super fun unconditional support. *Mohit Gohil* – for keeping company during boring work hours. Also, for your kind friendship and weird sense of humour.

Sandhu, Irderaj, Somi, Toby, Aditya Neeli, Shravani, Veena, Jimmy and Spotty for entertaining my stupors. For the times we cheered.

Jackson (Varun Parmar), Bhadda (Dheeraj Negi), Bhosale (Priyank Jain), Diggi, Appu and Rahul Bhatt – for the greenery we enjoyed during 'graffiti days'.

Abhinav Kaw and Arjun Chaddha for enduring my tiresome lectures and for the occasionally intellectual and always marvellous company.

Anshika Singh and Neha Arora – for the kind, caring friendship.

Rahul Agarwal (Taxi) – for the glorious friendship which we never shared at school. A million thanks for bringing life to every party, unending conversations and loyal friendship. Loads of success and happiness to you.

Alok Chaturvedi, KaranYadav and Amit Nayak – "Partners of Glory Days." For always providing a place to crash and comfortable hospitality served with a clean heart. For the brotherhood we share!

Captain Naresh Uniyal – for memories at and after school. A million thanks for always putting me ahead, whether in that extempore or when dining in the Officers' mess. A million thanks for your smiling presence.

Gurpreet Bali and Shobhit Bose – for the days we spent together running through the hills. (This was done intentionally!)

Mandeep Sharma, Amit Arora, Vikas Pilania, Roger Hawaibam and Maneesh Mangal: For the best graffiti of my life – *Live Fast, Die Young.*

Pritam Mohanty, Vivek Sharma, Komanna Bhavani, Swamy and the entire SAP team at Syntel for a highly creative, cheerful and peaceful work experience.

Nilesh Rajput, Tushar Ranjan, Ferror Alfred, Upasana Bhat, Snehal Bhonsale, Baljit Singh, Satish Tale, Bharat Vullanki, Sharada Doddi and Mahesh Khot for maintaining the vibrant humour at a drab of a workplace, and for your never ending encouragement.

Andy (Prabhat Dubey), Raavan (Shreyas), Vibsy (Vaibhav Gadkari), Faizal & Asim Ahmed, Sushil and Barun Agarwal for sharing their bad, BAD stories.

Nitin Nair for the tough times we endured, and the prize yet to be shared.

Jagdish Malvi, Mayuresh Pawar (Gondia), Pankaj Sonone for the good times we shared.

Adwit Sharma – I know, that you know, what I am thanking you for! Many thanks Bro.

Shreya and Priyank Talwar – for all your best wishes, guidance, hospitality and the endless rounds of dumb charades.

A million thanks to each one of you for all the crazy parties and awesome memories which you all have shared with me. A million thanks to each one of you for keeping the brotherhood alive.

For the Folks at Syntel

(Dreams come true if you believe in them... At times they really do!)
The entire Sales Enablement, Training
and Marketing Team at Syntel:

From football to alcohol to rain treks. This has been a very interesting year, which we spent together. From late nights, to the morning swipes - Starting from business strategy to highly informative conversations, skill sets, dreams, hobbies and passions. From long walks for a cup of tea to excursions around the lake and the dead church, and even the never ending humorous conversations. I have thoroughly enjoyed each and every moment I have spent with each one of you. Meanwhile, from a highly motivated work culture to the paranoia of layoffs; we have witnessed the demise of a company. At this point, I can confidently say that, together we are one of the best teams, and I feel glad that I have worked with you. Deep down, each one of you has inspired me, and I am glad that watching you all, I learnt a lot of lessons.

Francis Godad, Shoiab Patel, Akshay Joshi, Vaibhav Pingale, Yogesh Shette, Zafar Khan, Shruti Patkar, Vishaka Tikekar, Soccour Rodrigues, Apoorva Vajpayee, Prakhar Kamal, Prashant Pandey, Amit Saraf, Ankit Pai, Anish Sharma, Sanket Kaleshwarwar, Dhiren Gala, Sreemoyee Mukherjee, Aditya Sen, Prabhooti, Raghu Muralidharan, Sudarshan Rangarajan, Prince Wali, Preeti Anthal, Anubhav Pandey, Aman Dhingra, Varun Nair, Atish Sonkar and Mehershad Dilawarnijad for the pestering question, "When is your book releasing?" Also for lending your face for the many to come "BAD BAD STORIES" snippets.

Global Proposals Team: *Geeta Sadanandan, (Late) Ashish Kokaas, Amit Agrawal, Sharvari Bapat, Loylein Vaz, Russell Dalmeida, Aditya Kaul, Nitin Ekka, Mohd. Nizam, Amandeep Bajwa, Abhijeet Meshram, Samvedna Sibbal* and everybody else for creating a very trustworthy work environment and covering up for me. Also, for the endless parties and surviving threats from the near and dear ones.

Shonel Teke, for writing about *On A Bad Boy Note* in *Connect* which once upon a time, reached out to 25000 readers.

To all my ex bosses; you were right! I wasn't worth it.

Home

To boys and girls of Paradise Society: for keeping
the place where we live – a creative heaven.

Teachers

Benu Malik: Thanks for your blind faith, and everything that you did
for us... Beginning with language and all the fun. A million thanks, for
the strokes and spanks. Both were required with hooligans like us. A
million thanks for being my mother and a half.

To *Suman Saxena, Meghna McFarland, (Late) R.D. Sharma* for enriching
and explaining the purpose of language. Also, for the beautiful memories
of an innocent childhood.

And to all my teachers because at the end, each one of you gave the same
advice; the advice of following "One's own heart."

To boys of Vincent Hill and girls of Shangri-La:
*(The Batch of I.C.S.E – 2002) Guess this is the factory
where "BAD" Boys and Girls are manufactured.*

To Mumbai University and its various colleges:
*For the brilliant memories it leaves with all
the students who pass from here.*

To the students and alumni of National Insurance Academy:
*To my batchmates, seniors and juniors and for
the splendid freedom we all enjoyed.*

Family

With blessings of My (Late) Grandparents – *Dadaji, Nanaji and Naniji.*

Rani Poddar: A million thanks for nurturing me, and never changing the
memories of our beautiful childhood.

Mira Poddar: A million thanks for always guiding the elder generation to keep an open mind towards self-induced intellectual growth.

Sanjeev Kumar, Saket and Sumit Gautam: A million thanks for being the ever supportive uncles. Also, for never inducing ill envious vibes in our crazy friendship.

My grandmother: A million thanks to *Dadiji* for always praying for my good heath, happiness and prosperity.

To my aunts, uncles, and all my cousins... **Well, this is not the right book for you to read.**

To my Source

In the memory of *Chenghis:* I just stayed with you for a week and you etched yourself in my heart. A million thanks for teaching me that love has no language, and sometimes it doesn't even require words. A mere silent response is enough.

To *Zuko:* Whenever I am in deep ambitious thoughts which surpass all need for human contact, a silent lick from you, brings me back to my humble reality. A million thanks for being the tether for an ambitious animal like me... You keep me human without a single word, buddy!

Most of All, *My parents: Maa and Pa*, for food and money... And also for the unconditional love, faith and support. I know how much ever I thank you, it would never be enough. Some debts in life can never be repaid, and in a very similar way, I am indebted to all the love with which you have raised me. I am nothing without you.

Million thanks *Maa,* for the hope that this endeavor would sort out things for us. Thank you for staying up late at nights waiting for me, and for the best food I can ever get in this world. Most of all, for always encouraging me and for understanding my moods and arranging for finances, whenever required. I really, very honestly, love you.

Million thanks *Papa,* for the unshakable belief in your prodigal son, and for teaching me the lessons of integrity, 'never giving up', self-dependency and hard work. Thank you for always bestowing positivity on us and building up our self-belief – that we are made for bigger and better things. I really wish I could live up to the standards with which you live each day, and someday... I could be the man you are. Also, on a lighter note, special thanks for all the whisky. Keep it coming please!

**To all Women: Life without you on this planet,
or otherwise, would be very boring!**

To all my friends and adversaries... "You complete my life!"

For the *friends:* As long as I am alive you will stay in my memories, but I hope your names stay forever in this scripture. For my *adversaries,* many thanks for building up the pressure to help me finish this book. Sadly though, you are not even worth my vengeance.

Gratitude to the Readers

(My lessons from the experience of writing this book)

After persistently dwelling in this manuscript for almost 2 years, I want to share a few lessons which I learnt during this apparently stagnant, yet endless journey.

1. Control like 'time', is an ever persistent illusion. When I started writing this book, I felt like I will complete it in three months. Those three months have repeated themselves over and over till I lost count. And every time I failed, it enraged me and left me with a lot of unsettling emotions. But 'time' worked its therapy and magically healed all my anger and frustrations. Thus all the unsettling emotions finally found peace when I accepted that dreams take their own time to manifest. One can just track the efforts they put in the direction of the dream.
2. Whether negative or positive, anything takes considerable effort to be built. There were many moments when I felt short of skills required for a seemingly simple activity like writing. But

when my brains gave up, it was just the heart which helped me sustain. Thus, reasons will always outweigh skill sets. Whereas about skills – they take their own time to develop, but if you continue practicing it will be just a tiny moment of this vast 'time', where you will know that you have learnt what you so badly wanted to learn.

3. Last, but never the least, rejections are the first sign of growth. It's a pretty strange observation, but any organic growth begins with rejections and failures. And perhaps that's what keeps us humble and learning. It helps us become what we need to become to bring home what we desire. The most stable structures present in this vast universe have faced a lot of rejections and challenges to make them what they really are. So the next time you face a rejection over something which you really want, consider it as a good omen!

A million thanks to all my friends, acquaintances and the strangers whom I met on the many journeys of life. I really cherished the smiles we all exchanged at the idea of this crazy book. Sincere gratitude for bestowing your hopes on me, because though they burdened my shoulders, but many times, if not for me I continued for you all. Because deep down, I always knew that I am being carried on your shoulders.

This is the happiest moment for me as the author of this book, because what happens ahead in this bad, BAD story is not in my control. Who reads this book, who doesn't, whether it becomes a best seller or not, what influence will it have on the world... none of it is in my control. But even about uncertainties, they have a very special purpose. Uncertainties keep life interesting.

Thus, on a very humble, relieved note - I am just glad that I finished what I started.

Statutory Warning:

"The dimension of 'time' is limited. Make hay before it runs out."

SOUNDTRACK

Like a Stone - Audioslave
Careless Whispers - George Michael
BC Sutta - Zeest
When Love And Hate Collide - Def Lepard
Lady - Modjo
No Woman No Cry - Bob Marley
Maria Maria - Carlos Santana
Vienna - Billy Joel
Turn the Page - Metallica
Goodbye my Lover - James Blunt

PROLOGUE

Time is a mysterious component. It's very difficult to understand or explain, or even quantify this strange dimension. The only truth about 'time' is that at one certain moment, it would end in its being; at least for me to witness it. Wise people call it 'death'. Ironically a strange truth about 'time' is that; it will still last even if everybody is dead. In my life, I never believed that one day my 'time' would be over. Until today, when she told me, that the 'time' I had, is actually over.

Perhaps it's human to believe only what they could see. "To each his own", and even that's how 'time' is to each one of us. I still thoroughly believe that there is sufficient 'time' for me to win her. Even at this hour I still have her, as she is not yet gone. But the biggest mystery which I feel in this dimension of 'time'; is that the agony and bliss of my life, seems like it happened just a moment ago.

It's a cloudy late afternoon and the fast highway looks relatively empty. I am pressing the gas pedal to its fullest and my brand new SUV responds appropriately as she takes off, making me feel every bit of her momentum. It feels strange to cry for a boy, or rather a grown up man which I am now. I open the windows of my speeding car to feel the harsh wind on my face. Perhaps it could prevent me from crying. Sadly even the cool evening wind couldn't dry the hot saline water drops pouring out of my eyes. Thankfully, my weary eyes were covered in my newly purchased bluish shades. A few more drops rolled down my cheeks and I felt choked in my glottis. "I so badly want to speak to her", I uttered in despair... Perhaps the after effects of the morning and "The last conversation" which I had with her aren't allowing me to pick up the phone. I don't know whether to acknowledge this as ego or self-respect but indeed, a sad devastated state of loneliness was soaring in my being. "I so want to talk to her", I mumble amidst tears clearing my choking throat.

In a moment of impulse I pull my visibly gigantic ride to the edge of the highway and bring it to a screeching halt. I desperately pull out a cigarette from my pocket, light it and suck the smoke out with a vicious ferocity. But neither the smoke, nor my ferocity could stop my tears. Much like my life, I was again standing at the edge of some road, perhaps again paved with an uncomfortable loneliness. But here on this highway of life, I had the view of a serene landscape to comfort my eyes, but my soul won't give away the anguish.

I walk out of the car, towards the edge of the road and look down the cliff at the serene landscapes of *Lonavala*[1]. The relatively small hills dried up by the persistent sun longed for the rains. They silently empathized with me as I longed for her. An impulse to call her was slowly taking over my senses, rushing through my nerves. My nostrils flare as I blow out a grunted breath. I realize that something about my desperation is not making me conscious today and I shamelessly scroll through my phonebook to click her number and make that call. My entire body feels the urge to cry to her and tell her how helpless I am feeling. But when I was about to do that, her reasons for leaving got louder in my ears... Till a moment arrived when they began to scream, "You didn't fulfill your promise." And I sob to her howls as they began to overshadow the soothing murmurs of the hilly wind.

"I can't call her", I said out loud as I swallowed the unfamiliar yet surging anguish. At times, 'urges' are the rush which can drive desire to insanity. My 'urge' to speak to her still pressed hard on me and my fingers trembled scrolling through my phone and instead of clicking my favorite number I clicked on the voice memos. I left an exhilarated breath of air, relieved on saving my self-respect. "Anyways, recording a voice note is quite similar to having a conversation with her", I murmur to console myself. Because in both cases my words were often reflected back after hitting 'silence' at her end. "You never wrote the book you promised!" her words howled again, in my ears, and a surging regret made my breath heavier. In the only hope of finding peace, I speak the words to my phone, foolishly wishing that she might hear my story on the other end....

---

[1]   *A hill station between Mumbai and Pune.*

ON A BAD BOY NOTE

"She left me, wanting me to grow; beyond my own limitations. But I realized that, I only wanted to grow up to her. Grow worthy of the beautiful essence, which I received from her all the while - in times of distress, or in times of sheer bliss, in times of confusion or in times of confidence and victory.

All the while, when she was here... right here with me, in my arms or hanging on to my shoulders. Smiling to whatever she heard and saw...

And now she is gone with a vow that perhaps she would never see me again...!

I wait to break free, to just fly and grow.
But to grow only with you, to watch the world together and... trust me it's amazing.
So watch it with your eyes,
And then watch it with mine.

To show you how beautiful it looks from your eyes, and even if you never accept to believe in your vision, well, you just have to look within. That's where I looked and guess what; I found you...

I am in awe of the view, of how things look between my eyes and yours, but the madness of the endless is too enchanting to leave.

But you go my love, it's dangerous and I shall travel it alone.
To love you is to not to change you.
And I am here as change.
It's just that I wanted to stop this 'time',
For you,
To be with you,
To choose the path of companionship and live and relive all that we saw. But I am glad that you made me aware of my own nature, my own self...

Who am I to judge what you are, when I could never understand what I am...

Very few well-wishers pray to show you your real nature and your path. I am sorry, but I felt you saw the beyond with me...

On a bad boy note...
It's beyond, and we stand to see the eternity. At least, that's what my God taught me. Just faith within yourself and nothing else can change your destiny. I was just waiting to meet it. I still feel, my destiny is commanded by my heart and my heart alone. Look around, there are a million hearts, do they collide???

On a bad boy note...
So confused...
What to choose
And what to leave.
A million paths
And my heart deceives...
Its own master...

Smitten by beauty,
And eaten by loath...
On a bad boy note...

It was my pride
Or just my guilt,
Good on fire,
And bad in the quilt...
And to my down
My head did tilt,
On a 'Whatever'...

So break my heart,
And get it even...
It's cool, girl!

I am man enough to take it,
Not cool enough to fake it,
But crazy for you
Enough to rake it...
I am coming just in 'time' to make it...

Or maybe not...

The last step is left with you..."

TRASH AND TREASURE

I reach my friend Arpan's place in a posh locality in *Pune*[2]. People around the building are staring at me as I walk out of the car which had stopped after a screeching halt. My flushed face and redder eyes definitely matched the profile of a rash driver. I looked straight at the small bunch of people but nobody dared to approach me. I briskly paced towards the lift and walked into a yellow cabinet adorned by a big mirror. I was startled to look at myself. I always believed that hanging a mirror in a lift is a very good idea. It had definitely helped me 'never get bored' as I always found company in the mirror. Perhaps it helped others too, at least good enough to keep their minds off the claustrophobia. But here I am, staring right back at me. A second look at myself could generally be re-assuring, but the more I look at the man in this mirror tonight, the more annoyed I feel... It was infuriating as all I could see was the face of a 'loser' and it was all over the mirror, howling in flames and screaming back at me... and slowly hisses to remind me of my loss. "How could I lose at something I was so good at?" I kept wondering and my red eyes bashed against their alter selves in the cursed mirror.

I turn my back to the mirror and waited to get off from the claustrophobia which was surprisingly because of myself. It's a disturbed feeling to be suffocated of one's very own self. In no time Arpan opened the door, the look of sympathy or empathy was already on his face. The news had spread. Romit came inside from the terrace and passed me a lit up joint. I rushed to take it, considering the possibility that this magic stick would decrease my pain, show me some hope or at least some way to make it to her. Or perhaps a way to whatever I wanted to gain, but could never reach. Very soon I was 'high' but not even an inch away

---

2   *Freckled with little hills, and blessed with a very pleasant weather – The Sister City of Mumbai.*

from her memories; our last conversation and how she broke my heart. The atmosphere around is still filled with love and friendship. While the couples cuddled, the singles enjoyed their personal space; even if they didn't – they pretended well. I try to seek the least attention as I don't want to display my state to others. Only close friends are allowed to see my weak and my vulnerable. The core of a person is supposed to be shared with the few you trust; who won't abuse it. I quickly rush to grab a beer to welcome my desired isolation from the people partying in Arpan's house. I pulled a green bottle out of the refrigerator; surprisingly it's her favorite brand *'Tuborg*[3]*'.*

"Gosh, her memories!" I mumble to myself and a drop of tear oozes out of my eyes with every sip; reminding me of the best times spend together. It's getting more annoying to be a sad soul amidst happy people. On a usual break up I would have never been bothered and quickly looked around for newer and fresher opportunities; but today nothing fascinates me. It feels like I had everything and I have lost everything. A delightful aroma of the freshly prepared dinner filled the ambience but it too doesn't fascinate me. Food was still important as something in my heart tells me that the battle to 'win her' is still not over. I quickly ate my dinner and left Arpan's place, as I wanted some solace to handle myself.

It was a strange and a totally new side of mine which I was witnessing. I had never seen myself like this before. I speed back to my house and rushed into my apartment, and entered my room. I keep swallowing my 'urge' to speak to her considering that now there was no point.

The strange feeling of despair which had met me in the morning, is still behaving like a stranger and it kept soaring up to new heights inside me, telling me that, "All that I ever wanted is gone... That I might still have all the name, fame and glory which the world has to offer but no one to share it with!" I always wanted to share it with her. Her smile haunted my eyes, the way she fought with me and the way we dreamt together were still circling in my thoughts. I have never cried for a girl in the recent past but I guess I am back at that door. Slowly hot drops

---

[3]   *Her favourite beer!*

of saline water start trickling down my eyes. I reach out for my laptop, open it and surf through my mails. It seems some 18 odd females have expressed interest in marrying me for my profile on the matrimonial websites, which I had just created to formally indicate my interest to marry her. "What an irony?" I chuckled amidst tears. The 'irony' which again happened, as ironically it was the first time in my life I really wanted to get married. I began laughing hysterically at the world which wants to indulge me in the vows of companionship but the only one who I wanted to marry is not there anymore. All the faces of my ex-girlfriends started circling in my head like a photo collage, especially filled up with those glimpses where they were in tears and had asked me to stay but I left for a more adventurous future.

But the only question which intrigued me for quite some time still remains unanswered. "Whatever that happens to us in our lives, is it our destiny or is it our 'karma' returning our deeds?"

I guess, 'karma' is indeed a bitch, that it follows you, and takes the count of every action and deed which you ever did and pays you back appropriately. I felt I had improved, let go of everybody and prayed for their happiness. And the fucking 'irony' now, is that I have to pray for the happiness of the one I wanted to keep happy. To watch her go away with her smiley presence and light someone else's house and life, leaving mine behind in the void of her memories.

I look at the wall and I see the old crayon painting which I had made long back when I began to date her. The painting was of a biker boy who looked smart with his long hair and ugly with his protruding teeth. He sat on his jazzy big bike and held his big heart in the center of the painting, giving it to a girl who looked down with a frown. It was very difficult to figure out whether she was shy or just not interested. Her heart had a puzzle which neither had an entry, nor an exit. On top of the painting, the text repeated itself, "Please Break It!"

A flush of surprise and anger simultaneously ran through my body. I violently rushed to take the painting off the wall and I scraped the adhesive tape. "Please break it, fuck!" I howled at myself as the words reminded me of how badly I wanted my redemption. How badly I wanted to punish myself for breaking the dreams and hearts of all those girls. At least now I should be happy that it happened. But with my redemption, I lost my dream of finding 'love' again. Or maybe, it's the loss in which I have found 'love' again.

Furiously, I took the paper painting to my balcony and I took out my lighter. The lighter, which was gifted to me by a cigarette shop owner and an old friend. Someone who always asked me about my marriage. And today was the day when I had asked him to pray for mine, as I have found the one I want to be with and I am so glad that even she wants to get married to me. The lighter bore the King of Spades. Looking at the black heart on the lighter I felt like destroying the curse which I carried with me all the while. I held the painting and set it on fire. It did catch fire but then it stopped burning, telling me as if the jinx is too strong to break. I lit up the painting again and then it finally burned. Few fire sparks rushed out of it with a crackling noise. It appeared as if a magic seal guarded the painting. Finally, I witnessed my wish for my heart to break, burn to ashes. The flames rushed towards the bloody tear coming out of the biker's eye and then, towards his frowning confused lover. At last I see the three words burn "PLZ BRK IT." I feel better as if I just turned around my destiny, as if now I am redeemed and that I will make it to her.

It was an easy option to let go of my dreams and be at peace. The thought of indulgence as the best way of moving on, occurred in my head. I thought of all the girls who want to party with me, have an affair or just have fun. For a moment I thought of going to them, and just be there... Just let all the pleasures of the world help me forget her presence and her existence. But then a following thought occurred which asked, "What next then?" I too wondered what next, anyways I have seen how indulgence will lead to attraction and then the dreaded phase will reoccur where I will be replacing every face I meet with hers and trying hard to live the dream in replacements. Well, I had given this advice to a few people and now, I don't want to live my own preaching. What a shame? But that's because I can see doom and an uncrossable void where I would live in her thoughts and her dreams, till my pain is numb... while I would have again broken a lot more hearts in my search for the perfect one.

She was perfect indeed, in her every aspect and especially the way she complimented me. I was a fool not to see what I have or maybe I had... I guess I just didn't have the faith and courage to take it. Just waited for her to confess her 'love' for me, and when she confessed, it was too late. And that too she did just before she left. I realized I can't go back to the way I was. Quitting my dream won't find me peace, especially when I think of her last lines. I gathered myself and asked all the Universe for a direction. Well the Universe did show me that too.

I went back to my room in my 'high' state. Maybe crying helped me lighten up and I started running through my old notes and journals. I was going through the inboxes of old phones and notebooks in which I wrote about us and more about me. The entire story of this 'fire' began to come alive and I saw myself again, with her and those pretty faces which perhaps left with tears, leaving behind wet eyes of mine.

The 'trash' which I was storing in my data space and on my bookshelves suddenly became the only 'treasure' which I had. Perhaps her only memories and the memories of everybody else. Things which I was planning to get rid of, and now suddenly those are the things which bring back her memories. But it also brings back the memories of my deeds and the vicious yet obvious cycle of 'karma'. It was a strange day, when the things I was most sure of – crashed, and my 'trash' became my 'treasure'.

Suddenly I realized the thing which I had promised her, perhaps the only thing which she was holding onto me to do and then she could settle down with me... It was the story which she wanted me to write. With tears in my eyes and a rather heavy heart I open my laptop and start typing. All that stuck creativity perhaps needed a trauma to unblock. I smile at the way she had requested me to write, and I see that dream of being the classiest writer and calling her on the stage when I receive my biggest award. I see her draped in a white dress with a smile which could even light up the brightest stars. I see her walk up to me to the stage where I hold her hand, kiss her and walk down with both my awards.

Daydreaming hasn't helped many people. And even though, it apparently is my favorite hobby, I can't dwell in the thoughts of a brilliant future when my immediate present is in crisis. I drag my sluggish self to the washroom. Red eyes stared back at me from the mirror and I splashed some water on my weary face. "Oh, okay I am back! I can't afford to be lost now. It's because of this fucking habit of day dreaming, I have ended up wasting so much time. I had promised her the world and all I could do was to waste my chances, in unreal thoughts and fantasies!" I breathed to my sad baked self in the mirror.

I know where I stand... At least I am thankful for whatever I have now. My story looks amazing! People came and people left. I just didn't understand one thing about life and now that I understand the only thing about life, is that – it's cyclic.

I had all the time to win her but lacked the courage to break my heart again. And I continue to wonder that whatever is happening with me, is it my destiny or just an outcome of 'karma'?

It's like "Why do people whom you want the most leave you at your lowest?"

Well it happens to everybody. I sit here in my room with her photographs pasted on the wall. I don't know what law or what secret of the universe would bring her back. I just chose happiness and... she chose her happiness. Sometimes in life, what you might think you are happy about, might not be the same for the person you are with. I have broken so many hearts, anyways it had to happen to me.

It's just that I was waiting for it to come to me. Why did I wait for it to happen? I should have just left it. Was I too guilty? Perhaps yes or perhaps no. When I look at everybody, I see each has their own intention. I don't need to feel sorry for myself. Its ok, it happened and thank God it happened!

The worst of lives, happiness of times. But perhaps it's the best of my life. At this point too, I still see new shades, new things, something else happening... but when I look at her snap I feel as if I left something there, something which was mine, not with me anymore. It rests there. I feel incomplete, but it's ok, it's a part of life... isn't it?

People talk about all practicality and professionalism and everything like that signifying the control of emotions. Emotions are such erratic things inside a human. You can't control them. It's like the waves of the ocean, which flows, moves and dances, and you cannot control them. If you can then perhaps you never felt them!

Call it a spin of time, but all of the most useless memories which I had termed as 'trash' has suddenly turned into the most precious moments which I always treasured.

I still don't know if she never loved me or it's my 'karma' returning my deeds. To figure out this mystery, I just have my gone life to look into.

This journal contains the memories which I began penning down more than a year ago. The only component then and even now, is that I feel, it all happened just yesterday....

CHAPTER 1
THE WARRANTY OF LOVE

The thoughts of Saturday evening are still very fresh in my head as I struggle restlessly to continue sitting at my desk. Glimpses of that darkened room and those two entwined bodies are still engulfing my nerves, and I can feel the goose bumps. The dim light on the air conditioner switchboard was turning the dark room into a candescence of a mild blue haze. I looked into her eyes for a brief while, but got easily distracted by her other assets. Soon I was down caressing her breasts and I realized that they are a little different in shape. One was bigger and fuller and the other one was comparatively smaller. The age old chauvinistic education of my country struck a violent chord in my head and I started massaging her breasts vigorously, with a charitable thought that I might help her equalize both. To my surprise she exhaled a breath of joy, and she said my name. I don't know what rushed into me when I heard my name being so passionately said by my last object of love, or perhaps my actual 'love'. But I was a little too skeptical to think about 'love' at that moment; I was more concerned about 'lust'. Somehow in my experiences of understanding, 'lust' has a very direct correlation with 'love'. I started nibbling on her breasts and violently sucking it, as if the last drop of life and peace would actually come out of her nipples and finally pacify me into tranquility. But I guess I was too restless and I swooped down to her inner, darker secrets. Something about her hidden treasure was very sexy. It was clean, with very minute hair. The very fact that she did it for me before she came to meet me turned me on even more. I touched her smoothness and couldn't resist giving it a lick. The moment my tongue touched it she shrieked out in excitement. I was going wild by then, with my fingers inside her, exploring her deeper secrets while my tongue danced on her clitoris. She started moaning my name, I was so proud. I remember I had read

1

somewhere that a woman is like a musical instrument, one is supposed to tune it properly. Maybe after all this 'time' I have become a master in tuning. Soon all I could hear was just my name, being called out louder and louder. I guess I never felt so proud of my name.

"Uday..... Udaaay.... Udaaay.... Don't stop.... Right there, right there..... Just there.... I am cuming, don't stop..... Your fingers got some magic.... Oh my God..." she screamed.

And she finally came down to peace. Watching her cum got me so 'turned on' that I was ready for action. She asked me to come up to her and she held me tightly, I tried to kiss her and she returned a mild insensitive kiss. I realized that her interim peace is making my 'little warrior' relax and go down. I got back again on top of her and she gently went down stroking my 'little warrior'. It's nice when you get a blowjob. Nothing makes the 'little warrior' as happy as a blowjob. I pushed her head a little more on it, till she gagged. A few more strokes and she laid down next to me. She said, "I am tired." So I turned onto her for my action session, where she closed her legs and said in a very cold tone, "No sex." I was getting furious, and thus I asked, "What about my orgasm?" To which she paused and sighed, "Just shag yourself." God; it was pathetic; the whole idea of working so hard to give someone an orgasm and then not getting your own is very frustrating. Unfortunately I realized that if I don't cum, I will become a possible social menace, so I started jerking off to my satisfied lady. It's just that there were no visual 'turn on memories' of the girl lying next to me, and her lack of interest in my gratification also turned me off. So I closed my eyes and I started revisiting old memories of those massive sexual escapades, about the time when I had a fall, and the glimpses of the naked bodies came back.

I was at peace in a while, while I saw Tanya almost dressed in the 'darkness' of the room. Putting the hook of her black bra she said "I have to reach home early, my parents are waiting." I also started getting dressed up hurriedly as I realized that my parents would be home any minute. We both left for my car and I drove her down to her place. On the way I lit up a cigarette, and was smoking peacefully to which Tanya got a little agitated. "You can't quit smoking right?" she demanded. I didn't pay much heed because though my semen left my body but the thoughts didn't. I silently ignored her with an excuse like, "Its temporary!" Tanya was anxiously waiting to reach home as her mother had called around five times and she had some relatives coming over. Moreover I drove fast because of the unsettling feeling inside me really wanted me to be alone. Soon I reached her apartment, and at a strategic point on the road which is not visible from her balcony, I stopped the car. She gave a very hurried peck on my lips as if she's sticking to the protocol, and rushed out slamming the door behind. I got further infuriated with her discourtesy. I lit another cigarette and started driving back home. The thoughts of the naked bodies was still running wild in my head, taking me back to those days and moments when life was much lighter with very few priorities. 'Making love' was one of them.

The next morning happened to be a Monday and I was driving down to my office from *Mumbai* to *Pune* while it rained on the express highway. I was in a big hurry to reach my office as my new boss had assigned the development of marketing flyers for our warranty management services. It was a new project and I was very particular to not to spoil my impression, which I almost always ended up doing. The thoughts of Saturday night still continued in my head. I was still struggling with the fact that Tanya doesn't give 'shit' about me. I had never been this type of a man. Maybe my male ego is hurt. "Chuck it", I said to myself, and soared up the volume of my car stereo. It was Chris Cornell of *Audioslave*[4] singing for me "Like a stone...."

And the song went on as I sang along, "I am waiting for you here... like a stone, I am still waiting for you here... all alone!" I realized that perhaps even I am waiting for her here just exactly like a stone. Waiting that she would come and move my heart and everything that has stopped since she left. How she made me feel, and how much I longed for that feeling. That single feeling of being so alive and so excited, of those moments which got me so 'turned on' that I could do anything just to take off her clothes. I remembered how her face turned every time I touched her. All the glimpses of those young college days were coming back and re-running in my head and in front of my eyes. Somehow it made me feel

---

[4]   *Hard Rock meets Alternative Rock with heart wrenching lyrics and mad videos.*

that perhaps I am not over her or perhaps no one can make better 'love' to me than her.

Soon I reached my office and was parking my car. So consumed in my own thoughts, I barely noticed people around. Moreover IT companies are full of so many people that noticing also doesn't help much. I ignored everybody and walked straight to my floor and was seated in my cubicle. I quickly switched on my computer system and checked out my inbox. My boss's mail was already waiting for me with its teeth clenched. I had to prepare the flyer and submit it on that Monday morning and I had not even started. I realized if I failed to produce the assigned document and the so called deliverable in the next two hours, then my old boss is going to rant off on my head like an irritating aunty, and especially with my disturbed love life running in my head I would have to bang my head on the computer screen.

So I collected myself and started working on the assignment. Very soon I realized that it was all Greek & Latin for me. Nevertheless I started researching on Warranties being used in the automotive industry. With a holistic understanding and copy pasting a lot of web articles I completed the task just two hours late from the time of delivery and mailed it. To my good stars my boss didn't realize it and nothing happened. That day I learnt something new called Warranties.

Now warranty is a promise given by a manufacturer that if a certain product malfunctions, then the producer shall repair or replace it. I wonder if an arrangement like this was possible in relationships. What if 'love stories' had a warranty; that if any party malfunctions in the relationship, it has to repair the relationship or even better, replace themselves with someone better. Imagine the peace with which most people would fall in 'love' and form relationships, knowing that even if things don't work out amongst them they still won't be left alone. If they are lucky they might even replace their spouses with someone who is better in looks, success... or in bed. What if people got greedy with such an arrangement, and abused it to derive a regular change to keep them happy? What if they are too scared to ask for a replacement, wondering if they end up missing the old defective piece? Well, perhaps it's difficult to give warranties on things which don't have any guarantees. Or perhaps the warranty might bring some peace in a world full of insecurities.

I look around my workstation. The woman sitting next to me is silently cribbing over the phone and trying to sound as low as possible. She is having a tough time in her relationship with her husband due to her mother in law. "I told you Vikram, I have no problems with your Mom, and it is she who doesn't like me", she said in a hushed voice but loud enough to travel to her coworker through her clenched teeth. "So you blame me for all the troubles your Mom is facing? Am I the cause of her health problems?" she mumbled angrily. "Why can't you see she doesn't like me being independent, she can't take you listening to me?" she said in anguish. She turned her head & saw me looking at her to which it became an embarrassing moment for both of us. Tears were held up on her eyelashes and I didn't want to see them fall. Especially when anything close to crying might jolt up my own emotional state and I start remembering those who cried because of me.

The hunky fresher on my office floor looks a little agitated today. He was popular for his vocals, his skills on the guitar strings and had a very pretty girlfriend on the same floor. I got up and left to have a cup of tea as that is the best thing to do, especially when I am not giving my sweet coworker her required privacy to fight with her husband because of her controlling mother-in-law. The hunky fresher joined me for tea on the way and we walked outside the office campus. He blankly kept staring at the hills around and silently sipped his tea. "What happened to you?" I asked him, when I couldn't resist questioning the lifeless creature who was once a breath of fresh air. He stared at me silently as if he was studying my eyes. Maybe he wanted to check whether I was actually concerned for him or not, or I am just another passerby who wants to gossip about his state.

After a long pause he said, "My girlfriend is getting married in three months." "How? I mean, why? You guys are dating, right?" I tried hard to empathize. "Her parents forced her to settle down with some *IIT*[5] guy",

---

5   *Indian Institute of Technology (According to the Indian mass folklore, IIT is a popular educational institute, where students generally stumble upon a huge salary job).*

he mumbled with his throat heavy. I remembered seeing his girl the same morning, but she looked fine! "What is the problem with marrying you?" I asked him considering that is what he wants. "I am not settled enough, I mean she says that she loves me and all, but her father thinks I am just a fresher with a nominal salary and I am not capable enough to take care of her", his voice turned pretty low. "Hey, don't worry about the girl's father, they have to be like that. Never mind, fuck her father, at least you have the girl", I said sounding casual and cool. "But she won't be here with me for long!" and now two thick drops of tears slithered through the corner of his eyes. Watching this talented sentimental fellow cry enraged me a little and I said, "Stop fucking crying! You are too good to cry for a girl. Listen, the only way to have her is either you go out and get an *IIT* degree and switch to a higher salaried job. But that you know can't happen in three months. So chuck bullshit and focus on the girl. Give her such a good romantic time, that no moronic *IITian*[6] can replace the way she feels with you."

The hunky fresher had a smile on his face and 'fire' in his eyes. "Thanks Uday, let me see who takes her away from me!" he said as his face flushed red. He shook hands with me and left, back for his cubicle. I felt good watching him walk back like a man, and I feared a little bit of consequences like obsessive compulsive behavior which generally happens when lovers resist a break up with someone they want. Nevertheless, I felt that her father was correct, in a salary of mere 25000 rupees, how is he going to buy his girlfriend her favorite designer *Vero Moda's*[7] stuff and then sponsor a lavish dinner and then last the month? I couldn't understand which side I was on, am I siding with her dad over my friend or am I asking my friend to fight till the end? I liked him because I saw a side of me in him as I was in college. I feel as if I am turning old into an uncle full of cynical beliefs, but I guess one of the few things that I had earned was 'fighting till the end'. I am glad I taught him the same lesson of how to survive a chance in this world full of insecurities.

---

[6]   *Alumni of the Indian Institute of Technology.*

[7]   *A very popular International Designer.*

I thought about the warranty assignment again, and I felt that perhaps if the hunky fresher had a warranty on his relationship with his girlfriend then maybe he wouldn't have been so upset today. My coworker would have shown the warranty contract to her husband and her mother-in-law and wouldn't have been so agitated. But I guess that is not possible, warranties do not exist in relationships. In a vague sense, I feel that perhaps it's the insecurities which make relationships beautiful and unpredictable. Except for the first time in 'love', the patterns of relationships become predictable.

"Except for the first time", I said to myself. "What if I had a warranty then; for my relationship? Perhaps it wouldn't have pushed me to break it. Or probably what if she had used it?" I chuckled to myself. "Or maybe we would have torn the agreement apart and dumped it in the dustbin", I sighed. Attraction couldn't be contained or governed by a piece of paper then; it was everywhere around… in our bodies, in our souls and in our eyes. At least the warranty did not exist in my relationship, especially when I was the one who malfunctioned.

All this 'time' has helped me move on, and if not move on, then at least helped me keep away from the pain. Although the human mind is very sharp and it brings the 'lost days' back, even when I try not to think about them. Her thoughts often take me back to those days when I met her and also serve as the temple of diminishing memories. Hovering in the glimpses of those days, I often return to how I was.

I could see myself 10 kilograms lighter and leaner, with a very sharp, boyish jaw line, jumping out of local trains in my favorite blue t-shirt and walking the last kilometer to my college daily. And on one of those days in a classroom full of new students of microbiology, a lame joke out of my mouth got me something, which I didn't know then is going to stay in my memories for the rest of my life.

It was the onset of my Graduation, where I was in a new classroom full of 55 odd students of various types with a majority of girls. I remember being very excited those days for the new lot of opportunities. The two years before graduation had been more or less a waste where I was moronically wasting my time over a mean *Gujarati*[8] chick who chose a guy a million times sadder than what I was or probably could ever have been. Perhaps the only way he got a chance with her was because of his big *4x4 Tata Safari*[9]. The 'time' I had seen them making out in his car around the big basketball court near our college had actually made me realize that she was not 'worth it'. And that I am too fragile... fucking much more hopeless than school kids. In fact the kids back at my boarding school were much braver than me. I often wondered, how many of them would have lost their virginities since the last two years after school had ended.

"Am I the last left virgin of my school batch?" the thought often disturbed me. I realized I had to do something about it, before it became a disgrace which will be very difficult to carry. I always held on to the decision which I had taken back in school about making things much better in college.

"Losing one's virginity" could possibly rank as the top most insecurity during adolescence for boys. Perhaps it's the loss of virginity which trumpets the onset of manhood. "What about those, who lose it in their late twenties or probably when they get married?" I often wondered about a dreadful fate like that. The pessimistic self which I had nurtured over my past years of mediocrity and failures, kept pricking back this question, "What if you are one amongst them?"

Nevertheless, I was keen to make some progress and thus in the first week of my Graduation, I was there in my new classroom with new classmates who did not have a clue about my single past and failures with chicks. With all the brimming enthusiasm to give myself a brand new chance I hoped to get at least a little closer to loving someone of the opposite gender. It began in that classroom of microbiology, where a very 'hot teacher' was teaching the basic principles of the microscope.

The male mind is highly trained in evaluating chicks, always checking out the jungle available to him to go bond and find a mate. Simultaneously

---

[8]   *Gujarat is a state in India full of smart, vegetarian, pretty females.*
[9]   *Tata Safari is a popular SUV in India.*

it also assesses the competition which he is going to face from his other male counterparts. It's highly conceivable that the feeling of insecurity which a boy's virginity could create is at times quite capable of writing his destiny. I had soon realized that I was a timid animal in this jungle, although with real time brawling experience from my boarding school. But unfortunately, kids out here in big cities use mobile phones to fight.

"Motherfucker wait here for 15 minutes! I will show you who I am. Let my friends come over. They will beat the shit out of you, so much so that your parents also won't recognize who you are!" I wished to scream this on the face of any kid I didn't like in college. Unfortunately, I didn't have anybody to call to come fight for me and I couldn't afford to get my timid simple parents into any mess, as they were already upset with my low *12th grades*[10]. The other fact that I couldn't make it to *M.B.B.S.*[11] added up to the ever consistent experience of being a failure. All in all, I couldn't nurture my ever existent and very persistent 'shit' to cause more trouble.

So there I was, checking out the chicks in my classroom, and somehow I could find something fascinating to do with each of their bodies.

Someone had good hair,
Someone had good skin,
Someone had a good face,
And some had other things,
Beautifully placed...

Some were hopeless with their looks,
And with them my chances didn't cook,
So their assets didn't matter,
But remember my dear ladies;
Your charms can always flatter...

---

[10]   *High School.*

[11]   *Bachelor of Medicine & Bachelor of Surgery.*

Yet some had ok faces,
But curvatures too good to ignore,
With the leaching diffidence of getting laid,
My curious eyes went sore...

As that's the gift of my past failures,
For I am checking all of you out to the core,
It has made me pretty reasonable,
And negotiable with everything in store...

Beggars can't have everything,
And to the circumstances they swear,
Our selves are often wounded by an unconfident sting,
Thus, I was ok with more or less anything...

Call it a wretched me,
Or just an insecure self,
But do look around once girls;
I am just like anyone else...

The lecture on microbiology was going on as the gorgeous teacher explained the compound microscope. "The most important thing required to view anything under the microscope is light. Without light you can't see anything under the microscope", she instructed and the students nodded. "Now tell me students, where does light come from?" the pretty teacher asked a question. Being good and obedient had never got me anything exciting. The only pat it got me was a 'good impression' in front of teachers and elders which could never get me laid. In my observation, the most outrageous kids in my school and college were the only primitives familiar with the treasure called girlfriends.

I instantly sprung up with an answer, "From the window!" The timing was impressive beating the geeks with the regular answer called "The Sun." To this remark the entire class started laughing. "Who was that?" asked the pretty teacher with her face blushed. I stood up proudly for my new found insolence ready for a probable punishment. I then began to see the faces of my target audience turn back. My excited roving eyes spotted the babe of the class looking at me with a smile. Her name was Poonam, perhaps one of the most common names in *India.* She had beautiful fair skin contrasting with her jet black shiny hair. Her lovely brown eyes focused on me while mine observed her big distorted nose which resembled a *pakoda*[12]. I felt then that I had my moment with her. Poonam's girlie 'cheerleaders' too gave me a look of approval; and so did their male counterparts.

And amongst these many faces I saw her smiling. With a gleam in her eyes and a very excited childlike laughter, I felt as if she really enjoyed my juvenile humor. I wondered if I was so funny but still, I almost felt a strange admiration coming from her. She looked 'weird' to my eyes, when I compared her to the other chicks in the class. She wore a denim jacket and had long plated hair, nothing like those of the other girls who dressed up just regular. My observation of the weird chick in the class was interrupted by the laughter of the pretty teacher. "Yes, light comes from the windows. Even from the doors. And also through that little hole in that wall behind you", the teacher pointed out sarcastically. The teacher's pink cheeks and her charming smile were potent enough for me to forget the rest of the females in the classroom. Such amazing incidents seldom happened with me.

The next day I was roaming around in the college as my usual thing hoping to make some friends who would connect with a loner like me and I reached the Zoology Lab. The lab still had the memory of my dear *Gujarati Chick* as we used to flirt a lot in there while we dissected frogs and rats. A little sadness crept inside me reminding me of those touches while we studied anatomy and identified the various organs of cut smelly animals. Sad for my infidel crush, I turned around just to find the same weirdo standing in the corridors. And in the next instance she smiled a big grin. She was tall, as tall as me, maybe a little more because of her shoes. She still wore a fitting rugged denim jacket and worn out jeans. The girls in college usually dressed up in t-shirts with cheeky slogans or frilled tops. It was different the way she was dressed, especially with the sharp end of her plated hair. Her eyes conveyed a familiarity which was significantly different from the insecurities omnipresent in every

---

[12]   *For those who don't know, it's an Indian vegetarian starter and is kind of shapeless.*

eye. I guess I was no different as I honestly got confused with her look of acknowledgement. I looked behind wondering if she was smiling at someone else. And when I looked around to confirm, it was me! My usual inferiority complex took over making me question myself, "Why would a girl actually smile at me?"

I ignored her and nervously walked away, still wondering if I should have smiled back. I hurried into a lecture hoping to bag a chance to introduce myself to Poonam. The lecture ended an hour later and Poonam was rushing out of the classroom with her girlfriends. I struggled to look at her through the hoard of leaving students when someone tapped me from behind. And when I turned, it was her again.

"Oh my holy God, a chick is actually chasing me!" an inner voice echoed, quickly wiping out Poonam and her big distorted nose out of my system.

"How can I help you?" I asked her very politely. She smiled, "I need your notes; I had missed the previous lecture on this subject." She spoke in an urban accent which I had rarely heard in my college. Her confident approach did make me realize my timidness and I hesitantly asked her, "Are you new in college?" "Yes, I am new here", she beamed. "Let me open the notes of the previous lecture", I said flipping through the pages of my notebook which I most certainly knew that I might not have.

I was really miserable with staying attentive in class and it was no surprise that throughout my life my notes had never been complete. I looked at her in dismay and with a heavier doubt I flipped through the pages of my notebook, knowing that it would fail me again.

"After such difficulties, prayers and struggle, today a chick has actually chased me down for, ok, notes and I guess I don't have them", I thought regretting the fact that I usually slept in lectures. I continued flipping the pages of my shabby notebook and my pace slowed down. The feeling of dismay sank deeper with every turning page. She stood patiently looking at my notebook and at times at me. To my great surprise I discovered the notes of the previous lecture. I looked back at her with a sudden surge of confidence and said, "Yes, here it is; now you may copy it here, because I would require it at home to prepare for the coming class tests."

The moment I said that, I felt like the biggest nerd born on this planet, who instead of giving his notes away like a stud, has actually asked her to copy it there because... accept it; he is a nerd, and he believes that his studies can accomplish great pathetic grades. If my school's best friend, Bose had seen me do this he would have given me a head lock. Even she gave me a bewildered look, but said, "Okay, I will do that." We sat down together for her to complete her notes. It then suddenly clicked me that I haven't asked her, her name. "By the way, Hi, I am Uday", I said extending my hand for a hand shake. She shook my hand and smiled, "I know." "Oh she knows! Didn't know that a joke could get me so popular", I wondered. "What's your name?" I asked her. "Hi, I am Anita, and I really like the t-shirt you are wearing", she grinned looking at the logo of my t-shirt. That was the first time in my life, something that my parents had shopped for me made me so proud. The twinkle eyed broad grin on her face, for a lousy t-shirt made me ask, "Thank you, but what did you like about it?" "The basketball", she said and her smile curved, and I could see dimples, which perhaps I didn't notice earlier. What an 'irony' it was? The dumbest thing on that t-shirt was actually the basketball. Kids in the college wore t-shirts which had these powerful slogans and I had a big basketball on mine. When I had asked my parents why this basketball, they had answered in unison, "It's cute!" I still couldn't believe her so I asked again, "What about the basketball?" to which she surprisingly said "It's cute", leaving me smitten to the beaming admiration of her eyes.

We sat together for an hour as she copied the notes, while I ate an apple as we chatted. "So Uday, didn't you try for Medicine? I mean, all students who pursue life sciences are more or less Medicine drop outs", she asked. I remembered my hopeless score and answered, "Yeah you are right. Even I did." "Where all did you try?" she continued as she copied the notes. "Everywhere. I appeared for *National PMT*[13] and *AFMC*[14]. What about you?" I replied half-heartedly avoiding the discussion.

---

[13]   *Pre Medical Test.*

[14]   *Armed Forces Medical College.*

"Even I applied everywhere. I had got admission for engineering but since it wasn't *IIT*, I didn't wanna go", she replied confidently. "Wow, you were all ambitious for these big institutes. How much did you score in 12th for getting admission in our college?" I asked intimidated by her confidence. "85%", she replied. An instant 'shame' knocked on me repeating my 12th grade results which were less by 20% compared to hers.

"How much did you score in the entrance examinations?" she asked. "I can't remember my *PMT* scores, but I scored 97 in *AFMC*", I said dubiously. "97 what? The marks or rank", she asked. "Rank", I lied. "What! You scored a 97 rank in *AFMC*. Why are you wasting your life in this college?" she asked bewildered at my superior proof of intelligence. I giggled and said, "No actually it's the marks. I scored no rank." Anita gave me a look of disbelief but she did make me feel better as she was the first person in my life who could believe that I could score a good result. My guilty giggle induced itself into her and she laughed along with me. Soon, we exchanged numbers & left for the day. While I walked back to the local railway station, I felt a little different about myself. Perhaps it was the simple click of being liked, like someone's biggest insecurity of being accepted just turns out be a simple mental block. I returned home standing in the local train, thinking about the day. The fast wind on my humid face blew along the glimpses of her eyelashes which were running in my mind, cooling me off, of every little resentment of unacceptance. I looked down at the basketball on my aqua blue t-shirt, and perhaps it was cute. The cuteness of the day was slowly withering off the little grudges of rejections which unknowingly I carried throughout my life.

The next few days we demonstrated the good behavior of social acquaintance which was slowly getting tainted with lingering gazes. From classrooms to laboratory, every time I looked around for Anita, I mostly found her looking at me. It began to feel like a creepy telepathy being developed between her and me. Her eyes fueled an unsaid enthusiasm in me which resulted in a lot of participation in the lectures. Every time I made a point, the next answer would generally come from her. The communication of teachers became friendlier. It was surprisingly new to me, to be adored by teachers, who were young and enthusiastic. The fellow students became friendly discussing the wonders of biology. The mega magnanimous system which resided in the very microscopically minute cell did draw everybody to awe. Everybody discussed biology, like putting together small pieces of a big puzzle called life.

Like life exists in various forms, from huge whales to infinitesimally small cells and atoms. The only common thing in all the life forms was growth and destruction. The cells grew and killed each other too, till a very strange observation about nature began to reflect. The entire nature wants to grow and kill itself at the same time. Even I did want to grow. But I hardly knew then, that I too have the tendencies to kill my own self.

Everybody more or less spoke to me except for Poonam. She did occasionally give a mute "Hi" but her lack of craving to have a conversation with me kept me intrigued. She was indeed gorgeous if that's the word one can use for a fair maiden. Her fair skin contrasted with her shiny black hair helping her stand out of the common genetic pool. Poonam was a trophy for a girlfriend, to date, to have, perhaps to even settle down, as in the ideal *Bollywood*[15] way of life. She always looked lost, at least with her eyes, rarely giving answers but very particular about every piece of her notes. And for her distorted nose, I could accommodate as long as she stays with me. Every other boy in class secretly hoped to have a chance with her, as they kept peeking glances on her when she didn't notice.

Till one day, Anita caught me giving Poonam one such glance in the laboratory. I felt a gentle nudge on my back and she asked me, "Who are you checking out Uday?" I was surprised for being caught in my moment of lost fantasies. It also remotely felt like I lost my chances with Anita. I wanted to tell her that honestly I was hitting on all the decent chicks and the list also included her. But I still said, "Well I like Poonam." To which she smiled and said, "Yeah, everybody likes her." The mischief

---

[15] *Perhaps a colonial cousin of Hollywood. The Indian Film Industry is called Bollywood. But it just doesn't end there – we have Tollywood, Kollywood and a lot of "Wood" prevalent in the second largest population of the world!*

in her eyes gave a girlie hoot but before she could complete it I said, "I even like Gurdeep and Rasika." Anita gave me a bewildered look and said, "You like all three of them!" I nodded emphasizing my choices. "But why would you like Gurdeep? She is so dumb!" Anita made a pitiful face. I considered what she thought and perhaps I didn't know the distinct meaning of "Being dumb!" Probably it could be that even I was pretty dumb, if that were to be the meaning of "Being dumb."

I retorted immediately, "It's like an order of preference, if I don't get Poonam, then I will go for Gurdeep and if not Gurdeep then I will go for Rasika." Anita looked at me for a few seconds giving me that look again which suddenly broke into a fit of laughter. I smiled back playfully. "Okay tell me one thing. I understand why you like Poonam. But Gurdeep is like these *Punjabi*[16] bimbos. You should rather date Rasika, at least she is cute!" she strongly suggested. "I liked Gurdeep just because she is fair. I mean, I don't know her as such. But yeah, Rasika is cute", I smiled, embarrassed. The practicals got over and Anita and I walked downstairs discussing my dating prospects. "Just in case Uday, if you don't get any of the three, what would you do then?" she asked jovially. I thought for a while and replied, "Then you be my girlfriend." "Very smart huh!" she laughed sarcastically. "That is, if you don't get a boyfriend" I humbly added. "In that case, fine. Actually, that's a good idea Uday", she grinned. "You see, I am so smart, I have already made a backup plan", I said making a canny face. We both laughed.

We both walked down together to the corridors and I bumped into my dearest *Gujarati Chick*. I was surprised to find her and she gave me her usual miser smile. "I am leaving college and going to *Canada*. You see, my Dad had started a business in *Canada* and now we are all shifting there", she said after a couple of pleasantries. "So when is your last day?" I asked her, shocked at the news of her departure. "Today is my last day", she said looking at Anita standing by my side. My face went low, thinking about the two years I wasted on this chick where a friend of mine (who was apparently good with females) had told me very clearly, "Uday, do not waste time getting stuck on a single chick. Either you

---

[16]   *Punjab: I don't really need to talk about this state of India. Just google it or ask any Indian, Australian, Brit, Canadian, American etc. etc.*

get laid or you don't, but in two years you can date at least eight girls, provided you change girlfriends every three months. Even considering your skills, a bare minimum of two girlfriends is the least you should have. This 'love' funda is all girlie bullshit, and it is not in college you waste time on it." The regret of wasting two years for nothing on this female came a little harsh on me.

From *Dadar*[17] to *Canada*[18] was indeed a long journey. In another few minutes she was ready to leave and said, "Goodbye Uday, it was nice knowing you. Keep in touch on *Orkut*[19]." She stepped ahead and gave me a light hug to which I reacted emotionally and grabbed her tightly. I exhaled a heavy breath on her neck and gave a light peck on it. Holding her I realized that all the passing students were looking at us. Somehow I felt good about this fact and kept embracing her, perhaps in vengeance for my wasted time. Soon I realized she was rubbing my chest and whispered, "I will miss you Uday, let me go now."

Anita walked back with me to her railway station and I realized that the place from where she took her train was on my way. I kept talking about my *Gujarati Chick* to Anita. "I had a crush on her for past two years and she also liked me but then she went with another very hopeless guy. I so wanted to set her ass on fire", I mumbled softly to her, revealing my embarrassment and 'shame'. "You should have told me, I would have had helped you make her jealous. That's what friends do right?" she replied instantly. It felt different to not to be judged for the little loser present in me. "I guess I had given her an over emotional hug", I pointed out with a silly smile. "Yeah right! It wasn't a hug Uday. You grabbed her as if you gonna take her home", smirked Anita. We parted on a jolly note where she turned to her station while I kept walking towards mine. Life in *Mumbai* is complicated, where three different train lines run through the large city which is spotted with multiple stations.

Walking back to our respective railway stations soon became a habit for the month. Either Anita or I would wait for each other to leave college.

---

[17]   *Very busy suburb of Mumbai.*

[18]   *Great White North.*

[19]   *Predecessor of Facebook: R.I.P.*

At times, other kids joined us on our stipulated way. The social air was soon buzzing with rumors about Anita and me. Our classmates usually huddled up in conversations and silenced when we passed by. It was awkward to notice the beginning of change in the social behavior of peers. Perhaps it was a filter to remove all the petty brained kids. When I hung out with the guys, a couple of them collectively jeered at Anita. I never retorted as I did not have anything for her as we were friends like anyone else. But it was pretty amusing to watch guys bitch about someone, whom they didn't even have a chance to date. I honestly was never sure of my chances to date her too.

But the implications of our growing friendship did reduce my personal prospective dating list. Poonam had become very distant and sad as her 'first love' were teachers and books. She always hovered around the first bench of the classroom. Moreover a long list of guys were already cued up in her list of fans. Gurdeep had become a close friend of Poonam along with a few other girls, who huddled and cuddled together. Rasika was still single in spite of guys who hovered around her trying to have a conversation. Only Ratish was the socially amicable chap amongst the boys, who would rather prefer a socially exciting life than huddling into lousy groups.

It was his idea to bunk a lecture and go for a movie. Anita was pretty game for such a plan and so was I. Perhaps the past two years where I attended every pathetic lecture for my *Gujarati Chick* strengthened my reasons to go out and explore the world. When I mentioned the plan to Anita, she got Rasika and Manjeet along. I was glad to see Rasika join us for the movie and so was Ratish. Rasika was open about 'getting bored' in class and the clinging nature of boys around her which I perceived as caution to build my chances with her. Manjeet's imposter phase of a "Teacher's pet" faded away, as she too rushed into the taxi outside our college.

Ratish kept cool with the girls; though he had a 'bad' image in college for picking up fights with people who were triple his size. He made his way through the hordes of students crowding the ticket line of the movie theatre, pushing his plump body to his advantage. The girls recognized his efforts as very sweet and adorable. An unsaid competition already brew up with the fact that who would sit next to Rasika without making it too obvious. Unfortunately, a mistimed nature's call got me delayed in the washroom and I reached the seating row to find Rasika between Manjeet and Ratish. Anita gave me a sarcastic pitiful smile for my loss of opportunity. "I am so sorry Uday. Only if you didn't have to go pee, you would be sitting next to her", mocked Anita. I pretended to be casual about losing the opportunity as if I really didn't care. "Well I came here to see the movie. Let Ratish have his chance", I replied generously. Throughout the movie Anita and I giggled over funny 'over dramatic' *Bollywood* scenes. I wasn't really missing Rasika's company as we were pretty engrossed in our self-created humor. When the movie ended, we walked down to a bistro at the end of road where Ratish continued hitting on Rasika with his silly jokes. It was funny for a guy with a reputation like Ratish to have such a silly sense of humor. Funnier was the fact that Manjeet enjoyed his jokes more than Rasika. I tried joining the trio for trying my luck at Rasika but I couldn't cope up with their sense of humor. Anita too tried in her ways but was soon disinterested.

Anita leaned towards me and slowly whispered in my ears, "I want to smoke, could you go and buy a cigarette for me?" Her husky whisper was followed by my alarming mental scream, "Smoker for a Girl!" "You smoke?" I asked astonished. "Sometimes", she winked. The little hope that was left in me came crashing down on Anita. I had never smoked except for a few mouth fags with the *Thai* guys in my boarding school. My resident lurking fear of mixing with people in a big city like *Mumbai* surfaced as I had always expected kids in an urban city to be different and perhaps more modern. Yet my old chivalrous values compelled me to ask her, "Which one do you want?" "*Marlboro Lights*[20]", she replied instantaneously. I walked across the road to a tuck shop and bought her stick. All the while, I kept thinking about girls who smoke and Anita was the first one I met. She walked with me to the corner of the bistro so as to not scandalize the other girls and lit up the cigarette there. She took a couple of drags and closed her eyes in relaxation. "She smokes shamelessly", I thought in retaliation. The entire value system,

---

[20] *Marlboro is the largest selling cigarette brand in the world, made by Philip Morris USA. Everyone who has smoked a Marlboro must have felt like the cowboy, at least once!*

TV commercials on "No smoking" replayed in my thoughts, while she enjoyed every puff of the clear white smoke circling out of her pouted lips.

A couple of passersby stared intensely at her. Perhaps in a country like *India*, "Smoker for a girl" is a direct reflection on her character. I got infuriated by their lewd glances, but still holding my social courtesy I asked her, "May I take a drag too?" "You smoke?" she asked in excitement as if she found a smoking partner. "Yeah sometimes", I replied disinterestedly trying to mask my rage on the lecherous onlookers. She gave me the lit cigarette, and I took a mild drag of smoke and held it in my mouth to make it look real. I slowly blew out the smoke. Anita eagerly waited for me to return her cigarette but I intentionally took another drag, and a longer one this time. When I blew out the smoke, she pointed out, "Hey, you are mouth fagging!" "Oh yes I am not much of a smoker", I tried to cover up the embarrassment. My boarding school education of dealing with chicks took over me I guess, which said, "Never stay behind in doing what a chick can do." But smoking wasn't my ball game. "You won't get the kick of a cigarette unless you take the smoke inside", Anita suggested taking another drag. "You have made the filter wet", she complained looking at the white butt of the cigarette. "Oh sorry", I dubiously apologized for spoiling her forbidden pleasure.

"Sharing a cigarette is practically like kissing", she chuckled. The idea of sharing a kiss via a cigarette was intriguing but was shattered soon enough by another onlooker. We began to walk in the alley behind the bistro. It felt like the small fantasy world which I had created of having Anita as my girlfriend was stubbed by the fact that she was a smoker. The thought of having a smoker for a girlfriend was further resentful to my naïve values. Another passerby gave her a sleazy look, while she hardly noticed anybody as she was too engrossed in her forbidden activity. She had reached half of the cigarette, when I asked her for another drag. She casually passed the lit cigarette to me. A new impulse took over as I threw the cigarette on the road and stubbed it with my shoes. "You shouldn't smoke here Anita. These people are giving all sorts of 'dirty' looks. Moreover you don't look good when you smoke", I said firmly. I wasn't anticipating her incoming reaction when she screamed, "How dare you stub my cigarette, who are you to tell me what to do and what not to? I don't give a fuck about all these people and what they think of me." I felt offended to the fact that she screamed at me but the mirth in the eyes of the onlookers for a free fight enraged me. "I am sorry, I thought I was your friend", I replied egoistically and began to walk away. Perhaps watching me walk away in anger cooled her of the loss of her half stubbed cigarette and she began to run behind me. "Uday stop! Why are you getting angry? You are the one who stubbed my cigarette!" she reasoned. I was still too offended to listen but I felt a strong grip on my elbow as she pulled me to a stop. "Ok look I am sorry. I know your intention was good but I am really not used to people telling me what to do and not to do", she told me affirmatively. "It's ok. I understand. Let's go back", I replied, still assimilating her way of life.

Soon we were back at the bistro and the mood had calmed down. I showed the kids a sample of the *Mithun*[21] dance I had recently learnt. They all laughed and Anita laughed with them. We smiled at each other as if we had preserved a little secret. "Since when are you smoking?" I asked her. "We started smoking in high school, me and my school friend Nikita. Her boyfriend always got it for us", she began. "So even your friend Nikita smokes?" I asked curiously. "At times; yes. Well she says that she only smokes with me", she explained. "Listen Uday, we are not some big time smokers and all. We just tried it", she explained defensively. "I feel like I have made friends with the drug mafia", I chuckled, breaking the awkwardness. Anita laughed and then gave me a long admiring look. "You know Uday, you are so much like my ex-boyfriend", she smiled. "Ex-boyfriend", I thought as I saw the last few shades of my idea of dating Anita dampen. The last thing I really wanted to know was whether or not she had dated someone before. My world was a little more shaken as I came to know some more about her. "Why does it feel so upsetting? That someone dated her before me, that someone touched her before me. What if she had already kissed that guy? Why does this feel so awkward? As if I am trying to woo a conquered territory. What if she had done 'it' with him?" and million other thoughts like this echoed in my head. The awkwardness of the moment was just left inside my heart which slowly crumpled to its own insecurities.

---

[21]   *Mithun Chakraborty is a three time National Film Award winning actor and very popular for his dance moves in Bollywood.*

21

"Hey my friend Nikita and me are planning to go for the *Xavier's College*[22] fest; I have heard it is very cool", she said. "Would you like to join us?" the brightness returned in her eyes. "I would have to ask my mother, and I would let you know", I replied still upset about the ex-boyfriend Anita had.

"Oh my God, she already had a boyfriend, what if she had done 'it' with him, what if she is not a virgin?" the forsaken thoughts of "What if..." kept repeating themselves on my way back home. "Are all kids in *Mumbai* corrupt? Back in the *North* it's not like that I guess", I consoled myself. To which reality dawned again, "All the kids are having fun other than me, because I am so unattractive and no six footer. Maybe I should go put on some muscles. Why the hell am I concerned if anyone is a virgin or not? It's just that I don't want to be a virgin."

My mother allowed me to go for the fest, looking at my miserable state of low 'self-worth'. She and an aunt laughed about it and joked that they would pray that I get a girlfriend soon. It was way more embarrassing that my mother has to pray for me to find a girlfriend. Anita and I bunked college and rushed to *Bandra*[23] on the event day. Nikita was supposed to catch up with us there and continue the train ride to *Churchgate*[24]. Finally, she joined us. Nikita was darker, shorter and plumper than Anita but she had a very posh accent. Well I was floored with the accent. We were soon at the gates of *Xavier's College* and the entry tickets were already unavailable. Nikita's accent definitely came to help as she got entries for all three of us inside the campus. The festival was a very different sight I had never seen before. There were boys and girls singing and dancing and most of all, so very comfortable with each other. There was a band performance going on at a corner stage. The *Mumbai* rains were 'on' those days, which meant it could rain anytime and it could rain heavily. The rain increased and Anita, Nikita and I found a covered corner which had a chair. Soon we were sitting in a pattern where either Anita sat on Nikita as Nikita was a little

---

[22]   *One of the coolest college in Mumbai, blessed with an ancient gothic building.*

[23]   *A posh suburb of Mumbai.*

[24]   *There is no Church or any gate, yet Churchgate is the first station of the Western Railway suburban network of Mumbai.*

plump. Or I sat on Anita's lap and Nikita stood up. But this time, Anita was going to sit on my lap and I had relatively low experience of this. When she sat down, I realized that my 'little warrior' is beginning to create some turbulence. "God that would be so sad, that a girl feels my erection when she is sitting on my lap", I thought in panic. I adjusted and adjusted till the bastard inside my pants reached its full length. The music changed just around that time and both Nikita and Anita started dancing. I breathed a sigh of relief. They started doing a dance called *Jive*[25], of which I was not just ignorant about, but in fact I had heard the name for the first time. They expected me to participate but I was too shy and nervous to dance. "I don't know how to *Jive* ladies", I said nervously. Anita made a kind face and offered to teach me, "Don't be shy Uday. Come, I will show you how to *Jive*." I tried to learn and soon I could *Jive* but just a little bit. Then Nikita suggested, "Let's do *Salsa*[26]." Anita and Nikita started with *Salsa*. Anita was a natural dancer and the way she swayed in the arms of Nikita was spectacular as many of the students stopped to watch them dance. A couple of teachers passed by but unlike my college, they smiled looking at the dancing girls. I must admit they were impressive. Even all the very 'cool' population of that college was noticing these two girls' saucy *Salsa* moves. And then it was my turn to *Salsa* and my benevolent dance coach was teaching me the first few moves. I could feel her breath on my face as we moved together. I held her slender waist feeling the muscular curve of her love handles. Moreover she was exactly my height, but now she looked taller. Nevertheless, she whispered in my ears, "You are a fast learner." And I replied, "I don't know *Salsa*, I just know *Khalsa*[27]." We giggled together as Anita taught me my first *Salsa* moves.

The dance ended, and we made a move. On the way back, a lot of people smiled at us. It felt good, as if I took a first step to see an open world of mixing cultures, where people danced and laughed together and gender differences didn't matter. I had a very sincere feeling to thank

---

[25] *A lively and uninhibited form of Swing dance style that originated in the United States from African Americans in the early 1930s.*

[26] *A social dance that originated in New York with strong influences from Latin America, particularly Cuba and Puerto Rico.*

[27] *A warrior sect in Sikhs popular for a dance called Bhangra.*

this wonderful new friend I got, or else I would have never seen what the very popular *Xavier's College* fest looked like. I was still enjoying my new found liberty, when on the way out Nikita gave me a grand goodbye hug and said, "You are really flexible Uday, you could be a very good dancer." I felt that she had really big boobs, and the moment she embraced me I had already missed a hundred heart beats. Shivering from the marvelous experience of my first hug, I had not even recovered, when Anita gave me a hug. I felt there was something different about her hug. When I embraced her, I realized that I did not feel like leaving her. Soon they left and I was in a train, soaked from head to toe with the unstoppable *Mumbai* shower. While going back, I just thought about Anita, and the dance, and the hug all the way.

Two weeks later she came running towards me when I was waiting for a veg roll outside our regular canteen. "Uday, would you like to come for my birthday party?" she asked. "It's your birthday? When?" I exclaimed. "Day after tomorrow", she replied. "What kind of a crazy girl is she, self-inviting people for her birthday?" I wondered. The people I knew rarely revealed their birthdays for the fear of paying up for a treat. Anita on the contrary was self-inviting people for a treat. "She must be a very rich girl", I thought and asked. "Who all would be there?" "You, Gando, Ratish and me", she said excitedly. "What about Rasika and Manjeet?" I asked confirming the presence of her so called girlfriends. "Well I asked them but they are giving me lame reasons that parents won't agree and bullshit like that", she replied, annoyed by the mention of their names. "Gando agreed to come", I chuckled trying to divert her attention to the uber obnoxious Gando. "I would love to come", I said politely.

Now, Gando was the biggest nerd on the planet. His naming ceremony was done appropriately. He displayed a super pseudo confidence, claimed to have beaten up two guys together and had an *AK-56*[28] hidden inside his father's bed cabinet. I didn't know then that keeping an *AK-56* under your bed can get you booked under *TADA (Terrorist and Disruptive Activities Act)*, by the *Indian Constitution*, the same one in which our

---

[28]   *From Russia with love: The most popular assault rifle in the world, officially known in the Soviet documentation as Avtomat Kalashnikova.*

dear *Sanju Baba*[29] is doing his time. Well, broke kids like me have to beg their parents for occasions like birthdays where they have to buy the seldom occasional gift and that too for a person of the opposite gender you have a special interest in. Luckily, my mother was kind enough to buy me a nice top for Anita out of her modest savings.

Finally her birthday arrived and I wished Anita at midnight. The next day, Gando saluted Anita a 'happy birthday' and reached out to give her a desperate hug, which he indeed tried to mask with chivalry but couldn't escape my cynical eyes. I reached out to shake her hand to wish her 'happy birthday' but instead she gave me a friendly hug. Ratish was just happy to bunk college. Gando, Ratish, Anita & I bunked college to go to *Bandra*. Anita treated us at *Subway*[30] to which I was going for the first time. She helped me order a chicken teriyaki sub. She looked very pretty that day with glittery blue eyeliner highlighting her feline eyes. She was an all denim girl, not at all dressed up like the other girls. She was a fan of cool t-shirts and fancy jeans. Anita also dug smart casual shoes. Rarely had I seen Anita dress up in traditional Indian wear, though she looked stunning in those too. Her tall height and lean figure made her look good in anything she wore. She wore a very cool metal band t-shirt and a pair of jeans that day, with her favorite denim jacket. In short, she wore a look of a kickass rock star.

We proceeded for a *Bollywood* movie. I was sitting next to Anita and the movie turned out to be really sad, till a melodious romantic song played up. In that moment I felt Anita's hand very close to mine. I slid my palm onto hers as she lightly touched mine. A few seconds later our palms were entwined into each other. I gently pulled it down below the arm rest of the chairs so that Gando & Ratish can't see. We watched the remaining movie like that. Ratish & Gando left after the movie, but I quite didn't feel like leaving. So we wandered off to her home.

She had an entire floor to live in, in a posh apartment in *Bandra*. I entered her house and went to her room. I was eager to go to the washroom and

---

29 *Nick name for a popular Bollywood actor – Sanjay Dutt.*
30 *An American fast food franchise popular for low calorie submarine sandwiches and salads.*

Anita showed me the direction. "Come out quickly, my Dad is at home." A shiver ran down my spine, and I thought what her dad would think about the situation. His daughter went to college and brought a guy back who is a little shorter than her. "I don't know what to talk to him about, is he like tough and all that?" I whimpered. "Yes, just answer what he asks, and that should be fine", she said calming me down. I didn't know how her father was, so I hurriedly washed up and came out. Anita was with her father, so I quickly took out her gift from my bag and put it into hers as I had planned. Then I had to face something I hadn't planned for. I went out of the room to face her dad. He was six feet, broad and bearded, wearing spectacles with high power through which I could see multiple images of his eyeballs. Nevertheless, the sharpness in his eyes could not be ignored. So I said my favorite, *"Namaste*[31] uncle." The Indian way of greeting is very amazing as it greets the other person without touching his ego and his body. "Hello, what's your name?" he asked me in a firm voice. "I am Uday... Uncle, nice to meet you", I replied. "Come sit, would you have lunch with us?" he asked. "No uncle, I just had a *'sub'* with Anita", I smiled. "So what does your father do?" he asked. "Well, he is a general manager for a leading pharmaceutical company", I replied. "Nice, and your mother?" he continued asking. "She was a teacher for ten years, now she is a housewife. And I have a younger sister, she is in school", I answered before he could ask about siblings. "Good, so why did you opt for science?" and he asked me the question which I was answering for the past four years. "I liked Biology a lot, in fact I was aspiring to become a doctor, but I am glad I am not doing it", I remarked. "Why is that so?" he looked serious. "My father and I celebrate the fact that I am not aspiring to be a doctor or else I would be studying for the next fifteen years of my life and probably start earning when I am thirty five years old", and I finally laughed. "So what are your hobbies?" he asked, unmoved by my futile attempt of humor. "I like playing football and watching movies", I replied quickly. "We often go out as a family to watch movies", I added. "What types of movies do you like to see?" he continued. "It depends on whose type of movie we are going to see. My dad likes action, and my mom likes romantic movies and my sister and I, like comedy", I replied after thinking for

---

[31] *The traditional Indian way of greeting people, with folded hands and head bowed in respect. Once upon a time, it meant – bowing to the God within each one of us.*

a moment. To which he finally laughed. I must admit he looked very cute when he laughed. "You see Uday, science is born out of art. Art is the mother of science", he started explaining. "What about commerce sir?" I participated. "It's all economics at the end of the day. Commerce is a part of economics", he further explained and paused. Pauses in such a conversation can be quite uncomfortable. "Does he want me to throw light on economics?" I thought. "Uncle, I don't know much about economics", I admitted before I was asked. Anita observed that the situation was getting sensitive and she came to my rescue. "Papa, lunch is served", she interrupted. "Uncle, I would leave, it was nice meeting you", I joined in. We shook hands and we left. Anita asked her father if she could see me downstairs and joined me.

"Oh my God, that was crazy; I didn't have any clue what to say. But did I piss him off by any means?" I quickly asked her. "Don't worry, I am surprised he spoke to you so much, he generally talks very little with my friends", she stroked my arm. We were crossing the road and we held hands again. Somehow I didn't feel like leaving her hand at all. "Wow, look at that car, it's a *Mercedes*[32] sports", she literally jumped. "Yes, it looks so good", I replied, sadly realizing the fact that I didn't even have a remote chance of getting her this car. "Nikita and others are waiting for me at *Mocha*[33], I would have to go there. My *Rotary Club*[34] friends are also calling to go clubbing. There is this guy Rohit who drives a *BMW*[35], he is always after my life and perhaps he might also come", she narrated her forthcoming busy day. "It's cool, you go, and I will rush home, take care and have a very happy birthday. Also thanks a lot for the treat", I

---

[32]   *Mercedes: The beauty of German engineering and probably the dream vehicle of the average Indian man.*

[33]   *Mocha: a popular eatery at Hill Road in Bandra. Now it's shut.*

[34]   *Rotary Club: Rotary International is an international service organization whose stated purpose is to bring people together to provide humanitarian services. There are 34,282 clubs and over 1.2 million members worldwide. Rotary's primary motto is "Service Above Self", and secondary is "One profits most who serves best."*

[35]   *Bayerische Motoren Werke AG (English: Bavarian Motor Works), commonly known as BMW is a German automobile manufacturer. Probably the new dream vehicle of the average Indian man!*

said preparing to leave for home. Anita gave me a goodbye hug and she left. I looked at her walking away and she turned back to give a glance. I boarded an auto-rickshaw, feeling insecure thinking about girls getting drunk while clubbing and the subsequent 'shit' that happens. "Who the fuck is this Rohit guy with a *BMW*?" I cursed, feeling helpless. All I could think as I left was, "I was almost there today but now Anita would go clubbing and I don't know what would happen."

At 11:30 in the night, my home phone rang. I was too upset lying on my bed thinking & worrying about Anita. My mother called me to take the call, "Some girl", she said and left. I answered and it was Anita on the other end, "You slept off?" she asked. "No, was about to", I answered. "You came back from the party?" I asked hesitantly. "No, I did not go", she sounded casual. "Why, Rohit didn't force you to come?" I asked, sounding a little jealous. "Rohit is an ass, he asked but I said I have to go for dinner with my family", she answered. "Why? Did you not feel like going for clubbing? You like dancing right?" I probed. "Stupid, you weren't there, that's why I didn't go", she said reluctantly. I was floored; I could feel butterflies in my stomach and stars flying around my head. In fact I was feeling a little dizzy but I still felt like dancing.

"I am a very pathetic dancer, you know it! Why would you wanna go clubbing with me?" I asked. "Come on, you are not so bad. Nikita told me later that day after the *Xavier fest* that you are very flexible", she said consoling my lowly self. "Yeah right! As if Nikita is a supreme authority in dancing", I challenged her. "She is a very good dancer Uday. Plus she has choreographed so many dances in our school. If she says that you can dance well then that means you can", she emphasized. "I probably agree. I am happy, at least I am good at something", I sighed. "Why are you saying things like these? I mean you are good at so many things", she encouraged my 'worthless' self. "Like what, tell me one thing", I argued trying hard to prove my uselessness to the girl of my interest.

"Do you know Uday, what you have?" she paused. I couldn't hold on the curiosity to know that one unique thing which Anita discovered in me. "What?" I asked. "Uday, you have the 'gift of gab'", she said in delight. "What's that?" I asked curiously. "How should I explain? It's like this thing you have to know the right thing to speak. Something like spontaneity in talking. Like, you have a nice sense of humor and perfect timing of saying things", she explained. "Really?" I asked in astonishment as it was probably the first time I heard someone praise me to that extent. "Yes stupid! No wonder all the chicks in our class dig you", she added. "Oh come on, nobody digs me", I rejected her opinion. "Oh yes they do. They might just never tell you. Girls are like that", she jeered. "But so what if I can talk? That doesn't make me sexy", I reasoned. "As far as I know, not many people can talk. Plus you can do the *Mithun* dance. Nobody can do that!" she giggled. I laughed along for the *Mithun* dance.

Anita finally relaxed after making me feel special of my abilities. "I feel so stupid. It's your birthday and instead of me making you feel special, you are trying to make me feel special", I apologized. "My birthday was yesterday. It's already past twelve", she said. "What time is it now?" I checked. "It's around two", she answered. I wondered if she discovered her gift which I had planted in her bag. I held on to the curiosity of knowing whether or not she found the gift lest I kill the surprise.

"By the way do you know that Mrs. Ragade is going to address us in the lab tomorrow morning?" she continued the conversation. "Really? The H.O.D is going to give us a lecture?" I asked startled by the information. "Yeah, you better be prepared", she insisted. "At times I am scared of her", I confessed. "Yeah, me too. I mean did you look at her face? She looks so ferocious. And I have heard that she doesn't compromise on discipline", she added. "You know Anita, I feel like she would have been very 'hot' during her youth. I mean have you looked at her eyes? They are gray", I said mischievously. "Yeah, I guess so. I wondered what went wrong that made her so ferocious", she wondered. "Probably she dated a guy who dumped her", I chuckled. "Yeah, probably, someone with the 'gift of gab'!" chuckled Anita. We laughed together.

"You are not much into reading books right?" she asked. "I have read but not much. I have just read the *Alchemist*[36]", I answered. "I really

---

[36]   *The Alchemist is a story of a shepherd who undertakes a journey to the mysterious Egypt in search of a treasure he often dreamt about. Quite explains the power of dreams upon the Human race!*

love that writer. *Paulo Coelho*[37] is amazing", she added. "Indeed, I could imagine every bit of what he wrote", I replied in admiration. "Have you read *The Godfather*[38] by *Mario Puzo*[39]?" she asked. "No I haven't. Though I have heard the name", I answered. "Do read it once Uday. It's one hell of an amazing read", she praised. "The exams are commencing next month. We have a lot to study", she said with concern. "Yeah, I have no clue of what happened in the classes in the last month, as we are bunking almost all lectures", I added up to her worries. "Yeah, thanks to Ratish and his plans. I wonder if they will raise an issue about attendance", she pointed. "You can't even put a proxy attendance here. It's like the teachers know us by our names. If the batch was larger, it would be simpler to ask someone to put proxy like we did earlier during high school", I explained. "Don't worry Uday, I am sure you will talk your way out", she taunted. "Why because I have the 'gift of gab'?" I chuckled. "Yeah. Even my ex-boyfriend had it. Life was so much easier for him", she replied. The mention of her ex-boyfriend again made me low, but this time my curiosity got the better of me and I asked, "Hey, tell me one thing, did you ever kiss your ex-boyfriend?" There was a momentary awkward pause and she replied, "No. Once we were about to but something happened and we didn't. Why did you ask?" I didn't have an answer to her question. "Just... I guess I was curious", I replied, sighing in relief for her not being touched, and remained silent.

We continued chatting about studies, teachers, books, movies and *Mumbai* and 'time' flew by to four in the morning. "What if you don't get Poonam?" she asked. "Then there is Gurdeep", I answered. "Gurdeep is sad. She is like a typical aunty", she taunted. "Then Rasika", I thought and answered. "What if you don't get Rasika too?" she challenged. "Then I have you in the end", I chuckled. "No way, I don't want to be your back

---

[37] *Paulo Coelho is a Brazilian lyricist and novelist. He is the recipient of numerous international awards. He had a rough start as a writer, but then some universal conspiracy brought him to where he is now. Deep down, his heart desired the same.*

[38] *Okay; let's be clear – Missing out on 'The Godfather' is terrible and you wouldn't even come to know what awesomeness you missed. Sad to say, it's like a lifetime wasted.*

[39] *The author of 'The Godfather'. I wonder what his life must have been like.*

up!" she teased. "Don't worry, I will keep you like a queen", I said with an ounce of passion pouring in my voice. What followed was a little silence which lasted for a short while.

"What time are you coming to college tomorrow?" she asked breaking the tensed silence. "For the morning practical class at 7", I answered. "Let us reach by 6:30, we will hangout a bit before class", she said making a plan. "Sure, but for that I have to get up at 5 and it's already 4. It's ok, let's sleep now, my mother will wake me up", I said realizing the strange absence of the ever persistent 'time'. "Ok take care bye", she said promptly. "Bye", I replied. I waited for her to cut the call, and she waited for me. "Hang up", I asked. "No you hang up", she demanded. "By the way Uday, thanks for the gift", she said softly. "What! You found it?" I asked in excitement. "Yeah, I opened my bag to take out the notes and there I saw it. You are so smart, you didn't even mention that you got it for me", she replied in excitement. "Then how did you figure out that it was me who got it for you?" I asked in surprise. "Just... Plus you just owned up to it right now", she giggled. "So, did you like it? I wasn't sure if you would like it", I asked in doubt. "Stupid I loved it. It's so cute", she replied happily. "Thank god. Ok let's sleep now, before my mother wakes up and catches me talking on the phone for the entire night", I said thinking about the embarrassing possibilities. "Ok let's count till 3 and hang up together", she suggested. "Ok... 1, 2... 3", we said in childlike unison and hung up. I slept relaxed and happy for all the undisturbed little insecurities I carried. I guess I had found what I was looking for.

The next morning my phone rang at six, then ten minutes later and then again twenty minutes later. When I woke up, it was 6:30 am and I realized that my mother had forgotten to wake me up. Anita would have waited for me for the past half an hour. I hurriedly left for college and made it to my lab at 7:45 am. I was mildly drenched as it was raining continuously in *Mumbai*. I tried calling Anita all the way but she did not answer. I was instantly denied entry in the lab since I was late. I tried to peep in the lab just to see Anita. My eyes roved around for a while till I spotted her. I looked straight in her eyes with the most romantic look I could muster; and in return, I just got a cold stare from her. The very moment our teacher in the lab screamed looking at me, "Uday, first of all you are late and then you want to disturb the other students who are here 'on time' to learn and study? Please get out of the lab, and don't even stand at the door!" I hurriedly rushed away, as I didn't want to face Mrs. Ragade, our beloved *H.O.D*[40] as she would have been out anytime to take a stroll. I really didn't want to be in her 'bad' books. So, I left and hung around the college for the next two hours. I must admit, I was really tense. Cursing everything that had gone wrong since morning and blaming everyone because of whom I couldn't make it to meet Anita. "I was so close to an actual girlfriend and I totally blew it!" I thought helplessly accusing my unpunctual self. I looked at my watch and realized that the lab practical is about to get over. I rushed to the lab. On the way I met a few classmates who looked very happy. It seems all the lectures post the practicals scheduled for that day had been cancelled. I hurriedly went looking for Anita. I saw her walking towards me in the corridor. The only thing different about her, was that, when she looked at me she started looking elsewhere and continued walking. I looked at her in dismay, and in a desperate attempt I did my famous *Mithun* dance. Anita couldn't ignore the saucy moves of the killer *Mithun* dance and burst out laughing. I knew I had my chance.

"I am so sorry, my mom didn't wake up and so I couldn't wake up", I apologized. "What time did you reach here?" I asked. "Six", she said bluntly, "And I waited for you for an hour till the class began." I looked at her like a puppy who had just spilt some milk on a carpet and now wants to be cuddled. "Sorry", I said in the softest voice I could mumble. "What about Ragade's lecture?" I asked curiously. "It got cancelled, it seems there is a meeting of the Principal with the H.O.D's of various departments", she answered. "That's what I was wondering. How could she cancel her lecture?" I remarked. "Count yourself lucky for today. If you would have entered her lecture so late, she would have surely taken your case", she warned. We began walking downstairs and soon were outside the college. We continued walking to the nearby football ground where the other guys of the class were playing cricket. "Gando was pretty upset for her lecture getting cancelled", laughed Anita. "He is such a nerd!" she cackled. I laughed along as we turned into an alley which was shadier and emptier. Our hands kept on coming closer till we were again hand in hand while we walked. The privacy of the single

---

[40]   *Head of Department.*

lane road slowed our pace and we walked looking at the small houses and the nearby college buildings. The damp withering walls of the old buildings narrated their stories of existence. The clouds huddled up to cast a dim curtain on their momentarily lost presence.

"These houses look so beautiful in this weather", she said slowly absorbing the dampness of the road. "Yeah it looks like we are walking in a painting", I said picturing the two of us strolling in an old alley on a rainy day. Anita gave me a soft gaze while I looked at her and continued taking the small next steps on the road. Our shoulders rubbed against each other and the gaze grew intense and insolent, disobeying the orders of courtesy. "What?" she gestured with her eyes. "You know what would be better in the painting?" I asked softly. "What?" she whispered with a smile.

I slid my palm onto hers and said, "This." Anita looked down hiding her coy glances. We walked up on the pavement. The reduced walking length of the pavement brought us closer. The road became lonelier and we stopped at the base of a beautiful lone tree. We chatted for a while about class and practicals. We looked at the enormous shade of the thick tree. It stood inside the playground of the adjacent college, just at its bricked boundary. Its branches spread out to the roof of a nearby single storey building. The distinct appearance of the tree beheld our attention as we marveled at its creation. Water drops trickling down from the leaves fell on us bringing us closer in the damp 'silence'.

We looked at each other and words made themselves scarce. Perhaps it was their way of showing respect and gratitude towards the conspiring nature which held us in its arms. I saw a tense vibration in her eyes where her pupils shrunk, and simultaneously I saw her emotions tearing up. I felt a similar tension rising in my belly and pushing towards my diaphragm. The 'life' in such heart throbbing moments often doesn't know the roads lesser traveled. Thus 'life' charges itself up in those who are present in the moment... waiting for an explosion to happen, in the beautiful uncertainties resting ahead in the next moment of 'time'.

She hesitantly embraced me and caused the much awaited explosion, of which I had no clue about how it would feel. It felt like something dropped inside my stomach. A shrill tension tickled my knees and I felt as if I am falling. The feeling of falling within one's own self often seeks something to hold onto... and I held her, tightening my grip around her waist. Till suddenly I realized we were physically a little too close. My eyes were locked into Anita's, and not even a single glance shifted to any other person or thing around us. We came so close that Anita ended up giving me a tight hug. My hands moved to her waist, and we held each other in the embrace for a while. It was the most beautiful hug and I could never forget it. She rubbed her cheeks on my neck while I gently kissed her temples. I curiously sniffed her neck and kissed lightly on her nape. Anita's rubbed my back while I just gasped out the tension. I hugged her with a surging desperation of unfulfilled desires as perhaps they only needed her touch to be fulfilled.

But lonely desires and feeble hearts need a lot more to be satiated. Anita leaned back looking at my face and like a curious child she leaned ahead and kissed me. Her tender lips gently held mine and there I was in the lip lock I never expected. Stroke after stroke of lips moistened by the rain or by our souls sucked each other. The tongue still needed a companion and made its coy advances to meet hers till it tasted cherry for the flavor of her lipstick. The heavens cried together for my little accomplishment and the clouds began to drizzle. The weather moved to an all-time 'high'.

It's timeless to look back at the peace of the first kiss which was so unexpected. But 'time' often takes us to a road where we begin expecting the unexpected. The spiraling energy built up in our systems made peace as we continued kissing only to be absorbed in nothing but each other. My ideal world of wants and preferences, imperfections and insecurities simply washed away. Maybe it's the magic of the moment when you get what you always wanted.

My tongue danced eagerly to lick her lips, as we kissed in the absence of 'time'. It continued raining but we didn't care to pull out our umbrellas. We stood there on the road, below the tree, while it poured and we continued to get wet. Finally the kiss was over and stilled in the embrace, I looked at her. She had watery eyes but her tears soon mixed up with the rains and I couldn't differentiate between the blend.

We regained ourselves. Before unnecessary thoughts could turn into words, nature presented its last gift and filled the atmosphere with the sound of trickling murmurs. I believe the weather too caught up with our accidental yet soaring passion as the mild drizzle turned into a heavy downpour. Anita opened her bag to take out her wind-cheater while I quickly opened my umbrella.

She smiled a demure laughter watching my spontaneity and moved under the umbrella. 'Time' was kind that day, as it left us in peace. The road back to college was longer than usual and we silently walked back with hands clasped into each other's under the shade of the umbrella.

It was the onset of a very romantic time, a 'time' I didn't know then, would still remain very fresh in my memories for years to come. Nobody cares for a warranty when they get their first kiss. The scary insecurities are indeed just illusions of the mind, and if warrantied, they will never come into play. 'Love' is the alter side of such insecurities. Perhaps there are moments where warranties can kill the pleasure. The pleasure of the strange kiss, at a strange place, with a stranger you just start finding 'hot', and before you know it, she suddenly turns more important than anyone else.

Though she lived in front of you for a few moments, yet you feel like you know her for a lifetime. I didn't need a warranty, for this beautiful 'time' would last forever. Because it had the beauty of forever even in that short while and I just hoped that Anita found it too.

My phone rang, jolting me back to the present and I answered it, "Dude, we are catching up for a drinking session at your place", an office colleague and friend was on the other end of the phone. "Sure, but suddenly a drinking session and that too on a Monday?" I wondered. "Bloody Uday, since when did you start differentiating between Mondays and Sundays?" he said, sounding very excited. "Obviously buddy", I reinforced his excitement, though a little disturbed by the intrusion of my friend in the memories of my first 'love'. Nevertheless, when 'love' is gone then only friends remain, and I didn't feel like discouraging my enthusiastic alcoholic friends. "But Ajay, we have office tomorrow *yaar*[41], can't afford to get late or my boss will grab my balls and then hang on it", I cautioned him. Ajay laughed out loud and said, "You are already 'high' or what? Tomorrow is *Gandhi Jayanti*[42], it's a holiday!"

"Oh I see", I said, now much more relaxed, "So tomorrow is a *dry day*[43]?" I smiled. "Yeah man, we need to stock up for the night and day", Ajay added. "Of course, bloody call everybody, I am in a very fucking awesome mood to drink", I added up to his enthusiasm. "And food?" I voiced out my concern. "Don't worry buddy, Poops is planning to cook a lot of chicken at your place", he added. "He better does, or else I will make you cook", I said in my usual friendly arrogance. Finally I shoved the warranty of availability of food on my friend and relaxed for some more time. I wander back to the thoughts of Anita and the rains as the weather around *Pune* is becoming dull, cloudy and windy. Very soon it is going to rain, and I wish Anita and me could get drenched together. Nevertheless, I guess I will get drenched in the booze and the 'blood' of the delicious poultry. Well, at least there was something to look forward to in the day. "Dude, I want to have some serious fun and good food as addictive as 'blood' to a tiger", I messaged Ajay. "The taste of 'blood' it is my friend", he replied quickly. "Just 'be on time' as it is your house", he added. I relaxed back in my chair and looked at my watch for the day to end and the party to begin. The rains started pouring and the winds blew in a fury. I stepped outside my office building just to get a little rain and wind on my face. The monsoons were ending but unfortunately the thoughts of Anita didn't end with it. The memories of that 'hot' kiss in the wet *Mumbai* shower is still running in my head and dancing on my lips.

---

[41]   *'Buddy' in Hindi.*

[42]   *Our Father of Nation was born on this day. Hence a dry day!*

[43]   *Alcohol is prohibited throughout India during dry days as a gesture of respect for the occasion.*

AND FINALLY THE LITTLE WARRIOR SPOKE...

Measuring the silence of the rains and its scope,
No one is clean and perhaps not even the 'Pope',
Making its way through the suffocated crotch,
Finally, the Little Warrior spoke....

Reminiscing the memories of the yester-years,
Which doesn't get washed away, even in the flood of tears,
How far you left, the one so dear...?
Radiating its heat, the Little Warrior knows no fear...

If you were perfect or just a flawed hare,
Whether you stepped up...?
Or didn't even dare,
Staying lost in the magnificence of those lovely eyes,
Ironically, the Little Warrior doesn't care...

For the insecurities your desires invoke,
Carry your expectations on your smile... or just drag them with a rope,
Even if you lose, it still carries hope,
Rising up to its full length,
The Little Warrior Spoke...

There are no Warranties in life,
Perfect are just moments,
If finding the perfect love is your greatest fear,
Then you have nothing...
But a lifetime stolen...!

Come back in the moment and clear out the smoke,
And that's why, the Little Warrior spoke....

CHAPTER 2
A TASTE OF BLOOD

I was leaving office in a hurry as if I am escaping the corporate prison, tip toeing out of those bars. The fear of looking happy and excited to my superiors could bring on more work…, and god forbid if I am incapable of doing that, it would mean that I am in deep shit. And then what if, I am put forward to some training, and that's where my biggest weakness reveals – my inability to learn from the drone-like instructions of the regular trainers at work. Just then, the plump and gorgeous trainer passed by. The little familiarity with her did bring a smile on her face, and I returned the smile. "Maybe attending your training won't be so bad", I murmured to her back in a tone loud enough that only I could hear. "Did you say something Uday?" she turned around. "Nothing… uh", I blurted the words in surprise. "Just saying a 'Hi'", I responded quickly. She nodded and was about to turn around when I added, "But Jasmine, the last training which you delivered was pretty good, especially the part on corporate culture." Her smile widened on my sincere compliment. "Thank you", she replied. "Which project are you a part of?" she asked. "Uh… Manufacturing", I replied sluggishly. "It takes a while for you to remember your project?" she interrogated with a whiff of contempt for the insincere employee that I was. "Oh my God, I forgot you are an HR!" I exclaimed with mild avoidance which she took with an agitated shock. "Aren't we humans first?" she argued. "Indeed you are. I rather believe; the evolved ones", I smiled with an obvious sarcasm. "Have you seen Harry Potter?" I asked. "Yes", she nodded a flat reply. "Wow, are you into fantasy movies too?" I asked excitedly. She replied an elongated "Yeah!" "In a corporate, HRs' are like those death eaters, similar to the ones after Harry to take his soul away", I giggled mildly. "I am not an HR, I am a trainer", she protested as the offence grew on her face. "But thank god, at least the HRs' here are beautiful to let poor Harrys like us in corporate, to happily let their souls be taken away", I smiled a wicked grin. Her eyes widened and her pupils dilated. Even her posture changed as her bosom sprung upwards towards me saying a "Hello!" I looked at her with a stretchy smile. "Hey, no offence huh! Was just kidding. See yaa", I responded gracefully to her welcoming aura and began walking away.

"Hey, where do you live Uday?" she asked interrupting my departure. "In *Saudagar*[44]", I replied. "With family?" she asked. "Uh… No. They are back in *Mumbai*", I replied. "So you stay alone here?" she asked. "Yeah, on rent", I added immediately. "So, how do you manage your food?" she continued. "Well a maid comes and cooks. Why, are you gonna take me home and… then feed me?" I smirked. "I wish I could. But you know what, I live with my parents", she smiled, elongating her coyness. "I totally understand", I replied formally. "But yes you can do one thing", I suggested looking straight in her eyes. "And what is that?" she asked flirtatiously. "Take me out for a treat, since I guess you know *Pune* better", I smiled and took a step closer to her. I looked intently at her face, observing her big eyes and her dilating pupils. My gaze fixated on her lips and then traveled back to her eyes. I mildly bit my lips and smiled. Neither could I resist the temptation to whisper to her face, "I guess, I still have a lot to learn from you." Jasmine's red pout appeared redder and her big eyes were filled with a conflict of excitement and intimidation. I took a step back to avoid unnecessary glances of fellow workers in the office premise. We exchanged numbers and parted on the idea of catching up someday. My phone vibrated, and rung my senses back to the important appointment, which I had totally forgotten about.

"Hey Uday where are you?" asked Ajay in his hoarse voice. "Buddy I am just getting in my car", I mentioned in a hurry. "You still in office?" he exclaimed in shock. "Yeah, I just bumped into Jasmine", I said excitedly. "Who Jasmine?" he asked with indifference. "Dude, that sultry red lipped HR. Sorry! Trainer", I corrected myself. "What's with her?" he asked. "She took my number. I guess it's 'on'", I cheered for the continuing excitement. "Asshole, we are all waiting here for you outside your apartment, with food and booze and everything. You still haven't left",

---

[44]   *A locality in Pune.*

he screamed. "Ajay, I found 'blood'", I re-emphasized my achievement of the little conquest of red lipped Jasmine. "You are such a bloody... 'Bloodhound'", screamed Ajay but he couldn't hold the following giggle. "I am driving as fast as I can, and I will reach..., just give me fifteen minutes", I yelled starting my car. "Dude, reach fast. Everybody is here. The beer is getting warm and the ice is melting. Even the chicken needs to be cooked", Ajay cited the concerns.

When in a gang of wild friends who are prepared for a lavish party, it generally makes a lot of sense to be proactively available if one is a host. Delays like these can occasionally call for a beating. So, to avoid my gang from going violent on me I drove fast and parked my car in a jiffy below my apartment. I checked my cellphone in the elevator and it already had twelve dreaded missed calls from different friends who were waiting outside the door of my apartment.

I rushed out of the elevator into red grumpy faces of ten of my friends impatiently waiting outside my apartment. Each had a black polybag of something in their hands.

"Motherfucker, your fifteen minutes aren't done yet", greeted Poops. Before I could speak to such a warm welcome of the late host, Mishra interrupted with, "Your twenty minutes are like an hour. Asshole, what do you think, we don't have any better work than to wait for you?" The furious faces were not as scary as the loud angry voices, since I didn't want to add another complaint from the residential society I lived in. I quickly took out my house keys to open the door. "Guys keep your voices low, I don't want another complaint on my head", I shushed cautiously. "Why shall we bloody keep quiet? We have been waiting for such a long time", yelled Poops. "Dude, I have to stay here. I can't afford another complaint, or else I will be fucking thrown out of the apartment by the landlord", I interrupted his loud cry. "What complaint did you manage to get?" interrupted Mishra in a concerned voice. "Rash driving, I guess", I answered. "Bloody kids in the society", added Mishra. "They are like piglets", chuckled Ajay with his humble smile.

The door finally opened and everybody rushed inside the way water entered *Titanic* when it had kissed the iceberg. Soon everybody was in their respective departments from the kitchen to bartending. None of my lousy roommates had reached back home from their mediocre and false work lives. Not like my work life was any fruitful, but I understood a simple reality that a lifelong job won't be sufficient to change my life. The question kept resurfacing in my observation that, "How fruitful is all the peer and superior pleasing which we all diligently do in our workplaces? Would all this hard work eventually change anybody's life? Or we are all going to end up the same – job, apartment, car and loads of mortgage? Plus, a commitment to work round the clock to help someone else become rich." At least, it wasn't my cup of tea to work for high values if the salary or even the future increments are not going to change my life financially or otherwise.

"Where are your roommates?" asked Ajay. "I don't know where the fuck are those pussies", I said with a smug face. "Why what happened with these new roomies?" asked Ajay. "I don't know *yaar*. I guess they are too conservative. One of them was bickering about smoking up in the house. One has complaints with loud music and parties. I don't know why they are even away from their homes? They should go snuggle back with their parents", I sniggered. "The worst part is, they observe all my activities with a lot of interest and then come and give me all these worldly advice. Don't drink, don't smoke, loud music is not good etc. etc. And when they cook, these fuckers don't even consider me amongst the people who are going to eat", I yapped my angst. "It's like they are the naïve conservative world, correcting the way the world is getting corrupted", and Ajay added his worldly wisdom.

"Why be concerned in the first place? Anyhow life sucks with work pressure. Doesn't it make sense just to chill?" I reasoned.

"You say that as if you work so hard Uday. As if you are going to make our organization the next two billion dollar company", replied Ajay with obvious sarcasm.

"Then what? Obviously!" I chuckled sheepishly as I was pretty aware of the hard work I was putting in my work life.

"Either ways, living through life is hard work. Even if you try to progress or if you try to scrape by. The ass slog part of life doesn't leave so easily", I smiled a disinterested smile at the ways of the world.

"Yes Uday, nobody dies a virgin. Life fucks everybody!" sighed Ajay. "I got an even better idea, let's corrupt the conservative naïve world. What say?" Ajay giggled a devilish grin.

"Yeah, it makes sense. Eventually they are all tempted to get corrupted. If nothing else, even then they are desperate to lose their virginities!" I giggled with thoughts of 'pity', thinking about the pretentious fools I lived with; who proclaimed to be righteous but can be corrupted with the slightest glimpse of temptation.

"I wish *Katrina Kaif*[45] could come home and party with us. Then I am sure your roomies will change their views on your lifestyle", laughed Ajay. "Forget *Katrina,* even if Jasmine with her red pouted lips comes home and smiles, these buggers would be all happy and partying", I added sarcastically.

Ajay laughed along. But a subsequent thought did make me sympathize with my roommates and fellow employees about the lack of options available to us in our daily lives to break free from this vicious cycle. Neither did I know of any better way to change our lives and break free, so somehow the wisdom in getting drunk to forget these tough questions of life made more sense. The only lesson I carry from my life is that nobody is perfect. Sinners too, do holy deeds while even saints would have a sin to hide.

"Talking about corruption is making me thirsty. Where is the booze?" Ajay's thirsty eyes looked around for the liquor.

"I hope the beer has not gone warm", I asked with concern only to be greeted by another howl of Mishra, "Asshole; you shouldn't be concerned about the beer as you are not getting any." I jeered at him saying, "Is this the brotherhood you keep bragging about? That one brother doesn't

---

[45] *An awesome example of intercontinental breeding and how gorgeous it could be.*

let the other brother drink in times of distress, just because he was late. That too, for a genuine reason." "Genuine reason; my ass", Poops screamed from the kitchen. "He must have found some girl or as he calls; 'blood'", added Poops. "Everybody, let's put a bottle of beer in the asshole of this asshole", chuckled Mishra. The remaining crowd cheered and howled, and before my dear co-employees and friends vented the frustration of their offices on me, I decided to go in my room and change into my favourite khakis.

I came out to the living room where alcohol was flowing freely and the boys were having fun. Short dark and muscular Mishra was physically harassing Poops, who was our regular chef. Poops was a lean lanky man with certain reptile like qualities; and his retaliation towards his molester came instantly where he tried to burn Mishra's crotch with the frying stick. Mishra retorted in shock and everybody laughed. Ajay was on the couch busy finishing his first peg of whisky, and soon was making another one. I spotted the empty place next to Ajay and took a seat there. "And tell me buddy, wassup?" I casually asked. "Nothing asshole, just quenching my thirst which I had developed for all the time we waited", he croaked in his trademark hoarse voice. "Friends, sorry I got late, now would you please drop this?" I replied with mild annoyance. "Chill buddy, just fucking around", Ajay consoled me. I smiled and began to drink. The conversation on the table traveled from the managers to movies and finally to the girls in our company. "Did you check out that Neha female, she is really sexy", added Mishra with a faint lecherous smile. "Oh yeah", I added extending the lecherous smile. "Uday, we should talk to the chick bandwagon of the training department", suggested Mishra. "Oh yeah, you should. And if you need any help, ask Uday. Or rather 'bloody' Uday", Ajay sarcastically added up to Mishra's idea. "Which chick you are talking about?" Mishra interrogated with enthusiasm. "Yeah which one Ajay?" I added. "She sounds like a flower", smirked Ajay. I gestured Ajay to stop talking about my little beginning with Jasmine. Though Ajay silenced with a mischievous grin, Mishra caught up and quickly blurted the words, "What are you guys hiding? Which chick are you talking about? You have to tell me", he pleaded to no heed. "Uday, you asshole, fucking speak up! You made all of us wait so much today. Now you better talk", demanded Mishra to which Ajay and I laughed and to God's grace, the mention of Jasmine didn't happen or my chance with her would have already been screwed, courtesy of my bloody gang of 'bloodhounds'.

Amidst all the conversation, an aroma of food filled the air as Poops entered the hall with a plate full of fried chicken. Drops of sweat trickled down his tanned brow. The hard work which he had put in the kitchen reflected on the dish. "If I look back at life and try to remember you people, the word 'blood' will always come to my mind", taunted Poops. "All you guys can talk about are girls, or as you all call them; 'chicks'", grinned Poops. "Yes, now that you are getting married Poops, you shouldn't listen to the 'chick' talks", jeered Mishra. "Fuck the 'chicks' and eat this chicken. I have fucking tolerated the heat of the kitchen to make it", insisted Poops.

Poops insistence was not really required as the boys pounced over the plate of chicken. The fresh fried pieces of chicken were pretty hot but due to the competition created by the number of eaters, most of us were comfortable burning our mouths with the hot chicken. The chicken was tasty and I went up eating the soft bone of it. When I broke the crown of the bone with my teeth, warm reddish bone marrow oozed out of it. It looked so much like blood. Mishra got a little grossed out with the scene of fresh blood being sucked by me with so much enticement. "This is so gross, you are a complete animal", said Mishra in his usual sarcasm. "Well, you wannabe non vegetarians would never learn the correct way of eating meat", I said still chewing my bone. "Even in my village, people chew the bones. They say that the real taste of meat is in the bones", added Poops.

"The real taste is in the 'blood'", I said out loud and then returned to my corner. I started drifting in a lonely space, slowly and slowly distancing myself from all the voices. They grew distant and soon they were just like a little intrusion in the void of my thoughts. I looked at everybody, so involved and engaged in each other's presence. "My dear friends", I thought to myself, and smiled at them. Thank god I have folks to live with. The 'change' life keeps bringing, often gets you in acceptance of getting used to people; and I feel my need too... But these guys are so good that they care to spend their time and emotions at my place as I am their friend. Maybe it's because they too, need me. I love the feel of being needed. It was the need that addicted me to her and perhaps it was her need to possess me which hooked both of us.

Ajay gave me a quizzical look. It appeared as if a gothic lean demon evaluated me and went back to his drink. This look of Ajay struck a chord in my head, making me realize that he wants to talk about something. People got drunk and after a while they started leaving. Ajay too, was pretty drunk by then. Mishra and Poops left together leaving behind some dinner for Ajay and me in the kitchen. I looked at Ajay and asked him, "What's the matter with you?" Ajay chuckled, stroked his thick goatee and made a funny face and said, "Nothing as such." I couldn't help probing, as the mere thought of Ajay in a dilemma appeared interesting. It was pretty contradictory to his socially perfect ways. I felt I knew my friends and insisted, "What shit is cooking in your sick head bro? Why don't you spit it out?" "For you to chew?" replied a drunk, arrogant Ajay.

I gave him a continuous cold stare and repeated my question. Ajay gave up his resistance and opened up, "Dude, can you share some of your experiences with 'chicks'? I guess I need some help." Ajay speaking hesitantly was a rare situation as he was a guy who always spoke loud and clear, often rendering the impression of the most sorted chap in the gang. I nibbled on another piece of chicken, and listened. "Dude, I kind of like this chick, and I guess even she likes me, but I just don't know whether I should ask her out or wait for her to be sure", blurted Ajay. I started laughing, and said, "Bro, you need this kind of advice from me? Come on, Ajay, you are much better than me in this subject, how can a 'bloodhound' like me help you?" Ajay looked at me again with a quizzical look and said, "It's because I am kind of getting fond of her but I am not sure if she feels the same, and if she doesn't then I don't want to ask her out and then get rejected and of course make a fool out of myself." Looking at the quizzical funny brown face of this sweet stud friend of mine I spoke, "Dude, don't ask her out and all that in the beginning." "You go ahead and first 'make out' with her, if she responds well that means you don't have to ask her out", I completed with a cunning smile.

Ajay laughed at me and said, "That's what, I don't know how to start it." "I mean I have done stuff before but there has been a long break, and what if she resists me or finds it cheap or whatever", he said thoughtfully. "Bro, the fear of rejection won't take you anywhere. You might as well give it a shot and see whether you have a chance or not. At least you won't waste time on this in your near future. Things would be sorted", I completed. "Ok now what way should I approach her, as in should I take her out for dinner, get drunk and then do something, or a movie perhaps?" Ajay asked, sounding confused. I thought for a while and looked back at him, and I smiled.

"I guess you should focus on the approach", I said. "That's what I asked you. Where should I take her to?" Ajay explained only to be interrupted by me. "No. Don't focus on the mechanics Ajay. Focus on the intent here. It is not about where you take her to. It is more about 'why' you take her to wherever you are taking her to. To cut it short, all I mean to say is, you go ahead, and intrude her aura", I explained. There was a momentary silence and Ajay lit up a cigarette still trying to figure out what I meant by intruding somebody's aura. "Kindly explain Uday", he asked with a smug look on his face as he blew out the smoke.

I took a deep breath and started, "We all have an aura, and it's like our essence. Everything that we know, we value, we carry, makes our essence. To explain it in a better way, whatever you are made up of, makes your aura. When you want to associate with anyone in a way to form a connection, you have to enter the aura of the respective person and get your aura accepted or even better acclimatized with theirs."

"Would you explain in a simpler language?" chuckled Ajay giving me the look of a deranged moron.

I laughed and continued, "Every human being has their own essence. Or simply understand that each person has their own energy, they are like a universe in themselves. Thus or so, you are a universe in yourself as you have your own energy. So when you want to mate with a girl or even when a girl wants to mate with a guy, one has to intrude the energy of the other person and present their own energy to them. The one whose aura is stronger attracts the other and if they accept, then they are connected. If you look at sexual intercourse, even that's an intrusion on one end and acceptance on the other. The beauty is in the fact that the entire nature moves and works on this phenomenon and often after such 'intrusions', peace for eternity is achieved", with a wink, I concluded.

"So you are asking me to intrude her aura?" he asked, stroking his goatee. "You must have already done that, and that's why you are in this dilemma", I gave a wise smile. "Similar to how you intruded Jasmine today?" he reciprocated quickly with the face of drunk yet enlightened monk. "Asshole, I did not intrude her as such. I guess I just took a step closer to her, hoping that she probably feels my energy", I nodded confidently.

"So tell me Mr. Intruder, how did you enter Jasmine?" he asked lecherously. "Dude, I didn't enter her, if you know what I mean", I giggled. "But still tell me, what did you do?" he interrupted. "Rather ask what should 'you' do", my index finger pointed towards him and he nodded sheepishly. Ajay's sudden interest to know my observations of human aura made me feel like a professor of aura sciences. I generally don't waste such opportunities to give a free lecture, as a token of gratitude to return the favor of all the boring monotonous lectures I had received all my life from teachers, elders and bosses.

"Well, now when you intrude the aura of a girl, you have two approaches to do so, as far as my experience is concerned", I began. "I am listening", said Ajay with a grin as he continued to stroke his goatee. "You can either touch her like 'fire' or blend with her like 'water'. When I say blend in like 'water', it works well if you want to stay for a longer while, get committed and take the relationship ahead. The 'water blend' makes you turn fluid; fluid enough to blend. You shed off your reservations just enough to accommodate hers, you laugh enough to make her laugh and both your laughters echo as one. When dreams, hopes and insecurities adjust and accommodate between both of you, and neither one of you feel the sacrifices you have made to accommodate each other; your shortcomings become her strengths and you overshadow her weaknesses as if they never existed. It soon begins to look like a dance in which two people complement each other in each and every move. So be like 'water' my friend, as it's 'water' that blends in, changes the color and comes out unaffected. But you don't come out of her aura Ajay, better stay with her forever. And that's a perfect relationship which you have got", satisfied with my 'good friend' advise I smiled and lit a cigarette.

"Dude, what is the 'fire' way?" he asked with higher curiosity. "Let it be dude, don't try the 'fire style', it needs you to burn, and not just burn, it requires you to burn with desire! You don't blend then, but you ask, call, perhaps grab or even take… At times by choice or at times by force! It's the nature of the 'fire' that it burns and it doesn't care. If controlled and kept, it's like a candle illuminating the world out of the darkness, but if left uncontrolled, it goes out to take all in the way and burn it down, and even burn itself", I completed sounding cautious to not to let Ajay take my advice.

"Why do you burn then?" he asked with a philosophical look on his face.

I wondered why I burn. I guess I burn for her beauty and what we shared and perhaps that's the only way I have of calling her back. By burning in her presence, and whatever she taught me and made me feel. "I just burn because it's sexy. I feel like a tiger burning to taste the blood at the end of its prey. Or even better, like a Vampire, who burns in his coldness just for a few drops of 'hot' fresh blood", I replied. "All in all, I like making that one fantasy of girls come true, that someone burns for you", I added, with a sadness entering my eyes, but I am too selfish to show my sadness, all I have with me is happiness and the eagerness to taste the 'blood'.

"Women are kind of ungrateful here, to fantasize having a guy burn for them so that they can feel desired", pondered Ajay. I nodded and said, "But if someone does that for you then imagine how 'hot' that is? It's like an entire aura just asking for you, and with you it completes itself", I hissed.

"I am too drunk I guess, you carry on with your intrusions, aura and 'blood'", he mumbled sluggishly. We were both pretty drunk till then to even have dinner. He conked off on the sofa and I dragged myself inside my room, still burning within. Whether it was the alcohol or the conversation but my little conquest of red lipped Jasmine was fading away. Soon, a previously experienced restlessness replaced every bit of my system. I knew I was burning for Anita, and the alcohol was taking me back to those days when I tasted my share of 'blood' with her. Tucking inside my bed, the moments of losing innocence came back, re running her glimpses. Though my sloshed eyes could barely open, but the detailed clarity of those moments spent with her were fresh. I felt her lap on which I often rested my head and her breath, which was so addictive. All I wanted was her, as somehow finding her is eventually turning out to be the purpose of my life, and perhaps my sole reason for survival.

TASTING BLOOD: INSINUATION

The monsoons had welcomed 'love' in my life that year. At least everybody around me called it 'love'; or something like that. Even I liked to call it 'love', to that feeling of the strange 'craving'. It was a tensed sensation filled with curiosity. From thoughts to body; the heightened uncertainty of every arriving moment kept my heart throbbing. I was drawn to her, like a young vulnerable predator is drawn to blood. Innocently tasting it for the first time; tasting the earthy fire of excitement. Yet that craving wouldn't stop to grow; like a certain thirst which is newly discovered and would never ever be quenched. My fingertips kept reaching out for hers. Now and again they kept finding each other and somehow yearned to stay interlocked, the way creepers entwine to make an earthy leafy crown. Creepers always find their kind, as if they were born just to find their complementary counterparts. Similarly, our fingers found each other. At times to remain together as a tight clasp – in moments of intimidation, or tied loosely – following each other around the city. From crowded local train compartments to fancy cinema halls, it was a different safety in distancing from every other entity, into a world of our own. The call to distance occurred after a small incident when I realized that even Anita could have a probable prospective dating list.

Life outside college began to appear 'cool'. Simultaneously, a little distance seeped in between us and the rest of the classmates. The pressure of the upcoming class exams also percolated in this uncertain brew. College was unavoidable and hanging out was expensive. *Mumbai* is a miserly city when it comes to privacy. People in this city work very hard to earn it and others just adjust. Broke kids learn faster to make peace with its lack. Anita and I were doing exactly the same, finding ways of being together; like partners in crime who shared a secret or rather curious with an 'urge' to create many more secrets.

The silence of the first kiss left a lot of turbulence inside me. It did comfort my insecurities temporarily, but a new set of insecurities began taking shape. Standing in the college corridors with Anita and other classmates I wondered if I would get a chance to kiss her again. Despite her attention, Anita was probably not on the same line of thoughts. She kept her social status unaffected, and never made advances towards me. Chattering with classmates on the second floor balcony of the college, I noticed her gazing at students hovering in the college ground. Her gaze specifically lingered on a boy laughing with his friends in a blue t-shirt. He had a fair chiseled face and brownish-black hair much longer than usual guys. He pretty much resembled the famous *Pakistani cricketer Imran Khan*[46].

Anita's gaze lingered on him and it made me feel something called 'envy'. Being totally forgotten by the girl I craved for, for someone who looked better than me stemmed up a certain new fear. The old insecurity of not finding 'love' was suddenly replaced with a fear of losing 'love' that too, to someone she actually digs. The thought of losing her to a lookalike of a famous guy pierced the juvenile yet nurturing feeling which I preferred to call 'love'.

I felt the surge of the icy heat of 'envy' for the blunt honesty of her eyes. It was something very close to anger but not exactly anger. I felt as if I had been wronged for not being her first preference. I looked at her with a hint of disdain in my eyes and I guess she got it. She didn't retaliate to my weary feelings as I soon realized that all the while I did consider myself 'unworthy' of even having a girlfriend. And when I had all the freedom to express my desires for other girls, it would be just for her to express the same. Neither does she refer me as her boyfriend, nor have I ever asked her out. All we shared was a secret kiss, which I indeed wanted to repeat but wasn't sure if she wanted it too.

The next day in college, Anita and I were going for a regular lecture when I saw the *Imran Khan* guy and a fellow senior pass us. They had a typical boyish mischief in their eyes and they both checked out Anita. I felt a little angry especially when I saw Anita return that typical coy look of hers. We started walking upstairs, when the senior came up

---

[46] *Pakistani politician and former cricketer. The most successful Pakistani cricket captain, leading his team to victory in the 1992 Cricket World Cup. Also, he was quite a heartthrob amongst women and had an 'interesting' personal life.*

to me and said, "Excuse me, are you Uday, can I speak with you for a minute?" Anita looked at him with surprise wondering what purpose he might have with me.

"You go to the class, I will join you", I instructed her formally avoiding any probable arguments. She began walking up while I walked with him to the corridors.

The senior had huge biceps and a very nice smile. He asked me gently, "What is your friend's name?" I looked at him and returned a quizzical look. "Which friend?" I tried to pretend to be as unaware as possible. I realized even my pitch had gone down, making my voice softer. His persistent grin broke into a frown. "That girl, with whom you had entered", he said gesturing upstairs. I felt a shudder inside for his obvious intent. He looked aside at I caught him sharing a glance with the *Imran Khan* guy, who gave him a kinky smile of acknowledgement from a distance. "Oh", my heart sank and bubbles of heartbroken thoughts burst in it.

"He wanted to set her up with him; it also means that *Imran Khan* has noticed Anita glancing at him. He knows that Anita checks him out?" I felt a little hurt for the tinge of impurity in her gleeful innocence.

"Should I give in to the seniors as they know that Anita is interested too? And why not; they are a lot cooler. Uday accept it, she will be happier there. They are her type! And look at him, he actually resembles the cricketer. He is even taller Uday; taller than you and taller than Anita. They would look so good together. Like the guy who is taller than the girl, as it happens in the movies and perhaps in a perfect world too", my thoughts flashed my picture in front of me, lonely and without friends, sad and scared.

"She is Anita", I gasped her name, and it felt a little like betrayal. I felt weak for my lack of self-belief and handicapped because of my umpteen several shortcomings.

But sometimes, 'acceptance' brings a lot more peace to a flame like 'shame'.

I stood silently and looked at him, in peace, of answering his question and accepting my mediocrity. It soon turned into an awkward moment of silence on his end.

Victory is a tricky question, and 'habit' is its simple answer. "Why?" I asked him with mellowed acceptance of his superiority.

"Are you guys seeing each other?" he asked curiously. I didn't know the answer to this question so I took a pause to answer. The question made me nervous but before I could think much, I blurted a 'Yes'.

It made me wonder the worst possibilities of this scenario as I began asking questions to myself, "Am I going to date Anita or are we already dating? Should I ask her out directly and settle this? What if this guy wants to set *Imran Khan* with Anita? Would I be able to handle this if it happens?" And last but not the least, "Is he the right guy for Anita?"

The 'craving' for her, answered these questions for my confused intimidated mind. Well the answer came to me when I asked this question to myself, "Would I able to see Anita kissing this *Imran Khan* guy or even this senior?" Well I knew my answer. So I said to my senior, "Actually, she is my girlfriend." My voice went a little low due to a minor lack of confidence for a lie and probable embarrassment if she actually wanted to date him.

"Yes, she is my girlfriend", I re-emphasized a little louder this time. He gave a funny smile and said, "It's cool", with a little embarrassment.

"I just wanted to know whether she is single", he smiled and continued, "But now that you guys are dating, so... it's cool." Watching him give up, fueled confidence in me and I said, "Thank you." He shook hands and even I smiled at this super courteous person, as such people were rarely found in my college, in fact in my life.

In grown-ups it's the amount of desires and not their bulk which rules. But in juveniles, the desire is nothing but a small 'craving'. A 'craving' much beyond the comprehensive ability of their logical minds. Perhaps if life is like 'desire', then being alive is just a bloody 'craving', which keeps insinuating our actions.

When I came upstairs, Anita was eagerly waiting for me. "You did not go inside the classroom?" I asked her only with a little surprise. "No, I was waiting for you to come. What did that guy want to talk about?" she asked curiously. "He wanted to know if you are single", I answered sheepishly. She made a coy shy face again and asked, "Then, what did you tell him?" "I said that you are my girlfriend", I replied with dwindling confidence. A little shock appeared on her face when she heard my answer. "Why did you tell him that I am your girlfriend?" she asked me with a little disappointment. "Just, to protect you, unless you want to date that guy?" I said trying to sound casual. "But then, am I your girlfriend?" she asked with a serious face. "I don't know", I said abruptly and gestured towards the classroom as the teacher just entered. We rushed inside the class before the door closed. Anita found a corner seat on the fourth row while I sat on the last bench with mixed thoughts. I felt a little humiliated for the fact that she had an obvious crush on the *Imran Khan* guy, and I like a fool, proclaimed her to be my girlfriend. It would be a matter of short time when the senior and *Imran Khan* would mock me as she would be dating him.

I kept looking at her throughout the lecture trying hard to imagine myself without her or probably just as a friend. The idea strangely appeared difficult even to think, as all I could finally see were the glimpses of our first kiss. The way she looked at me wearing the top I had gifted her, made me smile. "Should I let her go?" I wondered again. "Or should I just ask her out? At max, she says a 'no'. At least it would be better than the regret of not trying", I answered my doubts.

She walked out with the other students after the lecture ended. "Uday, did you make notes of this lecture? 'Protein synthesis in a cell' is an important topic for these coming exams", instructed Anita. I was surprised at her ability to stay focused, where she wrote down all the notes during the lecture and all I did was, think about her.

"No, I didn't", I mentioned with a smile. "Don't worry, I have written them down. You can copy from me", she said calmly. "Let's go for a walk", I said, totally ignoring the subject of notes and exams. "Ok", she returned a confused glance and began walking with me.

I led her to the same alley where we shared out first kiss. I looked around at the road to check if it was empty. Anita returned a sly smile which made me wonder if she already knew my intent. "Should I ask her out now?" I thought looking at her. "Or should I..?" and before any of my stupid logic could poison my brain, I impulsively grabbed her waist and pushed her on the wall adjacent to the big tree. I kissed her instantly, not giving her room for a single word.

She dug her finger nails in my chest, while I kept tightening my embrace. My lips forcefully sucked the life out of hers but the moment of surprise happened when she reciprocated with similar passion. A speeding car passed by, disturbing our passionate moment. We separated immediately and waited for the car to pass. I grinned victoriously at her as if it didn't matter to me anymore whether she dates *Imran Khan* or not. Her passion was my victory and I had claimed it.

She returned an embarrassed smile for her dormant 'urge', which she never acknowledged but I discovered. "What?" she whispered. "Would you like to be my girlfriend?" I asked her. All the love of the world poured out into my eyes watching her coy face when she heard my question. "What about Poonam and Rasika?" she asked mischievously. "You want me to pursue them?" I asked her in disbelief. "If you want to", she replied with a canny smile. I was too afraid to present her the opportunity to date her favorite *Imran Khan*. "What if I say, I want you to be my girlfriend?" I emphasized with authority.

I felt weak in the knees after what I had just said. She returned a coy smile with a hint of moisture in her eyes. After a short silence she nodded "Yes" with a smile on her pretty face. "You know what Anita?" I said softly. "What?" she whispered touching my face. "You are the first official girlfriend of my life. I have always wondered how will I find her? Maybe I am a little late, but it's better late than never", I gasped my confession and kissed her again, breathing small breaths of relief between the strokes. We walked back to college, victorious and hand in hand.

'Coveting' is a natural phenomenon. It happens to everyone, we all do crave for something in life. It's just that, sometimes we know exactly what we seek and at times we don't.

Exploring the vicinity of the college was a natural outcome to satisfy the 'craving' for space. The proximities pushed hard as they too craved to grow exceedingly close. Between Anita and me, people grew thinner and the world grew bigger.

Stranger 'cravings' to just be around her surged in my thoughts. A 'craving' to giggle with her and laugh at all her stories. A 'craving' to travel with her. The rains helped to keep us close and warm.

The suburb looked lush and beautiful. Old buildings reeked their stories to the rainy skies, and the skies drizzled in return. Some days later, we were back strolling in our favorite alley. "Anita, I can even walk the desert with you", I said hesitantly. She looked at me and grasped my palm and we slowed down. She turned around and I stopped walking. "What should I do?" I wondered. "Does she want to kiss, or talk?" I pondered taking a step closer. She leaned in and kissed me. I smiled and looked affirmatively at her. The mild drizzle sped up a gear as a strong wind swayed the tree nearby.

"This place is so beautiful", I said looking up in the clouded skies. We walked to the pavement as a car passed by. "I really like this house", said Anita pointing towards an ancient mansion. "Wow! This looks beautiful", I giggled. She looked at me briefly. I felt as if her eyes were asking me a different question. Maybe they waited for an affirmation. "Imagine if you owned this house!" I asked her. "Naaaice", she beamed. "Yeah, you can do so many nice things here. If I own this house, I will decorate the entrance with carnations", she exulted. "What are carnations?" I asked. "You haven't seen carnations!" she exclaimed. "Sorry, my vocabulary is not so good", I responded with an embarrassed smile. Anita was pretty sensitive as she immediately smiled back, "They are adorable flowers. Don't worry, someday I will show you what carnations look like."

"Hey look at that tree. It's so beautiful", Anita smiled. "Yes, it's so big", I smiled back; in fact I would have smiled to anything and everything she said. "Imagine how old would it be", she wondered out loud. "It would have seen so many lives", I wondered within. She stepped closer and I held her gently, pulling her towards me for a peaceful kiss. We looked back at the tree. The long slender branches with spread out leaves provided the best shade possible. The world distanced in the growing drizzle, but just then a dark big bird flew down and perched on one of the branches. I looked intently at it as it gyrated its head. The bird looked at us. "It's a crow", she mumbled. "No it's a raven. I remember", I exclaimed. "It's such a different bird. Big black and scary", I beamed in awe of the magnificent creature.

Ravens are supposed to be aggressive. A glimpse of my boarding days occurred when I had seen a bunch of ravens on a coniferous tree. It felt like a bad omen then. But this bird was different. It was alone, neither with fellow ravens nor with the inferior crows. It wasn't hungry or weary. The raven didn't bother drying up its wings. But it perched with confidence with its shaggy broad neck and dark feathers. It looked at me but instead of the expected aggression, it had confusion. I ignored the raven and went back to kissing Anita.

It was a strange sensation to feel the wetness around my lips. The mad attraction drove us, sucking for a little more of each other. The kisses grew desperate as they even sucked out the air in the distance between our tongues. I faintly opened my eyes to meet hers. "This is so embarrassing", I mumbled between the kiss. Anita paused and the drowsy affection in her eyes turned excited. "Don't you know it's rude to stare while kissing", giggled Anita. "You were the one staring", I laughed. We looked around to check for any uninvited passer-by.

The raven still perched on the branch staring at us. I ignored the little creepy feeling of being watched by the dark bird. "This bird is still here, isn't it a little weird!" I gestured towards the bird. Anita gave a deep look at the bird. "Isn't it a little scary?" I mumbled. "Shut up Uday", she immediately interrupted. "You know I don't like this kind of a conversation. The spooky ones", she said with a funny annoyance. "But look at the way it is watching us", I still protested to the possibility of the paranormal. At least, it was an insinuating idea to scare her.

"It's our 'Guardian Angel'", she clapped in a childlike excitement. Her natural frenzy made her look like a little girl who is very excited on a day out. I looked back at the raven but now it appeared gentle, like a black, friendly angel; an angel who flew down to the branch of the tree only to guard us. 'Love' is this feeling which makes the ugly look beautiful; a feeling so powerful to the extent that the negatives we know are totally ignored. "Our 'Guardian Angel'", I smiled with the happy mild innocence which love had casted.

The raven gently looked back at me. I curiously took a step closer to look. "I guess it's smiling", I said. Anita giggled, "Stupid! It's our 'Guardian Angel'." I smiled at the dark gentle angel and it looked back at me. Its black eyes had a faint gleam like the life present in 'darkness'. I mischievously moved my head mimicking its movements. The raven obliged me with participation as it moved its beak. It was a huge bird, twice the size of regular crow. "Thank you 'Guardian Angel'", I croaked. "It's about to rain Uday. Let's go back to college", she said, nervously looking at the graying clouds. "Just let me say goodbye to it", I said and turned. Suddenly, the raven croaked loudly. "What happened 'Guardian Angel'?" I chuckled. The raven croaked again and louder this time. The aggressive croaking of the raven discouraged me. "Did he get upset?" I asked her in doubt.

"Uday, please let's go. It's getting a little creepy", she panicked. "Okay; let's go", I giggled at the scared Anita and the angry bird. I gave several glances at the mysterious dark bird while we walked back. The raven kept croaking. I don't know if it wanted to tell us something but its hoarse croak was indeed ignored.

We walked back in haste towards the end of the road which turned onto the main road. The thought of scarce 'privacy' makes one realize the importance of it. It's like you want to say and do everything which you wouldn't want the big bad world to speculate on. I reached out for her hand and mildly touched it. My fingers stroked hers till they interlaced with each other. With a gentle nudge of fingers, I grabbed her palm. She slowed down and looked at me. Her eyes questioned my gentle yet bold move. "I love you", I said, stunned in her eyes. Her innocent lost eyes froze for a moment. She hesitantly looked down and returned a faint smile. Anita slowly began to walk again. Her lack of words left me a little dubious, but the heightened shimmer in her eyes somewhere still reaffirmed.

I held her warm palm and continued walking. "What was I thinking? Do I really love her? Is this called 'love'? Is it the right time to even confess it?" a lot of doubts echoed in my head. Perhaps they echo in everybody's head when they confess their 'love'.

How does 'love' sound as an idea? Whenever a boy and a girl come closer, does this idea cross everybody's mind? Whether many years later, will they still be together and happy? Living every day full of joy and each night is a passionate sleep. Would they never leave each other for someone else? What if they got bored of each other? What if they fought with each other? What if they separated? Is 'love' meant to be forever in this world full of uncertainties?

Anita's silent walk still challenged my doubts and they howled, "Do you really love her Uday? What if she leaves you? What if she doesn't love you? What if you lose her? What if you find someone else? Is this the right decision? Did you exaggerate your feelings Uday? Shouldn't you just be happy with her as your girlfriend?" and before my soul panicked to paralysis, Anita's wet lips touched mine. The rhythmic flow of her enchanting kiss silenced my doubts and uncertainties. Kissing is an interesting activity, sometimes so potent that it overwhelms all forms of verbal 'love'. The heaviness of my doubts was cleared by a mild hollow sensation in my belly. I kept kissing her like an involuntary action induced by her or by my own self. It made me feel lighter for saying those three words for the first time in my life.

"I love you Uday", she paused. I gasped for air. "I love you too Anita", I panted. Nobody exactly knows the definition of 'love'. It is just a feeling which is very difficult to define or explain. Whether it's a 'crave' or just an 'urge', the idea called 'love' insinuates everybody. The feeling of being alive often urges us to break limits. Like the limits of possibilities to the common mind, and the self-imposed limits of one's own self.

Neither of us were an exception to this idea. The insinuation did spread in our thoughts and fantasies and colored everything in its shade, like 'blood' colors the eyes of an innocent predator. Driving its breath to its only objective, the craving of what it desires. We craved for 'love', like innocent kids who always craved for a rainbow on a rainy day.

> To taste thy Blood, and then call it Love,
> But Shimmers in your eyes...
> Tastes like blood,
>
> Color me red, for a touch so wet,
> For the taste of your blood...
> My fears shed.
>
> Long after from now,
> And in your arms somehow,
> Love too; is an Idea... And my idea is 'Blood'...
>
> Even if it's Procrastination, or the surge...
> Of this never to forget Hallucination,
> Open your senses and feel the Insinuation,
> Love is the Ingredient... To a certain 'Crave' called Addiction.

TASTING BLOOD: ENTHRALLMENT

The three year graduation program was distributed into four examinations for each year. The first quarterly exams were about to commence. Passing in these examinations was important to everybody as it provided the faculty with a clear distinction of the serious students. My inclination towards life and the science which governed it, did make me a bright student. But the books on life sciences didn't have a subject on 'love'. A subject which I believed I could only learn through Anita. The concepts in the books were barely interesting when compared to the way she smiled. Her twisted nostrils and stories about *Bombay*[47] kept me engrossed. Our conversations would travel from classrooms in the day to phones at night. The books always stayed open in front of me, but I could barely understand them. My imagination was too consumed to accommodate anything other than Anita. Glimpses of her kisses kept replaying, creating a high stir in my senses which only craved to be with her.

I was sure that I was going to fail those exams, a strange feeling kept telling me. The students in the classroom kept busy framing answers to various questions, it was so important to them. But when something like 'love' happens for the first time, future has different answers... My thoughts revolved around the questions about whether or not Anita and I were for real.

Travelling for the exam with similar thoughts, I stood on the footboard of the local train. In the hot noon, my face was being cooled by the kind breeze which blew as the train clunked along. My eyes dwindled to the windy relief, as I badly needed sleep. The previous night's conversation with Anita lasted till 4 in the morning. I dragged myself to the college campus, tensed about not being prepared. "This is the first exam of the course. Freak, I am feeling too nervous as I don't know anything", I kept relenting till I walked past the college gate and bumped into her.

---

[47]   *Once upon a time, Mumbai was called Bombay.*

"Are you prepared?" asked a confident Anita. "Today is the first day of the exam and Chemistry is a relatively simple subject", she said. "I am not sure, I barely studied for a couple of hours", I answered sluggishly. "Why, what were you doing all night?" she asked in shock. "I was talking to you, right?" I replied in confusion. "Yes I know, but I finished the major questions", she said in disbelief for my inferior learning capabilities. A little insecurity surfaced on my face and I said, "I don't even know which ones are the important questions. I wonder how I would pass." She gave me a brave empathetic look and said, "Don't worry Uday, I will help you prepare."

The college entrance was buzzing with students as the examinations were about to commence in an hour and a half. "It's too crowded here Anita. Can we go somewhere else and study?" I panicked at the state of my preparation. "Alright, but where shall we go? To the library?" she suggested. "No, I guess the library will also be crowded as all these students will go there and study", I said. "Let's go to the classroom", she beamed. "Yes, that's a good idea", I nodded.

The classrooms were locked. On enquiring with the peons, we came to know that they will be opened ten minutes before the exams. "Shit! Why did we walk up two floors?" I lamented. "Uday, let's study here baby. You don't have much time", she voiced her concerns. The corridor led us to the auditorium which remained empty for most of the time. We walked inside the auditorium, took a seat and continued studying.

"This 'Atomic Hybridization' is a sure shot question. Plus it has high weightage. Just give it a quick read and tell me if you don't understand any part of it", she instructed. I began reading loudly and wandered off to the balcony of the auditorium. The dumbbell shaped atoms couldn't hold my attention for long. I looked down at the crowd preparing for the examinations. A sense of panic ran through me considering my previous year's result. "Would I do better this year or even worse than last year?" I kept thinking. Anita walked out to the balcony and stood in a corner studying her notes.

"Did you read?" she asked. "Yes, kind of", I replied and to avoid further questions, I began to walk towards the other end of the balcony which ran parallel to the stage of the auditorium. The end of the curved balcony had an open door on the right side of the wall. The door opened into the backstage. I walked inside the door into a dark wooden backstage. Sunlight through the door had mildly lit up the room. A wooden armless chair rested towards the center of the backstage. Anita followed me inside. "Which place is this?" she asked in amusement. "I guess this is the backstage. I have hardly explored the college building in the last two years", I answered in excitement.

I curiously walked towards the chair and sat down. I looked around the stage. It felt gregarious to be seated in the center stage of my existence. I looked at Anita who was still running through her notes. I looked at my watch in panic, "I better study", I murmured. She continued to walk, revising her notes. She paused and looked back at me. She gestured a "What?" with her eyes. I stared at her blankly. The beauty of closed spaces rests in the implied silence. "Why are you not reading?" she asked softly. "Are those your notes?" I asked her back. "Dumb... Of course. Why would I use someone else's notes?" she replied. "I meant to ask, did you make these notes?" I whispered in the stillness of the room. "Oh that way; yes", she answered. I looked away at the room quietly. The silence grew a bit awkward and I just waited for something to happen.

"This place is different!" she looked around. "I am sitting at the center stage", I smiled. I had my book closed in my hands, with my index finger still between the pages. She looked tall and lethal in her mauve tank top and blue denims. Her hair was tied up in a pig tail. Anita started walking towards me slowly like a cautious feline. My eyes glared back at her in excitement. She came closer and I reached out for her notes. The stapled pages were full of handwritten notes. "You have a very good handwriting. I wish I could write like this", I sighed. I put her notes in my book replacing my finger. Anita returned a silent look of disbelief.

I dropped the book on the floor and with the other hand pulled her towards me. A minor shock ran through her eyes as she hesitated but with a jerk she landed on my lap. It was a moment of silence. Silence is the absence of noise, yet 'silence' has an extreme presence, as it makes our muffled thoughts and desires echo back to us. When my thoughts and desires echoed back to me, I realized that 'silence' too, could be lethal. At pin drop silence, Anita turned and changed position. Now she faced me.

My heart pounded in excitement for the uncertainty of the next moment. I breathed heavily in disbelief at what just happened. My hands raced to her slender waist and my fingers craved to dig in. I leaned in to kiss her. She gently kissed back. My curious tongue dared to taste hers, tempted to feel her touch.

Anita pulled behind and looked at me while my tongue slowly rolled back. The gentle calm on her, turned aggressive. She grabbed my hair and pulled my head downwards. I looked up at the wooden ceiling, enthralled for the events which had never occurred before. Wet kisses and strokes of her tongue touched my bare throat. I gasped and shivered. She mercilessly kissed my throat and every stroke of her tongue, broke me a little. She had a strong grip on my hair and she pulled it down with all her strength. Her cruelty enthralled a lusty pain but her kisses had soothing warmth. I held her slender muscular body travelling through her breadth, venting out the pain.

Anita appeared like a powerful Goddess who dominated the center stage of my life. The taste of 'love' can be so unpredictable and enthralling that even worries fade away. Her touch was insinuating enough to lose my senses. I returned each of her strokes with equal ferocity as we made out on the chair, totally disconnected with anything else. Even dimensions like space and 'time' are lost in such moments. This is perhaps how carnivores feel when they dig into their first meat, their first 'taste of blood'. A taste so enchanting that even their souls can't leave.

Faint footsteps ignited a little fear, which crawled deep within. "What if we get caught here?" I thought and instantly acted. "I guess someone is coming", I warned immediately. She responded promptly and got up. I quickly handed her the notes while opened my book. Anita walked away while I sat on the chair, waiting, with my heart pounding. "Who would come? What would he think of us? What if, it is some teacher?" I kept thinking and eagerly waited for the intruder to appear. A short peon entered the room. We continued our pretense of studying while he looked at us with a scandalous gleam in his eyes. He observed us, questioning our presence in the forbidden place but didn't utter a word.

Anita and I totally ignored him and continued to look in our scriptures. "Hey Uday, there's only half an hour left for the examination to start", suggested a panicked Anita. "Let's go", I replied in a hurry. The peon continued to fidget around while we left the auditorium in a hurry, perhaps guilty of our deeds. She looked at me with mild embarrassment and giggled, while I laughed in excitement.

"Thank god, we didn't get caught", she panted. "Don't worry we wouldn't be caught", I smirked. "But did you study anything?" she asked. "I tried but the atomic diagrams just faded away to what you did to me inside", I accused her with pretentious innocence. Anita looked at me with higher embarrassment which trickled in my thoughts, as ideas to embarrass her further began to pop in my head. "I love you", I mumbled and we entered the examination hall.

For Anita and me, 'making out' in the balcony before an exam became a part of the daily schedule. For the entire quarterly examination, we sneaked inside the backstage to satisfy those certain yet undefined urges.

When your heart pounds,
To the whiff of the unpredictability in the air,

And your eyes slowly gnaw,
At the unseen in that cruel glare,

"Can't rest!" the pounding of your heart,
For the taste of 'blood',
This is just the start,

For the Enthrallment which you have never felt,
It was 'Sin' in the 'Insinuation',
Which did invent,

Growing with kisses like daisies on a grave,
Call it bloody love or just a bloody crave...

TASTING BLOOD: GRATIFICATION

During the exams, I could barely write complete answers and thus struggled with neighboring students for help. Being alert was the only way to cheat in an examination, as it is a series of little victories. Passing answer sheets under the supervisor's nose, kept me 'high' and giggling. Very few cooperated to share what they wrote. For a majority of the students, helping someone copy was a taboo; something which good kids didn't do. Beating the challenge to pass answer sheets, sneaking around in the presence of alert supervisors presented a different feel. The little feeling of breaking the rules driven by a helpless reason to copy, to just pass the examinations, had a different thrill. Maybe survival is something like that, when the need to just be alive surpasses all the deeds required to do so. Coming out unnoticed was the little crown of accomplishment to be won in every attempt to copy. Whether the attempt was fruitful or not, surviving through it felt like an accolade in itself. I didn't know whether the answers I wrote would help me pass, but the little shame incurred for being the unprepared student easily faded, replaced by the gratifying 'high' of survival. Because life could be long and boring, where every day isn't blessed with an accolade. Just getting by is an equal achievement.

Two weeks later, the results showed up. My fellow batch mates brimmed with happiness for passing whereas only five students had failed. I was one amongst the 'bad' lot. "Hey Uday, how many subjects did you flunk in?" asked a smirking geeky classmate. "Two", I replied hesitantly. "Which ones?" he probed. "Chemistry and Biochemistry", I sighed. He laughed mirthfully and said, "Chemistry was the simplest exam. I guess it's just you who failed in that subject." I looked angrily at him, feeling bad for my stupidity and lack of preparation for the exams. Anita walked in with her result and placed her arm around my waist. "It's ok, you will make up in the next exam", she consoled me for my horrible result. My jeering classmate shut up. He looked at Anita, who had passed in all the subjects and scored the second highest in chemistry. I looked at him and smiled for the 'love' of my intelligent girlfriend, which incidentally

66

grades couldn't buy. His eyes narrowed down to 'envy'. I ignored him and looked back at Anita, with a lot more affection than usual.

He walked away, ignored and silenced. Perhaps I wasn't that 'bad' at chemistry after all. At least, that was the only little accolade Anita bestowed upon me, by slowly turning me into the center of her world.

After that, failing in exams wasn't hurtful anymore. My results of the first quarterly exams never reached home and though my mother kept pestering me for it, I happily procrastinated till the next exam arrived. My immediate world often took it like a dutiful responsibility to shove 'shame' for not being a good student. But even 'shame' fell on deaf ears, as all I heard was Anita and her conversations.

The idea called 'love' wasn't an idea anymore. It kept maneuvering me day and night, keeping me thrilled, like the first taste of 'blood' keeps a young predator driven to explore it further. Perhaps 'love' was the 'blood' which I had never tasted.

The 'taste of blood' after invading and enthralling one's senses, often demands 'gratification'. But the 'urge' to gratify oneself, is often heard like a muffled whisper. Something unheard, yet too loud to ignore. I often heard such 'cravings' within me, driving me to explore her further. I just felt like touching her all day, as I kept finding reasons to be with her. She was well versed with my growing fondness and often reciprocated it, though careful of public speculation. But 'curiosity' is a very integral component of the 'taste', like a thirst which badly wants to be quenched. I was always curious to know her more and see her further, though I never knew how to achieve what I so badly craved for. Someone else also made its yearning pretty clear, but that someone stayed with me. My 'little warrior' behaved unusual as he stayed warm most of the time. There were erratic erections especially when I was with her or thinking about her. Maybe that's why I began to feel a 'hard on' all the time. Not that I did not have an erection earlier, but now the 'little warrior' pursued her too, erect and pushing forward in her direction.

September was about to end and the wounds of the horrible exams had surprisingly healed in only three weeks. Life had returned to normal with our usual outings. "I have to leave early today. I guess, I won't be able to join you guys for the movie", said Anita in hurry. "Why? What happened? Why aren't you coming along?" asked an enthusiastic Gando. Ratish along with Rasika and Manjeet waited downstairs in the college building. "It's a friend's birthday. I need to meet her", she explained. "Which friend?" I asked curiously. "It's Nikita's birthday today", she answered. "I have to go or else she'll be mad at me", she hurriedly explained and continued packing her bag. "Cool! Uday, then you come along with me. Ratish, Manjeet and Rasika are waiting for us downstairs", suggested Gando as his enthusiasm didn't mellow down. "Hey I guess I will pass this time", I said with an embarrassed smile. "Why what happened to you now?" asked a mildly infuriated Gando. "Nothing, I just realized that my family is going for the same movie in the evening. So why watch it again?" I added. Gando's enthusiasm finally mellowed down a little as he left alone to catch up with Ratish and the girls for the movie.

"Why didn't you go for the movie with them? Go for some other movie with your family", suggested Anita. "My family isn't going for any movie", I smirked. "Then... Why?" she returned a surprised look. "Because what would I do without you?" I said, helplessly staring in her eyes. She returned a shy smile and stepped ahead to give me a quick peck on my cheek. "I love you", she smiled. "I don't feel like letting you go", I said with admiration, touching her fingers.

Anita looked at me and it appeared as if an ocean of affection has poured out in her eyes. She grasped my palm in a tight grip and closed in her palm, as if she is just trying to feel the warmth. I stood there, in awe of the reaction a few words could create. "Uday", she finally spoke. "Why don't you come along?" she asked softly.

"Where?" I asked in confusion. "For Nikita's birthday", she winked. "But she hasn't invited me!" I protested in confusion. "It doesn't matter, you are always most welcome to join", she insisted with a wider smile. "Ok" I reluctantly said but 'blood' never lies for what it seeks as I felt the surge of excitement for spending some more time with her.

We quickly left to catch the local train to *Bandra*. The trains were relatively empty in the noon. Anita and I stood at the footboard of the local train as it slowly clanked its way to *Bandra*. "Where is her party?" I asked her as she gestured a rickshaw to stop. "The party is an hour later. But, before that I have to go to my place and change", she explained. "What's wrong with what you're wearing?" I asked. "Stupid, all our friends would come for the party. I don't want to be in this crushed T-shirt", she protested.

Anita guided the rickshaw driver to her home which was on a lone road covered with shady trees. Small residential buildings stood on both sides of the road. Expensive cars were parked alongside, adorning the residents of the posh suburb. Anita paid the rickshaw driver and he left. "Alright, you change and come. I will wait for you here", I said courteously. "Alright", she casually replied and began to leave. "Hey Anita, where can I pee?" I called her back. "Don't pee here on the road. Ok let's do one thing, you come upstairs", she reluctantly offered. "Who all are there at your place?" I asked fearfully. "No one. My parents are at work", she replied. "And your brother?" I asked. "He must be at his friend's place playing video games or something like that. His exams are near and that moron is happily wasting his time over stupid things", slammed Anita.

We began to walk inside the gate of the building where a lazy watchman adjusted himself on a metal chair. I gave his uninterested vigilance a rest as he drowsed away. Anita said in a hurried hushed voice, "Rush upstairs. I don't want my watchman to notice you coming with me." We quickly tiptoed upstairs to the third floor and she opened the door to her apartment. We giggled in the adrenaline rush for making it unnoticed by the world.

"Sit here while I change and come back", she said gesturing towards the couch in her living room. I obeyed and waited for a while on the sofa, fidgeting with the magazines. No piece of information was legible over the curiosity to follow her. The idea to be 'home alone' with her kept drawing the images of possibilities of things that could happen. Though saner thoughts did conflict but the 'taste of blood' can easily overpower timidness. I began to grow very restless and couldn't help entering her room. Anita was out of the washroom in her white party top. "Just give me two minutes, almost ready", she said as she quickly combed her hair. Her white tilted collars appeared different. "You are looking good, as in sexy", I smiled sheepishly feeling the similar urge to touch her again. "Nice collar. Pretty different than usual", I complimented as I walked towards her and stood behind her in the mirror.

Anita passed me an affectionate glance in the mirror. Encouraged with her admiration I embraced her from behind and gently kissed her neck. She tilted her head to kiss me and we witnessed ourselves kissing in the mirror. "Let's go. We are getting late", she whispered as soon as the kiss ended. The intriguing possibilities which were growing in my head a few moments ago were silenced. The thrill of the kiss was also mellowed as I realized that I didn't want to leave. The taste of her wet cherry flavored lips resulted in an impulsive move as I pounced on her and we fell on the single bed adjacent to her mirror.

"Uday", she said in her husky voice giving me an intimidated look as if she knew what my intent was. I silently kissed her, deafened by my desire. Her resistance melted with my growing touches. "We have to go Uday", she mumbled beneath me as I rested on top of her, still kissing and ignoring her defenses. My curiosity raced inside her top and I pulled it to reveal her 'hearts', which were covered properly beneath her bra. "My top will get crushed", she mumbled amidst kisses. Anita resisted and tried to pull her top down, but instead I started pulling her top off. "What are you doing Uday, you will spoil my shirt", she protested strongly. "Anyways your 'hearts' are partially out so why spoil the top. It's better if you take it off", I immediately suggested. "No", she giggled but the influx of the little 'shame' quivered in her guilty eyes as I hurriedly removed her top and threw it on the floor. I gave a similar treatment to my t-shirt, craving to feel her trapped bosom against my bare chest.

She was left in a black bra and denims. My hands raced behind her, craving to unhook them free. I never knew then that the bra hook could be so tricky and stubborn. It immediately killed my stylish attempt to open it with two fingers as I had seen in a popular banned commercial. I turned her around to open the hook with both my hands. My struggle with the tiny hook made her giggle. "Does it have a password?" I smirked. Anita continued laughing while I struggled to open the vault of the untasted 'blood'. Finally, her bra was open and I pulled it out setting free her gorgeous caramelized creamy breasts.

For a guy like me, I had only seen the human female mammary glands on a television set in porn movies which were played in my boarding school. At times I had also seen them in the *Debonair*[48] magazines which were also a very popular component in most of my batchmates' cupboards. Laying hands on porn in *Mumbai* was easy but watching it was horribly difficult. Most kids either saw it at a friend's place where generally the friend got caught by one of his family members, or at a cyber café. "This is better than porn", I exclaimed looking at her bare self. Her awesome pair of feminine blissful fruits smiled back at me, adorned with prim and proper tiny brown nipples. The view of real boobs in my face almost made me cry. I had never imagined that one day those curvy 'hearts' would actually come out of the television sets.

What was left behind were two bare chested individuals, breathing heavily into each other in such close proximity. The lips began kissing in pairs in mad frenzy. The touch of her bare torso on my chest felt like a dollop of butter on a frying pan. The heat which I had preserved over years of abstinence melted on the treasures of her heated body. I grabbed and massaged them and finally couldn't resist the urge to suck them.

I moved down to her navel and soon I was licking and kissing every bit of her bare upper torso. It felt like a desperate attempt to quench a lifelong thirst. Little freckled goose bumps appeared on her skin wherever my tongue traveled and all I could hear were soft hisses as I traveled her gorgeous landscapes. Her long slender fingers ran through my hair and I heard her call my name. "Uday..." she hissed in a husky voice.

"Yes", I whispered as I traveled back to her face. The look in Anita's eyes had an inert 'fire' burning beneath the 'guilt', somewhere asking me to free it. The more I looked into her eyes, the more 'turned on' I got. "Let's

---

48   *Debonair founded in 1971, an Indian men's magazine on the lines of Playboy.*

71

go", she said in a coy voice. I couldn't resist asking her, "Could you suck my thing?" I said amidst heavy breaths.

She looked at me with a little surprise in her eyes, while I anticipated my little fear of getting rejected. But when yearning for 'blood', often 'shame' and other reasons which might come in its way are mercilessly killed.

Perhaps even I lost my 'shame' or the little fear which had stopped me. I shamelessly unbuckled my belt and opened my jeans and pulled it down. The bulge on my underwear was soon revealed. Anita's eyes opened wide as she looked at my chaste 'little warrior' beaming at her, asking her to satiate his 'fire'. She hesitated with mild embarrassment but yet moved down and held my 'little warrior' which had grown enormously. She held it with both her hands and her fingers clasped around the hard piece of muscle. "It's so huge", she said in amusement. I felt good and I said softly, "Thank you." I eagerly waited for her to start while she looked back at me, unsure of what to do next.

She hesitantly went down, engulfed it in her mouth and I could feel her teeth digging my shaft. I got up in an instance, and looked at her face. Maybe my fear amused her as she laughed and tried to bite my shaft off. I screamed in a frightened voice, "Don't do that, it's very sensitive, no teeth please." She laughed louder like a power seeker belittling all my manhood. Although the 'little warrior' is the epitome of manhood and perhaps one of the strongest reason which keeps men alive and moving, but at times it can also be extremely vulnerable and sensitive. A man's happiest moment, is also his weakest, because the thing which makes you exhilarated is the only thing which can make you morose – making men very much like their inflatable and deflatable ego.

But Anita didn't intend to deflate it as she moved her head back. I laughed mildly, scared and relieved of avoiding a major massacre of my dear 'little warrior'. She kissed it lightly and then ran her tongue on his topography. I waited in exhilaration for her to advance. She glanced back at me, probably just to be sure... but in her eyes I saw the glimpses of what all I wanted to do. It was like my list of those unfulfilled desires which I had carried through life, surging like impulses of recurrent cravings for all that I wanted to feel and explore.

Maybe the 'unexperienced' starts our defining our idea of 'blood'; an idea we all muster and nurture in our hearts... and we keep yearning for its 'taste', hoping that one day we will 'tick it off' feeling satiated. Gratification is the little accomplishment for fulfilling a long carried desire, and mine got fulfilled when she engulfed my 'pride' in her wet mouth stroking it to a new 'high'. It was the most amazing feel I can ever describe, and it stands true in every man's context of that glorious list.

Enchanted in sensations, I pulled her head a little closer, till she choked on me. She immediately pulled her head back and coughed. She looked at me in disbelief. "Sorry", I apologized, feeling that perhaps I had gone too far. Suddenly, her phone rang and Anita rushed to check. It was her father's call. She panicked for a few seconds and signaled me to 'shut up'. She answered the phone and I shut myself up totally panicking at the thought of her father.

After a while the tension settled and I looked at my topless beautiful girlfriend talking on the phone. The endless list of unfulfilled desires resurfaced, and I traveled again to the thoughts – of the things I would want to do. My helpless need to know her, turned to touch, which eventually turned into a desire to be touched. I wondered if this 'urge' could ever be gratified. It just kept growing from one desire to another. Maybe that's the 'taste of blood', or the thing called 'being alive'.

It was a shocking yet pleasant difference between her clothed and her topless self. Anita saw me silently letching at her and she made a coy face. But perhaps her shyness also got colored with the 'crave' of being desired, or her 'taste of blood'. She raised her index finger and gestured me to come to her. Her sudden provocative call disrupted me before I could lose myself further into deep useless thoughts. I obediently tiptoed to her and sat on the bed, curious to touch her again. I silently sucked her bare brown 'hearts' while she continued talking on the phone, breathing cautiously to not be overheard by her father.

When the call was over, she realized Nikita had called several times. "Oh my god, she will kill me", she giggled. I saw a message from Gando. "You guys are big time ditchers. Ratish vanished with Rasika and Manjeet and no one answered my call. I would never hang out with you guys", I read it out to her. We continued giggling, slowly shedding off our 'shame' and embarrassment in our semi naked selves.

The urgency to leave, had mellowed down while 'time' continued to fly by. Anita and I struggled to keep away from touching and kissing each other to finally get dressed. "Anita, I would go home now sweetheart, it's pretty late already", I mumbled while kissing. "Yeah, it would be better. If Nikita sees me and you, she would get the wrong idea for me being late", she suggested. It was getting difficult to leave each other and we dragged ourselves to the door of her apartment. "I still don't feel like leaving you", I whispered in her mouth. She looked back at me with admiration. Dusk had begun to set in and we reluctantly walked out of her apartment. The sleepy watchman was wide awake and he passed us a suspicious look. Anita called a rickshaw for me. "You are very sexy Anita", I said stepping ahead to kiss her. But she stopped me by my chest, to avoid any public display of affection in her residential vicinity. "You are sexy too Uday", she said softly, looking into my eyes and we parted for our destinations.

Stirred up are my Senses,
Lower than ever are my Defenses,

Can't carry anymore these forsaken pretenses,
And I want you, in all my tenses...

The gleam of Forbidden glittered with Ice,
To have them Devoured, I shall pay any damn Price...

Too curious to resist the Temptation,
Touch of lips is the beginning of the Sensation...

Of the Thirst which Demands Satiation,
When Burning with Desire, the Ointment is Gratification...

TASTING BLOOD: ADDICTION

Blood once tasted can never be forgotten. And if you just discovered that what you tasted turned out to be your 'blood', then you will always yearn to taste it again. Sometimes this yearning can reach a point that it can possess you, driving you crazy in its pursuit. Only to discover that no gratification can ever satisfy this thirst. This thirst also begins to define our lives as knowingly and unknowingly we would always find a way to be around it.

As days passed by, I came to know Anita better. The more I knew her, the further I was mesmerized by her uniqueness. She was a very talented girl but she indeed had something much beyond mere talent. Her tall curvy silhouette and uber quick athletic responses didn't make her look like any sassy girl. In fact, they reflected on the culture of grace and substance, in which she was raised. She had topped in almost all exams throughout her academic life and yet was an excellent volleyball player. Her linguistic skills were far superior to any of her counterparts. When she spoke, even tough guys silenced to listen to her. Her long slender fingers adorned by her longer nails could maneuver a pencil into drawing beautiful abstract sketches which she often drew on the last pages of my notebook. Yet she would look at me, and her large feline eyes would pause me, waiting for a comment on each of her creative accidents. I would often wonder why she even needs my acknowledgement! No one there, including me were even close to her level. But whenever she received a compliment, she returned something which perhaps nobody could. It was her graceful smile, which left people in awe of unbiased friendship. She was kind to the weak, and treated the odd ones with respect, but when required she would voice her opinions loud enough for people to hear.

Her taste would often reflect in her pick of clothes and the way to carry them. In spite of a modest allowance, she picked clothes which looked rich. Whenever I looked at her, I could see a clear difference in the way she dressed up as compared to other girls. From light casual colors to grand ethnic Indian wear, Anita often made the idea of buying her gifts pretty interesting. Her versatility often reflected the traits of someone we would like to acknowledge as "Beauty with brains", but I felt a few more traits which I never knew then, I would miss so badly. They were things like substance of character, a big heart, loyalty and humility.

She would often quote a sentence which her father kept repeating. "Do you know Uday, why do *Punjabis*[49] have big faces?" she would often ask. "No", I often pretended ignorant. "Because it's a reflection of their big hearts", she would complete and her ethnic gorgeous face would beam with her gregarious smile guarded by pretty dimples. Thus, she would happily trot around from classrooms to pavements, casting an imaginary halo on the world. Perhaps it was her aura. An aura which created an influence of positive happy vibes on the world it interacted with. It was something which I had never seen before, and perhaps wouldn't ever see again. An aura too unique for anyone to ignore.

'Love' too, is like 'blood', thick and 'red' in color. Perhaps that's why people say, "Blood is thicker than water", to denote family ties and bonding, as even they are formed out of 'love'. And like blood connects the various organs and cells in a body, so does 'love' keeps a family connected.

But in the eyes of a predator who craves for love, 'love' often becomes its 'blood', its only reason to survive. Can 'love' also be so addictive? So much so, that it starts defining everything in our lives? Wise people always say that 'love' is a part of life. For the unwise, perhaps 'love' is life. She often told me, "You are like this 'always ready to make out' kind of a guy." "That's because I love you", I often replied out of embarrassment for such comments but my body behaved otherwise.

'Love' did cast its magic spell in form of the pink blush which often appeared on Anita's face. She started looking better day by day, as maybe a lot of 'making out' does that to you. I barely found time to notice myself as I was too engrossed in noticing her. At the same 'time', the feeling of someone waiting for me at college increased my affection for

---

[49] *People of Punjab.*

my educational premises and as a result I started spending much more time in college. On the other hand, I witnessed my life move around hers through the posh suburbs of *Bandra* which previously I had no reason to visit. I often thought about my previous two years in *Mumbai* when I had come down from the hills. All I did was go to college and come back home, like a mechanical monkey, each and every day. I avoided bunking lectures with crazy friends as if I was trying hard to look good to the other losers who attended the last lecture. My mediocre scores added up the deepest regret as 'time' gone by never comes back.

Like 'blood' adds life to a body, 'love' adds life to everything it touches. Anita often laughed at the fact that even after two years of staying in *Mumbai,* I had never seen *Bandra*. She had soon become my eyes to this marvelous city, in which I lived but never explored. We became inseparable; as if we were glued together by some invisible yet strong force. From classrooms to labs, to the intricacies of the big city, we wouldn't leave each other, deeply involved and yet so curious.

Our days passed by in college and its Vicinities,
Where we just found reasons to remain in Proximities.
I wondered if she could help answer my Curiosities,
Only for me to surface to my own Insecurities.
Yet her eyes continued to make my day,
Alluring me with Resistance,
On my Soul's advancing Insistence,
Her Coy shall always lay....

The incident which happened on Nikita's Birthday opened a different realm of 'being in a relationship'. I could never understand how Anita looked at it. She never said anything about how she felt with me, or rather what she felt for me. A week post this incident she came running towards me just before a lecture was about to begin.

"Uday you won't believe what happened yesterday!" beamed an enthusiastic Anita. "What?" I asked with curiosity. "I was hanging out in *Bandra*; with my *Rotary Club* friends. Even Nikita had joined us later. And guess who arrived?" she paused. "Who?" I asked dubiously but somewhere inside I kind of knew the answer. "It was Rohit", she answered. "The one with a *BMW*", I said conforming my doubt. "You remember him?" she exclaimed in surprise. "Yeah, you had told me about him. Anyways, what happened next?" I asked quickly. "He came and sat on the same table where Nikita and I were sitting. It seems he had been working out lately and of course he looked better. But then he just wouldn't leave me alone. He kept bragging about his Dad's business and then he kept making these stupid remarks, which were hell annoying", she continued. "Then what did you say?" I asked with mild anger. "Well, I remained silent and kept smiling. But it seems, Nikita quite liked him. And then she started flirting with him. She was very impressed with his car. And then she asks him to take her for a ride... But you know what he said?" she paused again. "What?" I asked curiously. "He said that he would only take her for a ride if I am willing to go on a ride with him", she chuckled.

"Oh boy, you should have seen her face!" she laughed. "Oh, then did you go for a ride with him?" I mumbled suppressing my 'envy'. The mention of a guy and that too handsome, rich or ambitious often shook my world when it came to Anita. "No I didn't. Though I like his car, but I really wasn't in a mood to go. Nikita kept on insisting but he just wouldn't take her along with her. I just told him that I would like to be here with everybody – as we all are meeting after such a long time", she answered, relieving me off my insecurities. "Indeed you look way sexier than Nikita", I forced a smile to keep up her enthusiasm. The idea of having a potential model for a girlfriend was like a dream come true. It sounded sexy, and it made me even fonder of her. But it also presented a negative feeling, that of an inferiority complex.

We rushed inside the classroom and sat together on the last bench. Anita quickly flipped from her glory and focused on the lecture while I deviated to my hidden insecurities. "Why does she like me? I am so dumb, poor and average looking. What if she had been topless with her ex-boyfriend? Should that affect me? What if she develops the 'hots' for this rich, well-built owner of a *BMW?* What if he asks her out, considering that he finds her 'hot'?" I pondered in the ocean of my negative thoughts.

'Love' in its true form is much about liberty, and to such inferior thoughts, liberty is the best answer. Her hands suddenly slid into mine and I quickly turned towards her. She was still busy penning notes from the lecture. I felt like the teddy bear which a little girl needs to hold every night to go off to sleep. I looked at her in awe and relief. "No, this Rohit guy doesn't have a chance. And about her ex-boyfriend, she isn't dating him anymore. So her past doesn't matter", I consoled my insecurities with my new found liberal views on life.

"Let's go for a walk towards the market", suggested Anita when the lecture ended. I agreed and we left. We passed a roadside bookseller. "Uday, can you buy me a bottle of almond milk?" she asked. "Of course", I said promptly to do anything to be her perfect indispensable boyfriend. I went to buy her beverage and when I returned I saw her standing at the bookseller. "Thank you Uday", she smiled giving a peck on my cheek. "What are you buying?" I asked curiously. "Nothing, just checking out", she smiled and we continued to walk towards the suburban railway station.

"Bye Anita", I smiled as we arrived at her station. "Uday, wait!" she called. "Yeah?" I turned. She opened her big blue haversack and took out a gift wrapped object and placed it in my palm. "Oh come on! You don't need to do that. It's not my birthday", I whined in self-respect. But her mushy eyes melted me instantly, as I felt her gift. "Open it", she grinned. I immediately shed off my modesty and opened the gift wrapper and inside was a book with a title which read *"The Godfather."* I felt weak in my knees and a little ashamed for my previous insecure thoughts. "You didn't need to", I said softly but I knew that words weren't enough for her affectionate surprise. I stepped forward and kissed her on the main road. She reciprocated with an initial resistance but was soon impassioned by her dubious lover. "Uday people are watching", she whispered softly. I reluctantly stepped back. "I love you Anita", I smiled, holding my tears on threshold. "I love you too", she smiled back answering my insecurities.

Thus 'love' began defining my life. Like 'blood' stains anything with its color, so did her 'love'… staining everything that comprised me. But I seldom knew then that 'love' too, has many shades, and its thirst drives many to explore, at times even to their doom. Though my insecurities were reassured, I still craved for Anita. Can anybody ever be satisfied with what they know of a person they 'love', or the curiosity to travel deeper, rules the relationship? The 'urge' to know her intricacies drove me consciously and subconsciously.

The Godfather was a timeless masterpiece and it kept me hooked whenever I wasn't with her. A month had passed since that day till on a holiday eve she called. "What are you doing tomorrow?" she asked. "Nothing. It's a holiday so I guess family time", I returned a confused answer. "My family members are going out of town for some work tomorrow as it's a public holiday. Uday, would you like to come here to *Bandra* and then we can go travel around? Or perhaps we can call Ratish, Gando and everyone else and hangout?" she enthusiastically added. The idea of enjoying privacy with Anita answered, "Yes, I guess we should do that. But why call anyone else? It's been ages since I have even kissed you properly", I replied with lingering passion. She giggled as perhaps she got the hint. "My father is honking wildly outside our house. We are going out for dinner", I flipped, disturbed by long aggressive honks. "It's ok Uday, you rush. Call me tomorrow when you are leaving", she added and quickly hung up. I rushed outside to face my father who was often angry with my casual delays.

The next morning I woke up excited for the awaiting privacy with Anita and quickly started getting dressed. My family had made plans for a movie. Watching me getting ready to leave, my suspicious mother asked, "Where are you going Uday?" I mustered all the seriousness I possibly could on my face and replied, "There is a special guest lecture in my college on genetic re-engineering and one of the faculty members of an internationally acclaimed institute is conducting it." My mother asked me sternly, "Are you serious? Who keeps lectures on an *Indian* public holiday?" Somehow I always felt as if my mother can make out whenever I am lying. "Yes, it's very stupid. But I am getting late Mummy, I have to leave", I mumbled with pretentious annoyance and before anyone could probe me further, I collected my bag, wore my favorite sport shoes and rushed out to catch the local train.

In about an hour I reached Anita's place. The local train was relatively less crowded, saving me from the aroma therapy of various kinds of sweats and odors. I tiptoed quickly upstairs dodging the sleepy watchman and rung her bell.

I was already excited wondering the possibilities the day could grant. The thought of "Getting Laid" often passed my mind and every time it did, I skipped a few heartbeats. Anita opened the door covered in a skimpy black spaghetti with orange hot pants. Her long hair was ruffled up in a ponytail. Her black bra straps ran parallel to the spaghetti straps while her hot pants wrapped around her rack revealing the broad curvatures of her tush. I could see the hair nodules rise on her silky waxed legs. I felt elated and grinned proudly to the thought that even the goose bumps on her skin were anticipating me.

I entered her apartment, and went straight to the washroom to clean my face off the dust and sweat I had endured on the train ride. Of course, I should look good when I am in front of my girlfriend especially when she had dressed down looking so 'hot' for me. I came out, and Anita stood with a glass of water in her hand. I gulped it down and crashed on the sofa. She continued to stand with both her hands on her waist. We made some small talk as I drooled over her raunchy appearance. Her sensual eyes made me feel adored. It's difficult to remember the words of the conversations in such moments. It's just the eyes and bodies which talk, making words pretty insignificant.

Without much delay I pounced on her like how a juvenile carnivore would pounce on its initial prey, kissing her wildly. The mild absence of opportunities to 'make out' with her swelled the thirst so much that we ended up on the floor of her living room. Neither did she hesitate to make advances as she took off my t-shirt. Her bold move left me enchanted, while her saucy curves provoked the burning curiosity. I reciprocated by pulling off her spaghetti to get a much clearer picture of her assets. I threw her spaghetti on the floor leaving her just in her bra and hot pants. Black and orange over her brown skin appeared 'red' to my thirsty eyes. She crawled like a feline and came down on the floor and began unbuckling my belt, perhaps craving to finish the previous incomplete business.

The chemistry between our bodies communicated in a controlled thirst, as we removed each piece of clothing, 'one at a time' appeasing our thirsty eyes of the 'blood' we had so fondly began to crave. She boldly pulled my underwear down to my hips, with a familiarity of a conquered territory. But the moment she saw it staring outright at her, she displayed a familiar hesitation as she held it tightly feeling its heat. "Do it", I whispered in arduous thirst. She looked at me perhaps to judge how badly I wanted her to go ahead. And without much ado she engulfed my already hard 'little warrior' in her wet mouth. She slowly kissed the hard muscle like a young predator explores its first kill, innocently playing with blood and bones. Her sensual tongue licked and danced on the surface of the stretched skin. But like when we taste 'blood' and realize that something inside us has changed and we are not what we were, anymore. We might leave whatever we think we want, only to taste what we just came to know. Often a young predator would lose that little inhibition to devour and similarly she continued with her undiscovered imprudence, pinning me down on the floor of her living room. I gasped and trembled when I couldn't handle the sensations she mercilessly created. When 'fire' meets 'water', what's left of it is a smoldering wetness which still pulsates with the heat which it tried to extinguish. Yet the flames still burn further demanding higher satiation.

But my curiosity was far away from being satiated as my unruly hands raced down to unhook her bra straps. Unfortunately, I again needed both of my hands to do it. I lustfully touched her 'hearts', rubbing my fingers over her tiny erect nipples. She gasped in passion and reciprocated by pushing her mouth deeper on my 'little warrior'. She moved down to my hanging grenades and began kissing and tonguing them. I looked at her, bewildered by her soaring courage. She didn't care much to notice me as she was engrossed in siphoning my 'little warrior'. But in a second glance, she looked straight into my eyes. Her cold stare asked a million questions which I apparently didn't bother thinking about, or perhaps I was too nervous to answer. The 'little warrior' and his huge pride bloomed with happiness as she slowly submitted.

I took off the ruffle band on her hair setting them free. She continued to stare into my eyes as she sucked my 'little warrior'. With her hair opened she appeared like a goddess of sex cleansing the dirty corrupt soul of her follower who slithered in ecstasy on the floor. I held her shoulders and pushed her back, and instantly walked out of the stuck pair of jeans into a completely naked and free man. She gasped for air, but I filled in with a kiss. From the living room we kissed to the master bedroom to a white cushy bed. "This is her parents' bedroom!" a voice shrieked Inside my clouded head. But my passionate frenzy suffocated the breath out of wasteful conscientious thoughts. I pushed Anita on the bed and grabbed her hot pants. There was this look of a skip in her eyes; as if her eyes said 'no' but her body said otherwise. I too skipped a thought which I didn't want to think.

'Love' had a moment to choose between curiosity and compassion. But when the 'blood' is 'love', curiosity often wins. And my curiosity finally pulled her pants off to reveal her inner secrets. She had beautiful thighs and my eyes opened wide as I stood at the bed post. When I separated them, she whispered, "No, Uday." When 'blood rush' meets 'blood lust' it often deafens senses and reasons, coloring everything in its hue. Where the victim and the victor both turn 'red', as it reddened me, surpassing my thoughts of unprotected sex and its consequences. The deception her lack of consent created conflicted with her heavy breaths and passionate eyes. Words ceased to be heard in my head as I dragged my hard erect self, closer to her. It felt like an external force driving me as I inserted my phallus inside her and pressed in. It was hot and wet inside, as if some high temperature liquid filled up the space, and bathed my 'little warrior' in an ecstatic feeling. Maybe 'fire' and 'water' coexist in the 'taste of blood', where 'fire' burns the thirst and 'water' promises to satiate it. My eyes opened wide and I gasped a heavier breath. Nature has its own program to run its beings and I thoughtlessly began to move as if I already knew the way to quench my thirst. But it's not just the warrior which was thirsty. Passion soared in her eyes like 'blood' mixing with 'water', coloring it 'red'. And in a moment it suddenly exploded. Her strong yet feminine hands pushed me away, thrusting me so hard that I was thrown on the floor. Anita screamed, "I told you not to do it."

All I didn't anticipate was, what if I was denied access to her deeper darker secrets? I didn't know how to react as my manhood was still charged up, but I was very embarrassed as the first female I had inserted had denied me. Moreover the fall made me feel so unmanly as if a woman had picked and thrown me on the floor. It was definitely the pride of the 'little warrior' which was hurt. "How could she say no to me?" the 'little warrior' questioned, getting enraged. A sudden fit of anger had taken over me and I furiously started collecting my clothes and wearing them. Anita rushed in the living room in her hot pants, quickly picking up her fallen clothes and wearing them. I was dressed in an instance, still 'hard' and angry.

She rushed to the washroom while I walked towards the door. "It's not her fault Uday", I reasoned with myself but glimpses of her melting down in the intrusion of the 'little warrior' returned. But so did the moment that had passed, when she threw me away. I felt wronged for not being allowed to enter her aura, but her passionate eyes continued to haunt. The hot wet fluids inside her still extended their sticky warm feel on the 'little warrior' provoking enough for me to leave.

I opened her house door and walked off, while Anita came running behind me. I took the stairs and stopped the first rickshaw I saw and got in it. I told the driver to drive me to the station. Anita called on my cellphone and I answered, "Why are you leaving?" she asked worriedly. "I just didn't like what happened in there, I am very angry right now, let me cool off, then we will talk", I screamed for my hurt juvenile ego. "Please Uday, please come back, we will sit and talk", she pleaded. Some rejections leave a scar of a lifetime. The glimpses replayed in my head again and I screamed, "Fuck off; I will call you when I feel like."

I kept disconnecting her calls in fury, while she kept calling back. The 'taste of blood' takes over predators defining their lives. In humans perhaps it's their 'pride', or it's their 'need'. I could never fully understand what offended me the most, when she denied intercourse... I was unsure of even doing it in the first place and logically I knew it was my fault as I didn't take her permission, before entering her!

Confused, embarrassed yet enraged, I rushed into the local train. But like 'blood' never lies, neither did my thoughts as all they saw were her heated eyes. The increasing wind cooled off my heated thoughts, but the 'taste of blood' had done its job. The 'taste of blood' is so enthralling that all it needs is 'satiation'. But if ungratified, it can make one angry and perhaps even dangerous.

This is often called 'addiction', which the 'taste of blood' can cause. A thirst so enchanting that quenching it becomes the purpose of life…! But the ironies of 'time' reveal the fact that this thirst can never ever be quenched…! All I could think about then was 'making love' to Anita, and I traveled back home with a 'hard on'. "I love you Anita. I swear", I mumbled to myself regretting the anger which I displayed.

The only ugly truth about addictions is that they come with withdrawal symptoms, when denied. The ugliness of these symptoms are lesser known till they actually happen. Was it just 'love', or was it an addiction nurturing way beyond my own understanding?

Damped in your wet thoughts,
Still intimidated with the Passion you brought,
Scared of the sensual…
Forever, for which I might rot,

Unexpected,
Even when it has already Arrived,
Before I touched…,
It's your curves which Derived

Licked it with Love, but it's Lust which I got,
Pushed in for thrill, which I so badly sought,

The twinkle in your eyes held me still,
For the urge of your fill,
Love returned with the kill,

The thirst of your Fire, and with you I am drenched,
How much ever I drink your Blood…?
This Damned thirst could never be Quenched…!

TASTING BLOOD:
ENTRAPMENT – BONDED OR BLINDED

Fumes of rage came out as cold water drops trickled down my heated head and heart. I stood in the shower and negotiated my reasons with my hurt pride. Anita had stopped messaging or calling me, but glimpses of our last encounter flooded my thoughts. The vivid thoughts of her body and the passion in her blasted eyes engrossed me, so much so that her rejection too, didn't matter. Maybe the thirst for 'blood' does that, helping one forget all the failures, rejections and hardships incurred in its pursuit. My 'little warrior' remained undeterred even in the cold shower, hard and stiff, still dwelling in her wet heat. "What if I have lost my chances with Anita?" I kept wondering. I stroked my manhood as together we completed what was left and so badly wanted, even if in a fantasy... Finally, the ever desired ecstasy arrived as white drops of tears poured out of my 'little warrior'.

The hope of 'love' too, drained down with water mixed with tears, as my phone beeped lesser frequently. "She is losing it on me", I gasped accepting defeat. An hour passed by and the 'silence' of the phone deepened her value. It wasn't a pleasing silence, but as it continued, I felt trapped in it, desperate to hear a voice, any voice, her voice. But this time 'What if's' too didn't play in my mind. It wasn't my regular insecurities anymore which made me sad, this time it was 'hope'. I sluggishly wiped myself dry, wishing I hadn't tried harder. The only conflict which didn't settle were her eyes. "Were they angry with me too? I felt that they loved me, the way she loves me", I struggled with the last drop of the drying 'hope'.

The 'silence' broke with the ringing of my phone. I rushed to my table, in a towel wrapped around me, to answer it. Heaven gave me another chance as it was Anita who was calling. With a breath of relief, I was pulled out of the spiraling silence, to a call of 'hope'.

"Hello", she said in a feeble voice, as perhaps even she was trapped in the 'silence'. 'Hope' is the best remedy, even for wounded pride, but she wasn't affected with my disease. She was disturbed with separation and the 'silence' of the loneliness which it brought along. Perhaps she called to check whether I was still mad at her.

When 'hope' left my body, I felt my diaphragm go down touching the burning hollow in my stomach. My heart on the contrary just wanted to weep. Something inside pushed the tears on the other side of my eyelids to fall off. A terrible experience like this just created a dreaded hollow inside me, where I could do nothing but wish against the deadly repercussions of regret. As often the consequences of reality are faded in outcomes of regrets. Perhaps 'blood', or 'love', is the root of gratitude. The gratitude we often need to have, for our only, most cherished, desire to get fulfilled.

Imagine people with no desires! How dry, life would be for them?
Pretty similar to the blood which dries off, to become a Clot,
Which slowly rots, from Red to Brown,
Losing the gleam of its only Crown,
Love is nothing but desire, as Life is nothing...
Than an outcome of Fire.....

A heat so Divine, that even the Righteous couldn't be free,
And even if the 'Evolved' despised the 'taste of blood',
An ocean of 'crave' filled their desire's flood,
And together they ferment to spice,
To rot to a life, so beautiful that even a lifetime can't suffice....

A heat so Divine, that even the Righteous couldn't be free,
Even their thoughts say so, hanging on the Wisdom tree...

Desires are nothing but 'cravings' gone mature.
So is 'Blood', Nothing... but pure.

"Hello", I said feebly, hoping forgiveness from her. An eternity of 'silence' can turn 'voice' into a stranger. I heard her breathe, and with her breath I restored mine. "I love you", I gasped in peace as I restored my locked soul out of the 'silence'. I took several heavy breaths relieved to know that she still cares. Maybe it's an alterside that even 'blood' likes its craver. Life could feel so incomplete, if no one craves for us.

"I love you", she wept. "I thought you will never see me again", she simmered. "Even I felt the same", I gasped. "I miss you here. Feeling too lonely", I softly mumbled. To a lonely one, romance is nothing but companionship whether alone in 'silence', or in the crowds. Maybe the 'taste of blood' is our companion through life. We either taste it or yearn to, but throughout life we seek it.

"Hello, my lovely babe", I murmured. "How are you angry boy?" she hissed in a husky voice. "I have lived today a thousand times over, still 'turned on' and sad", I mumbled. "I am sorry for today", I meekly apologized. "Don't know what had happened to me", I said recuperating from the dreadful silence. "It's ok. You shouldn't have left though!" she said in a softer voice.

"You looked so beautiful, in those hot pants. Can't forget the way you looked. Especially when you were stark naked", I tried to pause but my insolent 'crave' just blurted everything out. "Oh my god", I gasped.

"Shut up Uday", she resisted in her husky voice. "I love you and I can never forget what happened today", my voice broke a little. "Me neither", she gasped.

"Hey my house is empty for the weekend, would you like to come?" I murmured. "Ok. I can come", she answered in a while. "I so feel like kissing you", I whispered. "Can you stay here for the weekend?" I asked. "That won't be possible. I won't get permission", she answered. "It's ok. I just wanna be with you", I said, still relieved for her return.

"Can we...?" I murmured and paused. "What?" she whispered. "Should we.... Do it then?" I hesitantly asked. "You really want to do it?" she murmured. I just took a heavy breath expressing my consent. Anita didn't answer this question and we continued through the night till my mother woke up and came to my room. She always had a clue if I was talking to someone at nights.

The next early morning, a taxi waited outside my house to drop my mother and sister to the airport. My younger sister and my mother were flying to *Delhi* for the weekend to meet a few relatives. My father had left for a business trip to *Indonesia*. An empty house is the best gift they left behind for me.

As soon as they left I rushed to the medical store nearby. This time I did not want to make a single mistake and thus I came back home prepared. Just the part at the medical store was a little awkward, when the attendant had asked me what I wanted. I had said softly, "Condoms", too embarrassed to let the other customers know that what I had come there to buy. The attendant had replied, "Which one?" and it got me further confused.

Now condoms have a lot of variety. There is *Kamasutra*[50] which has a very 'hot' cover of naked bodies 'making love'. It is so porn like that it is very difficult to ignore and not ask for it. Plus there are these dotted and ribbed varieties for extra pleasure. Although I had never seen a live condom on my 'little warrior' and as a matter of fact, even held in my hand. The memory of boarding school stayed as few stupid kids used to blow balloons out of smuggled condoms. I remembered picking up a condom user manual on the road, and reading intently about "How to wear a condom?"

Nevertheless, I gathered courage and said *"Durex extra safe[51]"*, a little louder this time. A couple of other customers looked at me and gave me a weird look which I was so not prepared to see. I continued to look down at the counter. As soon as I got the tiny quintessential box to safe sex, I rushed towards home as fast as I could.

---

[50] *India's second largest condom brand. Currently, being exported to over 40 countries around the globe. No wonder, we taught the world – How to make love?*

[51] *An English condom company with its name abbreviated for the words "Durability, Reliability and Excellence", which they promised to provide in lovemaking. Also, the extra safe version – thicker with extra lubrication, yet promises no sacrifice of comfort... Wow!*

I eagerly waited for her to reach. The doorbell rang and the maid answered the door. Anita entered my room to find me nicely tucked in bed. She was buttoned in a floral sleeveless shirt with a pair of blue denims. The buttons on her top were of a very peculiar nature, they just had to be pulled hard, and they would open without breaking or tearing off. I had started to call that shirt of hers as the 'easy open shirt'.

"Close the door", I commanded, but she looked at me and made a dubious face and asked, "The maid?" "Don't bother", I said arrogantly. She reluctantly closed the door and walked up to me. I reached out for her hand and pulled her onto the bed. We quickly tucked ourselves inside the blanket. "I am sorry" I said kissing her. She gave me a tight hug and continued to kiss.

Having her back in my arms, was a storm of relief. I couldn't possibly imagine myself without her. As I took heavier breaths of an overwhelming completion, she grazed my lips with pounding kisses. Perhaps this is the only relation possible between the addict and the addiction. She glanced back like an innocent girl. Lost in her eyes, nothing felt obscure. Maybe it's just the way nature made its beings. Her deep lingering kisses were similar to the innocence of a young vulnerable predator, gently chewing and sucking through its prey. My body craved to touch her, and just keep touching her. My hands raced inside her 'easy open shirt' grabbing her belly, rubbing her navel. A spark of pleasure surfaced in her eyes. I wanted her even more and pulled the buttons of the 'easy open shirt'. They popped out instantly as the floral piece of cloth vanished exposing her bare upper torso.

It was like a certain new madness we just incurred to become one, as we removed every barrier between us. She couldn't stop kissing and soon we were two semi naked bodies, drowning in the burning fire. Although frenzied, yet we tasted each other like innocent kids. The 'taste of blood' washes away the thoughts of regrets or consequences. Bonding to become one, the taste of blood compels us to complete ourselves. Perhaps that is the nature of blood and those addicted by it. She didn't hesitate to siphon my imprudent 'little warrior' which didn't know any regret. Neither did I wanted to regret – not tasting her!

I embarrassedly took out the condoms from the drawer. She was kind of shocked to see the condoms while I quickly opened one to put on my hard 'little warrior'. I held it very carefully like a precious delicate feather. The moment I installed the condom on my shaft as instructed by the manual, I felt a strange suffocation on my manhood. I felt like he was screaming in suffocation where nobody would hear the muffled voice of the erect 'little warrior'.

She was lying naked on the bed in her panties. She immediately switched off the lights out of embarrassment. I slowly pulled her last piece of clothing out of her legs. My heart throbbed for her reluctant submission. I nervously came on top of her and slowly separated her legs. The 'little warrior' had anticipated the 'blood' coming his way as he urged inside her 'darkness'.

A couple of drops of tears oozed out of her eyes. I quickly whispered, "Does is hurt babes?" "A little", she said in a cranky voice. I moved very slowly, though my suffocated pecker felt nothing. She remained still and perhaps in pain, stopping me at times from moving. "Just stay inside and don't move Uday, it is nice that way", she mumbled with her eyes closed. I kissed her shut eyelids.

She slowly opened her eyes and looked into mine. I suddenly felt very weird to look back into hers, as if I have made an unbreakable bond with them. Her light brown eyes were filled with moist love, but didn't ask any question. She just smiled and so did her eyes. I felt as if I am fixed and bonded to this girl forever. Her affection had sadness, which slowly engulfed me, making me tremble. A reality dawned at me at the same time – the reality that I have lost my virginity to this beautiful girlfriend of mine, whom I have begun to love. The 'taste of love' is dual, like the coexistence of two extremities. Perhaps like affection blended with sadness, brewing to possess you yet yearning to give away... Or bonded like water, but still entrapped in the burning flames.

'Together forever' is what I traded, but my juvenile brain had a doubt. I was just not sure, if she would be the one I get married to or should I have kept my virginity for my future wife. "What if I marry her?" another thought argued. I stayed still for a longer while and barely moved. For the fucked up suffocating condom, I couldn't feel any of her heat or wetness like the previous time. After a long struggle I gave up the hopeful pursuit of an orgasm. I withdrew and hurriedly removed the suffocating latex tube off my shaft. A thought passed suggesting me to shag out my vengeance but another look in her eyes just mellowed me down.

Anita held me tightly while I was still haunted by her melancholic eyes smiling at their predator. My dubious 'pride' made me question, "Did you have an orgasm?" She nodded a weak "Yes." All I knew about orgasms were that it makes one happy. I wasn't really convinced so I asked her again. She reluctantly said "No, I didn't, it was hurting a lot." Even juvenile 'love' can level massive pride. My 'little' pride was nothing for the way she held me. I kissed her and said, "Its ok. Neither did I." She looked at me, touched my face and said, "Why do you look so sad?"

What I felt that day in that moment, lying in the arms of Anita was something which I hadn't felt for the past eighteen years of my life. I had always been very eager to lose my virginity since the day I had got an idea about sexual intercourse. My desire to lose it increased much more when I had seen my first porn movie in my boarding school. I wonder why I lost it so late. Probably that's the price I paid for being 'good', as 'bad' boys don't wait... they go all out to get what they want. There is such a huge pride associated with boys about losing their virginities. No wonder girls turn into objects of sex in such perspective. But when I actually lost it, it felt totally different. I felt that mine was not as important as the girl I am losing it with, because even she lost her virginity to me. Now, she would have to remember me for the rest of her life. And even I would remember her, but God forbid what if we separate?

How would I ever be able to replace her in my life? I stroked her head, and kissed her forehead. Looked at her with all the awe and admiration which this little desire of mine had mustered up in all these years, and now fulfilled. It's just that I had imagined myself very proud on the day I lose my virginity. But I was not so proud, only sad. At the same time I connected with a girl on 'love' and admiration and felt a very profound concern rising for her; a concern which would never ever let me forget her and not care for her. A concern which would always remind me of the 'time' I spent with her and the courage required to take care of her in times of need. I held Anita and mildly cried to myself, while Anita cuddled up with me and consoled her cranky boyfriend.

"I don't know, it's like I am feeling weird about having sex", I said in an almost cranky voice. "It's like I have lost my virginity", I said almost in tears. She embraced me tightly and I consoled myself. Anita softly whispered in my ears, "I love you Uday", and kissed on my nape. "I love you too", I mumbled to her shoulders and we continued to cuddle.

The eagerness to lose my virginity kept pushing me till I lost it. But then, all I could feel was sadness. Like the 'taste of blood' eventually brought sadness while it promised the ecstasy of a lifetime. Perhaps, achieving what one craves for the most brings nothing but emptiness, when their only desire is fulfilled. I was bonded to 'blood', which was 'love'. For a moment I felt trapped, as if I cannot 'love' anyone beyond her. "What if I met someone else, someone who maybe looks better?" I wondered cuddling in her arms. "Naah, that would be betrayal", another thought reasoned. Maybe losing one's virginity is more about the bond than the orgasm. And thus 'blood' bonds all those who seek it, entrapping them in its cursed quench forever.

Another few days in college, and I had almost gotten over the loss of my virginity. I was surprised that I behaved more girlie as compared to how Anita should have behaved. Nevertheless, coming back to the females of my college, my 'little warrior' had started showing some activity. Anita and I were openly dating now, and everybody knew about it. Some kids jeered and bitched about us behind our backs, and few kinder ones encouraged us. Nevertheless we were so involved in each other that the existence of anybody else didn't matter at all. We kissed in public, in coffee shops, in the local trains, in movie halls, in taxis, in the lab, in empty classrooms and every other place where it was exciting to kiss. We even scandalized people and often shared a laugh about it. Many a times we were very close to getting in trouble but we luckily always escaped. I had grown possessive about her, and I couldn't stand her with any other guy. Even her ex-boyfriend, other close guy friends from her school, everybody was hated and detested by me. Anita didn't like this trait but accommodated it. Anyways, we were too busy amongst ourselves to notice or be bothered by anyone else.

Losing one's virginity irrespective of one's gender is definitely the dearest 'blood' one can taste. It's that moment of actualization where human beings come to understand their extended purpose of existence – which is reproduction. In books of biology it might look like a simple biological phenomenon, but when subjected to oneself it's a plethora of emotions and feelings. It's not as simple as it looks, but yes human beings are smart creatures. They eventually learn to belittle the magnificence of the beautiful feelings like these and just go ahead to consume it. I had tasted my 'blood', and I barely knew then that it is going to be so addictive. That in the pursuit of 'blood', what all awaited my path.

Alcohol was something which I had never experimented with. Maybe a beer, once or twice and that too was met with a lot of disdain from my residential colony friends. Anita was drinking secretly with her girlfriends and often told me about it. I was still carrying the 'good' boy baggage and treated it with contempt till one day when we were at my place. I had then introduced Anita to my parents and sister. My younger sister really liked Anita and looked up to her. I admired the fact that my sister had finally found a counterpart who won't do her any harm and bully her as most of her school friends did. After a jolly brief conversation with Anita, my family had to leave for my father's friends get together. I chose to stay out saying that I had to complete a college project with Anita. As soon as they left, Anita looked at me and made a very cute face.

She had a way of making me agree, either with her raw sexuality or with a melting puppy face. I asked her, "What do you want now Nitu?" Slowly and steadily Anita had become Nitu for me, and I loved calling her Nitu with a lot more affection. She pointed towards my father's mini bar and said, "I want to drink something." I looked at her and firmly declined saying, "It's my father's bar, and he knows that I don't drink. If he comes to know that the alcohol level in any one of his bottles has decreased, he would kill me." Nitu made a growling face and said, "You are such a scared chimp. All I asked for was a little vodka and you are scared. We can fill up water and keep the level same. Please Uday!" The stretched "Please" by Anita, changed my mind. "Anyways, my father has got many bottles, but I cannot afford to look sissy in front of my girlfriend. After all, I am his son; he can definitely lend me some booze to look cool in front of my girlfriend", I thought in my head.

So I opened up my father's mini bar for the first time in my life, simultaneously consoling myself with my reasons for this treachery. I looked at Anita to choose a bottle. "Pick a bottle which is already opened", I suggested. She took a while studying each and every bottle, from Tennessee to Scotch to white rum to tequila. Finally she picked out a bottle of *Absolut Cranberry Vodka*[52]. I found some sprite to go with it, and we made two tall glasses of vodka on sprite and ice. We raised a toast to a common line which was obvious and that was, "I love you", as we said in unison. I took a hesitant first sip and it tasted fruity. Soon we were down two glasses and I was swinging. Anita surprisingly had a large capacity to drink, and she sat still drinking, making one peg after another. Anita helped me to my room as I was a little drunk, and already reciting vows of 'love' and marriage to her. On the bed, we lied down next to each other, and this time Anita was undressing me. Once I was naked, and lying drunk on the bed, I suddenly felt wet around my 'little warrior'. I realized that the bastard is getting erect. I looked down to see my lovely girlfriend demonstrating her newly acquired skills of giving a blowjob, that too, to her first time drunk boyfriend. In a short while Anita rested at the bed end with her legs apart and I stood there with my hard shaft just waiting to get inside her. "Come on Uday, go for it", she moaned. I wanted to tease her a little so I did not insert her. Instead I said, "Nitu, I want you say that you want to get fucked by me."

"I want to get fucked by you Uday", she said obediently. It really turned me on, but I wanted to play more. So I said, "Say, please fuck me Uday." Anita hesitated and finally said, "Please fuck me Uday." The moment I thrusted my heated organ inside, Anita gasped in amazement. Her eyes

---

[52]   *Absolut Vodka was introduced to the global market in 1979. Since its launch, Absolut has grown from 90,000 liters to 96.6 million liters in 2008. It has become the largest international spirit and is available in 126 countries. Available in a multitude of flavors.*

were wide open and a smile appeared on her face, and she moaned, "It's so huge Uday; your 'little warrior' is actually a 'huge monster'!" "Keep going Uday, it feels so good, when you are inside me", she mumbled and clawed her nails into my hind meat. I liked the pain it caused. We did it for a while till I saw the excitement in Anita's eyes appear more like sadness. "What happened Nitu", I asked as I kept moving. "You don't love me Uday", she said slowly. "You just want to fuck me", she added in a 'low' tone. I stopped that very moment. All the alcohol inside my system went absent with its effect. I embraced her face in my palms and said, "No Nitu, I really love you, I don't just want to fuck you."

"No, you just want to fuck me", she retorted like a cranky child and the 'little warrior'; the coward he was, subsided in his size and voracity. I pulled back her clothes and wore mine too. I dragged Anita to the center of the bed where she could take a small nap. Surprisingly Anita was very heavy for me to move. I tucked her in a warm bed sheet and started cleaning the drinking table. I was still wondering why she felt that way. I just wanted to have a good memorable time with her. I still felt a little 'guilty' for the incomplete act of the merciful alcoholic fuck.

Well in my observation, people generally forget the incidences which take place when they are drunk. Naturally even I had forgotten the feelings of the first time I had alcohol. Surprisingly my girlfriend was a lot sharper when it came to being drunk and remembering what had happened. Somehow, she recollected the line which she had said to me about "Not loving her but just wanting to have sex with her." There was coldness in her tone and she kept a little distance from me. I was already addicted to 'making love' to her and her coldness was making it difficult for me to stay close, yearning with all that I could give and be, just for the taste of her 'blood'.

The journey of 'blood' never ends at insinuation. It will keep seeking enthrallment, as that's the 'high' of 'blood' and perhaps 'love' too. From one thrill to another, 'love' blinds it seeker, as how 'blood' blinds its predator. Risks just increase the thrill, as 'blood' easily attained might not be respected. Perhaps that's why when blood is left open, it clots, trying to prevent any more of it to leak or get contaminated. That's why a predator needs to inflict a fresher wound each time to suck more of it.

Day after day we waited for lonely moments and a couple of weeks later, the moment arrived. Anita had come over to my house to do some common group study for an approaching class test. Anita took care of my studies like her own, starting from notes, tests and lectures. She kept me updated on everything. Sadly all I could think about was touching her. We were studying in my room and I couldn't lock the door as my family sat outside. I tried getting close to her but I just faced resistance. Till an instance arrived when I couldn't control myself anymore and pounced on her for a mild kiss. I was instantly thrown away by her firm attitude. After we were done with the studies, I set out to drop her to the nearest available conveyance to take her back home. On the way I turned the car to a nearby suburban railway station which was under construction. There was a lot of empty space in the parking lot and very few people frequented that area. We parked the car in the corner and I tried to kiss her again.

She resisted me for a while with her coldness but eventually I gained access to her inner beauty. We kissed and we kissed, like I was making up for all the lost while. "I want to suck you", I said to her in exasperation. Anita again gave me a colder stare but lifted up her t-shirt, and I was astonished to see her readiness. I did not waste time in reasoning. It felt so nice to lick the bosom of pleasure. When I was finally a little satisfied, I asked her, "Nitu, what happened to you suddenly?" I mean you were so against making out and now you are fine with it." "Yes, I was in a state of thinking that what I am doing is correct or not. Whether my family would be happy to know this about me", she said with contempt and her 'guilt' saddened me. I looked at her sadly as her reason was justified and her choice was hard and even unacceptable to me, but the 'little bastard' heard his own music. I was soon about to accept that the last time we 'made out' was the 'last sexual encounter' I had with her, however then she added, "But then I eventually thought what the fuck! It's a normal thing, and that's the way you are, I don't think you will be able to do without it!" I smiled with relief for her decision and she smiled back coyly and we got back to kissing each other. Suddenly, Anita called out my name in fear and shrieked, "Uday, cops!" I turned to my right, and to my horror there were two cops on a bike who had just entered the parking lot. They were coming straight towards us. I pulled down Anita's top back to normal and started the car. Seeing the car move, the cops started waving their sticks and hurling abuses. I started racing my dad's little hatchback to run away from the menace of the cops.

In *Mumbai* or rather in entire *India,* moral policing is a way of satisfying old rotting values for beautiful things like 'couples in love' with each other. Sadly it's often labelled as the *'good Indian culture'.* The cops tried to chase, but gave up very early. We drove away laughing. It was laughter of relief and trust we shared as we could have been in a very embarrassing mess, which could have involved our parents and money, especially when my girlfriend would be associated with immoral behavior. Nitu looked at me with admiration and I regained my breath for a near escape from danger.

Like in the jungle, when a mate is attacked by other predators, it often requires valor by the other mate to protect its better half. Considering the threat the cops posed on us, Anita suddenly became my priority. Protecting her, topped my list. An epiphany occurred when we rested in peace and it again began with "What ifs?" The frustration of average *Indian* males struggling for a livelihood and menial comforts, often leaves them hungry to abuse the little ounce of power which they possess. I realized I couldn't trust anyone when it came to Anita or rather any woman I really cared about. I even knocked my head a couple of times wondering if I was blinded to not think of the consequences when it came to her. Maybe 'blood' blinds too, making one lose reasons in its thrills.

Post this incident, we stopped 'making out' for a while. We would spend the day with each other like before, only with a lot more socializing with others. The other kids had become our friends and slowly I realized that it was not just about us anymore. Ratish and I hung out a lot more. Ratish was himself getting involved in a little psychotic love triangle around two girls, Manjeet and Zaida, who were both good friends of Anita.

A month later our annual examinations were about to commence. With my disaster in the previous examinations, I was a little afraid to mess this one up. Especially when I knew that if I messed up the upcoming exams, my H.O.D, Mrs. Ragade will get my parents involved. I knew I wouldn't be able to handle my dad's anger over this disappointment. Anita, like a sweetheart helped me with all the possible notes for those exams, and we both studied at our respective homes, this time with a lot more focus and concentration. The exams finally commenced and got over. I was leaving for a couple of weeks to meet relatives all across the country and to attend the wedding of a close cousin.

A day before I was leaving, Anita had come over to my place. My family was already fond of her, so her coming over was greeted with a lot of joy and appreciation. After spending half a day with my family, Anita and I got some time off in front of the computer. My sister was leaving for her friend's birthday party and my parents went to take a nap after a heavy lunch. "You know Nitu, back in my hometown, especially in the events of marriage, there is a lot of groom hunting which goes down", I laughed. "So, you are also going there to look for a bride!" she bickered in a jealous tone. "Obviously not, why would I look for anybody else when I have you", I tried to pacify her. "Plus finding someone as sexy as you is impossible for a chimp like me", I further chuckled. "By the way, thanks for *The Godfather*. It was an amazing read", I added. There was a brief moment of 'silence' and Anita gave me a cute but grave look and said, "Uday, please fuck me." I was taken aback. But she was serious, and she started unbuttoning her jeans. I stood up instantly and locked the door, very silently. We could not afford to take off all clothes as anyone can knock on the door and it will look too suspicious or could be very embarrassing. So getting delayed was not an option. Anita pulled her jeans to her ankles and I pulled my boxers to my knees. I kept my hands on her knees as she was lying on the foot of the bed with her feet on the floor; I entered her. We 'made love' for a while and it was hurried and intense, till I heard someone waking up in the next room. We quickly got dressed up again, and I opened the bolt of the door. The moment I stepped back, the door opened. It was my father. "Why did you close the door?" he asked sternly. "Well, we were watching a movie on the computer and so we thought that the sound could disturb you", I replied immediately. Anita made a cute face in front of my father and I guess that worked.

I tried hard to ignore the little twitch on my father's face, though the gentleman in him left his prodigal son at peace with his girl who was apparently his friend. I reasoned with myself for being a guy and driven by 'lust'! But what was wrong with her? Couldn't she gauge the consequences of such a deed in such circumstances? Perhaps she was blinded by 'blood' too, messing with sensitive family ties at such close proximities. Maybe she was enthralled too, or just sad that her lover was leaving for a long vacation. I collected myself as soon as my father left, maybe after all, ignorance is actually blissful.

"That was so much like a quickie which *Sonny Corleone*[53] had had with the maid of honor", I remarked excitedly. "But you know what Uday, you are more like *Michael Corleone*[54] from *The Godfather*", she said affectionately. Well, can't help what Anita said as eventually the girl falls for the hero of any story. "Am I the hero of her story?" I asked myself. Before leaving; at the railway station platform, she said, "Please don't go there and find a bride for yourself." I silently but affirmatively nodded. We exchanged a tight hug and a goodbye kiss and parted. The local train arrived and Anita boarded it. She stood at the footboard and looked at me with a lot of affection as she hung out of the train door. There were a couple of tears in her eyes. I could never forget how she looked at that very moment. The train started moving and I stood at the platform looking in her eyes, as she stood at the door staring at mine. All the people who were trying to rush in the train could not bother the passionate eye lock we shared. I got a little pushed and she got a little pushed. Anita was very strong for the ladies compartment, as even being a girl, she had the guts to kick guys in their balls. She stood at the door unmoved as she passed me in the moving train. I kept looking at her head which kept on getting smaller and smaller as the train got further and further, and then so far that she appeared more or less like a dot, and then she vanished. I lesser knew then that in years to come, people would actually vanish from life like this. It's just the

---

[53]   *Santino 'Sonny' Corleone was the eldest child of the Corleone brothers, known for his temper, compulsive aggression, and rash decisions. A fictional character from "The Godfather."*

[54]   *Don Michael Corleone, son of Don Vito Corleone and Carmela Corleone. One of the most interesting character in fiction.*

memory which remains. I was a little melancholic and a little romantic. I still craved the warmth of her hug and the look in her marvelous eyes. I could just thank God for helping me find the most amazing girlfriend of my life! And I didn't know then, how much this unforgettable memory is going to cost me. I slowly started walking towards the parking lot, still lost in the thoughts of Anita and the day we spent together.

When I returned from my short vacation, I was dying to meet Anita. I guess I had missed her so much for all that while. Moreover, there were no other good looking females on the trip. Even the females that looked good somehow had made me feel that they socialized with boys with a strong, stubborn agenda of getting married. To add on to my hesitation in socializing with females of smaller cities and towns was majorly contributed because of the urge of their parents to get their daughter married to me. Perhaps it was their 'blood'. Not because I am prince Charles of Wales, but because the reputation of my family was commendable and they generally looked for such families to settle their daughters with. The reputation gave them an idea that even the son-in-law to be is going to turn out to be something nice and displayable in social circles. With the 'blood' I had tasted in the previous year and the addiction it had caused me, I had a bleak idea of what I was going to turn into. I felt bad for the girls too, as their parents considered them incapable of self-survival and marriage as their only hope.

Last, but never the least, even if I tried, I couldn't reach any close to compare my lovely girlfriend Anita with other females. I was back in *Mumbai,* and the city felt much better in spite of all the hassles it presented, because it was home to the girl who made *Mumbai* home for me.

Anita made a very sweet arrangement at her place and called me. There was nobody at the house. I rang the doorbell and it was answered shortly by a sexy lady dressed up in black spaghetti and a sea blue sarong. Her long black hair were loose and free. A sensual perfume enlightened my nostrils. But the best part of this fabulous diva that had opened the door for me to enter her house and her heart was her smile, a big brilliant smile composed of beautiful teeth. There was an awesome aroma of food in the house. I could also hear some *Persian* music playing in the living room. Anita quickly closed the door as soon as I entered. She gave me a warm hug, kissed me and then stepped backwards and asked, "How do I look?"

"You look so amazing!" I ogled at her from head to toe and then looked back in her eyes, so enchanting they were, that I lost myself for a while. I so wanted to go back to the eyes which I had left me there at the railway station. Throughout the vacation, her eyes haunted me and then I was finally back, in front of them. I stood speechless staring at her as she returned a diminished giggle and looked down. "Can you walk around and show me?" I asked as I wanted to enjoy more of her unconventional attire. She hesitated for a while and walked to one end of her living room, while I made myself comfortable on the sofa. "It's very embarrassing", she mumbled. "It's ok", I insisted with a smile. Anita started doing a ramp walk from one corner of the house to the other, while the *Persian* music grew faster into dance beats. She took a few steps and then did a few grooves and finally she came to a standstill in front of me. The pace of the music grew faster and she flexed her hips in a form of belly dancing. Her arms flung around as she did marvelous poses with a constant gyrating movement of her waist. When she shook her head, her long black hair followed. I couldn't resist myself at the sight of this sexy woman, doing sexier moves on a *Persian* belly dance number. "It's more of a mixture of belly dancing and *kathak*[55], something very extra ordinary and unique", I said with my breath getting heavier. I was so 'turned on' that I started undressing myself on the sofa, till I was left in my underwear. Anita walked to me and sat at my feet. She kissed the bulge on my underwear. She took out my 'little warrior', which was then paying a standing ovation and she looked at me with a much stronger spark in her eyes. She gasped at my erection, and returned a sly smile. I looked at her and she glanced back before she took me in her mouth. My jaw dropped in awe of the ticklish wet feel, while I grabbed the sofa edges and tried to relax. She moved her head deeper on my shaft, till she choked. "Let's go inside", she said and grabbed my 'little warrior' and pulled me up. I followed her to her room. We had a long session of 'love' making, till her breaths became shallow while she moaned louder. She pleasurably shrieked an exasperated cry and regained her breath.

---

[55] *A traditional Indian dance.*

I was far away from my orgasm so I continued beating myself against her pelvis, while she dug her nails in my back and clawed it so hard that I ended up screaming. I continued moving inside her with all the force I could muster. Every time my body clashed against her, a clapping sound occurred which began to sound louder, much louder than her passionate moaning. Anita moaned, "Don't stop, you are right there!" In a while she screamed to her second orgasm while I kissed her. She shrugged off my kiss, and instead bit my left cheek so hard that I screamed. I jerked off my orgasm to her. Anita brought her head closer and sucked me till I came splashing my hot juice all over her sweaty 'hot' bronze body. She wiped herself with a towel, and then wiped me. I wore the towel around my waist while she wore her sarong crossing it over her shoulders and tying a knot behind her neck. She tied her hair in a bun, and we stood in front of the mirror, where I grabbed her in my clutches from behind. We adored ourselves in the mirror, sweaty and shining in the glow of sex and 'love'. "We look like a perfect tribal couple", I snorted, and Anita laughed. I kissed her on her neck and kept rubbing my palms on her shoulders. "Come, I have cooked something for you", she said and then grabbed my hand and pulled me to the dining table, which was next to the balcony, and a clear view of the *Arabian* sea was visible. Cool wind blew in from the windows, which moved the curtains as if they were possessed by spirits. The wind chimes became the voice of the curtains and rung in unison. Anita took out a cooker full of steaming hot rice and served it on a plate. When I saw the entire cooker, I wondered how hungry she had assumed me to be.

She removed the lid of a big vessel and poured some steaming hot thick yellow *sambhar*[56] on the rice. *Sambhar* is pulses cooked in a curry with cumin seeds and tamarind. It is a specialty cuisine of *South India.* I noticed a bowl kept on the dining table. I removed the lid of it to discover white homemade butter. "I love this", I said in excitement, carving a big dollop of the hard butter. Anita fed the delicious food to me and to herself, with her own hands. After we were done eating, we cleaned up the table. Working in the kitchen along with my beloved was a very beautiful feel. Once done, we were sitting at the dining table, and I sat behind Anita with my arms around her while my head rested on

---

[56]   *Sambhar is pulses cooked in a curry with cumin seeds and tamarind. Try it!*

her shoulders. I kept kissing her shoulders intermittently and she kept turning back and pecked on my jaw line. I ran my hands from under her sarong to finally touch her bare smooth legs. I pulled her sarong up to find and entry to her groin. I touched her clitoris and flicked it gently. She turned back and started kissing me. Anita got up, turned around, and sat on her knees and she then removed my towel. I looked at her in amazement and asked, "You want to do it again?"

"Yes", she said in a huskier voice, and again started blowing me. I was instantly ready, and untied the knot of her sarong. Her sarong dropped on the floor in the light of the cloudy noon, where the sea breeze entering from the windows draped the white lacy curtains around her naked dusky body. The sea breeze blew my hair and hers too. I asked her to stand up. Anita never wanted me to see her naked ass, and she covered it. She always said that its 'ugly', but I somehow liked the natural stretch marks on her bum. I leaned my head in and carefully separated the tiny minute hair around her kitty and licked it with my tongue. She lost a couple of breaths. I probed in a few fingers and rubbed her inners, while with the other hand grabbed her curvy broad ass and dug my nails inside it. Anita pushed my head behind from her inner secret and sat on top of me. "I want you to cum now Uday. I want you to have an orgasm", she instructed as she moved on top of me and I laid down on the chair, watching my beloved pound me. The sea breeze kept blowing into her hair, while she moved to the rhythmic *Persian* beats. I synced up, grabbing her rack and encouraging her motion. She moved faster till a point of recklessness and I realized the surge in my 'little warrior'. I immediately pulled him out and he shot 'hot' sprays of my 'love' on her thighs and on the floor. I breathed a charged up joy in the gasp of an orgasm. "I love you Nitu", I gasped as I pulled her neck down to kiss. She came close to my ears and stroked my face with her long slender fingers. Her long nails grazed the tiny whiskers growing on my face. She kissed my jaw and chuckled in a husky playful voice, "You fuck like a tiger, Uday. You so fuck like a tiger!" I grabbed her, tightly dampening her with my sweat. She continued to kiss while I just happily growled.

Bonded or blinded, it was 'love'; my 'blood', my only 'craving'. The only thing I ever desired for, and it was there in front of me, breathing with my soul, possessing me and enchanting me. Perhaps it was preparing me for one hell of a lifetime of a journey called life.

In the end, I had tasted 'blood' and that too of different kinds. From the touch of soft 'hearts', to the tongue on my 'little warrior'. It just grew on me for I had tasted her heat, which was hotter than the alcohol stolen from my father's bar. I had tasted the look in the eyes full of excitement and the agony in tears of sadness which comes out when lovers separate. I had tasted the escape one makes with a loved one from danger, and tasted submission and possession of a lover. The 'taste' of the moment of heat when the brains stop working, still haunts like the unforgettable ecstasy of an orgasm. I had tasted 'blood' and so did my beloved. Life seems so much more exciting and alive when there is a little 'blood' to taste, and it's even better when you have someone special to share it with. When 'love' becomes 'blood', lovers become predators, happy and confident together, living the blush.

I had intruded her aura and she intruded mine. I don't know if we were like 'water' or 'fire' but I am sure that we burnt in desire for each other and the essence of our union rested in our eyes in the form of fluidic blended 'love' – with which we grazed each other for endless hours, paving the glimpses of our forthcoming memory lanes.

> *To Color me Red is Rubricate,*
> *To Color you Love is intimate,*
> *When Color me You, it's fornicate...*

> *Entrapped in your fragrance,*
> *Delighted by the loose ends,*
> *Like a Madman blinded in your pursuit,*
> *Mix us together,*
> *like 'Blood' we blend...*

> *Away from you and still in your embrace,*
> *When Colored with you, I can't wander in space,*
> *"'Red' is your love", I often Grimace,*
> *Tall claims of Adornment, I wish I couldn't disgrace,*
> *For you are my Conquest, immersed in my face...*

A TASTE OF BLOOD

The more I want, the more I crave,
So much you give, but more I will take...
It's never enough, as you can never fake,
Sipping Tears of love or drowning in a Bloody lake...

So with every drop that poured into this Fiction,
And as I foolishly hoped it to be the Prescription,
To drink my fill and Indulge this Fixation,
But trapped in the coy of your eyes,
Your touch is my Addiction...

TASTES LIKE BLOOD

Tastes like blood,
When you are breathing beside,
Chaste like a bud,
When I am stealing your hide,

It tastes like blood,
When your eyes open wide,
Tastes like love,
I am still trying to decide....

The blood tastes warm,
As I am not done with it,
The more I taste,
The more I crave,

Tastes like blood,
When you are stroking my pride,
Tastes like love,
When in my arms you cried.....

Tastes like blood,
When you put me to sleep,
For a waste like me,
I still have feelings so deep,

For you taste like blood,
I am glued with the mushy paste,
In your body's flood,
My heart is misplaced,

ANSH SETH

Moist like blood,
Is the touch of your skin,
My heart stopped thud,
With my thoughts disgraced,
And my wit went shut,

When you embraced...
Till I found my fear,
What if you leave...?
Have someone else,
But we interlaced...

Replaced like blood,
As there is plenty to find,
But like you,
No one can taste,
And I will make all haste,
To be inside,

Inside you,
Because you taste like blood,

And you taste like love,
When I am holding your waist,

Waiting to slide....
The look in your eyes,

Just tastes like blood,
Cause I am your stud,

As you are my bride...
In you I confide,

As you taste like blood,
For you my love,
As you are my blood,
And you are my love.......
You are my love.......
And you are my blood.

CHAPTER 3

ON THE PROWL

Life is a journey, of stranger experiences... and so is 'blood'. When we know and accept that what comes ahead, would always be much more than what we already know. There is no point resisting the pursuit of knowledge as it is an outcome of a humble acceptance of one's lack. This realization just instills a 'craving' within us, only to learn more. I knew, that one day I will die in its cursed pursuit, but I will still continue trying. It's just the way for me to be alive, at least for as long as I am living. Isn't it all about being and feeling alive, so is 'love', so is 'blood', and so is life.

Imagine a life full of stories. It would be much like the diary of a traveler. It would be just so beautiful to watch the world, and then witness it again. Like drowning in the ocean which swirls in every eye, the bubbles twinkle while the deep water trickles down as tears. A rich life is an ocean of stories; traveled in the depths of the world and collected like pearls in an oyster shell.

"Uday you fuck like a tiger", Anita moaned in peace as she cuddled. We cuddled naked on her balcony, shameless and callous, yet in 'love'. 'Blood' brings its own gifts. I looked at the tall distant buildings overlooking the sea. The cloudy sky and the rampant wind smothered our conversations. "I love you Uday", she whispered. My hands slowly caressed her naked body while my thoughts caressed my uncertainties. I marveled on the series of strange events which we call life. "Why are you smiling?" she asked curiously. "I was wondering how I reached here, on your balcony. When I look at these tall buildings, I wonder about the stories behind each of these windows. I feel that *Arabian Sea*[57] is nothing but an ocean of stories. Look at me, I was a confused boy who came down from the hills. And now I am here, naked with you, in the lap of the sea", I said caressing her buttocks. She kissed me again. "You look so gorgeous", I mumbled staring deep in her eyes. "I always wonder, what our story would be like?" she smiled. "Two naked lovers, shamelessly loathing themselves in front of the sea", I grinned. "And in front of people too. Let's go inside", she obscured the view of the painting, formed in my mind, of our naked selves together. "It's been too long we have been here like this", she said getting up. I nodded and moved inside with her.

"Don't you feel awkward dating me? I mean you are indeed taller than me, even if by a millimeter but yeah you are", I asked ogling her tall curvy figure. "I am certainly a mismatch for you", I said wearily accepting the reality that her picture could be, with someone better. As soon as we walked inside, she embraced me again and kissed me. "Do you know what the beauty of our story is?" she asked with a grin. "What?" I asked curiously. "I don't need to swoop down or crane my neck upwards to kiss you. I can just be and keep kissing you for as long as I want. That's the advantage of our heights. And trust me, it is kind of required, as no matter how much I kiss you, I can never be satisfied", she spoke the words amidst her lingering kiss. 'Love' in its true form is nothing but a never dying thirst. And thus, life with 'love' in it, is nothing but a never ending journey. A journey we all travel to quench a certain thirst and then probably end up calling it life. "I so fucking love you", I gasped impassioned in her kiss, and to my unending thirst called 'love'.

So that was our story, Anita and me, happily together and happily ever after. Life had finally found that someone who always seemed like an illusion; an unachievable dream. But yes, it happened and I was happily living it. Day in and day out just being with her was the most amazing thing about my story. The thirst we shared for each other promised to never ever be quenched.

---

[57] *The Arabian Sea is a region of the northern Indian Ocean bounded on the north by Pakistan and Iran, on the west by northeastern Somalia and the Arabian Peninsula, and on the east by India. One of the oldest sea trade route.*

Whenever we made 'love', it used to be atrociously naughty, as if we both are driven with an unexplained urge to explore the other ends of each other. Relationships are like Venn diagrams, where both circles keep pushing to intersect further. Of course, they do so with the idea of becoming one, only to realize, that one ends up being a subset of another. Perhaps that's the idea, 'blood' or 'love' insinuates, urging lovers to become one.

The chances of me and her making out were terribly low, due to our respectful humble ends and restrictions. Maybe such circumstances spiced up the entire affair as 'blood' difficult to taste is the 'blood' to yearn for. Any chance to pounce on each other was greeted with more than anticipation.

Alcohol added up further to such dangerous circumstances, elongating the fiery fusion of 'fire' in 'blood' as even that's called 'love'. Getting drunk and getting laid seemed to be the mantra of good times. Both of us never faltered on this, as we kept looking forward to any opportunity where Anita and I, could be making drunken 'love'. The most beautiful part of those days was the fact, that we didn't need much to be happy – a little pocket money which could buy food, booze and a few cigarettes for Anita. The dearth of space is a usual gift of big crowded cities and we struggled with it every day. The 'taste of blood' helps shed inhibitions. We managed to find a few generous rich friends, who at least had a place of their own. They often came for our rescue, as we never hesitated to borrow their rooms. Condoms killed the pleasure and always felt like a little wall between me and her and thus found its place back at the medical stores. Every time I was on top of her she clawed her nails in my back and said in her huskier than usual voice, "Uday, you are such a Tiger!" She would often dig her teeth in my chin after such compliments.

The deepest gratification is that of one's soul. To a naive soul, 'love' is both nourishment and nirvana. Much like peace and accomplishment, like the biggest mystery of life has just been solved. It's funny to acknowledge when wise people say that peace can only be achieved after death. Perhaps then, what we define peace as, is nothing but an ability to satiate a 'craving' at will. The urge of 'love' when satiated, does bring peace and accomplishment, and that is the most superior satisfaction. It's a pure feeling to have both, as ironies of 'time' tell many such stories when one was lost in the pursuit of another.

It felt good to be compared to the giant feline which rules the jungle and makes other animals shit in their pants. And the best part is that the first female I had ever touched, gave me this compliment. "I am good enough", I began to believe for her compliments. Thus, I would generally end up in sexual escapades pushing hard to win more of her compliments and I would not stop giving her orgasms after orgasms as a token of gratitude. In 'love', compliments work like a sugar rush, enraging the energy of the 'crave' to get more, as that's what drives both the receiver and the giver. The receiver does anything and everything to live up to the enchanting compliments while the giver just enjoys the vain magic which mere words can do. My girlfriend was indeed a 'rockstar' as she wouldn't stop shagging me to death, one orgasm after another. Her way of loving was turning into a habit, somewhat like a 'sugar rush'. She too was a lioness herself snarling ferociously for her share of 'blood'. The 'taste of blood' enthralls a 'superlative' feeling amongst predators, pushing them to try harder, to be the best. And so does 'love', for the lovers.

It's a feeling which only lovers can feel when they start looking at themselves in a better light than others. Perhaps companionship is the sole purpose of mankind. Anita and I felt it too, as being together was indeed a 'high'. A 'high' too difficult to explain to those who were not in 'love'. 'Love' like 'blood', withers away regular fears, as the 'high' becomes a part of life. The only aspect of life which broke our 'superlative spell' was our ordinary reality where at the end of the day we had to rush to our homes and be the sweet little kids that we were; at least to our parents and everybody else who could threaten our survival.

To survive, we often had no choice but to stay away from each other. A general break between our 'love making' encounters could stretch from a week to three months, depending on the availability of each other's house, or a common friend's pad. Nevertheless, 'cravings' don't wait as we compensated by making out in college, alleys or taxis or wherever we found a little privacy. The exams were near and group studies were popularly detested in homes of middle class kids. The age old Indian patriarchy held the value that kids need to study alone. They can't study with each other. On a wider angle perhaps they were correct; Anita and I would have definitely studied each other closely. Rather than the books, we would have studied our nudity and fantasies, lost in the beauty of the moments when we came together.

The exam fever mounted up, definitely creating distances in our meetings. We both had to rush home early due to parental pressure. At least Anita was a topper all her life; I was just an average kid with dull eyes. My mediocrity raised a plethora of concerns for my mother, as she knew me very well. My 'focus' was fragile and probably that's why my mother made it her keen priority to control my activities. On the contrary, Anita was focused on how she wanted to do in her exams. I didn't even feel like studying. My entire focus was on my 'little warrior', as he was more alive than he ever had been. He spoke to me day and night, telling me often, "Yes, I want more! I want to have way more fun. I want to be with Anita, who strokes and loves me; and in return I will just cuddle and kill her."

The moment a guy loses his virginity; 'sex' eventually turns to be the sole reason for his existence and perhaps his only purpose. I was also on similar lines, just waiting for her to call and tell me that her house was empty. If her parents had gone out, I would be absolutely happy to even travel for hours in local trains, crowded with people with all sorts of odor, just to reach her. Dangers make both 'love' and 'blood' interesting. The possibility of not tasting 'blood' will always rule higher than the few bleak chances of finding it. The pursuit of 'love' or 'blood', in its natural sense is designed to beat the odds and one's worst fears. Probably that's why predators and lovers feel superior in the blessed pursuit of their 'blood'. I guess amidst all possible dangers, the thought of being caught naked and "In the act" by her family members was the scariest. But still, both of us took our chances, undeterred by our fears or perhaps we began enjoying it, the mere thought of touching our 'scariest' and coming back unaffected. We constantly kept pushing our limits, pretty aware of unpleasant consequences that could happen. It was like fucking in a war, where a next bullet can have your name written on it, and all you care about is a last orgasm for your partner and yourself.

The 'taste of blood' is so sensual that no one can have a silent orgasm. And god forbid if they do, then they shall never speak again. Everything stops still in the thrill of a 'craving' being satiated. Even 'time' loses it mystique, becoming endless or rather non-existent. Deep inside her eyes and soul, I was never present to witness 'time'. So much so, that 'time' appeared like it never pushed forward, and always stayed within us, like we were living a lifetime of losing ourselves into each other. The more we lost, the more we found... 'Time' flowed or never moved, like the wise one said: the hands of a clock, the numbers on devices and the color of the passing day shall repeat. It would feel like the moment of 'time' just passed, or perhaps it never moved. Yet we lived everyday flowing with 'love', as how 'time' flows like a frozen river.

Our chances of meeting were getting bleaker as the exams approached, and we compensated this lack of availability over the phone where Anita gave me strict instructions to study specific subtopics and that later she would take my oral test, which she promised won't be sexual. The burden of my last failure in the exams still lingered but couldn't even come close to my desire for Anita. All I could do was to reach college early before the lectures began and be with her, and leave for home with everybody when the day ended. After I got back home, mostly we would be back on the phone at night in conversations which lasted till mornings.

'Time' is the first victim of 'love'. The dimension of 'time' keeps ticking the world for its whims and fancies, and for the whim called 'love', lovers lose the significance of the whims and fancies of 'time'. Perhaps 'love' or 'blood', is just a whimsy outcome of a feeling of forever which it carries for the ones enchanted by it. Even for Anita and me, 'time' was more like a forgotten entity, lost in our togetherness. It was only remembered in the moments we met, and in moments we reluctantly left for our homes. Perhaps that's why none of us wore wrist watches, as the hands which follow 'love' often forget 'time'. For me personally, a wrist watch would only restrict my eager frisky hands to further explore her inner beauty.

'Not living by the watch' had another collateral damage and that was sleep. The night long conversations and the early morning meet ups had soon become a habit and I began living a sleep deprived life. Soon lectures and train rides became the place where I was making up for my lost sleep. Not like if I was sleeping at night then I wouldn't be sleeping in the lectures or in trains. My dearest teachers put me off to sleep in a way better manner, while sleeping in the train was an alert snooze. Only the sleep in my bed suffered, as I was often restless for the lack of cuddles along with her conversations.

The state of peace achieved in the sleep during daily lectures was relaxed and deep. It too had consequences; soon I was the 'Mr. Sleep-on-the-first-bench' of the class, and teachers loved to throw me back to the last bench. In my defense, I always suggested slyly, that they could try teaching in a rather interesting manner by adding humor and creativity to boring subjects. I guess it was too much of an expectation out of their salaries, or probably my idea wasn't worth their effort.

Being with Anita had cleansed my desires which were once lustful but now sacred and full of 'love'. The dirty thoughts which often occurred to me were 'sexy' to my girlfriend. Thus, 'love' cleansed me, till one day when my filthy thoughts returned. And they just left me wondering, "What do I want to prove?"

That sunny day I left college and boarded the local train back to home. The noon blessed *Mumbai* with a comparable low rush in the local trains. I got an airy window seat in no time. After I got seated, I dozed off to a very sweet slumber. It was ages since I had gotten a haircut. My eyes opened just before my station arrived and I had to rush out of the train carrying my messed up sleepy self. I walked down the platform to the subway which opened up towards the residential side of my suburb. The little dark shade of the subway was about to end in the sun. I saw two girls walking towards the subway. They were distinctly noticeable in the sparse commuter crowd. I realized one of their faces seemed familiar. A little surprise was the fact that even I appeared familiar to her.

A week before this moment, I was hanging out with a local *Sardar*[58] friend called Kirat. A game of cricket has just ended and were winding

---

[58]   *People who follow Sikhism.*

up below Kirat's house. The familiar chick passed us by. Kirat called out her name and engaged her in a conversation. He introduced her as Anuradha to me. She did have a faint resemblance to my dear *Gujarati Chick* and I realized I was already attracted to her. Her plump ass, totally wrapped around her jeans giving me a little dirty passing thought of pulling her jeans down to witness white panties on her brown skin. She left after having a brief chitchat with Kirat. "She seems cool", I said with a smile. Kirat leaned in and whispered in my ears, "Stay away from her, she thinks she is too cool but she is just a wannabe." I looked at him, still wondering who actually was a wannabe, but I silently nodded.

It was Anuradha with another female who was an inch 'hotter' than her with her huge curves and a majority of her face covered with her hair. I waved a sleepy "Hi, how are you?" to her. Both the girls stopped and I had a friendly sleepy conversation with them. "You generally return from college at this time?" she asked. "Yeah. Around this time only, actually my exams are approaching so need to get home and start studying", I answered. "She is my friend here and he is Uday", she said introducing me to her friend. I looked at her friend and before she could say her name I said, "Hi friend." I was yawning again as if the sudden presence of these girls in my life was the most boring part of the day. "You seem to be very sleepy" said Anuradha with a sarcastic smile. I nodded my head and mumbled, "Yeah, have been up all night studying." An idea to exchange numbers with her crossed my mind and was immediately mellowed with the possibility of being turned down by the girls. "So what, if they turn me down. I anyways don't have anything to lose. I already have a girlfriend", I encouraged myself. "Hey Anuradha, what's your number?" I asked pretending to be in a hurry to leave. "It's ok, just take it down. I guess you have to go study", she replied. "Shit loads to study, and I am already nervous", I smiled meekly as she dictated her number to me. Her friend stood silently and watched us exchange numbers. I dropped a missed call to confirm my number on her cellphone and we left with a friendly goodbye.

I started walking back home and the two females went there way. On the way back I thought about how bad I can mess up. I wasn't presentable, looked totally messed and on top of that all I could do was just yawn. I had a chance of keeping a local girls bandwagon to have some fun and I messed it up. It felt like a sick urge, crossing boundaries of my conscious. "Fuck I am so full of dirty thoughts", I blasted myself and ignored my sloppy behavior. Very soon I was consumed by the thoughts of Anita and the instructions she had given me for the upcoming exams.

The next day I was in my classroom on the second last bench, mildly dozing off in a lecture of biochemistry where we were being taught the molecular arrangement of carbon in a glucose molecule. The long carbon chains and their behavior coming out of the mouth of one of our 'hottest' teachers kept me mildly awake. I saw a text on my cellphone, which read "Hey, how are you?" It was an unknown number, and I replied, "I am good, but who is this?"

A reply came, "I am someone you recently met, and guess what – I think we should be friends."

I tried to recollect meeting someone, and a rush of strange excitement shot up thinking the possibilities of the person to be a female. But I really didn't recollect meeting anyone and so I replied, "Really, I don't remember much, but still what should I call you?"

A reply came in a while, "My name is Nisha, and I would like to know you more, do you have a girlfriend?"

For the first time in my life after finding the woman who was highly capable of rocking my world, I was being contacted by a stranger, not to be known whether it's a guy or a girl to make friends with, or to make something interesting! I didn't know what to say, whether to be honest or just lie to see who was there on the other side. I grabbed Anita's thigh under the desk. She returned a distracted kinky look and returned to writing her notes. I dug my fingers in her muscular soft thighs over her blue denims. Perhaps I was looking for a direction. It was still a dilemma but then, "What's the harm in knowing?" I consoled myself. An age old dream of being chased by girls with their sandals in their hands to thrash me, revisited my thoughts. I giggled on the recurrence of that stupid dream. I had no clue where this road would take me but still I thought, "Let's see... who else finds me cute?"

So I replied, "Nah, I am single, do you have a boyfriend?" My phone vibrated as a message popped, "No, of course I don't, why would I be texting you in that case?" Her reply was politically correct, to an extent of appearing 'absolutely' correct. "So she texted me because she doesn't have a boyfriend, and she is so blunt about it! It's obviously a prank. Someone is trying to set me up!" I reasoned. "Is this planted by Anita? To check whether I am a loyal boyfriend or not? What if she got influenced by those stupid scripted reality shows which thrives on adultery in relationships and moronic emotional outbursts?" I wondered and looked at her with suspicion. "What?" she gestured silently looking back at me. She quietly scribbled in her notebook and forwarded it to me, to read. "Are you angry for any reason?" I read in her notebook. I looked back into her innocent eyes. I grinned mischievously and scribbled back, "No... Horny for a lot of reasons." Anita read the words and giggled. My frisky fingers secretly caressed her belly button. She gasped for the sudden intrusion, but controlled herself in the classroom. She quickly moved my hand away and stared back into her notebook. "It can't be her", I breathed a sigh of relief.

My cellphone vibrated again. "Did you sleep off?" it read. "Sarcasm", I thought reading her question. I didn't know what to reply next, a feeling slowly crept inside and asked me, "Am I cheating on my girlfriend?" The curiosity to know who was on the other end was still exciting. I mustered a reply and sent, "No I am awake. Sorry, was in a lecture. I guess it would be a great idea to talk. I will call you in a while." "I won't talk on the phone" she texted. "Why?" I replied, flabbergasted by her absurd reason. Bluntness was all that occurred to me and I bluntly put across my point, "Oh ok, well then, let's just meet, where do you stay?" "That's such a horrible desperate reply" I immediately thought, cursing myself for being so obvious. Her words returned and read, "I stay near your place. Don't worry, but I will meet you when I feel like."

"She has me", I smiled reading her message, turning further curious to look at her face. Resisting was no point anymore so I gave in honestly, "See, you have already made me very curious, I guess I won't be able to handle this for long. Nevertheless, what did you like about me?"

I guess I wanted to know what I was liked for, and I also hoped for a total loss of interest from her side...while the delay of her reply intensified the feel. "I think you are very cute and sleepy with the unkempt hair of yours", she replied after a while.

This statement suddenly rang a bell in my head that, "Is she Anuradha?" I tried calling the number but the call was disconnected. I kept myself from taking a chance with prompting a name to this unknown fan of mine. Soon it was two days of chatting with that stranger and we discussed almost everything from her college to her taste in boys to my taste in women. She liked guys who were tall and muscular, chiseled with huge biceps. I liked girls who were simply cute and curvy. I did not share my sexual experience or preferences with her over the messages and neither did she. Nor did I know what I preferred sexually other than Anita. I guess I hadn't even explored my jungle. I didn't know if she had any, but considering the kind of description of guys she liked, she was more or less pointing towards someone like *John Abraham*[59] who is tall, beefy and one hell of a stud. I was nowhere close. I wasn't tall or beefy or even super chiseled. In fact I didn't even have a sport bike or as a matter of fact – a normal bike. I was of average height, lean and sleepy. I didn't need a twelve lakhs sport bike to commute, as I didn't have a remote chance of buying it. I felt pride to use a one crore train to travel through the city. She never mentioned qualities like sense of humor or agility in sports which I was good at. It's not like I had a super funny sense of humor, but instead, more of an annoying kind. Anita always pointed out to my side where I deliberately did what I was told not to do. "You feel it's funny, but at times Uday, you can be hell annoying!" she often complained. I can't deny the fact that it gave me a huge kick to push people to the edge where they don't want to go. The benefits of this quality still remains to be seen, and I never knew then, that in years to come, how useful this simple trait could be.

I was still wondering what this girl wants out of me, or in fact, what she even liked in me. I fancied the outcome of my sinful thoughts turning into dirty realities. Thoughts of Anuradha's brown spankable ass flashed in my fantasy. The idea of fucking a total stranger appeared

---

[59] *A famous Bollywood actor, quite a heartthrob in his time.*

like 'blood' which destiny can offer. Anita left me lonely as she was busy with exams. My 'little warrior' ridiculously diminished the significance of exams for his own fantasies, making me come thrice to the thought of pulling down Anuradha's jeans to spank her brown ass. Anita's occasional calls had gone low; while I remained distracted to a different possibility, which was slowly ruling me, making itself a priority.

Perhaps the universe heard my excitement as she texted from the other end, "Lets meet tonight."

It was Thursday night and I was waiting for this stranger to text. And soon it arrived, it read, "Boarded the train, will be at your station in twenty minutes." Luckily my father was out of town for one of his regular official business trips. The best part about it was that I had the car to myself. I was dressed up in a denim jacket, with my unkempt long hair, stylishly pulled back. I picked up my father's hatchback and drove off to the station. A little nervousness about meeting her mixed with the thought of not having a driver's license and everything else an eighteen year old could be scared of. I drove to the station and waited in my car, in the parking lot. I witnessed the rail lines at a distance, waiting for a local train to pass. Finally a train arrived, and my phone rang. When I answered, it was a very husky voice on the other end and said, "Hey Uday, where are you?" I replied, "In the parking lot, just get out of the platform and keep walking, you will see a silver *Santro*[60] on your right hand side, I am sitting in that car."

I waited anxiously looking at the stairway towards the platform for this strange woman to come. "What if she was 'hot'? What if she fucked me? What if she found me boring and annoying?" I anxiously thought about my "What if's" again. I saw a sexy silhouette of a woman, dressed in black with long blackish brown perhaps bleached, straightened yet unkempt hair walk towards me. She opened the car door and sat inside. She wore a weird perfume, a little on the slutty side which intruded my olfactory lobes and directly reached for the 'little warrior's' directive to smell her closely or perhaps even eat her. Her hair was all over her

---

[60]   *Hyundai Santro (launched in 23 September 1998) was the once the second most popular hatchback being sold in India.*

face and I recognized Anuradha's friend, and yes she was 'hotter' than her. To my surprise she wore a silver nose ring, which was definitely a 'turn on'.

"Hi, it's you!" I blurted in surprise. "Yes, it's me" she smiled a naughty grin. "You are that friend of Anuradha. Oh my god, how did this happen?" I spoke in surprise. "Jussst..." she said coldly. "Let's just go somewhere from here", she hurriedly said, pointing me to drive away.

I started the car, silently obeying her. We drove around the neighborhood. I noticed the lack of words to speak in my mouth, as generally I never ever had such a problem. Probably the two day chat didn't leave much for me to ask or talk about. Anita was still a secret as probably I could go on for hours talking about her. The two day frenzy of texting this stranger was slowly settling down. I wondered why it was such a 'high'. Speaking something was still better than staying silent, so I just mumbled whatever came to my mouth. "So Nisha tell me, what did you actually find cute about me? I was all sleepy and messed up when I met you guys", I asked perhaps hoping for something to stroke my vanity. "It's just that you look cute. Maybe when you are sleepy", she said coldly. Her nonchalant voice made the word 'cute' sound so casual; as if there are a million other faces which are cute. I wondered why she was so numb. "Did someone 'cute' break her heart and turned her into this?" I wondered sneaking a peek at her. "And if that happened, then why is she looking out for someone cute again? I guess it's her fix. She is addicted to cute", I chuckled to myself. "And by the way, my name is Priya, not Nisha", she interjected my silence.

I was momentarily shocked, "You lied to me about your name Nisha.... umm... sorry Priya." "Sorry, initially I didn't feel like telling you my real name", she said looking at me. "Why are you telling me now?" I asked bluntly realizing there is nothing much to care about. "Because I feel that I can trust you", she said meekly. 'Trust'; the word knocked in my head. It was a heavy word for someone my age. Anita never mentioned words like these. She always spoke about lighter words like 'cool', 'cute', 'hot' etc. "Why does Nisha or Priya, trust me? She barely knows me?" I wondered. Call it a lack of experience in my long dry life or just the lack of people, but words like 'trust' were alien to my vocabulary.

"So you are Priya, as in Priya what?" I laughed trying to make small talk to divert from heavy words and emotions which I felt incapable to handle. "Priya Menon", she smiled. "Are you hungry Nisha, I mean Priya?" I asked her, trying to be a gentleman. "We can eat if you are hungry", she said, trying to sound modest. I reconsidered the thought about how much money my mother gave me before I left to meet Nisha, or sorry, Priya. With just 200 bucks in my pocket, I ended up in a dilemma. "Where should I take her? To the nearest newly built mall where there is a food court or to some cheap roadside *dhaba*[61]. Somewhere, where I could at least afford two full servings of chicken *Manchow*[62] soups for a romantic dinner!" I thought hard, circling my car around the neighborhood.

"I am not very hungry, is it ok if we park somewhere and talk?" I asked her dubiously. "But we can go to the nearest mall if you want to eat something", I said trying hard to sound caring enough, at least for the 'trust' she bestowed on a stranger. "It's ok, I am not really hungry, we can sit somewhere and talk", she responded in a disinterested way.

"So Priya Menon, since you are from *Kerala*, are you a *Mallu*[63]?" I tried to keep her engaged for a while, till we drove down to my favorite under construction station area, where generally Anita and I seldom did our car 'make outs'. I parked my car in a dark corner, and reclined my seat. I looked at her and she was looking at me with an insane boldness on her face. Which was strange, because I expected more of that cute coyness which a regular girl would demonstrate. She wore more of a challenge with her flared nostrils. I was intimidated, scared to make a move. Fearing a rejection or worse, I actually felt like the timid one. So I thought of talking something else with her but no brilliance came to my head. Without a second thought of what is appropriate or not for a first date, I said almost abruptly, "Since we are chatting over messages for the past two days, I guess we have nothing left to talk about, so... can we

---

[61] *A small roadside eatery which promises good food. Often visited by travelers and truck drivers.*

[62] *A blackish Chinese soup served with fried noodles... but probably that's the Indian version.*

[63] *Mallus (Malayalis): People of Kerala.*

just kiss?" I suppressed my shock for my direct insolent question and then I stared deep in eyes. Her big watery eyes totally contrasted with her boldness. To my surprise, she said "Ok."

I grabbed her head, and her hair felt smooth. I pulled her closer to reach her thick lips. She gullibly kissed, but her kiss was dull for her raunchy appearance. My other hand was as restless as I was, and struggled its way inside her top to feel her assets, caressing them and trying hard to find a way inside her clothes. Her nipples surfaced on her shirt, drawing pictures of her bare breasts in my head. She resisted firmly and put my hands away but persistence was my middle name when it came to 'making out'. After a short, partially successful struggle, I made it to her bra, but could not, to her nipples. After a certain amount of forceful tonguing each other we separated as she pushed me behind. I rested back in my seat. I tried again till she got a little weary of my advances, and I found something stuck to my lips. It was some powdery substance which was kind of shining orange in color. I looked closely at her lips amidst the very dim yellow street light coming in the car. The powdery substance was on her lips, it was her lipstick. I was grossed out with her cheap lipstick and said, "Is your lipstick coming off, it's in my mouth?" "It must have got a little loose", she looked embarrassed while she said this. I got out of my bad taste into a recent victory over a second female, and I asked her with a mute desire to stroke my ego, "How was it?" "Well I have never kissed a stranger before", I sheepishly admitted for my rookie courage. I wondered if she would tease me into telling her about all the girls I had kissed, and that might take the topic to Anita. But she said something otherwise, she said "It was nice, but I have to ask you something before we get any further with this." "What?" I asked her enthusiastically with a feeling that with the answer to this question, my 'little warrior' would be soon inside her and she would also be howling my name. I still chuckle to the thought, "How juvenile I used to be those days!"

"Would you get committed to me?" she asked. Her boldness was perhaps more of a reflection of her honesty rather than a challenge. Her eyes were still watery as if they promised to do anything for a word called 'commitment'. But the hint to the answer of her question, definitely gave my opportunistic self; an orgasm.

The 'taste of blood' is actually hope... Perhaps it's 'cravings' for which people live for.... Even to live a life without 'cravings' is actually a 'craving' in itself..... For her, perhaps it was an ego massage; the 'commitment'from a guy. And to me, I am so sure that my 'little warrior' defined commitment for his own thirst.

I didn't know what to reply to her question. I never knew the meaning of the word 'commitment' especially when it came to guys and girls dating, and I seriously didn't know what obligations it would bring. I wondered why Anita never asked me for a 'commitment'. In fact I never recalled that word in her regular vocabulary. She used words like, 'ass', 'hot', 'cute' etc. Uncertainty and intimidation answered her question for me. With my expectations getting a bit low and disappointed, I said, "I will think about it."

Perhaps it was surprising for her too. It's easy for a guy to nod a "Yes" and do the rest! She leaned in to kiss further, and though her shabby lipstick still rubbed off on me, I was elated to see her boldness work into play. To my surprise, I quite liked the answer I gave and wondered that all my past life, this was more or less the same answer I had got from any female I had proposed.

The kiss had to end on account of her delay. We kissed a quick goodbye, when I dropped her off at the station. I saw my phone and to my shock I saw around five missed calls of Anita. I rushed back home to call her. Anita enquired about my whereabouts and I lied to her that I was with Kirat.

I waited for Priya to revert. Later that night she texted, "I had a good time today. Let's do it again." I liked the message but the shabby lipstick was still turning me off. "Please take care not to wear any lipstick", I replied. The answer came back quickly, "Ass, Muah."

A satisfied animal is as good as dead. Perhaps that's why predators in the wilderness strive very hard to survive. Every kill comes with a lot of effort and the chances of failure are very high. In the human realm too, a 'satisfied' human being is a myth. Humans can never be satisfied, they will always end up finding something more to desire, something more to conquer. This basic instinct keeps pushing their limits. At least for the ones who feel alive!

The 'taste of blood' drives everybody to exceed their own benchmarks.

I was no alien to this subconscious drive. Perhaps having what you desire brings a momentary satisfaction and a lot of emptiness. I had everything which I ever wanted in my life and that was 'love'. I was too stupid to understand worldly or materialistic desires. But the drive to push limits and exceed myself didn't diminish. Looking back at 'time', all I can now wonder is, "Was it for 'blood' or was it an attempt to fulfill the emptiness which I felt out of the satisfaction being bonded to Anita?"

The next afternoon I was in a nearby mall with Kirat and another common friend called Sanky. Sanky was a lean guy desperate to build up his muscles as he considered a 'hot' physique would get him a girlfriend. Kirat knew Sanky since they were kids and continuously bombarded Sanky with his mediocre and introvertish useless advices which were nothing but derivatives of his own perceptions. In return, he was only treated like a Godfather by Sanky. Sanky obeyed Kirat on everything from what clothes to wear, what kind of friends he should keep and the career choices he should make. Somehow my boarding school experience had left me very selective of people and opinions. Kids from cities carried a lot of baggage; especially the social courtesy and a psychopathic need to cast a good impression on others. Well, even I wasn't much of an exception to these rules, but the boarding school experience left a certain undefined urge to prove things, especially when it came to breaking the rules.

Malls were always exciting, especially for broke kids who can view the beauty of the franchise world for free, without buying anything. Especially in a country like *India,* the constant air conditioning and escalators provided the ambience of a really progressive world. Another 'high' malls provided kids was a constant crowd of good looking guys and girls. A promotion booth of *Gillette*[64] was set up on display where a few girls in white tops and denim skirts were approaching men to

---

[64]   *A famous shaving products brand – "The best a Man can get."*

shave. I stood with my friends on the first floor as we checked out the girls working for the promotional campaign. "Let's try to get one", I smirked to Sanky and Kirat looking at the girls. "Yeah Uday, I don't mind trying!" added an excited Sanky. Sanky, out of habit looked at Kirat for perhaps an approval to indulge in my devious idea. "Dude, that's not possible. I mean look at them and look at us. What if these girls create a scene? We will get a public beating", said Kirat with a wise arrogance on his face which to me, appeared nothing but paranoia. Sanky shrugged on going forward with me. "I mean come on guys, what's the worst that can happen? A girl would just say a 'no' to us. I mean that's not gonna break our hearts anyways. And who is asking you to marry her Kirat?" I urged my fellow friends to jump into the idea with me. Sanky's mood swung like a pendulum as he was again excited to take his chances. Yet he still looked at Kirat for approval. "Uday, why don't you go ahead and give us a demo. Perhaps we get an idea whether you get any or none!" grinned Kirat. Sanky laughed mildly to massage his chicken hearted pseudo intelligent 'Godfather'. Their jeering faces triggered me, only to react with abusive words which I swallowed before they poured out of my mouth. "You know; what you guys should do?" I asked with a serious face. They looked curiously at me and asked in unison, "What?" "You both should go home and shag. Because it seems like the only possibility of you getting laid, at least in this lifetime. You call me every time for checking out girls, and I am kind of bored of it. Mere checking out girls is a waste of time, like checking out expensive property which we know that we might never buy in a lifetime. A guy should have the balls to go get a woman randomly in public", I said passionately.

Perhaps a little mockery was required to push me to put in a little effort to demonstrate to my geeky friends how it is done.

I angrily marched downstairs to the center of the ground floor of the mall looking for the girl whom I had chosen. When I reached downstairs, I looked around only to find that the very girl was missing. I felt like returning but I wondered what I would tell Kirat and Sanky. I looked up at the first floor only to spot both of them watching me with a suppressed grin. "Going back with an excuse to the geeks would just buy me more mockery", I mumbled looking at their faces which were eager to watch me fail. And if that happens, my non celibate pride would be hurt.

So I still looked around for the girl and instead spotted another girl with really huge 'hearts'. Perhaps it could be a good virtue for her to pass as 'hot'. I walked towards her and pretended to pass by, hoping that my stubble would definitely encourage her to ask me to use their razor and shave. To my surprise, she didn't even notice me. I looked upstairs only to see my two dear friends already laughing. I turned around, and scratched my stubble. My heart pounded as I walked straight to her. "Excuse me, could I check out your razor please?" I asked politely. She smiled and gave me a professional memorized sales script of how the razor worked and its long list of advantages, of which, I didn't understand or even recollect anything. My eyes swooped down, so badly wanting to ogle at her 'hearts', but I forcibly controlled them to keep looking at her face. It's a strange fact I learnt in that instance that if a girl has voluptuous 'hearts' then it becomes very difficult for a man to keep looking at her face. There is a sudden weight experienced around the eyes, which pulls the vision downstairs to the massive beautiful objects of affection which have a lot more utility value. "So, would you like to take a test shave? And then, you can probably even buy one!" she asked with a straight face adorned with a cold professional smile.

The moment I heard money getting involved, it gave me two simultaneous shocks. First; that what she was demonstrating was an expensive shaving razor. As she talked me into buying it, I realized I didn't have money in my pocket. The worst part would be telling her that I was broke. Second, I would look like an utter fool who had gone to woo the salesgirl, but instead, ended up buying a razor from her, slashed by her cold courteous smile. The 'high' always remains in melting the ice, so I spoke with my head tilted and my gaze softer, "May I know your name please?" "It's Pricilia, Sir", she said politely. I took a moment to calmly enjoy her. Pricilia was slightly plump, had a milky chocolaty skin and black eyes. She had dark hair tied up in a ruffle and she wore a white sleeveless t-shirt with a blue denim skirt. "Perhaps it's a marketing stunt to dress up huge girls in tight revealing clothes. Maybe raunchy sells", I silently let my wicked thoughts pass. "Maybe she is already fed up of men who must have approached her for her raunchy appearance and her vulnerable job", another thought crossed my mind as I looked into her dark dim eyes.

"You know Pricilia, I already have this razor, and I did not get a single word of what you said", I said softly to her. Her eyes narrowed as her face expressed a minor confusion. And to my satisfaction her cold smile lost its courtesy and straightened. To enter an aura, the first thing needed is disruption. The constant state of one's being must be stunned and off balanced to help enter a new idea, a fresher thought. I quickly added to cover up the confusion I caused, "I just came to you because I wanted to know you." My voice became a little shaky by the time I finished the sentence. I wondered what would be her reaction.

To my surprise Pricilia smiled and her narrow dim eyes enlarged. She blushed and her brown cheeks turned pink. She alertly looked around for any of her supervisors watching her and whispered, "Ok, take my number." I quickly took out my cellphone and started taking her number. "Where do you study?" I asked her. "I study at *National College* in *Bandra*", she replied. "Then where do you live?" I asked. "I also live in *Bandra*. Can you call me later?" she retorted. "Oh yes, you do your work, I will call you later", I obliged and left. I walked back upstairs and spotted Kirat and Sanky looking at me with wide open eyes. The guys had an astonishing respect in their eyes when I came back and I showed them my cellphone with her number saved in it. I didn't feel like saying anything but couldn't resist the urge to tell Sanky, "Bro, you should have tried your luck!"

The tiger inside felt good, and it roared with pride. Perhaps the identity of my 'blood' was changing as it wasn't just 'love' which I craved for. It was incomprehensible to put it in simple words, but it was definitely beyond. Maybe it was an urge to prove myself. An 'urge' which often compels us to cross our own self defined limits, only to prove it to no one but ourselves. Probably that is what 'being alive' is all about. I took a peaceful breath of air but I barely knew that my 'craving' to 'be alive' had just started and was headed towards doom.

In the pursuit of 'blood', there are high chances of collateral damages. In the pursuit of 'love', many with their timid hearts end up being the collateral damage.

While I was discovering my tiger, it seems Ratish had already discovered his elephant inside, which was going berserk daily in college as he was picking up fights with other kids every day. Probably it was because of his break up with Zaida. Earlier that year, Ratish's love scene with Zaida had picked up and it was everywhere in the rumor circle. Anita and I were temporarily glad as someone else had taken away the rumor paparazzi from us. The four of us often hung out together, obviously flanked by Gando and other harmless friends. The only drawback of this scenario was that neither Rasika nor Poonam were anywhere close to us. Ratish and I both missed having Rasika around but the possessive duo of Anita and Zaida had the better of us. Zaida was the shortest girl in our classroom, and fit very appropriately for the short heighted Ratish. She had a cute face but a dragging nasal voice. Though, in the initial days, Ratish along with other kids secretly chuckled about her nasal voice, but since they started dating, he quite seemed to enjoy it. 'Love' and such things often do that, as one starts liking the most annoying things about the other person.

The only person not happy about the brand new couple of our class was Manjeet as she had made a huge menstrual sulking melodrama out of it. Probably she had put on weight and her eyes appeared to pop out all the time, very similar to the symptoms of exophthalmic goitre. She had an outright crush on Ratish but covered it with clichés like "He is just a friend" for most of the time. The repercussions of her anger often reflected in her behavior she became callous with her huge body, rubbing guys accidentally with her huge 'hearts'. Once, I was also an accidental victim of her envious callousness. No matter how much I enjoyed the voracity of her fleshy 'hearts' massaging my back in a crowded huddle over a genetic experiment in the lab, still I couldn't succumb to such forbidden temptations. I had to force myself to tell Anita that perhaps Manjeet needed help.

Eventually Anita and I had cooled off Manjeet with a lot of consoling and counselling. But many a times, evil wishes too, have their way. Ratish and Zaida dated for a few weeks but their friend circles were different. Ratish had his dear buddies who were a bunch of shallow rich brawlers who drove around in a small red car and kept on picking up fights. Zaida had simpler people like her, who sipped cold coffee and chit chatted together about the regular unproductive things. Ratish liked Zaida but his friends teased him a lot about it, especially for her peculiarities. Zaida's friends on the contrary were scared of Ratish and filled Zaida with ideas of dating someone who was decent and actually spent time with her. A nearby café was our daily hangout and soon the cute couple of Ratish and Zaida who once held hands and sipped cold coffee, now argued and fought daily. The separation of Ratish and Zaida was only mourned by Anita and me, as we lost our only 'couple' friends.

The other kids were scared of Ratish for his erratic anger outbursts and his proud gang of angry brawlers. I liked him for his fun side and his silly sense of humor. Manjeet was happy to have Ratish's availability again and got back to behaving like a social bitch. Ratish appeared to harbor a secret interest in Poonam and probably hoped that Manjeet could help him increase proximities with her, as she was her good friend.

Anita and Ratish shared a jolly good chemistry and most often were seen laughing together. Around these days, once Ratish had a major fight which went on to become very popular amongst other kids in college where he had single handedly bashed two guys and scared away their gang of five other friends. When I heard the news, I went looking out for Ratish, till I found him sitting and smoking in the cafe. He waved to me and I asked him curiously, "Hey Rat, how did you manage to scare an entire gang?" Ratish sipped his coffee, flared up his nostrils and put his hand inside his pocket and said, "With this." He took out a chrome metallic knuckle, which was a popular weapon in my boarding school. He wore it on his fingers under the table and showed it to me. "Did you use this on them?" I asked him, with a little intimidation. "No, I just scared them with this", he said bravely. I excitedly took it from him and wore it on my fingers.It looked very fierce. I felt as if the tiger got his paws. The edges of the knuckles were sharp and it was made of pure thick heavy metal. The chrome gave it a marvelous shine. I couldn't resist the urge to ask Ratish, "Can I keep this?" "No, it's illegal to have this", he said bluntly. "Please fatso, please let me have it, I know it's illegal to have this but I will keep it hidden in my drawer", I pleaded. "Ok fine, but only for the exam period", Ratish agreed. I hid my new metal paws in my pocket. Possessing that knuckle had a different feel. It was a very powerful feeling that I could distort anybody's face and even demolish a gang of foes with a mere touch of my metallic paw.

My conversation with Ratish was disrupted by Anita as she joined us with a bunch of notes for the exams beginning in the next two days. I went to the washroom, leaving Anita and Ratish on the coffee table. When I returned, they were missing with their belongings and my bag rested on one of the chairs. I wondered where they had gone and furiously started looking for them. For a moment, some pathetic trash ran through my head, till I discovered them in an alley behind the café. Both of them were hiding and smoking. They had a secretive laugh, which felt piercing as if they were laughing at me, for being such a loser who cannot take his girlfriend out for a smoke. They looked at me and they gave me a casual smile. Anita caught the anger in my eyes and silenced, while I ramped up to her and exploded, "You are smoking here!" "You left my bag unattended on the table, and you know... I so don't like you smoking!" I continued exploding. Ratish caught a glimpse of a couple of his friends at the entrance of the alley and raced to them. Anita couldn't handle me screaming at her in front of Ratish, and she retaliated, "What is your problem if I smoke? As if I smoke all day, it's just one cigarette!" "But why are you smoking in this shady alley?" I retorted. "Because I don't want the world to see me smoking", she replied with a logical point. In *India,* the habit of smoking, especially for women has a very low acceptance, though all the sick hypocrite men, do find it sexy to watch a woman smoke, unless and until it is to do with some women who are close to them. For the rest, they dislike it unless and until it is someone who is at grief for the loss of someone dear, probably with cancer, or either the person is a cancer specialist who watches many smokers die daily!

I was losing the conversation and in a fit of higher rage induced by a valid point thrown by my intelligent girlfriend. I screamed, "Do you know how slutty you look when you smoke?" I realized just after the words left my mouth, regretting what I shouldn't have said. Nevertheless Anita didn't leave much of a room for me to regret, and slammed a slap right across my face. I had never been slapped by a woman, other than my Mom, my sister and a few aunts, and some teachers in my school. I looked back at the entrance of the alley and no one was there. But before I could turn my head back to react, I saw a couple of kids from college entering the alley. I couldn't react and I started walking away. A few moments later

Anita followed me and called me to stop. I rushed straight to the first taxi I saw and got inside it.

Anita was athletic and a national level marathon runner. She ran and stopped the cab before the lazy driver could even start it. She said, "Look I am sorry, I shouldn't have slapped you." Her powerful dominating tone triggered me off even more, and I said, "I have to leave." I signaled the taxi driver to go, but before the bugger could start the engine of his old cranky cab, Anita quickly opened the door and got inside. The whole way she pleaded me to forgive her. She wanted to see my cheek which was slapped. I was furious, breathing heavily and flaring my nostrils. "It's all about smoking a cigarette to you, right? And I must be such an uncool boyfriend who doesn't smoke", I mumbled angrily. We were about to reach the railway station and I took out the cash from my wallet. The cab stopped and I dumped the cash on the driver's lap and rushed out. Anita rushed behind me. I paced towards the platform and just then a train arrived. I started running towards the train, and I turned to see Anita run behind me. The train stopped, and I rushed in. By the time Anita could reach my compartment, the train started moving. I looked back at Anita, who stood there with a disappointed look on her face which wanted to apologize. The train gained speed and started moving faster. Anita still stood there looking at me, wearing a white sleeveless top with a heavy blue backpack and her ponytail. Slowly Anita became smaller and smaller and finally disappeared. A very weird feeling encroached me, and I wasn't angry anymore. "What if I had waited?" I repeatedly asked questioned myself. I had very little idea of what it can do when you don't get a chance to apologize, and even worse when your apologies fall on deaf ears. Ears deafened by the tricks and ironical situations created by 'time'.

By the time I reached home, I was already full of remorse for reacting so horribly to my lovely girlfriend. I sent her an apology message to which she replied, asking me to focus on my exam preparation as I was hardly prepared. Well, she knew me well. Maybe I just didn't know myself properly, or perhaps what I was turning into.

I sat down to study as I realized the gravity of my grades which were falling deeper than the gravity of the situation. I tried hard to concentrate, but the events of the day kept running in my head. My cellphone beeped, and I checked it. It was a message from Priya which read, "Want to catch up, my cutie pie?" My mood got a little better as my attention moved from the day's misery to the thoughts of spanking Priya's sweet ass. "Yes, bombshell, come over, let's meet", I replied knowing that amassing my concentration was anyways difficult at that moment.

Priya walked out of the railway station where I waited for her in the parking lot. She wore a black *kurta*[65] on a pair of blue jeans. Her bleached straightened yet unruffled hair still covered a major part of her face. She hurriedly came and opened the door of my car and got in. She still wore the slutty perfume and it was already turning me on. The idea of spanking her ass still played in my head. She hugged me as soon as she got inside while I grabbed her neck from behind, and without much haste began kissing her. She pushed me away and said, "Can you please quickly drive away from here, as a lot of people know me here." Priya looked worried, so I started the car. "Where should we go?" I asked her. "Let's drive down to the empty road at *Kharghar*[66]", she hurriedly suggested. "There we can sit in the car and talk peacefully", she added and she ran her hands on my thighs.

I felt good and started driving, but inside my head I was thinking about the cops who came patrolling the road to harass couples in the car. We soon reached the road and it was deserted. A cop patrolling van just overtook us and sent a shiver down my spine. I was scared to get caught as I didn't even have a legal driving license. Moreover I was there at the hunting grounds of the cops with an intention to 'make out' in the car. If I am caught as a person who has nobody in the city, then I wouldn't have been scared. The part which scared me the most was the mere thought of a phone call to my father, to inform him... that I am caught by the cops for involving myself with a girl in doing some immoral activities. I was sure that if my father got involved, then I would definitely get spanked by a couple of shoes on my head by his broad muscular hands. The incident of running away with Anita was still fresh in my head. "What if the cops knew my car and its number?" I thought to myself, as I parked

---

[65]   *An Indian unisex garment for the upper torso.*

[66]   *A remote suburb in New Mumbai.*

the car in a corner of the road. Five minutes later, the cop van passed us again. Luckily, they didn't stop and continued moving. It is a rare scene in *Mumbai* in which cops do not harass couples who are enjoying a little candid time in the corner. Finally at peace, Priya and I started talking. "How was your week?" she asked me. "Very busy", I answered. "Yours?" I asked, with my hands on her thighs, slowly reaching towards her groin. "Don't go there", she retaliated, not bothering to answer my question. "Why?" I asked in a softer voice, as my hands tiptoed to her waist while my head leaning in closer towards her face.

We began to kiss but the moment her lips touched mine I thought of her sad cheap lipstick. The lipstick she wore then was not wearing out by god's grace, but it still had a sad taste. It wasn't like the nice fruity lip glosses Anita wore. We kissed for a short while, where I focused more on touching her body. Priya's phone rang and we stopped. It was Anuradha calling, and Priya answered. She spoke to her in *Malyalam*[67], which is the world's second toughest language after *Cantonese* and thus left me no chance of understanding it. The more she spoke; the more it started sounding like some coded language which guerrilla warriors would use to send encrypted messages in a jungle. I tried understanding and the only thing I could figure out was that they are talking about me. "Talk later", I said and gestured to Priya, as I realized I should go home and study. Priya paid no heed to what I said and I began to grow restless. I went close to her available ear and started licking it; a few seconds later I tried to lightly chew it. "Ouch", she shrieked. "Don't do that, it hurts", she yelled. I relaxed back in my seat and continued being restless. "*Patti karna kudala*", she laughed. Now '*Patti*' was a familiar word with my *Mallu* friends as it meant a dog. "Did you just call me a dog for biting your ear?" I asked in surprise. I didn't like the fact that Priya was sharing so many details with Anuradha. Obviously, my chances to spank Anuradha's brown ass will reduce. The call ended and Priya turned to me. "Let's make out", I said pouring my head in her space. She made a serious face and asked, "Uday, I had asked you a question last time we met, you remember?" "What question?" I barely remembered and even if I did I really did not feel like talking about it. Clearly I wanted some of her tongue in my mouth and inside my pants.

---

[67] *Native language of the people of Kerala.*

"About giving me a 'commitment', remember?" she reminded me. "Oh yes", I pretended to recollect. "So what do you mean by 'commitment'?" I asked trying to face the toughest question of my life. "What is expected of me to do and not to do when I am committed to you?" I emphasized to be crystal clear of a heavy word like 'commitment' and its implications in my normal life. "Well you can do whatever you like, but you can't be with any other girl at the same time", she said sternly. I frowned, thinking about the criterion. "Plus if you are ready then let's go now and you can do me", she winked, came closer and kissed me.

I kissed her too and this time with tongue. Priya looked at me for an answer. The 'little warrior' was eager to answer for her tempting offer. I struggled to think against my carnal urges and weighed pros and cons for getting committed to Priya. I realized that it would become too much of a hassle to have a local girlfriend. I would lose my privacy with Anita. Moreover Anita is awesome at so many things and she could teach, cook and fuck. I chose otherwise. "Priya, it sounds too heavy for me, I want something more casual. I got a lot to study and do something big in life", I answered confidently. Well the latter reason sounded pretty lame to me too as I knew what I was doing to my grades. Her face straightened and she looked at the road. "Let's go, it getting dark here", she said coldly. I nodded a defeated "Yes" and began driving back to the station. "Don't go to your locality, just drop me to the nearest station from here, I will go home", she added. I kept silent and drove. Soon we were at a nearby railway station. The car stopped and Priya gave me a goodbye hug. "Keep in touch", she smiled dryly. "Priya, if you feel like we can do this again", I couldn't help being more shameless. She nodded, said "Bye" and left. I stayed in the car watching her walk to the station. Her head was low and her straightened hair flew in the passing wind. I felt bad for I just might have hurt her. At the same time I felt good for being honest. She disappeared in the shadows of the ticket counter line and I prepared to drive back home. The thought of the upcoming exams distracted me from the weird events of the day. I smiled for having a girl bold enough to 'do' me as soon as I got committed. I absorbed myself in glimpses of her brown face and her bleached straightened hair, still smiling to the idea of having a girl who stalked me.

Anita called up at night to know about my progress. I honestly admitted to her that I had made none. I hesitantly said, "I couldn't study much Nitu. Plus I am kind of sure, that I am going to fail again. I feel ashamed for my lack of needed preparation. Instead of covering up for my failures in the past exams, here I am doubtful to even attempt the coming exams." Like a caring girlfriend Anita cooled me down. "Just relax Uday. Don't panic please. Just do as I say and for sure you will pass the examinations", she suggested calmly. "Let me draw a study plan for you. I will tell you very specific topics to study, and these are sure shot questions of high importance. Even if you do these well, you will pass for sure Uday. Everything will be fine", she suggested calmly. "Yeah", I sighed. "But promise me Uday, that you will listen to me and do as I say", she insisted. Her stable voice and confident planning talked me out of my paranoia. I felt relaxed. "I promise, I will read all the pages in the notes. I will pass, I have to", I assured vowing to complete her assigned tasks at priority. "And if you don't then I will spank the hell out of your cute ass", she giggled. I laughed with her. "Then I will rather choose to disobey you, if you promise such punishments to me", I grinned with lewd thoughts. The thought of Anita spanking my butt for not studying appealed like an erotic punishment. The 'taste of blood' had always been a distraction but surprisingly this time it brought back my focus. We continued studying together on the phone for the night and the night after. I was twice interrupted by my mother for my over indulgence with the phone to which I could lesser explain.

The day of exam finally arrived and I had barely slept all night, partially studying and partially fantasizing about the cuddly moments spent with Anita. The exam was scheduled to begin sharp at eight in the morning. I left home two hours earlier to catch an early morning train with strict instructions given by my mother to study in the train. I did take out the book, but the cool morning wind tucked me to sleep for the entire train ride while the book loosely rested in my palms. The sun hadn't risen in *Mumbai,* and the morning twilight was beginning to turn into dawn. My eyes barely dwindled when I saw the train halted at my station. I quickly got up, collected my stuff and rushed for the door, as I knew that local trains in *Mumbai* hardly stop for ten seconds at a station. By the time I reached the door, the train began moving and I jumped off the train in the direction of its motion. I jogged for a while on the platform till I slowed my pace and finally stopped.

The madness for 'blood' is too outrageous, and spawns our tiny vices making them big. Very rarely, it replaces our vices, again with an extremity.

I walked the over bridge watching sleepy morning passengers going to their respective destinations. There were school students in uniforms who traveled in small clusters, busy chit chatting with each other while college students were clad in casuals, usually with earphones in their ears, detached from each other. The office goers dressed in formals, walked swiftly to make their daily living as they knew that their count would increase in a few hours. There were women who carried fish in big baskets over their heads and often crammed the entrance of the ladies compartment of the train. The laborers crowded around the train doors in their humble shabby clothes with oiled hair, mostly with an icky smell. At times, there were spectacular beautiful girls and women who drew the attention of everybody on the platform. I walked out of the station to the road which led to my college. Till my attention was drawn to a small tea and cigarette stall which still had its night bulb lit, hanging from a wire. The owner poured hot tea through a netted sieve from a big vessel into a tapped vessel. The taxi drivers waited eagerly for the tea to get ready. I considered taking a taxi, but the pleasant morning twilight and the little relaxing sleep in the train encouraged me to walk the two kilometers to college.

I continued trotting towards college and in a few meters ahead, I saw a man opening his *tapri*[68]. *Tapris* are small pavement shops in *India* which sell *paan*[69], tea and cigarettes. The thought of Anita smoking the previous day re-played in my head. I walked up to the *tapri* and asked

---

[68]   *A small tea shop.*

[69]   *Paan is a preparation of combining betel leaf with areca nut and sometimes also with tobacco. Although positioned as a mouth freshener, it is also chewed for its stimulant and psychoactive effects. If you traveling through India, the reddened walls are often an outcome of paan being spit by its consumers. A 100% Indian heritage, and definitely a must try! Also, it comes in a lot of varieties and flavors.*

the shop keeper to give me a menthol cigarette. I remembered the smell and taste of a normal brown filter cigarette which I had tried in my boarding school and it was very pungent. He gave me the cigarette and a match box. I paid him five rupees and looked at the cigarette. I felt the similar dislike for smokers I had all the years, even when I held the plain white cigarette stick between my fingers. I thought about the boyfriend of my *Gujarati Chick* who also smoked. I always wondered what did my *Gujarati Chick* like in him, as he had already started walking the path towards impotency and weak lungs. His breath would stink and even his lips would turn black. "What a loser", I mumbled feeling good about my physical agility to do a back flip with a football. "Weird girl, she didn't dig physical abilities", I wondered. I don't know what this cancer stick does to people and I don't know why girls dig smokers in spite of knowing the risks and hazards of smoking.

Nevertheless, I lit the cigarette and continued walking. I puffed a few mouth fags and a thought passed my head that maybe I should try taking the smoke inside and see how it feels. "What about it would make Anita and Ratish crave it so much. Why are people not able to quit it? What if I get addicted?" I thought to myself. My hurt ego reconciled the last thought and I saw the faces of Anita and Ratish in the alley with those cunning smiles and I pulled a long drag of the menthol cigarette. I tried hard to swallow the smoke like I was swallowing my anguish for not being a smoker. I coughed loudly with the smoke rushing out of my mouth. Perhaps it wasn't for me and I just discovered that my list of inabilities included smoking as well. My eyes went red while I coughed. I became more agitated, and sucked a lighter drag of smoke and tried to swallow it. It itched my throat with the coolness of the menthol, but I controlled the urge to cough. I left the smoke which came directly out of my lungs following through my mouth and nostrils. I repeated my previous effort and then something happened...

My knees felt weak initially and then I felt as if I didn't have any legs. I felt weightless... I continued walking while my head lightened as if the weight of my brain casted on my skull had been suddenly reduced. I swayed and walked slowly to my college and puffed better drags of the cool menthol cigarette resting between the first two fingers of my right hand. The bag hanging on my shoulders felt heavier, and I walked along. I reached the college gate and saw Anita and others studying. Watching me smoke, the kids gave a wide mouthed, jaw dropping reaction. Finally when I reached them, I realized I was still swinging. The exam was about to begin in fifteen minutes, and I began to laugh. I laughed about everything I could remember and see. I made fun of everybody standing around me and the kids looked surprised. Anita tried asking me questions and helping me revise but watching me in such a jolly funny mood, she laughed with me too. We entered the hall and the exam began. I still sat on my bench and laughed alone for another fifteen minutes. A slow yet powerful sobering effect came on me when I saw the kids racing their hands on the answer sheets. It finally occurred to me that the exam is important and I looked into the question paper. I took quite a while to understand that I needed to pass those examinations or else it would become bad for my peace in college and at home. The examinations went by peacefully but I picked up a new hobby called smoking; a socially detested activity but yet a very thrilling experience. I only figured out many years later that something which started because of a hurt ego for 'love' would require a lot more 'love' to quit.

The exams finally got over, and I had little clue of how it went. Anyways, thinking about the exams had no point when they are over. At least I wasn't the type who would sit and analyze my performance in the exams. Especially when my life had become so happening with friends, booze, girlfriend and the latest 'blood' called a cigarette. On one such occasion when I was at home, the curiosity of smoking a cigarette sprung back inside me. I left my home slowly tiptoeing to the nearest *tapri*. While I was leaving, I saw a tall lean guy walking out of the same compound where I lived. He was around six feet, fair skinned with black hair. He wore geeky spectacles and walked confidently yet barely sought any attention. After a short walk, I was at the *tapri*, buying my cigarette. I lit my cigarette and quickly moved behind a big roadside advertisement banner to hide so that even if an acquaintance passes by, they cannot spot me smoking. In a few minutes, the lean guy also joined in and hid behind the banner. I looked at him with a quizzical face and asked him, "Do you live in the housing complex next to the church?" He nodded and smiled and I smiled too understanding that we both were hiding because of the same reason. That was the day I met

Vini. Vini was also called 'Doctor' primarily because he was studying medicine and much later I came to know of his abilities to dissect any situation into bits and pieces of analyzable information. Even if he was good at it, nobody around would ever perceive so, as perhaps his simplicity was a mask which he wore. Though he appeared simple, and lived simple, his thoughts weren't the same. Over time I came to know that he was pretty athletic. I never knew that day, that I met a friend for life, and especially – that all the wildness and crazy adventures would be awaiting us in the near future.

We walked back together discussing biology and medicine. Perhaps maybe it never showed in my scores but the subject was the most interesting subject I had ever read. It talked about nature, behavior and the interesting things which runs behind the naked human eye and makes life as 'life'. Even in my college laboratory I used to love the way micro-organisms functioned. They come as two and make a million progenies. It was very creepy but yet amazing to know about the powerful things they could do. I developed a fascination for this subject. The age old stories of animals in the jungle and the way they lived...

A couple of days later Kirat called up to discuss a plan to go to the prom night happening that evening in his college. Kirat, Sanky, Gino and I met in the afternoon to discuss the idea of going to the Prom Night. Gino was the guy who had introduced me to Kirat and Sanky. He was a *sardar* who had cut his hair against the religious sentiments of his family. His only reason to do so was a hope to date a girl. But since he cut his long hair, Gino had been picking up on the modelling scene happening in his college. "Dude, we have the college festival going on and tonight is the Prom Night", bragged Kirat in excitement. "What say, let's go", Sanky suggested considering the fact that it might be loaded with gorgeous chicks. Gino was the most excited. He had all the reasons to exploit this opportunity for his little accomplishment of making it to the modelling ramp of his college in a small fashion show. He somewhere knew that he was getting the required opportunities to make a flamboyant college life. "Let's go *yaar*, it would be fun", Gino insisted with enthusiasm. "What say Uday?" asked Gino with a spark in his eyes. "Let's go, I mean do I need to have a partner to get in?" I asked doubtfully. The faces of all four of us looked dubious as we struggled with our insecurities of attending a big college party. "Dude, I guess we can enter as stags too. I got friends in the security, they can help", Gino answered the query lightening up the faces of the disappointed adolescents. "Ok, then I will call Anita too. She and I will dance together and you guys can find your partners", I suggested to my brilliant idea of romancing in the prom, only to be welcomed by dubious faces again. I ignored their single faces and called up Anita. The idea of Anita and me rocking the dance floor together rocked my system.

"Hi Hottie!" Anita answered. "Hey Nitu, guess what?" I responded. "What?" she responded with curiosity. "Would you like to go to a prom with me?" I tried asking in the James Bond style. Anita laughed and said, "Why are you sounding so filmy?" "Just, imagine you and me dancing together, arms in arms and eyes in eyes", I started. "And the whole world watching us, and you look 'hot' and sexy when you groove with me", I continued. "Well that sounds interesting", she said coyly. "But Mummy is angry with me", she said in a tensed voice. "Why, what happened?" I asked her, already feeling the tension which happens before a disappointment. "Day before yesterday I returned late after I visited your place. That angered Mummy", she answered with a little hint of blame and louder disappointment. "I guess you should still ask her. Tell Aunty that even Nikita is going", I said trying to find the best excuse. "What if she calls Nikita?" she asked hesitantly. "I don't like lying to my parents", she mumbled in an almost cranky voice. "Oh ok then, even I won't go there alone", I replied sadly. Anita remained silent for a while and muttered, "It's ok, I will still ask", she said with a faint hint of courage. "Ok. Ask aunty and call me", I hurriedly added and we disconnected and I went back to my friends.

Anita called after a while. "Hello", I answered. "I won't be able to come", she said in a low voice. "Why what happened?" I asked. "Mummy scolded me for going out so much. She said 'we are not spending so much on your education for you to just go out and party all the time'", she said with a heavy throat as she was almost about to cry. After a pause, Anita cried out over the phone, "I got a first class again, all my life I had been scoring good grades." I tried to console her but I was consumed with a thought which kind of pricked me for not scoring a first class for the entire year and a half. I wondered what happened to the studious boy inside me who 'once upon a time' was so concerned with his grades throughout school and junior college. I guess I hadn't tasted the 'blood' then. "Please don't cry Nitu, it's ok, parents are like that at times. Even my father doesn't allow me to go for night out's at Kirat's place. At least you score good grades, I don't even do that", I tried to sympathize. "It's cool, I won't go then, anyways I will get bored if I go alone", I added sadly. "No Uday, you go and have fun there, but just don't get too close to any girl", Anita tried to cheer me up in her possessive way. "We will go some other time", she added. "Alright. If you say so. I love you Nitu", I mumbled with sadness. "I love you too Uday", she replied softly. We spoke for a while and ended the conversation.

It was decided that the four of us are going to our first prom night. In *India* prom nights were rare as the concept is western but I guess *Mumbai* is the place in *India* where the west comes alive. We dressed up in semi formals, since wearing a jacket in the *Mumbai* humidity would be too uncomfortable. In the evening, all four of us boarded the local train and set out for *Bandra*. The train was crowded and we made our way to the door and stood at the footboard of the moving train. It's a little dangerous especially when everyday people die of falling out due to standing at the doors of *Mumbai* local trains, as they are not blessed with automatic doors which close once the passengers have boarded. But for the common train commuters, it's a part of the culture. At least it gave some space to breath and fresh air to survive the aroma therapy inside the usual crowded compartments. Sometimes space is more required than being safe!

We reached *Bandra* Station and we took a rickshaw to the college. I realized I was going to a different college where I wasn't a student so perhaps I didn't know what I might get into. Maybe that's why I carried Ratish's metal knuckles with me in my pocket. I knew *Mumbai* was peaceful as such, but the lessons learnt in my boarding school still remained with me and kept echoing in my head, 'be prepared for a massive fight especially when girls are involved'. The rickshaw stopped at the college and the view looked amazing. Beautiful girls stood around the gate, with well-groomed boys. People looked pretty rich in an average *Bandra* college. The iron gates were brightly lit up with LED lights spiraling around the metal bars. The college had a magnificent feel in spite of its small campus. I guess it was because of the crowd. Any place in this world is liked the most for its people. I guess maybe that's why a *Delhi* campus is so unsafe. I got off the rickshaw and went to the nearest *tapri* in front of the college and bought two cigarettes. At least, I knew that a cigarette is one of the coolest things in college to easily get accepted with the cool ones; and a little style of a smoker should do well. I lit up a cigarette before entering inside the college and observed around. I remembered the knuckle in my pocket and I never wanted it to get confiscated as Ratish was pretty possessive about his weapon of mass destruction. I thought of asking my friends Gino, Kirat and Sanky for help but looking at their faces I thought that maybe they will leave me behind here. So I went to the corner of the wall of college building and hid the knuckle in my socks. The security that frisked entrants consisted of fat beefy guys and everybody was being frisked for illegal substances which were not allowed inside the college campus. When it was my turn, I cleared it effortlessly as nobody went down to my socks.

The vibe inside was amazing. The music was loud and went out to the streets. The crowd was really 'hot', at least with the types of girls in there. Sadly most of the 'hot' ones had their guys with them. All four of us looked around with sad eyes watching the happy couples dance together and the music was also pretty romantic, which left us no chance to join in. I really missed Anita in that moment, and glimpses of her in a red single piece dress ran through my head. I so wished that if she was there with me at that point of 'time', I would have definitely felt more confident. I would have had a stunning partner to dance with. Looking back, maybe they were my inhibitions or insecurities when it came to being accepted in the world. I saw a big 'bad' world around me where I would be judged on money, looks, height or even for the clothes I was wearing.

I began to feel low when suddenly the music changed into a loud peppy college number. The other stags that stood around the dance floor gazing at the gorgeous girls and dreaming about them suddenly had a sparkle in their eyes. Bright smiles ran across their faces as they jumped in the dancing arena of the college ground. The crowd suddenly increased and Kirat and Gino got separated from Sanky and me. I forced myself to dance, still trying to enjoy my individuality despite of an uncomfortable fact for being at a party without the girl who taught me how to party. Sanky and I continued dancing till we reached the center of the dance arena. I turned around to witness two cute girls dancing with each other. Surprisingly in the crowd there were no other girls dancing together. Everybody had a male partner. A faint memory of my boarding school annual fete came back to life where I had hesitantly walked up to a girl to 'propose' to her.

I began walking towards them. Sanky held my arm and pulled me behind. I signaled him to come along with a wink in my eye. He looked nervous but gathered his courage and walked in with me. The very moment the music dulled back to the romantic numbers. The stags began to leave the dancing arena making space for the couples to continue the prom. The change in music was a pretty evident signal to me and Sanky too.

I looked at the two girls and a closing window of opportunity surged courage inside me.

I evaluated my reasons to come to the prom. "I am here at the prom to carry a good memory of a romantic dance with my girlfriend Anita. But if I am here without her what should I do?" I asked myself. "At least, I should still try my luck here or else I would never know if I had a chance of sharing a dance with the girls here. That shall do no harm", I consoled myself making a move. I went close to the girls and Sanky followed me. Both of them were fair, curvy and cute. They stood at the perfect height for Sanky and me.

"Excuse me, since you girls are dancing alone. Would you like to dance with us?" I asked one of the girls. She looked at me and smiled, "Yes sure, you can join us." she answered cheerfully. The other girl didn't look too happy about her friend's open mindedness to include the guys in their solely pleasure. I picked up the cheerful girl and started grooving with her. Sanky danced with the other girl. "Hi, I am Uday", I introduced myself. "Hi, I am Megha", she answered blushing with a smile. We did some small talk and danced for a while, till I looked at Sanky who was barely even talking to the other girl and both of them looked pretty uncomfortable with each other.

Sanky caught me looking at him and I felt I made a mistake. With a lot of courage Sanky asked Megha and me, "Would you like to swap partners?" I looked at Megha and she answered anticipatively, "Sure why not?" I had no choice but to follow and I landed up with the intruded unhappy girl Sanky was dancing with.

"Hi, I am Uday", I said to her looking straight in her eyes as I mildly embraced her to dance. "I am Rita, hi", she answered in a mellow voice yet loud enough for me to hear. She looked cute with a fair face and full cheeks. Her hairstyle was pretty trendy and streaked and a little part of her hair covered her face. I could still see her eyes through the gaps in the hair. "So where do you study Rita?" I asked. "I study here, in this college", she spoke without any expressions. "Don't mind me asking but are you uncomfortable dancing with me?" I couldn't help being blunt. "Yes, kind of", she replied looking at the floor. "I guess we shouldn't have intruded your dance", I apologized. "It's ok", she said flatly. "But you know what, you look very cute Rita, and it's just a compliment", I said with my gaze piercing her eyes. "Thank you", she said with a faint smile. I went closer to her ear and whispered in the loud music. "So if you don't mind, would you like me to hold you? So that we can dance properly", I grinned. "Ok, let's dance", she agreed timidly mildly nodding her head. We embraced each other a little tighter and began moving to the music. It was a strange feeling to match up the groove, but our gaze remained fixed. There was a certain mischievous spark in her eyes, something like desire mixed with abandonment. Her twinkly eyes peeped through her colored hair which over casted her fair gloomy face, as if they promised an oasis in a forlorn desert.

I realized, after all I was just collecting a story. Whether 'love' was my story or was it 'blood', was still left to be figured out. But the madness caused by my 'craving' for 'blood' never let the other schools of thought get the better of me.

The music progressed into a very popular number called *Careless Whispers* sung by *George Michael.* The romance in the music eventually began to spread in the crowd and Rita and I were also engulfed in the spreading passion. "Can I hold your waist and dance?" I asked her in a very polite tone. She looked at me and finally smiled and said, "Yes." I held her waist and pulled her closer. We grooved together unknowingly enslaving ourselves to the music. When the music went up; we went up, and when it went down we came closer. In that moment my gaze broke from her and I looked around at the crowd. We had made a little space for ourselves and couples around were checking us out. I held her close again, digging my fingers in her waist while she placed her arms around my shoulders which slowly hovered towards my chest. Our eyes found their way and gazed at each other, softer this time. "Everybody is checking us out", I remarked looking at her. She smiled and looked around. Her fair cheeks warmed up with the attention, and they blushed pink. "Now the night seems worth it", a thought smiled at me when I stared in her dreamy eyes.

The night stayed still,
For the girl with the golden hair,
Was it bleached, or was it for real?
"How does it matter... who cares?"

I wanted to dance with someone, and I danced with someone else.

But how can you ignore the blush of her cheeks,
They just turned 'pink', burning her golden streaks.
And when the golden veil made some space,
Stared back her eyes, astonished and dazed...

What a brilliant night, I am living tonight,
Grooved my way and I held her tight!
But the way she looks at me, makes me feel, I know her for so long,
And then she smiled, as if she knew me all along...

I wanted to dance with someone, and I danced with someone else.

The gift of 'blood' had taught me well, served with kisses in a hazy smell,
As I kiss the one with whom I couldn't be... When Careless for love, 'too much' means free.

But the night went along, Whispering around in the Careless song,
As for the 'guilty' dance I shared with the damsel,
I liked her fragrance... but I really couldn't tell...

I wanted to dance with someone, and I danced with someone else,

Stared the strangers, for the way we grooved,
The way I held her and the way she moved...

What a fate of intentions so swappy,
A night for us and everyone is happy.

I smiled with a breath of peace.
As I wanted to dance with someone..., and I danced with someone else...

The stillness of that glorious moment was interrupted as Megha and Sanky intruded, "Let's go eat something from the food counter." Rita regained herself and followed her friend Megha. I kept holding her hand in the crowd and soon I was making way for her and me. The sudden surge of confidence had taken over after a little dance with a stranger. The vibe of the dance was still running in our bodies till we reached the counter. I was too consumed in the passionate dance I just had with the cute stranger, and the glimpses kept urging me subconsciously to engulf her. I pulled her to the corner and pulled out the knuckle from my pocket. "Check this out", I said. She held it in her palms and gave it back. "What is this?" she exclaimed in a mild panicky voice. "Are you a hooligan or something like that?" she asked with wide open eyes. "No *yaar*, just in case", I said arrogantly and put it back. We exchanged numbers and said 'goodbye'. I gave Rita a tight hug, feeling the dance again. When I released her of my embrace, she had reluctance in her eyes but her body responded otherwise. I winked at her, and Sanky and I, went out of the gate where Gino and Kirat were waiting. I lit the last cigarette and started puffing it. Kirat and Gino looked at us and asked, "Where were you guys?" Both Sanky and I smiled a brave confident smile and said, "We were dancing with the girls." The pride of the hunt had a crazy feel, which I felt that day. Eventually I had a great dance in a strange prom night with a cute stranger. Sanky looked happy too with Megha's phone number. My body still felt her while her perfume was fresh in my nostrils, in spite of the smoke which was now coming out of them. I quickly messaged Rita my number with a note saying, "Hey this is Uday here. Thanks a lot for a nice romantic dance." We left back for home like glorious warriors, at least Sanky and I were.

The next day when all four of us met Sanky was in a very happy state. Anita called and asked, "Hey 'hottie', how was the prom night?" "It was fine", I answered casually. "So, you had fun?" she asked with a cute yet stern hint to her tone. "How can I have fun without you?" I asked her softly. "So you didn't do anything?" she asked in surprise. "I didn't say that", I returned her question. "In the sense...?" she asked. Her voice sounded doubtful and so I answered, "To be honest, it was boring without you. We just danced a little and left. We drank beer for a major time last night." "Where?" she asked curiously. "On the road. We bought some beer cans from a liquor shop and finished it on the road", I answered pacifying her doubts. "Aww you missed me", she cuddled sympathetically for her 'loser' boyfriend. But I was ok to let her consider me that. Somehow something inside, stopped me from telling her about the dance with Rita. "Ok Anita, I need to go now. My friends are waiting. I will call you at night", I added and we disconnected.

Sanky showed me his cellphone. He had sent over hundred messages to Megha in twelve hours of knowing her. I had a gut feeling which probed me to give him an advice. "Take it easy Sanky, don't message her so much. She will feel suffocated, and you will end up looking too desperate", I said with genuine concern. Sanky retaliated with a little angry face to my humble advice and said, "It's ok dude, I know how to handle this." I smiled with him. Gino and Kirat stayed distracted for the most part as Sanky and I were busy discussing our accomplishments from the previous night.

Two days later, Sanky looked upset. It seems Megha got suffocated and felt the lack of space from the needy Sanky. She broke up with him, at least that's what he said. "I don't know what did I do wrong?" Sanky kept asking in sadness. I remained silent as I knew that correcting him is going to make him sadder or god forbid angry. It's strange about women that how they like to be needed but yet detest the 'needy' at the same time; especially someone who is 'needy' for love. I had my needs covered. I hadn't called Rita till then but then I realized it was 'time' to call her.

It was around eleven in the night. I had just finished a conversation with Anita but she had to leave with her parents for dinner. I dialed Rita's number from my cellphone. The phone rang and she answered. "Hey Uday, hi how are you?" she said with a faint excitement in her voice. I was glad at the anticipated answer. I was sure she had thought about me. "So, you still up, were you studying?" I asked casually. "No *yaar*, I was just passing time", she answered casually. We started talking a normal conversation about college and places. It was a different feel when I engaged in a conversation with Rita that too when I was hiding something deep down. The only vibe which I remembered was of the dance floor and especially the song kept re-running in my head. "I still can't forget the song, it is still running in my head", I said in a soft voice. "Yes, I have also started liking that song", she replied immediately. "I never gonna dance again, guilty feeling got no rhythm, though it's easy to pretend, I know you are not a fool", I sang it out. Rita listened peacefully and then said, "You sing pretty well Uday." I felt good watching the charm work and said, "Thank you Rita." "Do you sing too?" I asked her. "Yes, I am more of a bathroom singer", she replied. "Nice, but it was just too strange right, we met in a prom night and danced like we knew each other for ages", I added. There was silence on Rita's end for a while.

I looked at my phone. Anita was calling; I guess she was back home. But I still continued talking to Rita. The silence finally broke and she said, "Do you have a girlfriend Uday?" I felt doomed for her question. I didn't feel like lying but when I answered, I still couldn't reveal the truth to her. "I have an ex-girlfriend. We were pretty serious but we broke up", I said weakly. Rita's voice suddenly turned sympathetic and concerned and she said, "Why what happened?" "Nothing *yaar*, she and I were serious but she had an affair with someone else", I blatantly lied. "Oh my sweetheart, it must have been hard on you", she exclaimed. "Yes, kind of, but I am fine now, it's just that the other guy was rich, and could afford a lot of things for her, which I couldn't", I added in a pretentious low voice. Rita was flushed with my sob story of a heart break, rejection and abandonment.

She tried to divert the topic of conversation. "Uday, have you heard that song called *Behenchod Sutta*[70]?" asked Rita. "Yeah", I answered. "Can

---

[70] *The literal translation is "Sisterfucker Cigarette!" A popular song for smokers and dopers.*

you please sing it for me?" She asked in a pleading girlie voice. Perhaps she wanted to remove the memory of my fictional ex-girlfriend. "Fine, but my voice is not so good, so kindly bear with it", I obliged her request and her latent desire.

I sang the entire song, and she listened through, singing along with me. The conversation continued for a long time doing small talk, and then we disconnected. Anita had called thrice since then. Whenever she called, I felt a power too strong urging me to cut the call and talk to her. Maybe that's the strength of a true romantic connect. Nevertheless, I was driven by my male ego, which with a 'hard on' was driving me good enough to continue focusing on Rita. At the same time the essence of the bodies which had submerged together dancing which each other, held on to my system. I finally put Rita to sleep and called Anita. She had dropped a message which read, "Who are you so busy talking to? Anyways I am going to sleep as we have an early morning practical. Please be there in college on time."

Anita didn't answer and I disconnected the call and dozed off, with thoughts of the dance I shared with Rita. It was indeed a guilty feeling but yet very addictive, as the prom night kept replaying in front of my eyes in glimpses. The prowl was successful as my first time seduction got me some success. The cub tiger that I was, at least came to learn, what it was to hunt.

A couple of days later I was sitting in the class with Anita. Sitting closely with Anita used to be the biggest treat for me in college. So much so that the lectures and lecturers lost importance. In fact, another side of me strongly suggests that they weren't of any importance. The only perk of sitting in the lectures was attendance because that rested with the faculty and I had started to get used to the differential treatment bestowed upon me.

I still wonder why I was so surprised at being treated like an outcast. I simply didn't match the herd. My classmates were into their subjects and so was I, it's just that my subject was 'love' or 'blood', as I would like to call it now. Anita was still a topper material so everything else about her could easily be overlooked. Though often she got indirect suggestions to find a better boyfriend. But she too, like me was too enchanted by the thing called 'love' to listen to anyone.

If not for my grades, my influence on my classmates was strong and inspiring but seldom appreciated. At least I would like to believe so. 'Good' and 'bad' both cast their aura on people and things in their vicinity. It's just, at times 'bad' shadows 'good', instigating it to fight back.

Nevertheless, sitting through the lectures with Anita on the last few benches of the classroom was pure and untainted. The attraction and connect we drew from each other kept bringing our bodies closer. The strong sensual clingy bond we shared could always be felt. Though we looked at the lecturer throughout, between us, our hands always remained entwined in each other's.

I often wrote passionate and vulgar remarks in her notebook. Once in a lecture after the glorious prom, I wrote, "I love your eyes when you are looking at me just when I am on top of you." Anita read the line as I wrote it. She looked around hurriedly to check if nobody is looking at her notebook for what I had just written in it. She looked at me with the same passion in her eyes, and I looked back at her. The way her eyes looked in that moment made my soul melt. I wrote back, "And when your eyelashes move, it feels as if it just lifted my soul." Anita lightly bit her lips and her hand slipped out of my grip and reached my thighs. My breath raced a bit considering her sudden move. Her hand slowly moved towards my crotch where my 'little warrior' had already made some space on the surface of my jeans. I began to lose my breath but I still controlled myself, considering the dangers of being caught in a classroom for immoral behavior. Out of a sudden impulse, my hand grabbed her thighs. Anita retaliated quickly to remove my hand from her thighs but to her dismay my grip was too tight. She struggled for a while but her breath kept getting heavier. Our sudden movements created a minor chaos just enough to break the silence of the nearby benches. The sudden head turns of the other students caught the attention of the lecturer. The lecturer was a thin young lady with spectacles and a bob cut. Although she looked cute and had the admiration of a major male population of the class, but that didn't give her much admiration for herself as she was infamous for being very strict. She looked at our row of benches and screamed, "What is going on there?" Anita and I were pretty startled with the interruption and the caused embarrassment ran down from my eyes to Anita's only to be converted into anger, in the eyes of the 'hot teacher'.

Ratish sat with Manjeet on the next bench in front of ours. "Ratish, is there something wrong?" asked the lecturer. I felt a sigh of relief and looked straight down at my notebook and pretended to take notes from the blackboard. Ratish answered hurriedly, "No, nothing Ma'am." "Please concentrate and if you are not interested then please leave the class", the lecturer retorted in a rude tone. Ratish's nostrils flared again with anger and his face flushed red. "Ma'am, I didn't do anything", he answered in a rather loud voice. "Please leave the class", the lecturer said authoritatively signaling towards the door of the classroom. It appeared more like a mood swing when the good looking teacher suddenly went crazy and angry. Probably it's acceptable for all 'hot' women.

I looked around at the faces of my other classmates. Most of the back bencher boys had a muffled smile on their faces and a look of awe in their eyes for their beloved teacher. "But I really didn't do anything Ma'am", Ratish retaliated with an almost hint of anger. "I won't continue the lecture if he doesn't leave the classroom", screamed the lecturer with her hands on her waist creating a sense of panic amongst the studious, who looked at Ratish with insistence to leave the classroom. Ratish gave in and quickly packed up his stuff and began to leave. He turned around to look at Anita and me. Anita gave him a guilty look while I tried to cover a smile encroaching on my face. Ratish smiled back and tried hard to cover his breaking smile as he began to walk out of the class with his head down. Just as he was out of the classroom door, the lecturer continued the lecture. But Ratish didn't leave; he turned around outside the gate, not visible to the lecturer and gave a 'stab in his heart' gesture with a broad grin. The students looking outside found it too unbearable to resist and burst out laughing. The lecturer immediately walked to the classroom door and saw Ratish making a move. Sadly she lost her cool and reprimanded Ratish to the H.O.D's office.

The classroom was back to joy but the joy was only celebrated by the backbenchers. The majority of studious kids made sad disgusting faces. Anita and I laughed while she pinched me hard on my waist. I shrieked in pain but I realized a vibration in my pocket and my message tone rang out loud. I put my hand inside my pocket and pulled out my cellphone suffering with the sudden pain caused on my fleshy waist. Anita curiously looked at my cellphone. There was a message from Rita. Luckily I had saved her number as Gino. I didn't open the message to check but quickly put my phone back in my pocket. Before Anita could ask anything, I pinched her waist. We both laughed in pain and fought a little. The next lecture was cancelled and the students began to leave the classroom. I said to Anita, "Why are you creating scenes in the classroom? See because of you, poor Ratish is thrown out." Anita hurled a stiff punch in my belly and retaliated, "It's because of you, you ass. Poor Ratish, he got badly screwed up because of us." We began to laugh again, and I got up from my desk signaling my little finger to her which meant that I was going to the washroom. Anita nodded and I left.

As soon as I got outside, I checked my cellphone to check Rita's message. "Hey Uday, wanna meet today? Megha, her boyfriend and I are coming to *Andheri*. Would you like to join us?" read the message. I walked swiftly to the washroom and called Rita. Her phone rang and she answered. "Hey Uday, how are you? Did you get my message?" she asked. "Yes I did, but when did Megha get a boyfriend?" I curiously asked her. "Oh that, he is Mehul, pretty nice guy", she answered. "But I thought, Megha and Sanky had a scene?" I commented with a little 'bad' feeling which encroached inside me, making me think about the day Sanky had been sad because Megha had asked him to stop messaging her. "Sanky was nice but he was suffocating Megha. He barely knew her for two days and he was already so possessive about her", mocked Rita. "Anyways, are you coming? Let's meet, what say?" enquired Rita with a muffled excitement in her voice. "What time are we meeting?" I asked. "Around four in the evening", said Rita. "Alright", I answered in a normal tone. "Ok, see you at *Andheri* railway station at four", said Rita and disconnected the call.

I walked out of the washroom to bump into Anita and Ratish. "Hey we are planning to go for a movie, other kids are also coming", said an excited Anita. I looked at Ratish and burst out laughing, "What happened with you, what did the H.O.D say?" "Nothing much buddy, she called my parents for misbehaving in the classroom. I didn't even do anything. All thanks to you both", he replied with a sarcastic smile. I apologized to Ratish but couldn't control the laughter thinking about the incident. Anita and I felt a fond affection for a friend like Ratish. "I wouldn't be able to come for the movie, I have to leave for home", I said sheepishly. "Why? Let us go for the movie please", Anita pleaded. "Yeah, let's go", insisted Ratish. "I would love to but my Mom just called me up and asked me to take her to the hospital. She has a sudden pain in her ears. I guess I have to take her to an ENT", I lied with a helpless smile. The lie was perfect and I knew nobody could counter argue it but the only thing imperfect in that entire moment were Anita's pleading eyes. And I felt a little sad thinking about the excitement in her eyes for the movie which I was killing. The thought of meeting Rita and what waited with her still pushed my fantasies, and the desire to see the unseen drove me towards it. I left college but instead of boarding the local train to my home, I took the train to *Andheri*[71]. Anita continued for the movie with Ratish and other classmates after a lot of insistence, but sadly she left with an upset face. Somehow her upset face kept haunting me throughout the train ride, invoking thoughts about "How would she feel if she comes to know what I am doing?" The rush in the local train pushed my thoughts back to my wits along with the predominant one which said – "Whatever is happening with Rita is definitely going to be temporary."

"Hey Uday have you reached?" asked Rita on the phone. "Yes I am at the *Andheri* station exit", I answered. "Come outside *McDonalds,* we are waiting in a white *Honda Civic*", said Rita. I reached the restaurant and saw a white *Honda* struggling through the horrible traffic outside. I quickly rushed and opened the back door of the car and got in. Rita waited in the car wearing a black thin jacket with a pair of jeans. Her hair was colored with hues of golden brown. She wore a nice perfume. I looked ahead and Megha said a bright "Hi." "Uday meet Mehul and Mehul meet Uday", Megha introduced me to the guy in the driver's seat. He was tall, darker than Megha and a little flabby. I felt a surge of brashness regarding the fact that Sanky looked better than him. "Hi

---

[71] *Andheri is a western suburb of Mumbai. In Hindi, 'Andheri' means dark.*

Mehul, I am Uday", I introduced myself with a smile. "Megha and Mehul sound pretty rhyming", I chuckled to Rita and she laughed along. Megha was a little embarrassed while Mehul just smiled. The car went to *Juhu*[72] beach and stopped. Rita and I got out of the car. Megha and Mehul didn't. "We have some work ahead so we will get that done and pick you guys on the way back", said Megha. "Till then you guys have fun", laughed Megha. Rita and I waved back and started walking towards the beach. We reached the beach and walked towards the shore. I took off my shoes and held them in my hands while Rita also did the same. We talked and walked while the slow evening waves of the sea washed our feet. There were people everywhere so the privacy was missing. We kept walking till we reached the end of the beach. The sun was about to set and the patch looked a little empty. We sat down at the beach and waited for the sunset. Anita's upset face still ran intermittently in my thoughts.

"It is a beautiful sunset", I said looking at the drowning sun. "Yes, it is so beautiful!" Rita answered. "You are looking really 'hot'. I couldn't figure out that you looked so pretty, on the prom night", I complimented her. Rita looked at me and said, "You could have done better." The laughter filled words pierced my little ego. I looked at the setting sun; it still reminded me of the fact that, "I had lied to Anita some time back to be here with Rita to see what chances I have." For a moment I felt like drowning with 'guilt', along with the setting sun. "Have you ever kissed?" I asked Rita still forcing a smile out of my wounded ego. "No, I haven't and why are you asking?" she answered with intimidation. "Just, felt like", I smiled. "No way, don't even think about it", said Rita with a playful smile.

Anita's compliments flashed in my head about the ferocious feline she always compared me to. Watching the resistance in Rita's eyes, I mumbled in a low voice, "I meant, I just felt like asking." The exciting idea which I had imagined since the prom, slowly diminished, like the light which diminished with the setting sun. Although the beauty of the setting sun was much more than the reality of my falling hopes… A little fear rested inside my head when a thought occurred, "What if I kissed Rita? What would be the worst that could happen?"

---

[72]   *Famous yet a highly littered beach in Mumbai, also a posh locality.*

The sun peacefully drowned in the sea leaving bubbles of darkness culminating an ambience called twilight. I barely knew then, that when 'light' leaves with the falling hopes, even 'darkness' comes forth to present a chance. A sudden hope surged in my thoughts again, because I could see the worst that could happen if I kissed Rita. The pride of the ferocious tiger which Anita had made me believe to be, yearned to go back to her. Endless thoughts ran in my head while we sat on the beach in the mournful silence of the dead sun. "I am not here to settle down with Rita. This is supposed to be an adventure trip. Just to be here with Rita, I had saddened Anita in the day. I had refused her for the first time. And after all this, what am I taking back from here? A rejection. No, I am better than that..." an array of endless thoughts flipped in my system, perhaps slowly building up the momentum... often required beforea kill.

Out of sudden impulse I grabbed Rita's head and pulled her closer. I kissed her lips, pushing my face into hers. After a brief kiss, Rita pulled herself back and rammed a hard slap across my face. "This was the worst that could happen", I chuckled to myself. The sting of the slap didn't deter my urge to take her. I grabbed her head again and kissed her, only to stay a little longer this time till she pulled back again and slapped me, a little lighter this time. I just couldn't stop anymore. There was no 'shame', no 'guilt', just the feeling of victory and the taste of sweet moist lips which in spite of all the resistance, moved as I wanted them to move. I grabbed her head again and this time with both hands, and continued kissing her. Her hands kept ramming across my body but nothing moved other than her lips and mine. Till she mellowed down, and continued kissing the beast she didn't want to. My tongue slithered inside her mouth to meet hers. The rejected kiss continued for an exceptionally long time and the last remaining rays of the setting sun were nowhere to be seen, leaving us in the darkness and strangely, the 'darkness' set in my heart too. Maybe that is the nature of the predator, which left on the prowl looking out for varieties of tasty 'blood', but instead of returning 'red', it came back a hue darker.

Rita finally freed herself and cried, "Why did you kiss me? I was saving it for someone special!" Her little cranky voice had no effect on me. I felt elated for the fact that I would always be the special person for her to remember. "I don't know, I just felt like", I said softly, still touching her face. "But how was it?" I asked with the excitement returning in my eyes. Rita's eyes met mine and she let out a playful smile again coupled with moist mushy eyes. "It was nice", she muttered hesitantly. I grabbed her again, but much lightly this time. We kissed for a long while. Rita's phone rang as Megha was back with Mehul to pick us up. Some passersby too paid attention to our candid kiss and we left with mild embarrassment. On our way back, I held Rita by her plump waist in the backseat of the car while she cuddled with fond affection. "Uday, you are such a rapist!" she whispered the derogatory word in my ears and mildly kissed my cheek.

I growled lightly to the demure humor of the horrible word. It's like falling for someone's sickness, and enjoying every freaking bit of it. I had found my sickness, the gift of the 'taste of blood'. It pushed itself up to my throat and finally into my eyes. The sickness mirrored in Rita's eyes too and the tongues did the talking. It's evolution, I suppose, when people start craving for pure sickness than the adulterated 'light' of just 'being around'. And then, they keep prowling for more.

PROWLING FOR BLOOD

Not like the conscious didn't knock,
Was it just plain nature or did it meet the 'dark',
Prowling for the blood,
And snarling for its taste,
Finding your own sickness can often lead you,
Looking for blood in haste,
As the 'dark' is ever so pure,
For the 'light' which is always graded,
And in the lust for the blood,
My conscious faded...

Was it innocence?
Blended with gluttony,
But it all mixed up,
As smooth as a symphony,
Of the smiles of the eyes,
Or the thought of the spice,
Demanding its identity,
Truth mixed up with lies...!

But the last ray of light,
Whispered as it faded,
In the purity of the 'dark',
Enchanting us for ages,
That it's endless,
But still it rose with curiosity growling,
As for the bloodlust,
The predator went prowling,
And as it locked the crave of her smell,
An ancient wisdom rung a bell,
Says, "Son, no matter how far you travel to the deep,
As you sow, and so shall you reap."

THE DARK DREAM:

WHAT IF IT COMES BACK?

It happened during one of those confused nights, when I often struggled with my conscience. I knew that what I was trying to do was wrong. At least the world referred to it in a manner like that. Those who knew what I was up to did call it 'wrong', yet they rewarded me with a certain strange respect. Like a mischievous grin which acknowledged that they knew what I was up to. At times I took it as an ode to the glorious; the one who does more than regular people. Often when I looked for the glory at those eyes in the mirror, I searched for it in the victory of my spoils, which rested in the twinkle of my so called 'innocent eyes'. I became fonder of them, happier that they had traveled to find the similar twinkle in so many eyes. Eyes leave imprints on souls and I had flipped through the glimpses of so many eyes in which I had looked in so closely.

But at times it appeared as though the twinkle had faded, making my search of glory difficult. The victorious spark had turned into plain 'dark' sadness, which often questioned me to reveal the consequences of my prowl. "How many hearts can I break?" I wondered, sometimes elated with mischief, and sometimes with sadness for someone who would leave. I didn't want anybody to go. I just wanted them to stay cheerfully through all the different worlds which I had created.

Perhaps I was confused with my own idea of 'love'. Probably I didn't even have an idea. It was just a feeling of constant excitement and curiosity. And it's true, as 'love' does make you feel both, elated and curious with desire and passion to know more. In my understanding everyone loves like that. Even if it's a sin which you 'love' to commit again and again, you would do it with a child-like enthusiasm. Enthusiasm makes you feel alive and curiosity doesn't let you lose interest. Your object of love is the one who cherishes the 'light' and 'dark' sides of 'love'.

The world of humans was made to keep human beings together. And to achieve this, they developed a social protocol, which eventually culminated owing to the mere detrimental helpless need of human beings to live together as social animals. Indeed they needed to be social to survive in the wild ruthless nature. "But imagine the wildness of human beings of a social and comfortable world; 'scary' isn't it?" The social protocol is thus the well-founded guideline for humans to accommodate and adjust with each other. They like to call it 'harmony'. Harmony often constricts the focus of the limitless human being. Like how my focus on knowing the opposite gender was restricted by the social guidelines for a harmonious lovey-dovey relationship. Pretty much like the ray of 'light' limited by 'darkness' on both sides and yet lightening up the darkness of the endless universe.

I didn't feel much wrong with a little curiosity which had made life suddenly so exciting. But the social protocol does influence each one of us, beginning from the things we know, the choices we make and even the dreams we are likely to pursue. The acknowledgement of right and wrong is an outcome of the protocol. And it kept screaming in my ears that I was wrong.

Mother Nature designed each to supersede the other. Though nature does define that each of her species have a place in this world, but in the human world of possibilities each define their own place.

I seldom knew then, that the strange respect which the world bestowed on me had an unknown eeriness. Though the world will always respect the one who has more (at least on the face of it) and yet, given one instance to take it all away from the one who has more, the world will never hesitate. They aspire to have more, but yearn to be equal, and probably that's how the world balances itself. On one end, they focus on desire and on the other they preach harmony. The social protocol was wearing me down as accordingly, loving more than one person in an intimate relationship is wrong doing. The innocence of such an adventure doesn't stay naive for long and is often tainted by one's own self accusations.

I had begun to lose my balance of focus and harmony since I got close to Rita. Her way of loving me was innocent which left a strange feeling of 'guilt'. I often imagined Anita with sadness in her eyes if she came to know of my disloyalty. For many nights I struggled with a realization of being the culprit who could destroy words like 'trust' and 'love' for the very people I adored, cherished and desired the most.

And one night the Universe communicated my worst fears in the form of a dream. Probably that's why there ain't no word for good dreams but the bad ones are called 'nightmares'. Ironically the good dreams fuzz out and are easily forgotten, but the bad ones often stay in our memories and haunt us for a very long time.

The glimpses of that nightmare still runs fresh in my head – the vision of the 'dark dream'.

In my vision I saw a building which looked somewhat like my college campus. However the populated road outside was replaced by lush green gardens. The old *French* architecture of the building looked serene on a hilly landscape covered with green grass which danced with the winds.

I traveled the college campus, walking through the corridors of the cream colored gothic building. The building was empty and devoid of students. I walked up two floors to my regular laboratory. The empty laboratory had microscopes evenly placed on each table as usual. The laboratory had a rear door which opened up into a balcony. I cautiously peeped into the balcony, and before I realized I was already walking into the balcony and suddenly, the balcony started transforming into a beautiful garden. I could see the balcony and the metal cupboards rapidly fading away. What was left; was me, in the garden.

I started wandering into the garden, not knowing where it leads to. I looked around and saw I was amidst short fruit laden trees which spanned the garden. I looked up at the sky, and saw the blue sky turn gray, covered with gloomy clouds. The cloudy graying skies made me realize the change happening around me and I felt anxious. I started looking ahead again, and saw myself, in the middle of an orchard of dwarf trees. I had lost sense of where I was, and was just neutrally floating through what later turned out to be my dream.

Red fruits hung on the low branches of the trees. I traveled further into the endless garden till I saw two naked bodies stubbed against the smooth bark of a thick tree. I wondered if I had wandered into the Garden of Eden.

Reddened was the tree by small circular fruits,
While its shade was rubricated by the fawn bodies.
The sight of their love was innocent and divine,
Naked and pure like a holy shrine...

Underneath the comforting clouded sky,
Fondled Adam, and for her blush he did try,
And when he saw Eve, missing in her eyes
"Where is she?" in a graying despair he cried...

Curiously I stepped closer to their fusion,
Their sound of lust ignited my passion,
She had him entrapped in her golden fleeces,
And grabbed his head and kissed him to pieces.

She was fair from head to toe, fused with him in a clasp,
Desire often makes one vicious, as he felt her voracity with a cruel grasp,
Lost he was in her fair feminine, cuddly and gorgeous from the start,
And thus engulfed him the gloomy skies, Conquering her 'Red', from 'heart' to 'heart'...

And still perplexed by the naked lovers,
Adorning my dream with their lusty cover,
I wondered if in their eyes, "Was it Love or her coyness worked like wine?"
Still steaming each other in frenzy, a pair was of Rita while the other was mine...

I cautiously walked closer to see a mildly plump woman and a mildly hairy man ferociously kissing each other. She was fair with golden streaked black hair falling over her face. She tried to resist his advances while he embraced her. Their passionate fusion appeared like Adam and Eve together in paradise. And then, I saw their faces. I was stunned to recognize them – it was Rita and me.

I slowly simmered in the dream of love. She physically resisted her assailant, yet invited him with her mischievous twinkly eyes.

But glimpses of 'love' didn't make the dream a nightmare. It was for an unsettling feeling which a thought invoked in my dreamy mind. "Where is Anita?" I thought anxiously in my dream. I guess I was surprised that how could any dream of mine could be complete without her.

Soon enough, the garden disappeared and in broken glimpses I saw myself running through the corridors of the college building. I walked up the wooden stairs which turned spiral. I looked down at the slant stairs. And when I looked up I was ascending up in a tower like structure. The college building appeared more like a castle with places which never existed or perhaps which I had never seen before. The spiral staircase ended in a shady lobby which had a thick wooden door.

I slowly walked towards the wooden door,
Approached me a feeling which I had never felt before,
The thick ridged planks were striped across with metal plates,
Guarded a certain secret for they were studded with big iron nails.

An anxious feeling had already found it,
"Where is Anita?" and with the thought... my heart still pounded,
Intrigued by the places which I had never seen,
"What secret would lurk behind that door?" I wondered in my dream.

I turned towards my right to a little hole in the wall,
The castle was huge and its tower was tall,
The window of the tower ran adjacent to a huge tree with many branches,
And I waited for that which had lesser chances...

WHAT IF IT COMES BACK?

Suddenly a big black Raven flew up and perched on the high branch (apparently, I could see a long branch outside, through the hole). It had a thick shiny black plumage. Its crown gleamed and as it clawed on the branch and looked at me. After a momentary stillness its beaks parted as if it's saying something. I gazed intensely at the dark bird wondering what it was doing in my dream.

"What are you doing in my dream?" I asked in surprise,
It clawed the wooden bark and cawed in the skies,
Its throat enlarged while its crest had begun to rise,
The dark angel shed off, its calm disguise!

"My 'Guardian Angel'", I did have it recognized,
But it croaked in anger as if he is preparing for a fight,
With irate voice and self-ruffled feathers,
Charging at me, it added up to my plight.

"Where is Anita?" I asked him with faith,
As such a deep haunting experience is called wraith,
The graying clouds casted fear blended with Sin,
From the booty of Rita I sought Anita's Skin...

And then my eyes met his 'dark',
Little convex eye bulbs, glimmered with a mysterious spark,
From breast to wings, flanked by 'darkness',
The old friend had brought, a glimpse of sadness...

I intensely gazed into the glint of the illuminated illusion,
Till the light in its dark eyes appeared like a watery reflection,
And the ripples of darkness stilled in its eyes,
To a shudder, as I witnessed the outcome of my vice...

Suddenly I saw vivid glimpses of a lean dusky girl curled up with a man. Their naked torsos rubbed against each other on a circular bed covered with a shiny black blanket. She was passionately kissing him with her half closed eyelids. I hurriedly rushed towards them to see their faces.

I don't know why I felt it's very important to check their faces. Probably I just wanted to clear my doubts. I looked at her and to my horror it was Anita. I skipped a heart-beat. A bad intuition arose. I so wished that the dream ends. But on the other hand, it was important to know the vague truth. And finally I saw the face of the man whose hair were being ruffled by her. It wasn't me.

He was the *Imran Khan* look alike from college. I froze, stunned to find her with another man. They appeared to be in deep 'love'. Cuddling and nibbling each other after a tiring love making affair. It was so much like me and her. "Anita" I murmured in a frightened voice.

She didn't hear me, probably. She kept looking at him affectionately. And then she turned towards me and stared in my eyes. As if she already knew that I stood there and watched her with her new flame. I felt the spectrum of hell from 'envy' to 'rage'.

And all my questions accusingly stared back, hoping to find 'guilt' in her eyes. But there was not even an ounce of 'shame' or 'guilt'. Just sadness prevailed in her moist brown eyes. And then a drop of tear trickled down from the side of her eyelashes. Maybe it was her 'shame' or her 'guilt' as either one of them often leads to another. Or perhaps it was her 'grief' as she was sad all the while and the deep 'love' in her unfaithful affair was just an illusion.

"Why?" "Why did you do this?" "Anita let's go", I screamed, howled and cried. But she remained there, silent and still. And then she began to grow distant from me as the dark waters in the raven's eye encroached in the space between me and her, perhaps dissolving everything in that moment into plain 'darkness'. I tried to reach out for her but she slowly vanished into the dark ripples.

The horror of the moment,
Which had just been surpassed...,
Haunting me forever,
As long as it lasts...

In the gloomy castle,
With gray in the skies and gray on the floor,
And so did the dark dream unravel,
While behind me was the wooden door.

"No" I screamed in denial,
For the payback of pushing loyalty to a trial,
But gone was she in my melancholic verse,
'Irony' was that, I had invited my curse...

I woke up with drops of sweat trickling down my brow. "Fuck", I gasped switching on the lights. "That was a horrible nightmare!" I mumbled still trying to retain the memories of the dream. The glimpses of the naked bodies kept replaying in my head.

Momentarily the glimpses of Rita and me, naked in the fruity garden excited my 'little warrior'. But the vivid ripples in the eye of the black raven stopped my heartbeat. "Fucking 'Guardian Angel'!" I gasped angrily feeling cheated by the bird on which Anita and I had bestowed the holy word called 'angel'. The glimpses of Anita passionately with someone else, kept excruciating me and all I could do was to curse the black raven. The black raven can never be an angel for its 'darkness'. Anita's tears bubbled up in my eyes. "I can't see Anita with anyone else," I hissed into the void with possessiveness, as 'envy' set my skin on fire.

"It's such a dark dream and why did it happen to me?" I pondered saddened by an anxious helpless feeling. "I guess I am not innocent anymore. My curiosity is no more like that of a child. It's tainted with adultery", I cursed myself. I looked at the books around on the table. I picked up an old book of poetry to pull myself out of the dream. I flipped through the pages and rested on a poem – *The Inchcape Rock*[73]. A quote ended the poem and as much as I wanted to return back to my reality, it pushed me back in the 'dark dream'. It read, "As you sow, and so shall you reap." It resonated like the words of the grim reaper. I switched off the light and struggled to sleep again. My screams of despair kept echoing in my ears and thoughts.

---

[73] *"The Inchcape Rock" is a ballad written by English poet Robert Southey.*

"What if it comes back?" I mumbled in fear. "Karma follows", I reasoned thinking about Anita's messages, which were all full of 'love' and cuddles. "My 'Guardian Angel'", I grinned sarcastically trying to recollect myself. "The black raven that encircled us, and in its 'dark' eyes which rippled with glimpses of Anita, with someone else, and someone I hate now", I rambled. "What if my 'Guardian Angel' is leading my way to the consequences of venturing into 'darkness'?" I tried hard to make sense of the dream and felt a little angry at Anita and a lot angrier at myself. "Can I fix all this?" I wondered. "Or I am too much into the 'dark' to come out of it?" I gasped a breath of desperation. With a thought of giving up, I got back in bed.

The 'dark dream' changed something inside which was difficult to gauge in that moment, but someone was still at pleasure and remained unbothered. It was my 'little warrior' boldly beaming outwards for the lewd glimpses of the dream. The 'little warrior' is deaf and listens only to his urges. He stayed erect, hard and unmoved, still yearning selfishly only for what he seeks.

My terrified conscience didn't allow my gullible self to satisfy the selfish urge of my 'little warrior'. I struggled to sleep for the next hour till it was six in the morning. My struggle with my inner 'voice' was disturbed by my mother who woke up for her daily early morning walk.

"You awake so early?" she asked in surprise. "Just *Ma*..." I struggled with words. Before I could complete, she poured out her regular doubts. "Were you talking on the phone all night?" she asked irritably. "No *Ma*. Actually I had a nightmare", I said in a dim sleepy voice. "Why? What did you see?" she asked curiously. I indeed couldn't describe my lewd disgusting dream to my mother. The only mentionable character of the dream was the raven. "I saw my college, Anita and a big black raven in the dream. I don't know what it meant but it was a disturbing dream", I described with a frown.

"What time did you see the dream?" she worriedly asked me. "An hour back. I guess around 5 in the morning", I replied quickly. "It's not a good omen. You must go to the *Shani*[74] temple. Today is Saturday and it's his day", she instructed with concern. "Why *Shani*?" I asked in confusion for my limited knowledge of *Hindu* mythology. "Because crows and ravens are symbols of *Shani*. He is the 'God of Judgment' and it's not easy to please him. I will speak to the astrologer too, will even get your horoscope checked", she hurriedly narrated. "Why are you getting so disturbed *Ma*? It's just a dream, don't be so superstitious", I said dryly, dismissing her concerns. "Shut up Uday! You think you know everything! Just let me do what I am doing. I am worried", she retaliated angrily.

I tried to pacify my superstitious mother by taking interest in her knowledge of the *Hindu* gods. "What is with *Shani*? As a God too, why is everybody so scared of him? I mean he should be loving as all gods are" I asked her disinterestedly.

"*Shani* is the son of Sun. But he was born dark. At his birth, the Sun God refused to acknowledge him as his son owing to the difference in their appearance. Sun was beautiful with a very strong powerful aura which lights up our universe. *Shani* was dark as night. *Shani* got agitated and angry with his father, and since then he became the 'God of Judgment', as he was judged by his own father at his birth" she narrated the story of *Shani* empathizing with the pain of the mighty god.

"And what does crows and ravens have to do with *Shani*?" I asked curiously. "They are his vehicles and messengers. Crows, ravens, deer, donkeys and a black dog are supposed to be his messengers for bad omens. When *Shani* enters a person's horoscope, he often casts a seven and a half year curse on them for their 'karma'", she explained with seriousness while I sheepishly looked away from my mother's eyes, intimidated with a fear of my own 'karma'.

"I am feeling sleepy *Ma*. Can I sleep for a while?" I asked trying to stop the discomforting conversation. "Yes Uday, sleep. Once you wake up, then we will visit the *Shani* temple", she instructed tucking me back in bed.

---

[74]   *Shani: A Hindu embodiment of Saturn – The God of Karma and Judgment.*

I closed my eyes thinking about the God who was disowned by his own father. "The 'God of Judgment'", I mumbled as I prayed in fear to not to be cursed. Thoughts of my caring mother put me back at peace. I was surprised at her knowledge of *Hindu* mythology. It's my religion too but I hardly know anything.

The glimpses of the black raven again took over my thoughts as it was the hero of my 'dark dream'. I wondered if the 'God of Judgment' is going to curse me. I wish I had looked at the raven as a fallen angel who was still trying to show me my destiny. Or perhaps I should have understood then, that I was going to become the 'fallen' one.

THE GOD OF JUDGMENT

Please forgive me,
"Oh, Lord of darkness!"
I was totally unaware,
Of the extent of your vastness...

Of what I may reap,
But now that I know,
Wanted to plant it with love,
And look what I have grown...

I am filthy with vice,
And I can't look straight in your eyes,

I 'm scared of your sharp claws,
And your long beak...
But most scary are your dark ripples,
And the view has made me weak.

But give me a chance to fix it again,
'Guilty' with my Sins,
And drowning in 'Shame',
As lies pulls me down,
Burdening me in chains...

Bowing in plight,
Praying with faith,
Forgive me my God,
And don't return my fate,

I know your pain,
As I try stepping in your shoes.

And being your child, if you can't forgive me...

ON A BAD BOY NOTE

Then growls my 'Red' blood,
Don't worry,
Just disown me...

The 'King of Darkness' summoned through its vastness,
Like in a blink of an eye and many such corners,
Whispers his words and his blessings on us...
'Silence' is his gift and it says in honor...

Don't give me choices,
You stupid cunning fool...!

There were many more before you
Along with 'time', I have always ruled.
I live in moments which are very narrow,
Sometimes in your heart and sometimes in your Shadow...

Silence is my gift
And Karma is my judgment,
Your 'Red' screwed it up
And that's the Fate of an Indulgent...

I will come back for you,
When you are lost in your destiny,
And in such dark flashes
Will surface an epiphany...

Even if you close your mind,
You shall never forget,
Of the deeds you did,
And if they caused a Regret...

You will find me when you need me,
But I don't belong in the Lustrous,
Sometimes look into your Shadow,
There I rest, "The God of Justice."

CHAPTER 4
THE RED COUCH FANTASY

Is the pursuit of 'love' also a fantasy? Every fairy tale ever told to each one of us is more or less about 'love'. It appears like we are born on this planet only to find 'love' and thus that would remain our pursuit for the rest of our lives. The entire experience of the human race throughout 'time', eventually juices down to one feeling called 'love'.

'Love' like 'blood', connects each one of us. Thus we all are nothing, but a universal connection of 'love'. From cinema to music to art, everything beautiful, whether good or bad has to do something with 'love'. Like the entire mankind has spent their lifetime just experiencing various shades of it. Its influence drives us, pursuing our virtues and vices only to understand what we truly love. What do we 'so badly' want? With whom do we want to spend the rest of our lives? And thus life is nothing but a journey of 'love', paved with good and bad experiences.

Human beings are born travelers, and they undergo two kinds of journeys in their lives. One within the world, and the other traveling within one's own self.

My journey within the world was tainted with a bad omen. The omen of the 'dark dream', which conveyed my blissful deeds and its consequences. The last few glimpses were my worst fears. The 'dark dream' had changed something inside me, it had smothered my innocence that night. It thus became a regular toil for me to sleep at night. For many nights I struggled with my conscience. The worst part, I couldn't talk to anyone about it because in a social context, I was 'wrong'.

When the roads of the world appear constricted, traveling the roads of the soul gives the way. The journey within my own self remained to be traveled. I had no clue about such a journey then. But on one out of many such nights, I discovered a new shade of 'red'.

At 2 o'clock mid night, my cellphone rang and I rushed to pick it up. The two hours of playing hide and seek with sleep hadn't helped me much. I was further irritated by the inaccessibility to my computer system. The three piece desktop computer worked at the mercy of a multiple point extension wire. This punishment was bestowed by my concerned family who had a regular complaint of finding me up, late at nights. Since they couldn't take the phone, the extension wire was held hostage to ensure I sleep early. My attempts to find that little point of leverage were futile as it was hidden somewhere in my cluttered house. "Somewhere in front of me, where I can't see."

I chose some private time with myself as 'love' and 'guilt' began conflicting which each other. Computer games were better playgrounds where 'good' and 'bad' deeds do not affect our realities. If not games, then *Oksana and Monica Roccaforte*[75] would put me to sleep. My 'little warrior' waited for the glimpses of these beautiful European porn stars. Being a male, sleep often becomes a missing component if one is not really tired; the only other thing which can put a man to sleep, is an orgasm, even if it is self-induced.

There was no guilt in watching these gorgeous women. Just pure admiration, and the exciting possibilities which I received from their promiscuous adventures.

My cellphone rang. It was Anita calling. I answered, "Hi sexy, wassup?" "Why you are still awake?" she enquired in a sleepy voice. Looked like I wasn't the only one robbed of sleep that night...

"I was hanging out with Doctor", I answered. "Who's Doctor?" she asked in confusion. "Oh! Vini" I added. "We call him Doctor. We were out with

---

[75] *Europe's most gorgeous porn stars. They, along with many others bring peace to the world. Bless them for their noble work!*

some of his medical friends. We had beer and did some time pass at the railway station" I replied instantaneously.

With the incoming call bulk increasing on my cellphone, caution was something which was essential. Moreover I couldn't piss off Anita. She had already suspected me of cheating. The call waiting alerts on my phone had become more frequent. The number of messages received on my cellphone had tripled. She would often notice the busy traffic on my cellphone and ask "Who messages you so much?" I generally smiled and mentioned any friend's name which popped first in my head.

"What is it with Vini these days, all the time you are hanging out with him? Are you guys dating or what?" she chuckled teasingly. "Date the Doctor? Wow, that's so cool!" she further laughed.

I got a little infuriated. "I found a nice guy for a friend after such a long time, and someone with whom I really get along. And it's not necessary for me to date everyone I hang out with", I retaliated. "Like I spend the entire day at college hanging out with you, that doesn't mean we are dating", I said trying to sound playful. But I knew I had stepped on a nerve.

"Oh I see Uday! I didn't realize that I wasn't dating you!" she recovered with curt politeness. Her sluggish sleepy voice became all alert and awake.

"Oh my God, that means I still have a chance with the *Imran Khan* guy? He is so adorable. You know Uday, he has such an amazing jawline and such cute hairstyle", she attacked flirtatiously while enjoying every word of what she said.

I felt that shudder again, as if that 'dark dream' was actually taking shape into reality. I could again see the glimpses of Anita 'making love' to him. Where she passionately grabbed the guy who was on top of her. The glimpses of her passionate face set my skin on fire.

I didn't know how to react or respond. "Should I go interrupt them in between or wait for my love to finish her orgasm?" my thoughts tormented me. An envious retaliation showed me a visual of how perhaps I might look when I am on top of Rita, in a very similar position.

"Do you think you would get a chance to look around when you are having your eleventh orgasm in a row, when I am on top of you?" I replied almost without a second thought. "Eleventh, seriously?" she mocked my retaliation. I bet she felt the anger in my voice, but a little coaxing was her usual innocent 'craving'. It came very naturally to her to challenge her surroundings. Like she perhaps experimented with dominance and control, as these feelings prevail the entire animal kingdom. It's Nature, which bestows its being with the little 'crave' of having what they most want As Mother Nature controls all, at times with abundance or at times by mere scarcity. Anita provided me both, her absence haunted of her, while her presence dissolved 'time'. And then 'time' took me to a recent memory, where resting in her arms I had looked so closely in her eyes.

"The last time you had nine" I replied with a sly grin coupled with her haunting thoughts. She paused and gasped a heavy breath. The memory of our last day-long intercourse must have replayed in her mind. "That is why I can never feel single with my *Jaan*[76] Uday, especially with your skill to….." and she paused again. "Skill to…?" I asked arrogantly. Anita breathed heavily and with a little breaking laughter said, "…Give me so many orgasms. So many…"

The breaks and pauses of a sexual conversation are pretty intricate. It's equivalent to the journey of heavy breaths and shallow pauses. Like the 'shy' smiles evoke steamy sensations. The scarcity and abundance of mere breathing presents us to 'love'. It often takes us to darker shades of ourselves. Our lesser explored corner of 'darkness' is deep and perhaps endless. Like a black hole, which keeps sucking us in.

Later I realized that the ounce of love rests in 'darkness' too. Like the 'light' in the darkest corner of our selves. Often it is where the true connect of mating happens. It's in these moments you come to know who you really are? You also come to know who you are actually with?

---

[76] *'Jaan' in Hindi, Urdu and Farsi means 'life'; it's a term of endearment for darling or beloved. Especially for the person, in whom your life would rest!*

Often in such journeys…, in one such moment, you might come to know how 'dark' you really are and where is your 'light' headed towards!

But I was too scared of the destination of my 'light'. The consequences of my journey had already occurred in the 'dark dream'. "I don't wanna think about the fucking dream!" I mumbled taking a deep breath.

I calmed down and simply asked her, "What are you wearing?" "T-shirt and shorts, and you?" she replied after a longer pause. "Even I am wearing T-shirts and shorts", I replied quickly.

"So what are you wearing beneath your T-shirt and shorts?" I realized my need for better images to see. "Why?" she teased. "I am missing my computer" I said with desperation. "So, am I a pornstar to keep you entertained?" she asked in an accusing tone. "No no, you are much better than them *Jaan*" I said with minor insistence. "No, I don't feel comfortable Uday", she mildly resisted. "You won't be uncomfortable when you do it!" I mumbled softly.

"Fine! I am not wearing a bra, but yeah I am wearing a panty", she hesitantly replied. "What color is the panty?" I probed. "Black", she replied with her huskier voice over the phone. I rushed to the door of my room and bolted it from inside. "Do you have lingerie in red?" I asked her with my hands inside my pants. "Yeah maybe, an old one I guess", she answered.

"Let's get you one, a nice pair of lingerie 'blood red' in color, and you strip your clothes and groove in front of me in those", I said lustfully. She paused again while I waited for her to answer. "Can I wear my heels also?" she asked with sly innocence slating me for playing along.

"No heels will make you way taller", I corrected. To which she laughed and then I said, "Stay bare feet, I will lick your feet I promise. I will lick you from your toes to your lips, I will lick your entire geography", I groaned, feeling an enormous 'hard on'. Her audible breaths grew louder.

"Nitu, tell me one thing, where do you want me to 'make love' to you?" I asked and silenced. It was her turn to answer. And then she held her breath and said, "As in when and where you wanna do me?"

"I want to do you now, just tell me where do you want to do it, on a bed, in a Jacuzzi, back seat of a car, where?" I spoke restlessly. *"Jaan* what about standing in back of a truck?" I added.

"Let's do it on a red couch", she said with a soothing calm. "Red couch!" I exclaimed excited for her idea. "Yes a very big comfy couch with a leather cover", she explained. "Like the ones in *Cafe Coffee Day*[77]?" I asked curiously. "No redder, like 'blood red' and bigger" she added the words with a rising surge of desperation in her voice.

"Yeah, and the wall behind the couch should be covered with cushiony black leather" I added to her imagination. "With a rough wooden floor", she said completing the image of our venue.

"What about soft romantic music in the background and candles lit everywhere?" I asked caring for the regular girlie likes which I knew. "Naah; that's fine. I just want you Uday. Just wanna hear your voice. The only music I want to hear is of you and me sweating together" she demanded in a soft lonely voice.

"What do you want me to wear *Jaan*?" she asked with a mild excitement.

"Nothing, I just want you to be in your lingerie, the red one... I can visualize you in it Nitu... it makes you look so sexy...! Yeah, you look so sexy in that red lingerie...you get me so 'hot' when you wear that..." the image of Nitu stripped to her red lingerie, was dancing in front of my eyes.

"Jaan, will it make you hard if I tell you that I'm talking using one hand only, because my other hand just got busy..?" she asked wickedly.

---

[77]   *A popular coffee chain in India.*

My body immediately swelled up further speaking for itself. "Oh God Nitu... how I wish I was there to do it myself..." I replied with a labored breath...

"What do you want me to wear?" I asked "I want you to be in your boxers, the black one", she said, with her breath getting heavy. "Any underwear", I asked. "Yes the red one, I'd love to remove it", she said with her voice getting huskier. Anita's vocal tone was picking up the actual excitement. Even on the phone, I could feel her breath.

"Yeah, I want you to dance to that music of yours, play with your body, all the while looking at me. Oh Nitu, I love the look you have in your eyes", I said imagining her grooving on the couch with her slender curvy body and broad hips, her wheatish skin shining at her cleavage under her red bra, and her curvy broad ass rubbing against the black leather walls. I could imagine her bright eyes brimming with a sinful resistance. The deeper I peeped into her imaginary eyes, the further they enchanted me, locking my gaze in the glimpses of her fantastic eyes...

An ounce of 'water' shimmered in her eyes and the gaze softened as if they are looking at my soul. Calling me to look into her soul, to watch her 'light' and then swim in her 'darkness'. Bright excited eyes drenched with moist sad 'love'. Whenever she expressed 'love', she did it with a certain sadness in her eyes, as if something I did overwhelmed her. A different intoxication influenced my thoughts, possessing me in my own imagination.

"And then?" she interrupted, but instead of coming back to reality I was pushed further in the fantasy. "Then I come over to you, and grab you by the waist and start kissing you. I kiss you really deep and deeper, with my tongue inside your mouth. Would you like to lick my tongue?" I slithered. "Oh yes, I would love that", she said amidst heavy breaths.

"And then my hands are traveling down your back, inside the band of your panty to grab your ass... Your sexy brown ass, oh my god Nitu, I so want to grab you right now", I continued with my passion fired to a degree that was mildly alarming. "Yes Uday, grab me", she moaned in a higher pitch.

"Then I want to grab your boobs and massage it... You have great tits...I love playing with them... they fit into my hands perfectly..." I continued.

"Keep doing it, it feels so good when you massage them... Take them into your mouth..." she urged me on. "I love the way your tongue twirls around my areole...sucking and tugging by turns...I can actually feel your stubble scraping my soft flesh right now...Its driving me crazy..." she slowly moaned.

"What would you like to do then?" I asked her to lead on.

"I would grab your hair, and pull your head behind so that you can't kiss me anymore. I want to see you 'crave' to kiss me, while I go kissing your entire neck. Then I would trace feathery kisses to your ear and nibble on your earlobe... before dipping my tongue in your ear and lick you all over your ear shell..." she hissed with a certain cruelty in her husky voice.

I felt a shudder go through my body. Each word she said induced a sensation as if I could really feel her doing those thing to me, right then, and right there. And I was simply losing myself to the visuals. Pure beautiful 'lust' is generally hard to forget especially when it's given so uninhibitedly.

"And then Nitu?" I coughed the words as I clearly wanted more. "And then I am kneeling down to pull your boxers off, and rub the outside of your underwear.....slowly up and down your thighs, reaching between your legs..." I could feel my breath becoming shallow anticipating more.

"Your thing is already hard Uday, and it's bulging out of your under wear. I pull your underwear down and grab your animal", she continued. I grabbed myself harder obliging to the moment.

"Take it in your mouth Nitu "I commanded, sounding aggressive.

"I have your beast in my mouth right now; it's pushing in to my throat. And I am caressing your sacs with my hands... Do you like it Uday?" she asked with a submitted obedience. "Don't just caress my sacs... I want more out of you" I commanded. "Oh yes *Jaan*, I am sucking your balls", she replied in a vulgar lustful tone.

"Yes I am loving it, please keep sucking my animal *Jaan*. Your tongue rolling on me feels so good. Oh Nitu, you make me feel so loved. Slobber it with all your saliva and look at me as you suck me off", I breathed out in enchantment.

"Yes Uday I am still sucking on you. It's grown so big in my mouth", she continued. "I wanna fuck you now Nitu. I am too hard and too horny. I want to take all of your remaining clothes off now and touch you. Are you wet *Jaan*?" I moaned almost losing all control.

"Yeah it's all wet and it wants you inside", she purred like a cat.

"*Jaan*, I want to take you from behind", I said. The call of the basic instincts of being close to nature often makes you crude. We love to stroke the feel of dominance. And in such moments of vulnerability, you often feel like reaching out to the soul and dominating it.

"Oh please, be my master, I want to feel you grabbing my ass as you take me from behind... have your way with me..." she said in muffled voice gasping for breath.

"I am inside you *Jaan*, you are so wet and it's so hot", I said almost about to scream. "Oh yeah Uday I can feel you inside. I love the smell and feel of our bodies together...so 'hot' and sweaty... just stay inside and keep moving", she breathed heavily as if she is moving along with me.

"Oh yes I am moving, moving really fast. You like being fucked hard and fast right..? You like it hard...You are a bad girl who likes it hard... You like it more when I fuck you hard and rough... You like that, don't you..? Tell me, you like it hard and rough..." I insisted.

"Yes! I like it hard and rough..." she squealed. "Yeah, I'm a bad girl, fuck me hard...I love it here on the red couch...fuck me hard and fast...." she screamed.

"Your ass looks so good, protruding up in the air, as I pound you from behind...can I spank you for making me jealous?" I growled getting wilder. "Oh yes *Jaan*, spank me I am all yours. Grab my ass, spank it, please spank it hard", she said obediently. Her obedient compliance with my whims turned me on even more. "Come on top of me Uday, I want to see your naughty eyes filled with desire just for me...and I would love to dig my nails inside your super sexy shoulders while you do me", she said in a flattering tone. "Oh yes *Jaan*, I am on top of you. I want you to spread your legs", I commanded.

"Yes Uday, I have... you like it when I spread my legs and take you in, right?" she said with her voice getting huskier. "Yes I am inside you *Jaan*, I love pleasing you and the sound of your pleasure drives me crazy... you look so pretty when you are beneath me on the red couch", I said losing my breath.

"Please don't stop... it's nice on the red couch. You are looking so 'hot' on top of me, your amazing jaw line and your dull yet naughty eyes eating me", she cajoled.

"Go on...don't stop...faster....deeper...harder...I am going to cum Uday", she shrieked. "Oh yes baby, I want to see you cum. You look so sexy when you cum", I said thirsty for her orgasm.

"Oh yes Uday, I am cuming... Oh yeah, Uday, you fuck so well", she screamed.

"Wait up *Jaan*...I am cuming too...Lets go over together this time..." and I soon joined her going over the cliff.

"Come all over me *Jaan*, and then I will suck you", she moaned sounding really dirty and I exploded.

Finally I had my orgasm and Anita had hers. It was so peaceful. I really wanted to hold her tight in my arms, and maybe 'make love' to her again.

"I so want to kiss you Nitu", I urged craving for her lips. "Even me *Jaan*, I so want to be in your arms. I love you Uday", she said softly. I always loved the way she said the magical words. "I love you too *Jaan*. The red couch with black leather walls and you in a pair of red lingerie looks really sexy", I sighed.

"I wanna take you from behind, on the red couch. I can't forget your ass", I hissed again. "You are 'hard' again! What are you?" she giggled. "It's around 4 in the morning Uday. Let's sleep. We have morning practicals" she cuddled. "Ok just talk to me for a little more time and then sleep", I insisted.

"I have to go wash up, it's all on my tummy", I hurried up to the washroom. She laughed, "Go clean yourself you 'bad' boy, and then call me."

The word *'Jaan'* kept echoing in my ears in her soft husky voice. Perhaps it really proved its meaning as it was all so alive, being with her. Even unreal fantasies were so alive for her presence.

And thus 'red' became my favorite color, where 'good', 'bad' and 'love' all can rest peacefully. Anita and I too, dwelled in the tricolor. The dark leathery walls highlighted the red couch. The couch of endless possibilities with some so vivid that it becomes a fantasy. Anita was the only 'light'. If not for her, then the dark walls and the red couch were lifeless.

And we did it again and again on the 'Red Couch'. For many nights, we kept revisiting the 'Red Couch' to fulfill our fantasies which perhaps had lesser chances of coming true in our realities. The 'Red Couch' was the most intimate place we discovered in our imaginations.

But there is something very unique about fantasies. Though they are imaginations, but their essence stays back in the realities of the ones who dreamt it.

I went and I washed up. When I checked my cellphone, there it was, four missed calls from Rita which shook me out of the bouncy trance of the 'Red Couch'.

I started feeling that little creepy fear of answering her questions. I called Anita and said, "*Jaan*, I so wanna kiss you first thing in the morning tomorrow." "I do too Uday", she said. "Alright, let us both sleep now, so that we can reach college an hour before the practicals", I suggested to which she happily complied. We gave our goodbye kisses over the phone and I hung up.

When I checked my cellphone again I saw a message from Rita, it read, "Who the fuck are you talking to for past hour and half?" I panicked and I called her, she answered after a couple of rings.

"Who the fuck were you talking to?" she commanded in a very angry voice. "Sweetheart, Vini and I got into a major fight this evening, he was totally drunk and I was handling him", I lied boldly.

"He is a very good friend, you know, I cannot afford to hurt him", I added the required emotions to my premise. "What did you do to him?" she asked. "Nothing Ritzy, it's just we were out drinking and throughout the evening I was busy messaging you, so he got upset that I don't have time for him. Now you have caught my attention in such a way that my friends are getting jealous of you", I flattered her by giving her all the importance.

"Oh really", she was back with her usual sarcastic humor and thank god I was relieved. We chitchatted for a while till her mother was up and entered her room. She disconnected the call and we went to sleep.

All that I could think about that night was the 'Red Couch' fantasy of Nitu and me. I felt proud of having such a 'hot' girlfriend, who is so sexy with her imagination. I held my pillow tight and stubbed my erection in it. And slowly I felt I was sleeping on the 'red couch' with the leather walls. Nitu was snuggling inside my arms with our bodies touching each other, and I kept looking in her eyes.

At dawn, my mother woke me up at five in the morning. Sluggish with barely an hour of sleep, in the shower, all I could think of was the 'Red Couch' fantasy. I felt like shagging myself to it, but I realized I might miss my local train to college. Very soon I was in the train, standing on the footboard of the train door, watching the sun rise. I could feel the cool morning breeze of the sea blowing on my face as the train crossed a bridge. I hurriedly ate the sandwich which my mother had packed, before it got too crowded inside the train. I could still feel my erection as the train started getting crowded. I tried to position myself in such a way that my 'little warrior' doesn't touch anyone. Moreover there are many homosexuals who fish for chances in the crowded *Mumbai* local trains. Coming off as one could be a very creepy and embarrassing experience.

After a long forty five minutes struggle I was back on the station walking towards the nearest available cab. I saw Anita's message that she is waiting for me to pick her up on the way. I bought a cigarette, lit it up, and boarded a cab.

I picked her up on the way. She was wearing a pink full sleeved top and jeans. Her eyes had dark circles due to lack of sleep. The moment I touched her, I was 'turned on' again. Anita took a few drags from my cigarette, and I could see the eyes of the scandalized taxi driver looking behind in the rear view mirror.

Inside college, we hurried upstairs to find an empty classroom, as very few people turn up to college so early in the morning. We ended up reaching the auditorium, the place where our romance kind of picked up. The door to the backstage was locked, and the front curtains of the stage were removed. There was no space for privacy left in the auditorium. Just then I noticed the last curtain covering the wall. "Let's go behind those curtains", I signaled to her. "Are you sure? This is risky Uday!" she pulled me back. I pulled her to rush along with me. We sneaked behind the curtains. The view from the other side of the curtains was very translucent. I kissed Anita. She kissed me back. "So let's find a 'red couch'", I said intermittently while kissing her. "I don't know where I would find that", she replied sarcastically. "Your lingerie?" I asked. "You can see it the next time we find a better place", she taunted. Kissing and talking behind the curtains was a 'little' risky. The time of the day was early morning and that was the only hope. I felt 'something' pushing really hard from within, till I unzipped it out. I pulled her hand to it, and she reluctantly grabbed it. After giving it a few strokes, she went down on the floor and pulled her hair back in a ponytail. It was a little hard to believe. For a moment I felt like crying and looking up at God that even such moments could happen in life.

There was hardly any space between the wall and the curtains. We went on for another fifteen minutes till I realized that I am almost there. I asked her in a hushed voice, "I am 'cuming'." She moved her head back, and I shrieked, "It will drop over your clothes." Anita didn't know what to do and she took me in her mouth. I couldn't keep my voice low any longer. I sighed in relief and then we heard some voices.

To our dismay there were two kids who had just entered the auditorium. I pulled my finger on my mouth and signaled Anita to stay quiet and not to move. I felt as if the kids were looking at the wall. We stood like statues. They looked around and they left. A breath of fresh air entered us. Getting caught in such an ambience could be pretty embarrassing and the worst part is that gossip like this spreads very quickly. Soon we also hurried out of the curtains and jumped down the stage and quickly made it out of the auditorium.

We couldn't share our 'Red Couch' with the colors of the world. I was paranoid of people especially when it came to trusting them with the girl I loved the most. Much later I realized it was me who was not to be trusted.

In the gallery we saw students and mixed with the morning crowd of the college. "That was like wow", I exclaimed. "I can't hold my breath till now", I said breathing heavily and looked at her. She smiled one of her cutest smiles and her eyes appeared drenched with 'love' and confidence. She knew how to keep me 'on' and breathless. She was at par with me. Even she had evolved to slay her lover. I was falling in 'love', all over again with Anita as the glimpses of the curtains were mixing with the glimpses of the 'Red Couch' fantasy. I held her hand and said with a heavy breath, "I love you Anita. Please marry me; I don't think I can live without you and all this. It's too exciting and too sexy." Anita looked down in embarrassment and kept looking for a few seconds. "I love you Anita", I humped it out again. And finally she looked up with a strange softness in her mushy eyes and grinned, "I love you too Uday."

I guess 'love' is a journey from reality to fantasies and back, only to see how many of them came true. Probably that's why lovers keep dreaming together of an unreal lucid world of fantasies. The fantastic dreams keep pushing to come true, at least in the realm of the lovers.

I almost dozed off the whole day in college, got thrown out of a lecture, and even dozed off in the train. It was night and Rita had been messaging me since the evening to stay free at night so that we can talk. Before Anita gave her usual call, I called her up and told her that my mother would be sleeping with me tonight as she had caught me talking on the phone the previous night. Anita agreed reluctantly, and I waited for Rita to call me. During those days, we felt a little pain in keeping down the phone after every conversation each night. During the day there were multiple activities, but at night sleep was a much lesser priority when compared to being with each other.

The dreams of the unseen are always enchanting, especially when the two of you are mixing your curiosity with your innocence. The entire blend of such emotions comes boiling down to a courageous risky cocktail; a cocktail of such a nature, which makes one confident and unsure at the same time. But few want to live this, or maybe deep down we all have felt it and we would always want to live it.

My phone rang on one such midnight. I had ensured that my parents were asleep and my younger sister was studying in her room. "Hi Uday, how are you doing, you rapist?" said Rita on the other end. "I am good Ritzy, I wonder how you manage your posture with such heaviness hanging on your beautiful 'hearts'", I said trying hard to sound as absurd as I could, understanding the context I was asking in.

I was again missing my computer for past two days and Rita was the angel who had put me off to sleep that night. "I didn't understand what you just said", she replied in a confused tone. "I just meant how your big juicy fleshy boobies are doing?" I lustfully said clearing out the confusion.

I busted out laughing. Rita felt the crudeness wrapped in the lewd remark I made. "Don't talk to me like that, it's disgusting", she revolted, in an annoyed tone. "Sorry for that, but seriously I cannot get the image of your 'hearts' out of my mind", I said, a wild feeling of pushing her buttons began to take over. "You are so sick Uday, all you guys want is just 'sex'", she taunted angrily.

I was sick; wasn't I? I was just about to share the 'Red Couch' fantasy with Rita. I was again going to cheat on an unaware Anita. I would again give away something she so dearly values for a selfish need and a moment of glory. I felt a very brief disgust for myself. But her rude words and an annoyed tone, smothered with something else. It was the tiger which Anita loved me for. I took a deep breath and spoke.

"Well I just wanted to compliment you, if that makes you feel so bad about your 'hearts', then I am sorry", I reverted. She felt the coldness in my voice and said in a sweeter tone, "I don't like it this way." "Then what way do you like?" I asked with a little laugh. "Why should I tell you?" she replied in her playful voice.

"Ok I wanted to ask one question", I said trying to divert the conversation. "Ask", she said. "Or let it be, you don't seem like you want to talk", I said coldly. "Now I am curious, you better tell me", she demanded. "It's ok; I don't want to force you in the conversation", I said, dismissing her curiosity. "Please tell me", she insisted, softer this time.

"Don't tell her and she wants to know it. Don't give her and she will take it all!" Hearing her crave, I felt that joy a little more till I just simply asked…

"What kind of a guy do you think would be sexy in bed?" I tried to sound genuine. She thought for a while and answered, "Hmmm, he should be cute, strong and sensitive." "How can someone be cute and strong at the same time?" I wondered. "If he is strong then I am sure he is going to go all out on you", I mocked playfully. "That's ok, if he does so", she replied coldly after a pause. "What if he forces you in bed?" I probed. "That would be nice… stupid. Of course he must force me", she replied immediately. "What? You would like to be forced in bed?" I asked with mild astonishment.

"A man should be dominant in bed", she announced. "That's weird, I ask you about your lovely gorgeous 'hearts' and so I am 'dirty' and if I force you in bed then it's cool. How do you justify that?" I said with the hint of challenge flinching in my tongue.

"Why do women generally like to be dominated by men, especially in bed?" I wondered thinking about both the girls I loved. Their inherent need to submit to a force mightier than them, to someone who can make them do things which they might never do.

"I said I want someone handsome forcing me", she retaliated with a cold sweet laughter. I guess the blow thrown at one's 'worth' is the killer most aspect in defining the fate of conversations. Of course, I felt the blow too, but a little intelligence prevailed, before my wounded ego spoke. "Well", I began calmly, "I guess I look handsome, at least the last time I saw myself in your eyes." Rita remained silent on the other end. "But stupid, you forcing me in bed, how is that going to happen?" she tried to tease and laugh her way out. I felt annoyed for her dumb sense of humor. "Well, I shall drug you and tie you to a bed. And then I will force myself on you", I replied with obscurity as an attempt to embarrass her. "Shut up Uday", she snapped. "Goodnight Rita", I lost my patience for her false righteous purity and her super dumb counter attacks.

"What happened?" she asked in surprise. "I am getting bored", I lied bluntly. "Why? Did I do something?" she asked innocently. "How stupid could she be?" I wondered. "No. I am just tired of being horny. And you being my girlfriend are not helping here. I got loads to study. So I will rather try watching porn", I answered coldly. "No Uday. Please stay. What were you asking?" she submitted to my lack of interest. Her submission got my interest back.

"You like to wear leather, right?" I asked. "Yes, I love leather", she replied enthusiastically. "Ok well just imagine you are in your favorite leather hot pants. Well, do you actually have leather hot pants?" I asked. "No, I don't have hot pants. I just have a pair of full leather pants", she replied. "Why? Did you live in Mexico?" I chuckled. "What?" she asked in confusion.

"Nothing. I was wondering why you have leather pants in a humid climate like *Mumbai*? But I guess you would look good in leather hot pants", I said quickly covering up for my sly remarks. "Because I always wanted to have them", she answered innocently. "Along with a black top", I interjected before she could complete. "And your long wavy hair culminating the essence of the 90's Bollywood actress", I said imagining if she was a look alike combination of *Divya Bharti*[78] and *Raveena Tandon*[79]. Rita had that hint of Bollywood. The songs which she kept humming were those of 90's Bollywood, where in all the movies, the songs were just about her kind of 'love'.

"I guess I would look good", she said with shy laughter. It was not shyness that I wanted in her voice. I wanted to see her 'darkness', but for that I had to darken her innocence. "What if I come from behind and tie a black piece of cloth around your eyes and blindfold you?" I began. "Then I push you on a bed which has a white mattress, and then tie your hands to the bed post. What would you do then?" I said with every word forcing her to oblige.

I couldn't take her to the 'Red Couch'. It still belonged to Anita and me. Any unknown place was better. My 'red' was only for Anita.

Rita waited for a while, took a deeper breath and said, "I don't know, my hands are tied by a rapist, what can I do?" she still tried to sound playful.

Her swift submission to my ruthless advances fondled my feeling of domination. Dominance is all about control, a superior feel of being when one knows the power of providing something or taking something away. "What all can I take away from her?" I thought with a 'hard on'. The erect 'little warrior' answered, "It was just her pretentious innocence which I could take away from her." Perhaps then, I could see her real hues of 'red'.

---

[78]   *(Late) Divya Bharti: An Indian actress.*

[79]   *Raveena Tandon: Former Indian actress and model.*

"What if I take a pair of scissors and cut your top and take it off? You are now tied with your top gone and all you have left is a black leather bra, and from its corners your big heavy 'hearts' are spreading out. Now what would you do?" I said with my breath heavy and feeling the excitement of stripping her. In return, even I could hear her labored breaths.

"Stop it Uday", she tried to hold her thoughts but her breath remained heavy. It was in this moment of reaching the threshold where a step ahead was equivalent to racing years ahead in each of our minds. I was already there, she just had to follow. "Ok, just if you are in this situation, what would you do?" I asked with my tone getting colder. Rita sensed that I am again beginning to lose interest.

"What can I do? But can you take off the blindfold? I really want to see you", she said in her cutest possible tone. And just in another instance, I was already melting inside.

"Imagine me licking your bare 'heart', one at a time", I continued. "You are so helpless Rita, your hands are tied up and then I come up to your face and kiss you. Would you like to see me kiss you?" I hissed in the phone but in my view I could think of that face of Rita which I looked at, at the prom night.

"When are we meeting next?" Rita interrupted. "I don't know. Anytime. You say", I said gaining back my conscious and also my conscience as thoughts of Anita ran back in my head. I realized I am about to lose the growl of my animal. "You could be very 'hot' Rita", I said finally giving up.

As I was done trying to fantasize her, she asked, "Are you done, you rapist?" I laughed and we continued the conversation. "You know Uday, you looked so cute on the prom night", she sounded cuddly. "Can I seriously have you?" I asked still enchanted in the thoughts of the leather on her leather. "Come and get me and I am yours", she replied playfully. She was stupid yet such a tease. The way Rita talked, a guy can have her walk in his fantasy, play with her and she can still walk out untouched. Either her tease, or my need to explore, somehow made it very interesting.

We talked for a little longer till my mother opened the door. I had forgotten to lock it that night. I quickly hurried back inside my bed sheet hoping that my mother doesn't check on me and finds out that I was talking on the phone. I quickly disconnected the call and pretended to be asleep. My mother walked around the room, checked my cellphone and left. When she was just outside my room, my phone rang as Rita called up. I quickly disconnected and my mother entered the room. She thankfully switched on the study light and asked me, "So this is your new discipline, talking all night on the phone. Who were you talking to? When I touched the phone it was hot, I knew you were talking to someone. Which decent boy talks to people or a girl at 3:00 am in the morning?" I made a helpless face and said, "It was a friend." To which I was greeted with another loud scolding, "Which friend of yours wants to talk to you at 3AM?" I tried to make my face even more helpless and said, "Don't scream *Ma,* papa will get up." "He should get up and see what you are doing", screamed my Mother. "Mummy, I have to get up in the morning, can we talk about this tomorrow?" I said putting on a shameless smile. My mother left in anger. I messaged Rita that I am caught and we cannot speak anymore tonight. When all the chaos subsided, thoughts of tying and stripping Rita returned and conquered me. I wanted to do so many things to her. But would she let me do them? Would she like it, if those things happen to her?

Next day I was in college and I reached late owing to the last night's dark fantasy shared with Rita. I reached our classroom just to find out that the lectures had been cancelled. The studious kids had left for their homes, and the better ones remained chilling out in college. I entered the classroom and saw Anita and Zaida having a deep conversation. Zaida appeared to be cranky and Anita seemed to be consoling her. I reached the two girls and greeted them. Zaida still looked upset, so I tried to cheer her up. "Why do you look so upset Zaida?" I asked her. "Nothing Uday", she said with upset eyes but a natural smile appeared on her face. "See, I just know one thing, people who are cute shouldn't look so sad", I said in a kind voice. Zaida and Anita looked at me and I left from their desk. Anita joined me in a while and she had a different admiration on her face for me. I asked her with a smug face, "How come… you are looking so good today?" Anita quickly came over and gave me a quick peck on my cheek. I returned her a look with a similar admiration. She held my hand and pulled me out of the classroom.

I walked with her and she quickly turned around and said, "Let's go." "Where?" I asked her. "Just come along", she said and I followed my powerful girlfriend obediently. Soon we were at the bus stop waiting for a bus, but the route was different. I was confused with the sudden outbursts of affection from Anita but I thought it's better to just play along. A bus arrived with the destination labelled as *Worli*[80]. Anita boarded the bus happily and I followed. Once seated, she asked the conductor to give her two tickets to *Worli*.

The weather was a little clouded and I suspected the rains to follow. The only hitch in getting wet in the *Mumbai* rains is that a very short shower is good enough to wet someone down to their underwear. The struggle begins when one has to survive the journey back home through the crowded local trains and public transport with a wet crotch. The idea of getting wet was already making me panic. But watching Anita's excitement I really didn't feel like complaining. The bus stopped at *Worli* and both of us got off. Anita crossed the road to the sea facing side. "Welcome to *Worli* sea face", she brimmed. I looked at the sea waves which were getting wilder coupled with the untamed winds which were blowing towards the promenade of *Worli* sea face. The clouds above grew a shade darker. Anita sat down at the bench nearby. I sat down next to her. She opened her bag and with excitement, took out a gift wrapped in blue glittering paper. I was shocked as she handed over the gift to me. The package was cylindrical. I looked at her and asked her in surprise, "What is this for?" "Happy Anniversary *Jaan*", she said softly and came close and gave me a peck on my lips. I trembled under my clothes, in fact much under my skin too. "Open it", she said with excitement. I followed her instructions and opened the parcel to find a beautiful sports watch. It had blue leather straps with a stylish blue dial. Blue was Anita's favorite color and so it had become mine.

---

[80]   *Worli: A sea facing locality of South Mumbai.*

I looked at her with eyes wide open in amazement thanking my stars for getting me a gift on our anniversary, which I never remembered. I kept looking at Anita, shocked and surprised with tears brimming in my eyes. "Thank you", I said in a heavy voice. "Sorry, I didn't remember and I didn't get you anything", I said in an apologetic tone. "It's ok", she said with 'no expectations'. "Do you like it?" she asked with a hint of uncertainty in her voice and eyes. "I love it", I said instantaneously. "Happy Anniversary *Jaan*", I gasped, almost in tears. I grabbed Anita and gave her a tight and a very long hug. I guess the only hug which lasted longer was the 'time' when we were parting some years later.

Like 'love' belongs to us, we belong to 'love'. Much like the sensuality of the fantasy was real, so was the 'love'. Though unreal, still keeping us hooked, and somewhere it feels like... it did happen! A feeling so powerful that even 'time' stops to flow in a moment filled with 'love'. And then it remains like a vivid memory, very much like the fantasy – which actually happened!

DIRTY TALKING

Please don't hang up,
For I yet have to remove your stockings,
Just keep slithering beneath me baby,
As we do some dirty talking...

These conversations could be sharp like a knife,
It's designed to bring your fantasies to life,
And if not, then you can just keep rocking,
Don't stop baby, please do some dirty talking....

You are allowed to be ruthless,
You can even do the stalking,
Even if you can't make me moan,
It doesn't matter in the playground of dirty talking....

So keep talking dirty baby,
As with my words I will do the corking,
I can still imagine the way you look at me baby,
And it feels like my heart dropping....

Talk some more with your uncouth words,
You can even make some feline advances towards,
If you play, you won't feel like stopping,
As that's the beauty of our dirty talking...

Heated it is to witness your own robbing,
Such filthy words can also start your heart throbbing,
As I am really not sleepy baby,
So please don't stop your dirty talking....

CHAPTER 5
BEYOND THE RAINBOW

The humble occasion of my first ever anniversary amazed my tiny 'guilty' heart, with a brighter hope of a fresher start.

We kissed on the bench. The passerby traffic was negligible and none of us cared in that moment. It began to drizzle mildly. We paused and again began kissing in the shower of mild water droplets.

I whispered to her amidst kissing, "This is the first time I am celebrating an anniversary. I never knew what it felt like to be a part of one. I feel very special. Thank you Nitu. I will get you whatever you want. And I will never forget this day in my life", and I kept kissing the words in her mouth.

"I love you Uday", she said withdrawing from the kiss. Her eyes shone with happiness, of that of an enlightened 'love'. Like somehow she had reached the destination of her pursuit of 'love'. Even I did, just with an ounce of 'guilt'. It pricked, but her divine eyes comforted my tired soul. And then the rainfall began to increase.

The water drops grew thicker and splashed on our wet skin. We sprang up from the public bench and ran across the road to the bus stop. The poorly covered bus stop had very little space to protect people from getting wet in the rains. I didn't have any rain protection like an umbrella or a wind-cheater. Nor like, having one can keep people of *Mumbai* any drier from the wild unpredictable *Mumbai* rains.

I stepped on the little 'safe spot' of the almost roofless bus stop. Anita covered me from the front draped in her wind-cheater. The waves in the

Arabian Sea splashed against the high pavement of *Worli* sea face. The size of the waves increased and so did the wind. I was soaking wet and shivered mildly in the pouring rain. There was no sign of the damned red bus on the road...

I held her by her love handles and pulled her closer to me. Her muscular handles were perfect and were amongst the best things in her body. The empty bus stop had no one to bother our snuggled effort to keep warm. The water drops still felt on my skin, very much like my 'guilt'. Anita held me in her embrace and kept kissing me intermittently, and at times checking out for the bus and passersby.

The damp atmosphere did set us up on 'fire'. It's strange to acknowledge the heat, 'water' can induce in the ones who are wetted by it. Water is the symbol of 'pleasure', the only thing which we want to experience. Human beings can shun an experience only for two reasons. One; they are too scared of the experience and thus, they have never really experienced. Second; the feeling that they don't deserve the experience, probably because they are not 'worthy' of it. Experiencing 'pleasure' can only be restricted by 'guilt' and at times, by 'cowardice'.

Even in times of a flood or catastrophic disaster or in simple conflicting moments of 'desire' and 'sin'. Both ways, 'water' brings people together as it brought Anita and me.

"I love you Nitu", I said with all the affection I could muster. And just in that moment, a bus arrived for our rescue. I looked up in the haze of the falling water drops. Perhaps someone up there judged my affection to be true, along with my curiosity and conscience. We rushed inside the bus and took the last seat. The damped seats didn't matter as not much of us was dry. The 'heat' we had brewed was enough to keep us warm. "Thank god!" she said relieved for the bus. "Thank you", I mumbled to her with affection. "I love you Uday", she said again touching my wet face. I smiled with admiration.

"By the way Zaida said that I am very lucky to have you as a boyfriend", said Anita with an air of pride. "She said that you are very cute", and she kissed me with admiration. The social approval of her gang just added up to her adornment of her shady boyfriend. I felt better for a certain appreciation, as I couldn't really appreciate myself much. The compliments mattered, but Zaida specifically didn't matter. The anniversary gift shook my foundation. I felt a strange attachment to Anita, a feeling of connect that I would never be able to 'let go' of.

The bus traveled through *Mumbai's* busy streets which were drenched with traffic, people and the rains. The rainfall decreased. The cloudy overcast still covered our 'city of dreams'.

"Hey look... Rainbow!" said an excited Anita pointing towards the mirage of the seven colors in the clouded sky. "Wow!" I added.

"It looks like a bridge between the clouds. Where we can walk from one cloud to another", she said like a little girl. "I feel like flying, so high, to the rainbow and just get to touch it, it would be so beautiful!" she continued to express her innocent desires.

"And what if you get to know that it was never there in the first place? Like an oasis in the desert of clouds", I dryly added reflecting my downtrodden self-worth on the miraculous rainbow. Anita returned a curious look.

"You know what, at times I so feel like eating a cloud. By the way, I am kinda hungry", I said jovially. "Yeah me too. Let's eat a *Frankie*[81] at college", she replied cheerfully distracted from my 'guilty' shades. "Yeah, he makes it so amazing. Especially with that *chaat masala*[82]", I added with the images of the delicious tangy potato roll.

"Yeah! Sunshine and rainbows always make me happy", said a chirpy Anita. She was pretty much like my sunshine who often shone like the rainbow in my clouded times. I smiled to the thought. But clouded thoughts weren't what I wanted to dwell in at that lively moment. The rainbow was brighter, happier and still full of hope.

---

[81] *Meat or vegetables and spices rolled in a circular Indian bread made of wheat flour.*

[82] *A mixture of Indian spices... have it to believe it!*

"So the VIBGYOR is there for real, huh!" I asked stroking a strand of hair off her face. "Yeah.... Dumb!" she gave me a look of disbelief. "I loved that experiment in physics", I added. "The prism one!" she said with an enthusiasm of familiarity. "Yeah! I was amazed to know that a single ray of light can be broken down into so many colors", I added. "Although, it's just seven colors", I remarked dryly.

"But stupid, there would be so many sub shades between those seven colors!" she corrected my lack of observation. "Oh yeah", I nodded. "And when you mix these colors, you get so many hues in between. So called secondary colors and tertiary colors. A majority of the colors on the color palette are nothing but a broken ray of sunlight!" she said with an aura of brilliance. I felt enlightened by her perspective on the few ignored things in life.

"What is your favorite color?" I asked. "You know it's blue. That's my most favorite of all the colors, and the color of your new watch", she smiled. I smiled back for her cheesy way of winning appreciations. "What would be yours?" she asked. "Dunno... Black or.... Red" I dubiously answered.

"Ok tell me, what is before violet and what is after red?" I continued to ask. "Ultraviolet and infrared?" she answered with doubt.

"I wonder what you would look like in a pair of violet lingerie in the 'Red Couch' fantasy", I smirked grabbing her lean muscular thighs. She gasped for the sudden carnal intrusion.

"Like the whole ray of light is nothing but various shades of you. I can see you on that couch. And trust me, I want to explore all your colors. Bit by bit; inch by inch. I am so cold and wet and yet I am so hard", I gasped pulling a heavy breath.

"I am so 'turned on'!" she shivered. "You wet?" I asked curiously. She nodded with mild embarrassment. I pulled my hand to her groin. I slipped it inside her jeans while she covered my hand beneath her bag. I quickly surpassed the fencing of her underwear and there she was, wet and warm.

The bus took a steep turn at a signal tossing the two of us in the corner. She shrieked mildly and held her breath while I continued to pleasure her. "Stop it *Jaan*!" she pleaded digging her pink claws in my forearm.

"Imagine the beauty of nature. The rainbow is like a baby. And it took so much fucking for the Sun and the clouds to make one. And when the rains left the clouds, the sunshine penetrated through the prism of the broken clouds making a rainbow" I whispered in her ears. She giggled. "I so feel like taking you back to the 'Red Couch'", I mumbled lustfully, totally ignorant of her orgasmic pleading. "And you will be my rainbow when I penetrate you. Wet in our love, as if we rain on each other... floating through our clouded dreams", I whispered in her ears and couldn't resist biting her nape.

She bit her lips and shrugged. "*Jaan* our stop has arrived", she gasped taking mild control of herself.

"Yeah! Fuck!" I muttered in defeat and quickly slipped my hand out of her jeans. I sprang up and she adjusted herself. The bus screeched at our stop. I rushed to the exit door while she struggled to get up. "Hold on. We are getting down", I screamed to the unbothered bus conductor. Finally, we were off the damned red bus but still simmered in our 'Red Couch' fantasy.

We quickly lit two cigarettes at a *tapri* next to the bus stop to fetch us some more warmth amidst the wet shivers. We walked hand in hand to a nearest taxi to our respective stations. Anita bestowed her wild kisses on me in the hind seat. The cab driver didn't matter. Neither did he try to make any nuisance, other than sneaking a quick glance, once a while. The day ended and we parted for our respective homes.

Throughout the train ride I could see the rainbow as I stood at the door hoping to dry off in the passing wind. *Mumbai* was indeed the 'city of dreams'. Slipping through its busy wet streets, and long shiny railway lines, it did find us a fantasy. The fantasy of our little 'Red Couch', which was enormous enough to create our world.

I wondered about physics. It would take so much of magnificence in the universe to arrange so many water droplets to make an enormous prism which dissociates light to make a large rainbow. I wondered if my clouded deeds will ever dissociate my 'light' and turn me into a rainbow. I guess it was too much of an expectation out of the universe. I was just the 'cloud' while she was the 'rainbow'; the only 'rainbow' which is up there to bring a smile on all its sultry patrons. But yet, the 'cloud' is too possessive to let go of his rainbow.

The spectrum of light is very much like a beautiful dream, mixed with colors. Like the universe blessed us with everything to see in a single ray of light. I still wondered, "What is before violet and what is after red?" The answer was simple but incomplete – it was indeed a ray of light. But it's the 'darkness' of the endless universe which makes a ray of 'light' so special. It gives a background to these magnificent colors.

Every color has its own significance. But why was I so stuck at 'red'? Even 'red' was pure and it was a fantasy which my 'love' and I shared. It was 'time' to cleanse.

Rita and I kept the communication all that while through discreet messages, which were humorous and raunchy. Yet I felt the loss of interest in her; especially after the anniversary. The honesty in Anita's eyes haunted me, I felt burdened with 'guilt'. Lightening up was necessary.

It's the intensity of love, which defines 'love'. Very much like the intensity of 'blood', wet and so 'red'. So was the bloody rainbow.

I felt the need to end it with Rita. She had been asking for quite some time to catch up but the huge traveling distance to go meet her seemed like a mammoth task. Two crowded train routes and three train changes is a lot of travel in *Mumbai.* But then, since I had to end it, I decided to take the last ride to meet Rita.

Just this time I borrowed a friend's bike to travel to meet her. I rode a long highway to her suburb. Riding a bike was new and refreshing, dodging vehicles and controlling the sprinting beast. It felt dangerous in the crowded erratic traffic, but the highways provided good space to throttle.

My cellphone kept vibrating and I finally reached my destination. I realized I was late. Rita had been waiting to meet me at a nearby mall. I messaged her to come out. Barely in ten minutes, she arrived. Rita was dressed in a white shirt and trousers and her fair face was flushed, 'red' with anger. "You made me wait so much, you rapist", she said angrily. "I am sorry, just hop on", I said in a cool unconcerned tone. She stomped her feet and obeyed.

"Where are we going?" I asked her. "Nowhere I don't wanna go anywhere with you!" she bickered. "Okay, no problem" I said relaxing on the bike. "Ok, don't stay here. Start riding I will show you the way", she said in panic and I obeyed.

After a few kilometers I felt her breath on my neck. She came closer to me and whispered in my ears, "Your perfume is very seductive, it's turning me on." I didn't know what to say. "It's my father's", I said.

"Just take a turn from here and keep going straight", instructed Rita. I kept riding to her instructions. Soon we were on an isolated road and I could taste the salt in the breeze. She held me tight and kept frisking me from my chest to my thighs. We were headed towards the non-crowded beaches of *Mumbai* set in *Marve*[83]. Her instructions led me to *Aksa*[84] beach which had a beautiful view and barely any people.

I parked the bike and looked at Rita. Her anger had subsided and a sweet smile spanned her face. "Do you have cigarettes?" she asked me. "Yes I have a few cigarettes but why are you asking?" I asked back in confusion. "I want to try one", she said in her playful voice. "Why do you want to smoke?" I insisted. "Stupid! I feel like trying", she asserted loudly.

---

[83]   *A beach suburb at the outskirts of Mumbai.*

[84]   *Aksa Beach is a popular beach and a vacation spot in Aksa village at Malad, Mumbai. This beach was one of the most silent and least visited beaches.*

I agreed and we began to trek down towards the beach. Once we were at the foot of the beach, the sea was distant and towards the corner there were a few huge rocks. "Let us go sit there on the rocks", said Rita pointing towards the sea shore boulders. I nodded and followed her.

Rita was seated at the rocks and I stood in front of her. I looked around and the road was barely visible. "Will you light a cigarette quickly?" commanded Rita. I obeyed her command and began to light two cigarettes, one for her and one for myself. The wind was strong and lighting the matchstick was difficult. I came close to Rita and she covered me. I lit the match stick in her embrace and quickly torched the tip of the cigarettes in the rapid winds.

We began puffing on the white cancer sticks. I remained puzzled for most of the conversation as I kept wondering on how to begin the conversation of our end. "Why do you look so serious, Uday?" she asked. "I don't know", I said in confusion struggling to find the correct words. "Am I smoking it right?" she asked. "I guess so", I nodded. "You know, Mehul taught me to how to smoke", she narrated enthusiastically. "Megha's boyfriend?" I asked dryly. "Yup. He is such a cool guy!" she confirmed. "Nice", I smiled coldly.

"Come here", Rita signaled me to come closer. I followed her lead. Rita wrapped her arms around me and puffed her smoke on my face. I frowned in annoyance and looked at her. She smiled and said, "Do you know, you don't look good at all. Especially when you don't smile." I looked at her and nodded, still confused whether I should spoil her mood, the day and the beauty of the beach where she had got me with so much of enthusiasm. Rita took a longer drag of the smoke and came closer to my face and finally stuffed her thick 'red' lips in my mouth and blew the smoke. I sucked in the smoke and soon it left through my mouth and my nostrils. Her sudden smoky thrust made me feel something hard rising beneath my jeans. The 'little warrior' had spoken his judgment; as it was nothing but 'gluttony'. Very soon my 'guilt' was covered in fumes of 'lust'.

Like 'blood' which boils, and so does 'red'. If 'love' and 'blood' were similar, then perhaps every predator would have been a glutton of 'love'. Probably we all suffer from a similar vice; 'gluttony' for 'love'. We like to have much more of 'love' than what we can keep or reciprocate.

Her fair chubby face and streaked hair induced her heat in my formidable loins, setting my desires on fire. As we blew out the fumes of 'desire' as Rita and I kissed every drag of the remaining cigarette. When the cigarette got over, we began to kiss and the winds of the sea blew around us. Rita held me passionately, suffocating me with her thick lips.

'Blood' when heated is much more powerful than water. It just doesn't exert force like in a steam engine. 'Blood' is heated by a lot of emotions and emotions lead to actions. It's the direction of the action which counts. 'Hot blood' exerts force in specific directions; and some mindless directions can change everything forever.

My hands began to travel from her waist to her back and then slowly towards her chest. She didn't try to resist much. "Your perfume is so sexy Uday, I feel like eating you up", she mumbled amidst the kisses. Her cannibalistic urges for a vegetarian were a super 'turn on'. My breath became heavier as my hands began unbuttoning her shirt.

I pushed her behind on the rock and pulled her shirt apart just to catch a glimpse of her 'hearts'. She wore a gray spaghetti inside and her voluptuous 'hearts' shyly peeked out. I probed in on her assets to get a taste of them. She tried to push me behind and yet held me in a strong embrace. Her resistance heated my desire to touch the smoothness of her skin. My hands reached the bottom buttons of her shirt. After unbuttoning a few buttons, I touched her navel.

I still thought of Anita's sleek waist. But before any more 'guilt' could flicker, she inserted her tongue in my mouth. I was mildly confused if I was the capturer or the captured. Her wet tongue extinguished the reoccurring thoughts of Anita.

"Stop, stop.... Uday.... please stop", she begged confusing me further. I regained myself and leaned backwards giving her space to breathe. She quickly buttoned herself up. The crease of her neat white shirt was a little wrinkled. I still breathed heavily and looked at her. She glanced back a smile. I smiled letching at her blushed face.

She got off the rock and gave me a hug. I held her too. Hot drops of tears were trickling down her eyes. I was surprised to see her cry. "I love you Uday", she whispered in a mild cranky voice. She craned her neck and kissed me. I reciprocated to her warm strokes but the erect 'little warrior' had totally disturbed my plan of ending things with Rita, keeping me there with her while she confessed her 'love' for a liar like me.

Perhaps 'red' was her color too. 'Red' enough to surpass regular thoughts and reasons. I felt she was my kind, a soft vulnerable predator. I couldn't do anything else but lie. I don't know what I should have done in that moment... To someone who just confessed her love and was returned a confession of lies.

I looked up in the sky foolishly searching for the rainbow. There was no presence of the divine broken sunlight, just shady clouds. "I can't break her heart. It would be too rude and that's not me. I am kind enough to share my 'red'", I thought giving 'red' a faithful chance.

"I love you too Rita", I mumbled and kissed her. "Let's do it Uday! I like the way you touch me", she shrieked with excitement which replaced her tears. "My 'hot' rapist", she said kissing me. "Light another cigarette and let us kiss and smoke", she urged with a lovey dovey smile. I obliged to her wish and we continued to kiss and smoke witnessing the distant sea while the romantic sea breeze kept brushing us.

The 'light' of 'love' lit the air around, as the sun descended leaving behind its burning glow. The winds blew with it, leaving sensations of passions circling on our skins. The clouds danced with the downpour of rains and the winds played with them too. It was dusk again.

The encroaching 'darkness' revealed to me her hidden beauty while the 'light' in her eyes showed me 'love'. I kept kissing her, intoxicated into this beautiful cocktail of colors which had begun to infest our lives with fantasies. The 'hot' cocktail of 'red bloody love' blended everybody in its tide.

The only thing which I couldn't acknowledge then was the encroaching 'darkness', which wasn't just around, but it had also crept inside. Though somewhere I knew it existed, but I was blinded by all the 'light' around me.

Her bright eyes concealed the 'darkness' which had started to grow within me. So much in awe of all the fantasies, that I remained blinded from the fact – all the bright colorful 'love' I received would eventually just leave 'darkness' within me.

I finally got my answer. It's 'dark' what happens after 'red', and surprisingly that's what lies beyond the rainbow. Though I never knew then, where my journey into the deep hues of 'red' would lead me to?

A couple of days later, I reached college earlier than Anita. She had texted me to wait for her as she would be late.

In the corridors I bumped into Zaida and we exchanged casual greetings. "Has the lecture started?" I asked her. "I don't know, even I need to find out", she replied in her thin nasal voice. "Cool, let's go check out", I added enthusiastically and we began walking up the stairs to the classroom. I remembered the compliments she had given to Anita about me.

Walking up the stairs I happened to notice her ass. Zaida was a short girl with a prim proper body but her assets were well distinguished. Walking behind her, I watched her ass move, and we reached our regular classroom. The classroom was empty and we entered it.

"Oh my God, no lectures, and nobody informed", I said in surprise. "Did you know?" I asked her assertively. "Nobody informed me", she answered innocently. A sudden beep on my cellphone distracted me. It was a text message I was hoping from Anita. Instead it was a message from Vini, the Doctor.

It read, "Recipe for darkness: take a little ounce of 'guilt' which occurred for your last 'dark' deed. Since you cannot do anything about it, accept, you are gonna get fucked. So either foolishly pray for forgiveness, or since what happened cannot be changed... just accept what you have become now... if nothing else, it keeps you calm!"

I chuckled to the message and wondered if it was just an ordinary forward or Vini sent this specifically for me. Well he had little clue of what I was up to. "What is it? Show me", Zaida asked curiously. "Sure", I replied and handed my cellphone to her. She smiled after reading the message. "So true", she added.

"So true", I thought. "It's definitely true in my context. My 'guilt' fucking me up is something which I understand. But why is she guilty? Has she done shit too?" I wondered. Foolishly praying for forgiveness won't get me anywhere, since nothing can be changed. Just accept what I have become now. If nothing else it keeps me calm and smart", I uttered to myself.

"What? You said something?" asked Zaida. "Nothing as such. By the way Zaida, in these pair of jeans your ass is looking very cute", I said masking my hesitation with a smile. "Thank you", she said with a rush of 'pink' blush on her face. "Thank you! Seriously?" I wondered amused by her response.

Zaida turned around and a surge of impulse ran inside me and I spanked her small curvy ass. She glanced back, and returned a bewildered look. I was flabbergasted for my sudden courage to spank her. I realized in my sudden outburst of testing my guts, I had gotten myself in serious trouble.

Instead, her bewilderment turned into a smile. A smile which had a little victory and a little shyness. "She isn't outright offended. And if she is not, that means she might like a little more of what I have to offer", a wicked thought passed my mind.

That look on her face gave me a sudden boost of mischief, a boost of crossing lines and boundaries. I pulled her towards me and pinned her to the wall. I began to touch her, expecting her to resist me, which she eventually did but it was weak and halfhearted. I heard voices in the corridors and I pulled myself back. We hurriedly left the classroom. Both of us shared a look of 'guilt' and excitement at the same time.

Anita was walking up the stairs to the classroom and we bumped into her on the way. Anita greeted Zaida with a hug, delighted for the lecture getting cancelled. The three of us walked down to the canteen. I thanked my stars as for that little delay, or else Anita could have found us 'red' handed.

In the canteen I stayed with Anita. Although I sat down to eat with her; somehow I couldn't look into Zaida's eyes. Neither could she, and if she did, what just happened in the empty classroom replayed in our eyes. I left with Anita for a movie but my cellphone inbox had a new message and it read, "Thanks for the compliment Uday, it was a nice way of complimenting." I puffed a big cloud of smoke standing outside the theatre, and replied, "Just didn't get enough, but I really like cute things!"

I was simultaneously surprised and shocked for what I did that day with Zaida. I had respect for her as that of a mature lady. A lady who in spite of being heart-broken in 'love', would never resolve to a sin. I tried to continue thinking about her as a 'good girl'. Maybe it helped me feel righteous enough; to not to feel 'guilty'.

But even the most righteous beings cannot defy the 'taste of blood'. It will continue to haunt them for the life which they had lived and life yet to come by. Call it emptiness, addiction, thrill or 'craving'; nothing can ever erase its memory. And the moment the 'righteous' are free of their pseudo beliefs, they will just return to the 'taste of blood'.

Call it 'blood' or acknowledge it as 'love', the 'red' it carries bonds everybody... as perhaps that is the only true color of life.

I often thought those days that, "What if there is nothing called 'wrong'? Everything is just a plain need and we have both – 'right' and 'wrong' needs? My deeds dwell on both sides of judgment. All I am doing is fulfilling a void called 'love' in many like me!" Maybe saddened for the ones who are left lonely, I felt as if somewhere... a part of me loved them too! But the unexplained need to conquer all the 'red' which surpassed my way, didn't occur to me as a sin. It was pure knowledge of the 'unexperienced', and a certain compassion which I often felt... as if I was a saint who brought 'love' to many, out of his sinful deeds!

Two weeks passed since the encounter with Zaida. We secretly met a couple of times in this span and it was all about crossing boundaries. None of us had much to speak to each other about, but yes crossing boundaries was the only thing which we shared. Zaida knew clearly that Anita and I were seeing each other and so she had no expectations, at least she never portrayed any. But then what she expected, I never knew. Neither did she say anything but it was a strange passion with which she met me that every time it felt as if it's the last time I am meeting her. She would take names of her God, whenever I intruded her presence. She appeared 'righteous', like the angel who had been tricked by the demon. She often appeared offended for indulging in something so out rightly forbidden, and yet she enjoyed it.

Why is forbidden so tempting? Why do the only few things which we aren't supposed to do, tempt us so much? I was still surprised on ending up passionately with Zaida. I guess I was lonely with my new found 'dark'. With her I found someone to share it with.

Our meetings were about submitting to a tormentor; one who would just cross her boundaries without permission or promises, in fact not even a word. During these visits she often took me out for treats and then waited for me to intrude her. When I did, she just resisted in her silent ways. All she communicated was in messages and most of them were forwards. It gives a strange 'high' to know that some people just like to be intruded by you, silently, without any expectations or complaints.

We kept our social distance and Zaida never intruded in the space shared by Anita and me. Neither did Anita ever sense this arrangement of domination and being dominated.

'Blood' bonds and so does 'love', and those who are bonded are trapped forever in its pleasurable insinuation. An idea so outrageous that it keeps pushing us to break our own limits, to experience the lesser known, whether it's regular or forbidden. Maybe it's an attempt to fulfill the emptiness, which ironically the 'taste of blood' brings along.

I was just looking out to discover and fulfill fantasies. And I did find the fantasies of the few pretty girls I knew. Their colored dreams were like the rainbow and I was the dull cloud without whom the rainbow would never be visible. I could definitely fulfill all their fantasies, both 'dark' and 'light', but I had lesser intuition in those moments, about the consequences of dwelling in both.

It was a lot of 'love' being bestowed on me and I had no clue if I was worth it. Too much 'love' for me from the world and it scared me. And when I was surrounded by the 'light' of love, which everybody had bestowed, I saw myself falling into my own 'darkness'.

The ray of 'light' ends in 'darkness', and in 'darkness' rests the spice. What happens after 'red' forms the deep dark connect between the colorful rainbow and shady clouds? Pretty much like the relationship between 'dreams' and 'deeds'.

The glittery 'dreams' will always need a shady background for them to be distinguished.

Such connects breed a strange comfort which is so thrilling for those who can see. The dreamy spectrum glitters around shady clouds, but when the 'cloud' accepts that he cannot change his color, he ends up feeling familiar with strangers. There are many like him...

I didn't know if it would be possible for a ray of 'darkness' to make a rainbow. If there was a way, I would have walked the colorful bridge of our dreams, but I was too shaded with 'guilt' to match the vibrance of our rainbow.

I wondered if, the reverse perspective of walking from 'darkness' to 'light' would also be possible. I wanted to explore the extent of their 'darkness' and their deep desires but ironically I ended up just exploring my own.

What happens beyond Red?
What happens beyond Red?
Nobody knows,
Nobody knows...

Why is that so?
Asked a drunk man,

Because in my Dream I saw a large crow...

Who brought me my violation,
Scarred me forever from salvation,

And thus with 'Red' I wake up every morning,
Was it mercy or just a plain warning!

What happens beyond Red?
What happens beyond Red?
Nobody knows,
Nobody knows...

Why So Red?
Why So Red?

It's dark down there,
Too red, too red...

For me,
And for you...
You might be lonely but friends are true,

Stop chumming to the red glaze,
The day just got brighter,
Humming away to a holiday...

ON A BAD BOY NOTE

Sang his melodies,
With a broad tooth line,
Stroking his goatee,
It was Ajay, a friend of mine...

Chumming away the Night's 'Red',
Humming the tune of the Morning Bread...

But;

What happens beyond Red?
What happens beyond Red?
And still...

Nobody knows,
Nobody knows...

Why is that so?
Asked a drunk man...

Because in his 'Dark Dream' he saw a Freaking Large Crow....

Where am I headed towards?
Nobody knows, nobody knows...

Where am I headed towards...?

Nobody knows, nobody knows...
Why...?
Nobody knows, nobody knows...

ANSH SETH

AFTER RED...

It begins with a ray of light,
Which goes as long as the Sun's sight,

Then with Violet it starts,
For which you need a piece of glass,

In the glass Prison,
Which we call a Prism,

Light breaks slowly to reveal its stains,
As Violet graduates to Indigo,
Without any refrain,

Indigo might be a mature tincture,
To blue it dissolves,
As the Cobalt punctures,

The Blue Oceans meet the Green,
As that is the color of leaves,
And the Nature's dream,

Mother Nature takes us back to light,
And that's when Yellow,
Begins its holy fight,

To grow up to Orange for the tint of a rebel,
Never knowing,
That one day it shall meet the rubble,

And then begins 'Red'...
'High' on frequency,
But a color most dread,

ON A BAD BOY NOTE

But the color of 'blood' is so true,
As that is me,
And so is you...

It's so fuckin Red,
It's so fuckin Red...

The color of life and the drop of death,
You can share some,
Still, in your last few breaths...

But what happens after the Crimson spark,
Sorry to say,
Beyond the Rainbow it's just Dark...!

CHAPTER 6
CHUMMING AND HUMMING

'Chumming and humming' is the cyclic pattern in many people's lives.
The rhyme might sound obnoxious but at times that is what life is.
'Chumming and humming' occurs when you explode because what you
had accumulated out of 'greed' is not what you actually needed.
At times, it's so much to handle... that it just spills over!
The walls of 'greed' are very weak to hold it. Greed is just a self-created
perfect illusion, which surrounds us with purpose-less 'gluttony'.
'Gluttony' is when, what you want is all and everything...
But even if you 'have it all', 'greed' is a very weak substrate to carry it!

What anyone eventually needs is 'love'. It is that force which defines reason in life.
It's a push towards getting better, breaking free...
At times the 'push' is given by the Universe as a chance
to free oneself, and to start all over again...

The next morning after the night long party with my office friends, I woke up to drop Ajay at his residence in *Pune.* The activities for a bachelor like me in *India* on a dry day appeared limited but I was still recovering from the hangover of the previous night, but the hangover of Anita's thoughts still prevailed as they had been prevailing for the past six years. I thought of going back home and resting but involuntarily drove down to the school building where it had all gone down.

'Chumming and humming', I stand here at the school gate where it happened six years ago. The day when the Universe showed its way and 'karma' was the messenger. It's generally not rainy in the month of October in *Pune.* It's the onset for winters but today, the clouds are present in thickness, over-casting the sun. Even the wind is blowing harsh, and subtly touching the soul of everything inside everyone. I see people around falling in 'love' again with the city and its beautiful moods. The cloudy overcast is making everything around look and feel beautiful. I park my car, come out and absorb the world. The clouds make me feel like smoking and I light a cigarette to the freedom with which we smoked here. As I lit the cigarette, the wind blew and ruffled my hair. I stand peacefully and watch the school building in front of me, where we were, six years ago.

Two and a half years had passed since I had last met Anita, and six years ago we all had come down to *Pune* to spend our summer vacations, preparing for the competitive exams which would come our way after the final graduation board examinations. Anita, Ratish and I were permitted by our families to go and enroll in the tuition classes in *Pune.* Students of the same subject from other colleges in *Mumbai* had also enrolled for the same coaching program. Zaida had also asked her parents but they had refused to send her. The three of us had made new friends in the tuition class in *Pune* which happened in the same school building. Life was at its best since there were no parents, no going home and all the freedom to do whatever our hearts would want. Lectures could be bunked and the world around had less traffic, lesser cops and a lot of students. Anita was putting up in a girls' hostel nearby and Ratish and I stayed in a boys' hostel at a walking distance from Anita's hostel.

The day used to be spent around the school building where our classes were conducted. There was a nearby mall which used to be our favorite hangout. There was a bookstore close by where Anita and I would spend a lot of 'time' reading about the different things in this world.

It was on one of those days when Anita had walked up to me, excitedly, after reading something. "Hey I found an amazing article in the mythology section", she exclaimed. "It talked about *Shiva*[85]", she said in her excited voice. "What does it say?" I asked. "*Shiva* means 'darkness'. It said that when thirty percent of the world sees 'light' then seventy percent of the world sees 'darkness'. It is the same with planet earth

---

[85]   *Shiva: The Supreme Most God. An Epitome of Manhood. The God of Kindness and Love and has the Power of Complete Annihilation.*

and the water present on it. When a very little portion of the planet is earth, an unknown extent of it is water, much more than the solid land. *Shiva* exists everywhere; in the 'light' and in the 'darkness', in the earth and in the water, and in you and in me. It is the 'light' which we all see but it is the 'darkness' which makes 'light' what it is. *Shiva* is that 'darkness' which illuminates the 'light' around", she explained with a calm glow on her face. "Wow; that sounds interesting. I didn't know all this about *Shiva*", I said with awe which reflected on my face. Somehow her inquisitiveness to know more always kept me intrigued with the world. The world looked way more interesting than I ever knew or had imagined.

"Do you know *Shiva* was also the biggest *Aghori*[86] sage?" she added. "Really, *Shiva* was also an *Aghori*?" that's interesting. "It means he ate dead corpses too?" I asked. "I don't know but I read one very interesting statement. If you understand the meaning of *Aghora*[87] it means deeper than deep. But I perceive it as darker than 'dark'. And that's why it is *Shiva*", she completed. Anita's fancy for *Shiva* was sweet and very innocent. "Do you know, in *Aghora* practice they have a ritual in which the *Aghori*s have sex with a woman in her periods?" I remarked. "Yuck, that is gross", exclaimed Anita in disdain. "Why is it gross?" I asked. "It is not like I know anything in this context but then what is the harm of doing it while a woman is in her periods?", I pondered. "No way, how can a man have sex with a woman when she is 'chumming'?" hissed Anita. "Why, I mean what is so gross about it?" I reasoned. "Uday you shouldn't see a woman chum, you might never have sex then", laughed Anita. "So 'chumming' means having one's periods?" I asked still dubious about the word I had heard for the first time in my life. Moreover it did not belong anywhere in my context or vocabulary because I was far away from the literal occurrence of the word. "It is the menstrual cycle, you fool", Anita stomped her feet and went back to her books.

Rita was in *Mumbai*. The last conversation I had with her was in *Mumbai* before leaving. I was Rita's boyfriend, as acknowledged in her close friend circle, but none of her friends were related to or associated with

---

[86] *The ascetic saints who practices Aghora.*

[87] *Aghora: Science of Tantra.*

me in any way. So I felt safe playing the 'once in a while' boyfriend. Since I was in *Pune* with Anita, I could barely find time to talk to Rita. But one night during those days, I had gone drinking with Ratish and his two new friends from the classes, Naman and Jai. They had rented an apartment, and had invited Ratish and me for a house party. That night was the only night when I had spoken to Rita properly.

"Uday you rapist, you don't have time to call me", sniggered Rita. "No sexy, I was pretty busy with the classes. How are you and of course your 'hearts'?" I coaxed. "I am good and I miss you with all my 'hearts'", she chuckled. "I miss them too", I said with a smile. "When are you coming back to *Mumbai*?" she asked. "Just one more month", I answered. "Come back quickly Uday, I miss you. Haven't seen you for a long time", she said with a little anguish in her voice. "Just a month more, my sexy teddy bear! And after that I am all yours", I said softly. The guys called me to come back and continue drinking. I asked for five minutes and went back to the conversation. "I feel as if you are forgetting me", complained Rita. "How can I forget you Ritzy?" I said passionately. "You are so 'hot' and wild, all at the same time!" I said trying to keep her warm. "Yes, that is what you remember of me", taunted Rita. "Tell me, how are the girls in your class?" she asked with her usual sarcasm.

"They are ok, nothing great. And why should I look at them when I have you?" I answered. "Liar liar, pants on fire", she laughed. I laughed with her. "I know you are a big flirt Uday", she continued. "Come on, Rita. I am an innocent nice boy", I pleaded. "The way you were looking at me at the Prom Night, I knew you were a big flirt", accused Rita. "And still you are with me", I laughed.

Rita went silent for a while. "I know one day you will leave me and go with someone else", she said in a sad voice. "Why do you say so?" I questioned. "Because that is what guys are like. They make a girl fall in love with them and then they leave her to find someone else. And it is all because, guys just want sex from a girl", said Rita in anguish. "Hey sexy, why do you say so? I never forced you for sex", I consoled. "But eventually that is what you would want from me and if you leave me, then also you would leave me to have sex with another girl", she argued in a highly cranky voice. Her tone got wetter as I heard her cry on the phone. I could not comprehend the 'insecurity' with which she was driven, the 'insecurity' with which she looked at guys or perhaps just me. "Hey Rita, why are you crying sweetheart?" I said. "Nothing I am just having mood swings", she cried. "Such extreme mood swings!" I exclaimed considering that her mood swing had almost probed in my reality. I was exactly doing what she expected me to do. I already had a girlfriend I really loved, and still I didn't hesitate to behave as her boyfriend.

"It is because I am in my periods", said Rita with a little embarrassment. "Oh, so you are 'chumming'?" I said with the familiarity of the new word which I had recently learnt in those days. "Yes I am 'chumming', you rapist", retaliated Rita in an annoyed tone. "Sexy, does it hurt when you chum?" I asked. "Yes Uday, my back and my stomach are hurting", said Rita in a painful voice. "Have a painkiller", I suggested "Or I can give you a massage" I couldn't help adding. "I would love a massage, but for that you have to come here", teased Rita. "I so want to be there", I said lustfully. "But for now Rita, be a good girl and have a painkiller", I instructed. "Yes, I will do that", she said obediently. "I love you Uday. Never cheat on me", she said the 'last words' which resonated with 'hope'. "I won't", I lied and then I felt a little bell tinkle in my forsaken conscience again. "But I can't help having female friends. I hope you don't have problems with that", I asked hesitant.

"Not your fault, your zodiac sign is that of a flirt. All the people of your zodiac sign are flirts", said Rita dryly. "No Rita, my zodiac sign is that of air", I defended. "And the 'air' flows, because it's freedom and it brings freshness. It's the 'air' which keeps the world alive", I added. "And Rita you are water. That is why you are so wet and sexy", I flirted back with my 'chumming' girlfriend. "Yuck, that is so dirty. I am wet right now and trust me I don't like this", she complained. "Okay the boys are getting angry, I have to leave Rita. You go to sleep sexy", I said in a hurry. "You are such an asshole... but I love you", she spoke the words slowly. "I love you sexy, dying to eat you up", I rushed the last words and we disconnected. I felt bad for Rita and all the pain she was going through. I had little idea then, about the pain which I was about to give her.

I joined the guys, where Naman greeted me with a statement, "Where are you flirting off to, bro? Girls will come and go. Come have some alcohol with us peacefully." Ratish was drunk and laughing. He was a guy who was just out in this world to get drunk and have fun and make a lot of friends. Well I guess even I was out for fun! Those days I used to be pretty careful in front of Ratish regarding the messages from Zaida. It was maybe because what Zaida and I shared was totally unacceptable. She was cheating her friend Anita by getting cozy with her boyfriend. I was cheating Anita, and Ratish by having a secret rendezvous with his ex-girlfriend. Zaida knew the limitations of our relationship and she never called. She only messaged. After Ratish had passed out, I checked my cellphone for messages. Rita had dropped a message which said, "If you are 'air', then I am the deep 'water' in which you will always float like a bubble... deep inside me." It felt nice being a bubble in her life, which brings her fantasies to life, refreshing the depth of her fluidic emotions with my airy vibe.

Zaida had left a few forwards and a "Miss you" message. I replied to Zaida, "Zaida, why do you miss me? I am nothing but a cheat!" I felt comfortable, being honest to someone. "No don't say that, I like you and you are a nice person", she replied with kindness.

"But all I do to you is touch you and torment you. I can never be your boyfriend and I can never fall in love with you", I replied with the familiar urge to torment. "I know and I don't even expect it from you", she messaged back. "Then why do you come to me and let me do those things to you? Why do you let me cross your boundaries?" I asked provocatively. To which she replied, "I don't know. I feel guilty at times." "I don't know what I like, I guess. I am just attracted to you", she messaged. "So attracted that you let me do anything which I would like to do to you?" I replied. "You have a different feel; I lose control when I am with you. I love you Uday. You can do anything you want to do to me", she replied. I felt the 'darkness' creep in furthermore, imagining all that I can do to Zaida and she will secretly enjoy, but thoughts of Anita prevailed again.

I realized I was falling in 'love' with the fantasies. I re-thought about the dream which I saw when I wasn't dating Anita. The dream had occurred when I was single. In my dream, I saw many girls throwing away their clothes and pouncing on me, begging me for my 'little warrior' and his cruelty. The way I turned into the God of manhood in that dream ran back in my drunken head. But then the faded memories of Anita in the recent 'dark dream' also returned. It often scared and made me paranoid when that aspect of the dream played in front of my eyes. Anita was someone I couldn't share even in my wildest dreams.

Though the fantasies were enchanting and I saw Rita stripping naked for me. I even saw Zaida acting out my whims. I saw Anita and me exploring each other even further. Life had become so interesting. The alcohol was getting to my eyes after my thoughts and I got pretty drowsy. I lit the last cigarette of my day and started cleaning my inbox of messages from Rita and Zaida. I realized I cannot afford getting caught or even suspected by Anita. I looked at the watch she had gifted me. I knew I can't lose her in any possible way. Anita was mine and I wanted to keep it that way. She was too perfect and too classy a girlfriend to have and I loved her.

I was turning into a witty predator that would cover his marks after he has attacked. Maybe that too for 'love' and for all the fantasies I always yearned for, and I finally had. I was too sure of never giving that chance away in which Anita would have got to know my reality.

But at times, the way, the Universe presents that dreaded chance, could be unbelievable. That chance was about to happen to me, to vanquish my achievements. The moment which I never wanted to face, but in life, like how dreams come true, at times, the 'worst fears' also come true. It is that moment when one is surrounded by the mirrors of perceptions from all sides. Perceptions created by one's self and by others. And amongst the many reflections of these mirrors, one discovers his true reality. And everything then awaits 'judgment', which would eventually define the fate of the 'change' – whether or not anything changes. Sadly, even 'change' begins with pain!

A couple of days before that doomed day, Anita had bought me a new shirt for which she had saved from her allowance. It was a handsome blue shirt and it fit me well. She was broke after buying me that gift. It was crazy 'being in love' and the way she loved..., she often left even survival behind on her priorities. The next day Anita looked upset in the class for an argument with her parents. I couldn't do much to help on her home front. Often menial arguments with her parents left her in a helpless jittery state. Probably our problems back home were totally different. Maybe it was the gender difference. My poor logic to deal with parental pressure, rarely convinced her. It was important to cheer her up, so I had called her in the evening and said, "Dress up quickly in half an hour and wear something nice." "Why? What happened? Where are we going?" she asked. "Just be ready and you shall know." Maybe she needed a surprise...

I took her to a posh restaurant to treat her with whatever was left of my pocket money. The city of *Pune* has many garden restaurants. They are open air and romantic. Anita was fond of fancy places. Being in college, the pocket money seldom allowed us to go and chill at these places. Anita looked gorgeous in a blue sleeveless top. Her smile chimed her way through the crowd. Pretty much, like a feather passing through many tiny dangling bells, touching them so gently that they resonated with mild vibrations. Many heads turned as she beamed through the crowd. But her gaze remained fixed at the corner table which I had picked for us.

Enjoying the splendid evening in the lost city of *Pune*. We remained engrossed in ourselves and had the most romantic dinner of our lives together. We spoke about just us, and looked nowhere else but in each other's eyes. The night ended with me dropping a little tipsy Anita at her hostel where Anita gave me a never ending kiss. *Pune* was not like *Mumbai* and people around were also conservative, though not bothersome. We didn't have a place to crash together or that night would have had a different meaning. I still remember the walk back to my hostel... I felt complete and a little funny, like perhaps I am about to find my destination in the dreaded journey of 'love'... I had no clue what the coming day had held for me.

The next morning Anita and I were sitting in the classroom. The desks were small and could accommodate only two people. Anita and I often sat together.

"Last night was so awesome. Thanks a lot *Jaan* for taking me out for dinner. It was so romantic. The shirt which I gave you looked so good on you. You were looking so 'hot'", whispered Anita with bright yet mushy eyes looking at me with the similar passion as the previous night. "Really, did I look that good?" I asked still a little nervous to handle compliments. "Uday, you were looking 'hot'. So 'hot' that I felt like eating you up", said Anita. "You were looking so gorgeous with that blue sleeveless you were wearing. I still remember nothing from last night but your eyes. I wish we had a place of our own here in this city. I couldn't let you go back to your hostel", I said still lost in the memory of the night before. "Yeah I wish we had a place. I am so 'turned on' thinking of that", said Anita slightly biting her lips. "Even me Nitu, I feel like kissing you right now", I said with a heavy breath. "Don't feel that way please. There are a lot of students in the class. I have faced a lot of embarrassment because of our regular public display of affection", blushed Anita. I looked at her and then looked around at the class. A lot of first benchers here too noticed us from the corner of their eyes. "I guess let us not scandalize the kids here", I affirmed and we both laughed.

"But there is one possibility which could be worked out", I said enthusiastically. "What is it?" asked Anita.

"Naman and Jai are putting up in Naman's family house in *Pune*. It is a three bedroom flat. We can take a room there", I suggested. "Are you kidding? No ways. I don't even know them properly", shrieked Anita to my idea of taking her to sleep over at my new friend's place. "They are nice guys. Ratish has become a very close friend of them. The last time we were drinking together, Naman had told me that I am most welcome at his place. We can seriously crash there one night. It's been so long", I explained with the 'urge' pouring into my eyes. "Yes *Jaan*, it's been so long. Remember the last time we did it. You just wouldn't stop", she cajoled in a shy voice. "How many times did you cum that day?" I asked with an ego surge stroking up my 'little warrior'. "I don't remember. But it was so awesome. You look so good when you come Uday", she added in her husky voice.

I grabbed her hand, and her fingers entwined in mine. We kept our hands below the desk so that no one could see. My arm touched hers, sitting so close to each other. Anita had goose bumps on her skin. And soon the goose bumps were rising on both ends. The weather caught the fire burning inside us and it became cloudy with the winds blowing heavily to cool us down. A window of the classroom started rattling and we looked outside.

"It's such an awesome weather outside", she said, delighted. "Yeah I know. I so still feel like bunking the class and getting a room", I chuckled. Both Anita and I looked out of the window at the blush green world outside, inviting us to complete what was left remaining from the previous night. "Let's bunk the class but only for today. Tomorrow if you ask me to bunk then I wouldn't bunk and I won't let you bunk either. Our parents have paid so much for these classes and thus we attend these classes here", she said buying into the plan but putting across her disclaimers. "Yeah we would, but let us leave for now. You can discipline me later out in the open", I said with my hands reaching out to her thighs.

The teacher entered and the lecture was about to begin. Anita and I got up from our desk. "Where are you kids going off to, the lecture is starting?" interrupted the teacher. "Actually Ma'am, I have an urgent work in the bank. My parents have transferred money and I need to pay my rent today. So I would be back in a while. I am just taking him along with me", said Anita with a sudden promptness and I nodded with a smile. The teacher agreed with a mere "Okay!" Perhaps teachers in coaching classes are paid enough to 'not care' or bother too much. I looked behind at the students. The kids who knew us gave a cunning smile. I smiled back at them and we left.

Outside the classroom, the weather was amazing on that cloudy day. The wind blew and enhanced the taste of the freedom which we were enjoying. I quickly rushed to the nearest *tapri* and bought a few cigarettes. We chose to walk in the weather instead of taking a rickshaw. We kept walking hand in hand as love poured out from the edges of our eyes. Soon we were away from the main road into a serene residential area. The houses were small and big... actually all sizes. The thin roads were covered with trees from both sides. We walked under the shady trees. Soon we reached the end of the road which started taking shape into a small hill.

I looked at Anita and asked her, "Should we go back or should we climb up?" "What the fuck would we go back and do? Let's climb up this hill", replied Anita in one of her arrogant tones. I held her hand and started walking up. She followed. The hill was a little steep but on the top it turned into a flat plateau. We walked to the other end of the plateau, till we saw the end of the hill and the way down. We sat down at the edge of the plateau. Anita took out my cigarette and lit one. I lit another and we sat down still holding hands and looking at the clouds. Anita and I came closer to each other and we began to kiss while the remaining smoke reeked out of our mouths and nostrils amidst the kiss. The kiss appeared to be never ending. After a long smooch, we separated and I looked affectionately at her.

"I love you Anita", I said and hugged her. "I just couldn't stop kissing you, the girl who has brought me to life. I feel like all these years I never had a girlfriend because I was just waiting to meet you", I said holding her hands in a tight clasp. "Will you please marry me someday?" I asked with my mouth gaped open. "I like staying in your arms. I would love to 'make love' to you all the time. At night and all day", I said, still drooling in her eyes. "The way you strip me and you kiss me... Nitu, I feel like I am gasping for breath. I won't be able to live without you", I mumbled and came closer to kiss her. "You know Uday, I love your jawline and your shoulders. The way you look when you have an orgasm. I just love holding you when you are inside me", she murmured and began kissing me.

"You know I feel like going on a long bike ride with you. It would be so nice to feel you holding me tight", I whispered in her ears as she rested in my embrace. I went closer to her and pulled her ponytail behind and saw her long neck. I began kissing it, with long strokes of my tongue. Anita reciprocated by licking my face. The embrace grew tighter and we kissed on the lonely hill beneath the clouds. The winds blew stronger and ruffled our hair.

"It's getting late Uday. Let's go back to the class", said Anita in a concerned voice and interrupted the kiss. "Let's go", I obeyed and we got up. We started walking back slowly, hands still entwined with slow steps. "I have a crazy idea", I beamed. "What is it Uday? You are too crazy at times", laughed Anita. "What if you, I, Uncle, Aunty, your brother along with my family are all seated on Harley Davidsons and we all set out for a ride? A long ride and you sit behind me and we travel all day. At night we will crash at a tavern. You sleep with me in my bed. In the morning we will have a shower together and then I will make you some amazing juice of all the healthy fruits so that all your dark circles go away." I kept narrating and we kept walking. Anita looked at me with a fondness I always loved to see in her eyes. We reached the school building and the kids were coming out. "No more lectures?" Anita asked Ratish. "No lecture, all remaining lectures got cancelled", screamed Ratish in excitement. Naman and Jai were standing with him. "Let us go party", suggested Naman. "Alright, let's go", I agreed immediately. I looked at Anita for her confirmation and she nodded with a smile. Naman and Jai left on Naman's bike and Anita, Ratish and I followed them in an auto rickshaw. We reached Naman's place and Naman and Jai left to get some beer. Ratish was busy playing a game on his cellphone. Anita and I were inside a room. I asked Anita to lock it.

"Nitu, please lock the door", I said. "No Uday, it is too embarrassing to lock the door. It's someone else's house. Even Ratish is sitting outside", she protested in embarrassment. I didn't know how to counter her logic but I just couldn't let go of the craving especially when the whole day we had been talking about it. "I so feel like doing it. Don't you *Jaan*?" I said holding Anita's hands and still pulling her towards me. "No I can't. I feel like *Jaan*, but I can't, I have started 'chumming'", said Anita, and her face turned low with embarrassment. "Oh don't tell me, you are 'chumming' now?" I said almost annoyed considering the repetition of the word so many times and now, which is the only thing stopping me from making 'love' to my love. Anita looked upset, though I couldn't make out whether it was because of my mood or because of her 'chumming'. But looking at the experience I had derived back home about female family members, I felt it's better to be kind. Anyways, the concept of chumming was beyond my comprehension and I don't see any fault in their 'chumming'.

"It's okay, come here", I said, finally pulling her to sit down on the side of the bed. My 'little warrior' was creating his usual troubles but it wasn't important anymore compared to Anita's low embarrassed face. I kissed Anita and kept my head in her lap. She stroked my hair and I kept looking at her. "Why is 'chumming' such a big issue? I mean everything is more or less the same when a girl chums. It's the same vagina but maybe with a little blood", I said trying to soothe her. "It's a lot more than what you think you know, but stop talking about 'chumming' for God's sake. It's grossing me out", she exasperated but in a better mood. "You know, in my family, a girl is not allowed to go inside a temple or a place of worship when they chum. It's strange naa *Jaan*?" I reasoned thinking about the cultural phenomena. "Yeah, they say that a female is impure during her chums", she said stroking my hair while I rested my head on her lap. "It's so strange *Jaan*, the same religion which doesn't teach us to discriminate amongst genders, differentiates amongst males and females because females chum. It's the way nature designed them I guess", I said looking at her. "Yeah, what is the girl's fault if she chums?" she reasoned helplessly. "Don't worry Nitu, I really don't subscribe to a God who differentiates. For me it's just nature", I smiled. Anita came close to my face which was resting on her lap and kissed me. She held my face in her palms and said, "I love you Uday." I looked at the honesty and affection in her eyes and said, "I love you too *Jaan*", and I came up to kiss her. Anita pushed my head back in her lap, and with the other hand pressed my nose really hard till I shrieked out in pain. "You look so cute with a squeezed nose", laughed Anita. I looked at her face with my hurting nostrils and slowly mellowed down on her lap. My eyes felt heavy and thus they began to close as we kept looking at each other.

It was such a loving moment, sleeping in Anita's lap, looking into her brilliant eyes, which were so fond of me. In no time I was asleep. I slept for quite a while which I don't recollect. The last glimpse of the brightness in her eyes is still remarkably fresh in my memories because I never woke up to those eyes again.

Putting me to rest, feathers of your soft skin,
Tired I am, of handling my sins,

Withered is my soul, for my self's disdain,

But dreams of you, still flows in my veins,
If the chums of 'red', are a boon or a bane?

With the heat within my loins, driving me insane,
The 'red' within yours is a lot of pain,

Snuggling in your lap,
From my vices I abstain,
The last glimpse of your brightness,
Is a drop of love and a lot of rain...?

Lost like a treasure, in the abyss of your eyes,
.... And sadly,
I never woke up to those eyes again....

When I woke up, I saw Anita sitting next to me where she was earlier. My head was on the bed and she looked still.

"Hey *Jaan*", I said as I woke up; still in the thoughts and visuals of her bright eyes. Anita's eyes had lost the shimmer and weren't bright anymore. She looked sick and shocked. Hot tears were swelled up in her eyes. Her lips quivered and she looked at me with a strange shock. "Is everything alright?" I asked. She nodded her head with disappointment and handed me my cellphone. I realized that I didn't have my cellphone in my pocket. The look in her eyes and my cellphone in her hand didn't look like good news to me.

"What happened Nitu, why are you looking so upset?" I asked in a strong tone either to push her out of her state of shock, or rather to make me look confident because I knew I was guilty. Tears rolled down her eyes and she mumbled with her throat choked, "I read the messages." I was shocked and surprised at the same time. I still held my cool to explain if anything went wrong, but a sudden flash of memories returned as I had deleted all the messages from my inbox. "What messages did you see *Jaan*, there is nothing?" I replied in the sweetest possible innocence I could muster in my state of panic. I opened the inbox and kept in front

227

of Anita. I ran through the messages in front of her. "What are you talking about? See the messages *Jaan*, and it has nothing which should possibly make you cry", I said in my calmest tone but was still unsure of what she might have seen. I felt internally that I am trying too hard to look normal. Well, that confidence didn't stay for long.

Anita took my cellphone and pressed a few buttons and showed me the messages I had sent to Rita, Zaida and even older messages to Priya. "How could this be possible?" I thought to myself. Then, to my horror I saw, it was my outbox which stored those messages. I had always cleaned my inbox but I never thought of the outbox. I never knew that the outbox contained the messages I had sent. This feature of the *Nokia*[88] phone didn't come with precautions to enable multiple dating. The phone was not designed to do that, and I realized that I am not so good at it either. My technological backwardness had fucked me. Anita was sobbing and looked at me, and before I could say anything she wailed, "How could you?" and then she began to cry.

I thought of consoling her but I knew it, "I am caught and I am at fault." I kept silent and watched her cry. No 'right' words came to me. After a while I tried to touch her to make her stop crying but she pushed me away. Still with eyes full of tears, she firmly said, "Don't touch me Uday." I looked at her and knew I couldn't do anything to undo what has happened between us. The commotion was increasing in the room in which Anita and I were sitting. I really didn't want Ratish and the other guys to know.

"Let's go out and talk", I pleaded in all my voices and tones. "I don't wanna go anywhere", she snapped, with tears still rolling down her eyes. "Please *Jaan*, not here, not in front of everybody", I pleaded. I tried to touch her and the moment I did, she said in a very cold tone with tears still bubbling out of her eyes, "I don't want to see your face Uday." Her face pushed hard to look straight but her eyes wouldn't stop crying. I looked at her and felt angry at myself. I picked my bag and left their

---

[88]   *Nokia is a Finnish multinational communications and information technology company whose mobile phones went on to become a rage till the Android and iPhones of the world arrived.*

apartment. I was feeling insecure leaving Anita behind there. But I knew there was no point insisting. She had never spoken to me in that tone. And she knows that I have cheated on her with other girls. Whether it was sexual or not, I can't even explain to her now, because even if I did, it wouldn't really matter. She always trusted me to be faithful and I turned out to be quite the opposite, considering the variations of affairs I was running simultaneously.

I took a rickshaw back to my hostel. I stopped outside the hostel gate and sat at a bench on the road. All I could think about was the fondness in Anita's eyes. And now all I recollect were her cold teary eyes, shocked and disappointed to the core. I looked at my cellphone again. All the messages I had sent to Rita, Zaida and Priya were there. Not a single one was missing. I felt pathetic watching the messages and knowing that Anita had read them. I knew she would never accept me, and even if she does it would never be the same.

I had lost my love. The only girl I loved and she loved me so much. I looked at the watch she had gifted me. She had saved money from her monthly allowance to buy me that watch. It continued to remind me of how Anita spent the month broke just to celebrate our anniversary. The anniversary of which I didn't even remember the date, neither did I understand its meaning or significance but she did, and gave me the most memorable day of my life. The first time I was loved to another level, and it was as simple as celebrating a year of being together. I thought about the times she fed me with her hands. All the train rides together. The times we 'made love' and her eyes, especially the way she looked at me.

I knew it then, that it was over, and I sobbed out tears of sorrow while my throat choked. It seems I hadn't cried since the football match at boarding school where I had hit an own goal only to make my team lose the match. It felt difficult to cry after such a long time. I had forgotten how to do it. I pushed hard to pour out my anguish. Just two drops of hot tears poured out. The feeling of restlessness and anxiety was still beating out loud in my heart. But I needed to cry or else I would have exploded. I pushed hard to cry and I did cry, though only a little. I wondered in that moment that all my life I never thought I would fall in love, and then so mysteriously the feeling of separation crept in, accompanied with such an enormous pain. Thus, I was sitting there, guilty and with a feeling of loss. A dawning thought occurred in my head, "If not Anita, then whom do I love and who else would love me?"

My head ached and slowly sitting in that park I felt uncontrollable with pain and regret. I knew I had to end this, but 'how' was the question. I couldn't go back to Anita; she would never accept me especially after reading my messages to Zaida. Zaida is a good friend of her and now their friendship turned sour, because of me. I wondered if there was any way I could have Anita back. Slowly my feelings for Rita and everybody else subsided. I felt nothing for them but just friendship. But for Anita, I felt the pain of being left alone and the 'guilt' of breaking her trust. The best thing to do in such moments is to get sloshed. Honestly, in that moment I felt like killing myself. "Let's drink to death", I murmured and left the park to buy some booze.

I walked a kilometer to a nearby wine shop. I wasn't much of a drinker, but nothing else made sense. The last time I was drunk I passed out in three mugs of beer and Anita had dragged me to the auto rickshaw. The walk was long and I walked angrily to the wine shop. I checked my wallet and I had the last five hundred bucks of my humble allowance. I wondered what drink shall bring me to a pathetic state, good enough that Anita comes and visits me in the hospital. I had never had rum till then, so though it was cheap, I didn't buy it. Vodka seemed like the only viable option. I took out the 500 rupee note and give it to the shopkeeper, "One bottle of *Alcazar*[89] vodka", I struggled to get the words out, holding back the tears. The shopkeeper returned 250 rupees along with the bottle in a black poly bag. I walked back to my hostel, opened my room and opened the bottle. Sitting on my bed, I thought about the time Anita and I spent together and took a huge gulp of neat hot vodka straight from the bottle. My throat burned and a very strong hurling sensation kicked in. I swallowed my urge to puke. A sip more and I felt as if I am rolling all over the floor. I pushed a sip more and I felt a vodka flavored fire, erupting in my throat.

---

[89]   *A cheap Indian vodka sold with a Russian Name.*

Anita's sad cranky face flashed in front of my eyes, I took another huge gulp of vodka and then I didn't stop drinking. Three more back to back sips of vodka purged a heavy volcano inside my stomach and with an instant reverse kick, I puked out on the floor. I threw up for long, till I had nothing left inside but still my body won't stop. My head felt very heavy and everything around me was revolving. In fact my whole body felt as if it were moving, or rather floating in space in a circular spherical motion. I crashed on the bed, still gagging.

But how much ever I tried I couldn't puke out the guilt. Still, the Vodka did give the required relief. The heat inside my stomach and my throat was as strong as the pain inside my heart. It even gave a hope of not waking up to the loneliness and perhaps a just apology to Anita for breaking her heart with my silent departure, out of her life and out of her existence. But no matter if I woke up or not, the scar on loyalty would always remain.

I guess the mighty Universe had a different plan. It wasn't ready to let me leave the world before showing me its marvels. 'Karma' is indeed a very strong force. It works in the way of a cycle of reaping what is sown and specifically to the one who sowed it. 'Karma' is the judge of nature which completes what was started, finally bringing peace and ending a cycle of events and deeds. My deeds still awaited their 'judgment', even though I had never realized their consequences.

I woke up after a couple of hours to the panicked face of my hostel roommate. My head felt heavy and the dizziness remained. My roommate saw my dim response towards his panic and that made him scream louder. Maybe he had no clue of my condition. The puke on the floor had begun to stink. "Dude, what have you done to the room?" he screamed. He was a kid who was mama fed, taken care of and strictly made to believe that being a law abiding citizen means to forget their inquisitiveness to explore the other side. "How much did you drink?" he ranted again as his volume increased. I looked at the bottle of Vodka. It was finished by three fourth, only a quarter left to go. I was shocked to see how much neat vodka I had consumed. My roommate kept on screaming and it began to annoy me. I pulled my finger towards my mouth and kept it on my lips, "Will you please shut up? I puked here...

so don't worry, I will get it cleaned, but don't fucking rant off on my head." I could barely speak but I coughed up the words with a straight face. I tried pulling myself out of the bed but it was very difficult. My roommate took pity on my state and got the hostel cleaner to clean the floor of our room. I kept lying down on the bed and saw the floor being cleaned. The cleaner hurled abuses for the extra work. I reached for my wallet and took out a ten rupee note and handed him the money. "Sorry and thank you", I mumbled with a broken voice. The abuses silenced and the floor continued to get cleaned silently. My mouth was in a bad state owing to the puke and acidity developed in my stomach. I dragged myself to the common toilets and started washing myself up. The other kids in the corridors looked at me and their look stayed. Once I was clean of the muck, I quickly changed my t-shirt and left the hostel. The feeling of dehydration after puking is very disgusting. As soon as I was out of the hostel gate, I lit a cigarette to change the taste. I reached a nearby juice stall and asked for lime juice. After drinking five glasses of lime juice I felt better. My headache didn't subside but my throat and my stomach were cooler.

But as relief was setting in my body the anguish inside my heart increased again. It was dusk when I got up. I had barely slept for two hours and I was surprised at my newly developed capacity for alcohol. I took out my cellphone and called Anita. She didn't answer. I called her several times but she didn't respond. The sadness was creeping in, but it wasn't just me who was sad. My phone rang and I hurriedly looked at it expecting Anita to call, but it was Rita calling.

"Hey Rita", I answered taking a hold on myself and my voice, "How are you?" All this while, prowling and tasting various kinds of 'blood' had led me to a different side of myself where I wouldn't let anyone see my pain, especially when I was lonely. Rita was still in love with me and in the worst possible scenario, I still had a backup insurance plan.

"How are you Rita?" I asked her again owing to her silence. "Not good", she said in a cranky voice, "I am 'chumming'." "Oh my god, even Rita was chumming. A month had passed since her last cycle", I thought to myself. "Are you alright sweetheart or is it hurting?" I asked sounding concerned. "Listen Uday I called you to ask you something specific", she said with her tone getting straighter than her usual romantic voice. "Yes, what happened, everything alright?" I asked.

"What is the name of your friend you hang out with in the classes?" she asked. I wondered who she is talking about. "I got a lot of friends here, which friend are you talking about?" I asked with a little confusion. "The tall girl you are with all the time", she said. I got a bit more alert thinking about the details with which it seemed she was describing Anita. "Oh yes, her name is Anita and she is a very good friend of mine, but how do you know all this?" I replied sounding casual. "Since when are you dating her Uday?" Rita came straight to the point. "Dating her?" I tried to sound confused. "She is a very good friend Rita, but I am dating no one but you", I replied agitatedly. "Really, that's why you guys hold hands when you sit in the class? And that's why you guys are always together whether in the classroom or outside?" she taunted in an accusing harsh voice. I was shocked knowing the level of details with which Rita knew about how Anita and I behaved in the classes. "How do you know all this Rita?" I asked foolishly not realizing that my question further incriminated me. "Because a friend's friend is in the same class in which you guys are. I had asked her if she knew you as you are my boyfriend. But she told me that you are with a girl all the time in the class. That's when I thought something is fishy and when she asked your other friends they confirmed that you guys are going around", she explained coldly. "You bastard!" she screamed with her voice slamming on the phone. I couldn't believe this occurrence that Rita in spite of being in *Mumbai* caught me cheating on her in *Pune*. The best part of the entire incident was that it all happened in a span of 24 hours.

"How could you do this Uday?" I trusted you, she said, angrily. "When you started being too nice and busy just after you left for *Pune*, I had an intuition which said that something is not right about you. You appeared to be too perfect", she accused. "And what about all those stories of your ex-girlfriend who dumped you for a rich guy?" she asked, perhaps with a little 'hope' that I still falsify everything she heard, and everything that she had believed remained the same. Perhaps that's what 'love' does to us, pushing us to believe what we think we know against all odds. Lying again was stupid, especially when my 'karma' was showing me the definite existence of a higher power which runs this world and governs the universe.

"It was all false!" I meekly admitted the truth. There was a brief silence on the other end. Perhaps Rita required it to assimilate my heart breaking reality. "Then all that you said about your ex-girlfriend... She never existed!" exclaimed Rita in shock. "Yeah, she was just imaginary. I only have... or rather, I only had one girlfriend and that's Anita", I confessed. The self-acknowledgement of losing Anita returned, choking me in my throat. But Rita was too shaken to her core, to empathise with my loss and console me.

"How could you do this Uday? You are such a liar, you are such a bastard!" she howled. I was silent again, with nothing more to explain. None of my wits gave me a solution to soothe her. All I could muster was, "I am sorry Rita."

"Fuck you and your sorry", screamed Rita. "I kept telling my friends how amazing you are. All of them told me that you seem risky and dangerous, but I kept fighting with them for you. Now I will tell them that you are a scumbag, an asshole. And the biggest liar, my friends were right about you", cried Rita. "Why did you do this to me? Why did you make me fall in love with you when you were already seeing someone else? You cheated on me and that's one thing, why did you cheat on Anita? How could you be so disgusting?" she continued to scream.

"You are very cute and I couldn't forget the way you looked at the prom night. I just wanted to know you more and maybe I wanted you to like me, but I never wanted to hurt you Rita. It might sound strange but I still do love you with all my shitty reality", I mumbled, trying to hold on to the 'last straws', with the moments spent with Rita running in my head. "Don't you dare talk about love Uday! Bastards like you will never know what 'love' is", she cried.

"Rita I understand you are in pain, abuse me as much as you want to... but why are you abusing my family?" I protested. "It's because that's what you deserve", growled Rita. I had never heard her so angry. I guess it was the day to see things which I had never expected to see, there's a first time for everything.

"You didn't leave me a kiss virgin, you didn't leave me a touch virgin", accused Rita, sobbing. It felt funny amidst all the pain and trauma when I heard the different distinctions of virginity. "Now what is a kiss virgin, and what is a touch virgin? There is only one type of virginity I know of, and that I haven't taken from you. You are still a virgin, Rita, I left you that", I said, trying to make it funny but it had a different effect on her.

"You think it's funny. You are so 'dark' Uday, you have left 'darkness' inside me forever. I would never be able to trust anyone. You are the first person who has touched me in my life. And all my life I have to remember you as the bastard I first kissed", she hissed.

> *I so wanted to tell her,*
> *That at the end 'darkness' completes 'light'.*
> *Without 'darkness' there is no 'light'.*
> *I shared their 'dark' passions, veiled in mine.*
> *Just the mere fact of realization that even I had 'darkness',*
> *Made them hate me...*
> *For being a creature not so divine!*

Something 'good' inside did make me feel that neither Anita nor Rita had done something to be in this situation. I felt mad at myself for causing all this pain to people I so liked being with. The anger finally spilled in my words too, "At least you can be thankful that I didn't 'make love' to you?"

"Yeah I am thankful that I didn't do it with you. Or else I would have gone crazy", she had started crying hysterically. There was silence on both ends; maybe we both did wonder how making love to each other would have been. Rita broke the silence, "But still Mr. Uday Singh, may you never find love in your life. Whoever you love shall leave you and that day you will understand what I am going through and it is because of you." She sounded choked, as tears would have been choking her voice. The silence which resumed after her last words kept me silent for a long time. Rita had cursed me. Though I never believed in curses, but the way it was said was very painful. I hardly knew in that moment how the curse would fulfill itself.

"Fuck off with your bitch", screamed Rita and slammed the phone. I felt angry when she referred Anita to her abuse. But I couldn't fight anymore. Not after what Rita had wished for me. My head still ached and I slowly walked back into my hostel to sleep, as there was nothing which I could do to change what had happened. I thought of Rita and her cute smile, and her childish attitude whenever she met me. The 'time' when she held me and cried on the beach re-played in glimpses. I didn't know what future she saw with me which had hurt her so much. My thoughts slowly came back to Anita and the passion with which she loved me till all I could recollect was her sad face, which was so, because of me.

I opened my hostel room and walked in. The floor was clean and displayed no traces of the day, neither the smell nor the color of the shit which I had puked out. My roommate was getting ready to sleep. "Hey how are you now?" he asked. I felt bad for being harsh to him during the day. "I am good buddy, just my head is aching", I said with a dry smile. "Take some rest Uday, I guess it had been a rough day for you", he said with kindness. "Hmmm kind of", I mumbled. I couldn't tell him how rough my day was. Nevertheless, the worst was over so I was settling down in my bed. Just then my phone rang, it was Zaida calling. I knew it then that the rough day still had some surprises. I answered the call, "Hi Zaida, how are you?" I asked. There was utter silence on the other end.

"Zaida, you there?" I asked again. "Uday", her voice cracked the silence but it was very low. This wasn't good news. The truth Zaida and I shared had definitely compelled Anita to confront her. "Anita had called up. She knows everything", she cried. All I heard after this line was crying.

"Ratish knows about this too and he even told my girlfriends in college. Everybody knows it", and she started wailing out her sobs. "Anita said so many things that I can't even tell you", she continued. "What did she say?" I asked, concerned and all the more guilty. "I can't tell you. I don't have any friends now", wailed Zaida. "How did this happen, how could you let it out?" she accused and continued crying.

"I didn't do it intentionally Zaida. I fell asleep and Anita checked my cellphone. I used to delete all the messages in my inbox but I never checked my outbox. And she read the outbox", I explained. "What should I do now?" she questioned amidst her sobs "I can't come to college anymore; it will be too awkward I won't be able to face Anita. Ratish was anyways angry with me because I broke up with him. He has a chance now to destroy my reputation", she kept crying as she spoke.

"Don't worry Zaida, everything will be fine", I said holding back my tears. There was a much higher level of comfort which I felt with her. I could cry with her as she was the only one who shared my guilt. Even though her sin weighed less compared to mine. She just crossed a line in friendship, for infatuation. I had broken three hearts in the same day.

"Uday, I won't be able to see you now", she reasoned. "Why did you do this?" she said and burst out wailing. I kept silent and heard her howl. The way she cried had a bitter feeling of regret which was slowly encroaching upon me. She hung up the phone. I messaged her, "I am sorry, really didn't mean to screw up like this. Take care." In a while she replied, "Uday, I always knew that we had no future but I don't want to regret what happened. I won't meet you again. You should have been careful." The last line of her message messed me up a lot. Often at times like these, people desperately try to find someone or something to blame their situation on. It gives a lot of relief to shed off the baggage of being the cause. Even I blamed my cellphone, and Anita's bad habit of fiddling with it. I also blamed my foolishness and my 'darkness', and most of all, my greed.

Zaida didn't message after that. I stayed awake for a while but slowly slept off to my headache and 'guilt'. I thought of life after that. After Anita, all I felt was a void, an empty space. Killing myself was useless, maybe I couldn't do that. I have to live with the emptiness and hope that Anita comes back. But the crack in our relationship would always remain; she would never be able to trust me. And it would never be the same again. I should forget about Rita, I stand no chance there too.

Here I am 'chumming' now, flushing that day out of my system. The day that changed my fate and cracked my conscience and the night in which I hated myself beyond all realms of possibility. Everybody chums in shame and I am ashamed too. So ashamed of myself that I feel numb.

I chum out Zaida's bitter tears, I chum out Rita's curse and I keep 'chumming' to Anita's sad shocked eyes.

But even in the saddest moments, there is always something to laugh about. I laugh out to the unbelievable way I got screwed up in a day; when all my sins grabbed me by the balls and shook my system. I laughed more thinking about Rita's virginity classification. I laughed to the 'irony' of Zaida and me. I laughed out the most to the day which started so beautifully and ended so miserably. That day, I also hummed to the fondness that I had for Rita. I hummed to Zaida's submission and still; the sad tear filled face of Anita didn't make me laugh. It still saddens me while the ironies of 'time' mock me.

The 'irony' often occurs when the smartest perceptions are just left to the will of Universe and one comes to know the real self. It happens in these moments when your wits and your chances are over casted, outnumbered and outplayed by 'karma'. It was my turn that day, in that moment when I was overruled and my walls of greed broke down. That was the day I broke a heart.

It was in that moment of dawning realization, which showed me the mirror of my perception about myself. In that moment I felt what I had accomplished was not what I needed. The only thing that was needed was 'love', and sadly I had a lot of it that day, much more than I could accommodate or handle.

The next day I reached late for the classes. The students could make out from my face that something had gone wrong. I had missed two lectures and the last one remained for that day. I looked out for Anita. She sat on the second last bench with Ratish. I looked at them. Ratish was expressionless. Anita still looked sad. I felt a sense of relief that at least she is still missing me.

I went and sat on the last bench, behind them. Anita looked at me and ignored me, while I walked past her. Naman and Jai sat on the bench adjacent to them. Naman and Jai greeted me to which I responded with a dry smile and nodded my head. Anita wore a collared blue sleeveless shirt and a pair of jeans. I liked the way she was dressed. She looked 'hotter' than usual maybe because of the melancholy on her face. I tried to hold her gaze but the wound was fresh. I felt the warmth and anger in her eyes.

I touched her waist from behind, and caressed her. Anita kept still for a while till her firm hand came and removed mine. The temporary moment of submission had a soothing effect on me; I felt a strange air of peace realizing that my touch still touches her. I whispered her name, but she didn't respond. The rest of the lecture continued with my futile efforts to talk to her. When the lecture got over, she quickly began to leave with Ratish, Naman and Jai. I reached out and grabbed her hand and said, "Anita, please listen to me." "Uday, I don't want to talk to you. You disgust me for whatever you have done to me!" she retaliated angrily. The sharp and never heard words from Anita's refreshed the sadness of the previous night to a deeper shade. "Please Nitu, please talk to me", I begged with regret and repentance creeping up in my voice. Anita pulled her hand off my grip and continued to walk out. I followed her out to the road in front of the school. By the time I could cross the road, she boarded an auto-rickshaw with Ratish and left. I screamed her name but she paid no heed. Maybe I didn't deserve any. The loneliness of being left by love when you are in a new city, just so you could be together at peace, is a very hurtful 'irony'. I stood there watching the disappearing auto rickshaw taking Anita with it. I lit a cigarette, as slow hot drops of tears start pouring out of my eyes. "Come on, I don't cry. I guess I haven't cried since school", I said to myself.

An impulse coupled with an insecurity rushed in my nervous system again, and a thought whispered, "What if Anita gets drunk and ends up making out with any of these guys?" The thought sent a shiver down my spine. The most primitive fear for 'love' started turning into a panicky impulse. I thought about of how Jai keeps hitting on Anita. "What if Ratish tries to get even with me by seducing her?" I thought to myself, "Or even worse, what if Anita seduces or gets seduced to get back at me?" I called for an auto-rickshaw and left for Naman's place. Sick frightening thoughts ran through my head on the way till I reached the lobby of Naman's apartment. I quickly start running up the stairs to reach his flat. Finally I reached the third floor and rang the bell. Nobody opened the door.

The creepy thoughts began racing at a full flow. Of course I couldn't trust any friend because I wasn't trustworthy myself. One often ends up seeing the world as they see themselves. I started ringing the bell incessantly till finally the door cracked open. It was Ratish who opened the door. He gave me an empty look. A can of beer shone in his hand. "I have to see Anita", I said and entered the apartment. Ratish stood silently behind and watched me go inside. Perhaps he was unaffected or he was just accommodating the emotions evoked due to my affair with Zaida. I reached the room inside to see Naman, Jai and Anita sharing a beer. Another girl sat there. She was Naman's girlfriend Urvi. I entered the room with tears in my eyes which yet hadn't dried. I looked at everybody and watching my face, their jovial faces turned serious. "Hey Uday, have a beer", invited Naman, asking me to join. I sat in the corner straight in front of Anita. The alcoholic massacre of the previous day was still hanging on to me, but drinking just to be with Anita felt fair. I sipped the beer, and she kept silent. She spoke to others but not a word to me. Her silence kept killing me. Soon Urvi and Naman got cuddly as they got drunk. Naman dragged Urvi to the other bedroom and closed the door. Jai, Anita and I sat together in an awkward silence. Ratish was playing games outside with his beer. Jai left to play with Ratish.

I reached out for Anita, and held her hand. "I am sorry *Jaan*, I am sorry, I am sorry, please forgive me", I begged. Hot tears dwelled up in her eyes. She clenched her teeth and mumbled angrily, "Don't touch me Uday. I hate you. I can never forgive you. I did everything for you, and you cheated on me", she cried. "Please forgive me; I never realized that I would end up making you feel like this. I am sorry, please give me one last chance", I cried back. I grabbed her and started crying; Anita stayed cold for a while till she held me and cried. We kept crying together. "I love you Nitu, I can't live without you", I mumbled on her neck and kissed it. "Why did you do this Uday?" she continued wailing. "I love you, I am sorry, please forgive me", I said, fighting my tears. "I loved you and you cheated on me", she accused.

I rubbed her back trying to console her. Her touch induced a peaceful tranquility in my anguish, I felt even more regretful for my foolishness in seeking out to find 'love', when it was dawning on me all while. And now even the thought of separation from Anita was too painful. It felt like I was missing an integral piece of my system.

I held her face in my palms and looked at her. I kiss her on the lips, still mumbling "Sorry", between the kisses. She kissed me back. I couldn't stop the urge to kiss her. The kisses fueled by the trauma and beer were very seductive. I inserted my tongue inside Anita's mouth and she sucked on it. I rushed quickly to the door of the room and closed it bolting it from the inside. I rushed back to Anita, and grabbed her waist while I rolled my tongue back into my mouth. I pushed her on the bed and I pounced on her. The kisses grew intense, as she held my body and continued kissing me. My hands raced inside her clothes and soon removed her top. Anita pulled my t-shirt off. Our bare bodies were touching each other. I moved to her upper torso, licking and kissing every bit of her. The noon had turned into dusk, and Anita and I stayed topless, still adoring the fondness for each other. In a brief moment of pause, she looked into my eyes and then pushed me away. "What happened *Jaan*?" I asked softly. "I can't be with you", she said coldly. "You still hate me, I know but I am sorry", I retorted and cribbed. Anita took a deep breath and said, "I don't hate you Uday and neither do I love you. Hate is not the opposite of love, indifference is", she said and paused for a long while. "I don't feel anything for you Uday. You cheated on me with those bitches", she said in a warm but firm tone. "Please don't be like this. I am seriously sorry Nitu", I said in shock.

Suddenly a big bang happened on the other side of the door. "Who's it?" I asked. "Uday, I don't want you to lock the door", screamed Ratish. "Yeah, okay, I would open it in a while", I answered with annoyance. "No, open it now", ordered Ratish. I wondered what had gone wrong with him. Anita wore back her clothes, while Ratish kept banging on the door. The constant banging irritated me as it was intruding the 'time' I so badly needed to spend with Anita. I rushed to open the door, and as soon as I opened it, I screamed, "What is your fucking problem Ratish?"

A punch was already waiting for me as I opened the door. Ratish landed a heavy punch on my face. I remained stunned, intimidated by the sudden blow. He charged up on me like a wild bull, pushing me to the wall while I lost balance on the way, tripped and fell. He descended on me, perhaps with an intention of pinning me to the floor and pounding my face. A sudden pang of anger ran into me as he pounced on me. In self-defense, I blocked him by my legs and like an eject button threw him to the other end of the room. Naman, Jai and Urvi entered the room. Naman held me while Jai held Ratish. Anita kept crying, watching Ratish and me fight.

Ratish hurled abuses, but said nothing about Zaida. But Anita and I knew why he was upset. I was fuming with anger caused by the punch which I had just received. I picked my bag and screamed, "Anita, let's go." She kept quiet and cried. I screamed again, "Anita let's go from here." She kept crying and mumbled, "I will stay here with Urvi." Urvi got the hint and told all the guys to leave the room and locked the door. Ratish still looked at me with anger but he didn't charge. I felt the pain of isolation; I knew I wasn't wanted there anymore. I was disowned by my love and my friend for my sinful indulgences. I slowly walked on the road with no destination. The outcast which I had become, had nowhere to go and no one to be with.

I hum the memories and chum out all the remorse and regret out of my being.
It's in these moments you cry out for all those who cried with you.
And in these moments you feel the pain which you caused.

Perhaps this is the way the Universe functions. The vicious cycle of 'karma', building up slowly towards your 'irony', where deeds are justified, and 'time' remains the only master. Your fate doesn't rest anymore within your control and neither in your wits.

Like nature when females chum, they end a cycle, and remove everything that was there but now, isn't needed. It's like the moment when sand castles of pride and greed mix into ashes and you can't differentiate the blend. What just stays back is a drop of tear and that was the 'love', that was my heart and I broke it out of sheer gluttony.

ON A BAD BOY NOTE

Here I am 'chumming' now, removing that day which
changed my fate and cracked my conscience.

I don't know why everybody chums in shame but I know that I am
ashamed too; so ashamed of myself that I don't feel shame anymore.
I hum to my fondness of Anita and I hum to the innocence of Rita. I hum
to the submission of Zaida and for the friend whom I cheated.

'Chumming' and 'Humming' that day,
Which just left shades of gray,
Graying my life for all these years,
Praying away for that only tear.

Maybe today also I stand here at that place, thinking about the memory
of the day I so badly want to redeem; the very day when I broke my
sweetheart's heart, along with the other girls who were so nice to me. Sadly,
even after many years, I feel that I had just broken my heart that day.

ANSH SETH

LET ME BREAK SOME HEART

Let me break some heart,
And let that heart be mine,
Dwelling in your thoughts,
And just with that I am fine....

With your gaze piercing so sharp,
Is just the end of the start,
As my sins left me tainted,
So just let me break some heart.....

The tragedy of the eyes,
Is that they cannot lie,
And they show the broken pieces,
Of your heart wrapped in your silky fleeces...

So let me break some heart,
And let that heart be mine,
As after breaking you my love,
No magic can make me fine....

This is how a heart breaks,
With dreamy memories still entwined,
But just let me break one heart,
And let that heart be mine....

CHAPTER 7
A SHADE CALLED GRAY

As I was driving back from the school building which still safely keeps the memories of the day when I broke Anita's heart…, and memories of those days kept re running in my head like fast moving images. "Anita, I so miss you", I mumble as I drive. The feeling of having everything and nothing at the same time leaves a hollow void. Sometimes so hollow, that it doesn't allow any other feeling to nurture up.

The success in my professional front seems hollow but it was the thing once upon a time I so badly wanted and now that I have it, it still feels so empty. The job, car, salary and my swanky lifestyle doesn't give me that happiness which being with Anita gave.

The noon had turned into an evening with gray clouds overcasting the city of *Pune*, giving clues of a heavy downpour coming ahead. People on the road appeared to be packing up for the day and rushing back to their homes. I switched off the air conditioner of the car and opened the window. A gush of heavy wind blew inside the car shaking me out of my sadness and guilt. It brought a smile back making me feel the unleashed weather outside, somewhere unleashing me again to touch the madness which can kick out all my sadness. I felt the instincts of love again especially in such a weather.

I unlock my cellphone and open my *WhatsApp*[90] to check on my cold girlfriend. Tanya had changed her display pic. It was a black and white photograph where her hair covered almost half of her face. She wore her cruel sexy smile with her face tilted, highlighting her sharp jawline.

---

[90]   *WhatsApp: Mr. Zuckerberg recently bought it.*

I check her status which read, "The color of human beings is gray. The degree of coloration depends on the situation and the characteristics."

I smile to the similarity in her status and my passing day. Both colored in the shades of gray. Even the situations and characteristics of my surrounding and my thoughts are all blended in the color. "What a color of my life!" I crib about the loneliness 'gray' brings back to my present moment. The idea of living the darkening weather with someone as cruel as her is still appealing. I text Tanya, "Hey, the weather is awesome out here. So wanna be with you!" I kept driving and after a while a message popped in from her, it was just a smiley. "Would you like to come to *Pune* tomorrow in the morning? You can take a bus from *Mumbai*. It will hardly take two hours", I text. "Not possible", she replies. Her replies are also as miserly as her, spending the least possible words. I guess being a *Sindhi*[91] it comes naturally to her. "Come on Tanya, it would be fun, it's super awesome. Moreover it is the weekend", I reply insisting her to change her mind. "Won't be able to come Uday", she replies. Her blunt 'no' did drive a primitive instinct of male ego which pushed the feeling to a higher notch to be with her. The 'blood' which is difficult to get has a different taste.

"Then I will come to *Mumbai*. We can catch up tomorrow", I text hoping to taste her tomorrow. "I have a family get together. I am sorry I won't be able to meet you", she replies increasing the loneliness of the weather for me. I curse her family and my life. The bloody urge for another human as long as not tasted, doesn't exist… but if tasted, it drives a craving of a different level, to just to be there with someone.

"Thank god, I am not in love with her", I say, still breathing the wind blowing on my face. "She has all the potential to fuck my peace", I mumble. But the suppressed 'urge' resulted in a surge of effect and I text her, "Why suddenly shades of gray, missing your dear ex or what?" I couldn't help being sarcastic. She texted back, "Nothing like that." Her responses were colder than herself.

---

[91]   *People of Sindh (Present-day Pakistan); who migrated to India after partition.*

Sometimes life can increase the extreme rarity of feelings to such an extent that I am even happy with her coldness. In fact hate is better than indifference. Hate can only be possible, if there was 'love' which went bad. Even an ounce of it would do. But indifference is an altogether lack of feelings.

I again visit the palace of my memories and try to relive the hatred bestowed on me by the people I loved and the shame, for the fact that it was caused by me.

"Anita was so right", I think as I drive in the graying day with her words still echoing inside me. I remember how badly I kept chasing her to take me back after she came to know what shit I had done. I was trying so hard just to confirm whether or not she still loves me.

Thoughts of Anita still feel too painful, something very difficult for me to face. So I deviate my thoughts, trying to concentrate on the gray.

> Gray, the color which happens when black meets white, and as they mix,
> White diffuses in the presence of black,
> While black fills up the entire void between the molecules of white.
> Finally the molecules of white slowly extinguish in the darkness of black,
> And black wins the fusion of the war between the two extreme ends of colors.
> When the war is over, black feels that it has 'won it all' and
> it peacefully rests in its endless 'darkness',
> But the dead corpses of light sing, that at some point of 'time' white existed here...
> And at that very moment, to the eye of an apparent observer it looks gray.

> Gray – the color which signifies the end of a fusion.
> Where white ends in black and changes it forever to a gloomy dull gray.
> The color of the fusion of nature.
> In the nature which is so full of opposites,
> Like night and day,
> Good and bad,
> Light and dark,
> And thus black and white.

Mother Nature could be so tricky.
She designed boys to go ahead and search their mate and the only way
she could hook them up was by letting the boy taste 'blood'.
The motherly nature is so sure that no boy would be able to forget
the 'blood' he tasted and defy the urge to taste it again.
We are humans, very perceptive beings designed to go to
the other end just for the sake of our curiosity.
I smiled at the phenomena of addiction so prevalent in something so pure called 'love'.
The fact that humans will keep trying to find it no matter how painful it gets
and this phenomenon is no less than an addiction in its own nature.

The journey to black from white is something like that... White
might reach black but it will never come back as white,
It will always remain gray,
Unless and until one day,
White pushes in with all its might and removes black.

A thunder roars in the skies and electrifying streaks of lightening pass the gray clouds. I feel as if the 'white' heaven has waged a war on the graying clouds asking me to see what I always ignored; the grayish deeds of my life and I start drifting again in the memory lane.

After I was caught indulging with different girls while holding my commitment to Anita, I became the despised kid of the class. Anita thoroughly ignored me while her friendship with others tremendously grew. Zaida stopped coming to college for quite a while. I could understand the shame and guilt she carried and I knew her innocence as well. I guess she just turned gray too as she was my only true partner in crime. Ratish too despised me but in the conduct of boys, showing hatred is considered a sign of weakness. I guess that's why he remained cordial with me, with empty smiles and words.

Rita did message me but her messages were the ones with hatred and despise. "Checked your girlfriend, she is good to clean your drawers", she texted. "Mind your tongue Rita, don't talk about Anita like that", I replied angrily as I sat in the classroom four benches behind Anita waiting for her to just give me a glance and I can look back at her with all the affection I have.

The tiny awesome dreams which Anita and I saw together kept re-running in my head. Crying didn't come naturally to me as the lessons of the boarding school still held its value more deeply engraved in my system.

For someone as clueless as me in their college days, often the roadmap of life is just a big thick dense cloud, perhaps grayish in color. The only road in my clouded future was paved with the tiny dreams which Anita shared with me and I kept imagining them. In her dreams I would see various colors, the colors of happiness and childish fantasies.

Like the brilliant colors of the big cars and bikes which Anita and I fantasized about owning and riding. Like the shades of the colors with which she wanted to paint our house with. All in all, those were the only colors of the only dream of my clouded confused life. I didn't know what I wanted to be, or where I wanted to stay. Whether I should do an MBA or pursue an MS for a doctorate degree. All I knew was being with Anita and every aspect of life she imagined with me. I never knew then how I would achieve those imaginations, but I just happily lived in those shades basking in her presence and my only direction.

Her dreams had mysterious colors, vague and beautiful. When I shared her dreams I often traveled deep within them. I realized that her dreams were so enchanting that I could never leave, not even now after so many years.

The colors of life are very vivid; very endless when it comes to imagination. I was walking mesmerized in the journey of dreamy fantasies, watching the endless shades of people. People whom I loved to be with, and with whom I wanted to share myself and my dreams. The thought fascinated me, making me curious to know someone's dream as I had no dreams of my own, just plain needs.

The 'curiosity' gave birth to an urge. The 'urge' to eventually know their dreams inculcated into a habit of painting their lives with the colors of their own dreams, as it had a promising fulfillment for my life of directionless needs and wants. I so wanted to paint Anita's dreams in and around her but my curiosity had no more innocence left in it.

Tainted with shame, I sat in the class room looking at Anita, watching her slowly distance from me, into a happier world.

Anita sat in the classroom and took notes in her journal. Somehow her sincerity in taking notes was very infectious. She was dressed up in a white tee and denims. She loved shoes and that too the sporty types with bright brilliant colors and fancy brand logos. Watching her sit, and attentively take notes, I felt the biggest alter realization of my life – the realization of a break up. I looked at my notebook and I realized that I was trying to draw her face for the major part of the entire lecture.

With the passing week since the breakup, Anita got better day by day while I got worse. The creeping reality of the world was harshly encroaching in my dreamy colorful connect with the girl I actually loved. The reality was simple, my girlfriend broke up with me, and now she will have someone else. The 'dark dream' was coming to life. I often thought about the dream and its glimpses returned bringing my worst fear alive. I cursed myself for indulging in other females, despite the dream which later appeared more like a warning from the universe. "What if she finds another guy and replaces me with him in her colorful dreams which she always shared with me?" I often thought as days passed by.

The thought of losing her often shook my ground as if there was nothing more left to imagine. The thoughts resulted into a dreadful nature of emptiness which cleared up my head, leaving nothing behind. Thoughts went blank and the leftover imaginations appeared hollow just like a torn painting. The various dreams and fantasies I had imagined with Anita, had just me missing in them.

The coaching classes in *Pune* ended. All of us were back to *Mumbai* attending college in the final year. Soon the graduation board examinations were going to commence to define our destinies. The fear of failing in the boards had much lesser impact on me than my break up with Anita. I still kept sitting in the classrooms always behind her, locking her in my gaze. The place on the bench next to her which was always reserved for me was now open to anybody and everybody other than me. Most days after college, I would walk behind Anita following her to her bus stop hoping to have a conversation. She would happily ignore me and continue with her girlfriends. On one such day as I was walking behind her as she walked chatting with her friends. I saw her turn back and look at me. A gush of her infamous anger ran up her nostrils and they flared as she walked towards me. The look on the face of the girls was something I was familiar with, it's the same look with which people look at the despised one, the 'ugly one' or the outcast.

Anita walked angrily towards me and yelled, "Why the fuck are you following me?" "Nothing, I just wanted to ensure that you board the bus safely", I answered in a low voice. "Stop bullshitting with me. I know you just wanna check if I am with another guy", she hissed. The mention of the idea of dating another guy brought back the horrors of the 'dark dream' which I so badly wanted to forget. "Please don't say that *Jaan*", I said almost cranky. The word '*Jaan*' did mellow her anger and the fiery look in her eyes. I guess it brought back some old untainted memories.

"Stop it Uday, you cheated on me with those stupid bitches!" she said firmly. "I am sorry, I was stupid. Please forgive me and take me back", I begged. "That's not happening Uday, you broke my trust", she said with the heat boiling in her eyes. "I am sorry", I pleaded. "Just leave me alone and go home. Study for the boards", she said coldly and turned to walk back. The people passing by looked at us with an insinuated interest. The look of mockery in their faces triggered a fit of rage in me. I instantly reached for her arm and grabbed it pulling her back. "Don't walk away on my face Anita", I trembled with anger. "Leave my hand", she said with an equal rage. "I am apologizing to you for the past three months now since *Pune*. And all you do is just walk away and ignore me", I ranted angrily. She twisted her arm and pulled it out of my grip. I was back again to awe, mesmerized with the display of her strength. "I swear all the shit I had with all those females is over. Please believe me", I said going back to begging again. "I never asked you to stop it. You are most welcome to go back", she said rudely. "I don't want to go back to them. I just wanna be with you and no one else", I insisted. "Listen Uday, what I had for you broke that day in *Pune*, when I saw those messages on your cellphone. I trusted you a lot and you broke it big time. There is no way it can come back. So stop wasting your time on me and study for your boards. All the teachers say that you have very low chances to even pass", she said firmly. "Fuck the teachers and fuck the boards! I don't care if I pass or not. I just wanna be with you", I said in anguish. "Sorry, that can't happen Uday. Please get a grip on yourself. Have some self-respect", she said firmly and turned around to walk. I called her name, "Anita wait, don't go please. Listen, once, please." I kept calling her and she continued walking to her bus stop.

When I was happily indulging with the other girls the thing called 'self-respect' never occurred. It was all just a sinful pleasure which stroked my ego which was already inflated because of Anita. Now that she pointed out to me to have some 'self-respect', it again fell on a wrong point. I felt humiliated as I walked to the railway station from where I took my train to go back home. I smoked a cigarette walking on the road to the station. "Shit how much have I started smoking, since *Pune*?" I regretfully asked myself and continued walking.

I reached home and my mother served me a lavish lunch. "Uday, have the chicken. I learnt this recipe on the cookery show on the television", said my excited mother. I nodded sadly and continued eating. "What happened Uday, you look so upset these days? You are not eating; you are listening to those sad songs all the time. You are not even on the phone these days?" asked my mother affectionately. "I am fine *Ma*", I said avoiding eye contact with her. "Is everything fine between you and Anita?" she asked. I tried hard to hide the misery and said, "Its fine *Ma*." I was surprised at the fact that mothers are such enlightened beings. She really doesn't need to ask to know the state of her child. But still, I couldn't share my problems with her as they would just add up to her tensions. The fact that she knew that Anita and I were dating was still a shock to me. "You know *Papa* and I often wonder how Anita and your kids would look like", she giggled. I looked up at her in astonishment. "Be nice to her Uday. I really like that girl. She is gorgeous, intelligent and hardworking. Most of all, what I really like about her is that she is an honest girl. She takes such good care of you. In spite of your terrible marks in your exams, if it wasn't for her, you wouldn't have even passed", she said completing her feelings for Anita which pushed me deeper in regret. "When is she coming home again?" asked my mother. I couldn't tell her the current scenario with Anita especially for the reason of its occurrence. It will directly lead to a series of questions which would just make her feel pathetic about her son. The fact that my mother could come to know of my indulgences was dreadful. The rule of the boarding school was to keep a guy's relationship problems to himself. It was critical for a peaceful life with lesser intervention from parents, so that one can live the wild fun which college offered. The survival lesson from school, still ruled.

I finished my lunch and went straight to my computer system to play a game. Somehow computer games diverted my attention from the misery caused because of the games I had played in my life. The game was my favorite first person stealth kill fest called "*Hitman*[92]", where a bald, well suited assassin killed enemies and hid their bodies. I was often inspired to play like him in my life too as I hopped from one girl to the next, covering my tracks as no girl would ever find about each other. But it was extremely difficult to kill the entire army of the *Colombian* drug lord and despite my repeated efforts to cross the level, I kept on dying in the game. Maybe I was dead in the game of my life too.

I shut off the game in frustration and sat looking at the computer screen flipping through photographs of Anita and me, while I thought about what my mother said. A chat window opened on my computer screen. It was from my boarding school best buddy Bose.

"Hey loser, how are you?" he pinged.

"I am fine *DK Bose*, how are you?" I asked.

"Life is awesome, just got into a relationship with a very 'hot' female", he replied.

"Wow, really, where in *Calcutta*[93]?" I replied.

"Yes nerd, in my dear *Kolkata*[94]", he replied.

---

[92]   *Play it and see.*

[93]   *The Capital of West Bengal (A state in India)...*

[94]   *Now called 'Kolkata'.*

"Is she a *Bong*[95]?" I asked.

"Yes she is a sultry *Bengali*[96] 'bomb'", he replied.

"I am happy for you buddy, *Bong* away to glory!" I replied.

"Did you get laid, you shag master?" he pinged.

"It's been five years since boarding school ended *Bose DK*. I have a girlfriend now", I replied. The reply felt like a lie to me. So I pinged, "And she just broke up with me."

"Why? What did you do?" he pinged.

"I cheated on her", I replied.

"Hope it's with another girl", he pinged.

"Of course Mr. *Bose DK*. Rather two girls", I replied.

"Oh yes, Uday Singh – the shag master now has three chicks", he teased.

"Stop teasing Bose, I feel miserable without her", I replied.

"Don't be sad Uday, what does she say?" he asked.

"She is not talking to me properly, not answering my calls, not replying to my messages. Even ignores me in class", I replied.

"Relax buddy, girls are like that", he replied.

"Like what?" I asked.

"The more you run after them the more they run away", he replied.

---

95   *Bong is a short form for Bengalis.*
96   *People of Bengal are called Bengalis.*

"So what should I do, stop chasing her?" I asked.

"Exactly", he replied.

"I am not able to live without her", I pinged.

"See, it's called 'chumming'. Girls do that all the time. You should just let her be. I suggest you go out and sit on the road, and light a cigarette, and walk out of yourself and then look at yourself again", he replied.

"Alright, then", I asked.

"Then you will know what to do, what is important to you and then do that", he replied.

"Ok, I will try that", I replied.

"Are you in touch with anyone from school?" he pinged.

"Bose you won't believe but I found Fatima on *Orkut*[97]", I replied excitedly going back to school memories.

"That nerdy girl from school who wore thick soda glass spectacles; in fact the first girl you ever gave chocolates to?" he pinged.

"You won't believe man but she has turned out to be so 'hot' and beautiful", I pinged.

"Really?" he replied.

"Yeah, she is in *Canada* and studying medicine", I pinged.

"Do you remember the story we read in our tenth grade; *Love across the Salt Desert*[98]?" pinged Bose.

---

[97]   *Orkut: Predecessor of FaceBook... R.I.P.*
[98]   *A story resting in the Rann of Kutch by K.N. Daruwalla.*

"About Najab and Fatima and how Najab crossed the salt desert of the *Rann of Kutch* to go meet his lover in *Pakistan*", I replied.

"Yeah, and our dear Uday crossed the hills in *Mussoorie*[99] to give chocolates to Fatima", teased Bose.

"Man; I miss those days", I replied, getting nostalgic.

"Me too man, come down to *Calcutta* someday, we will have fun", he replied.

We exchanged our goodbyes and I left for an evening walk. I walked to the *tapri*, bought a cigarette and sat smoking on the pavement of a lesser traveled road in my vicinity.

"What am I doing?" I thought. "Why am I being so desperate for Anita?" I reasoned. "I have anyways screwed it up, no matter how much I want her she would never take me back", I murmured to myself. "Anyways she has no dearth of options. She is all model material, all guys anyway dig her, plus she is so cool!" I mumbled. And as the cigarette finished itself, the gray smoke lightened up my head from the craving for Anita to accepting her loss. Though I felt like crying, but the smoke held back the tears which boiled up to an impulsive rage driving me to do something extreme.

The separation from Anita was killing me throughout college. Though I was guilty, but the hues of guilt were easily overshadowed by love. The 'love' with which Anita still looked at me in class and I felt as if it was diminishing in her eyes, slowly and slowly, day by day.

In her anguish, I didn't know how the day was turning into night and how nights turned into days. Every moment was just loaded with the anxiousness to be with her. I was not able to tolerate anybody, not even myself. Food did not taste as it should, despite the efforts of my mother to make it tastier. All I could do was listen to sad songs and regret. The

---

[99]   *A hill station in the state of Uttarakhand in India. Popular for the Winter Line seen only in Switzerland and Mussoorie.*

gray smoke did drive a need to 'get back' and in Anita's words, 'to get a grip on myself'. The only thing which could push me to be alive again was an extremity. A state which could cause a change in my head, and I kept pondering to do something which could help.

Finally an idea dawned and I walked to the nearby barber and sat down on his chair. "You want a haircut?" he asked. "Can you shave off my head?" I asked him angrily. "You want to shave off your hair?" he asked with mild astonishment. "Yes", I nodded. "Do you want me to use a razor or should I use a machine?" he confirmed. "I don't know, which one do you suggest?" I asked disinterestedly. "A razor will make you look like a boiled egg, while the machine will leave a millimeter long hairy carpet", he answered poetically. His description obviously discouraged me from using a razor and I opted for the machine. In a while I saw my black and spiky hair fall off in the mirror as the dark trimming machine traveled my head, chopping everything in its way. Perhaps I needed to do the same with my life.

I looked different to myself as if someone new. I stood up from the chair looking in the mirror. For a while I resembled a football player and it brought back a smile thinking about how Anita adored footballers. Football had kept me lean and I happily trotted back home feeling different as if I shed off my regret and anguish with my hair. My parents were shocked to see my new hairstyle. "What did you do?" asked my mother with 'wide open eyes'. "Just, felt like getting a haircut", I answered like a good son. My father laughed at my new hairstyle and said, "It's fine. Uday you remind me of my NCC[100] days now." "He is looking like a Buddhist to me", chuckled my mother recovering from the shock. My father patted my shoulders and asked me to take a shower and I obeyed happily for the encouragement.

The next day I wore my favorite white T-shirt to college. I was late for the lecture as it had already started. I stood at the door of the classroom and said, "May I come in ma'am?" The teacher looked up along with the class who turned back to see. There was a buzz amongst the students and I heard faint muffled laughter, as I just looked for Anita. She was

---

[100]   *National Cadet Corps.*

sitting on the corner of the first bench. She turned and looked at me and made a funny face, while I stayed expressionless. I took my seat on the last row and the lecture continued. A message pops in my cellphone, it was from Anita. It read, "You are looking 'hot' with a bald head." I felt amused thinking the fact that I just let her go last night and suddenly she finds me 'hot'. "Or my bald self is really sexy", an alter thought told me. "Thanks", I replied to her. The practicals were scheduled post lunch and we joined in the lab after the break.

I was glad that Bose's formula worked. I never knew it was so simple. Just 'don't want' her and she is yours. Well the sudden shock was not just limited to Anita. In the lab, the teachers guided us to an experiment on food microbiology. The experiment was to prepare a *French* fermented pickle called the '*Sauerkraut*[101]'. Anita was happily chirping, displaying her talents of cooking and her knowledge of soups and salads while I wandered around the huddling students watching Anita cut the cabbage into fine shreds. I stumbled upon Poonam. She looked at me and smiled. I said a friendly, "Hey", standing beside her and looking at the experiment. "Did you just smoke and come?" she asked. "Why, am I smelling of smoke or what?" I asked her feeling embarrassed. "A lot", she said inhaling in the odor. "I am sure you don't like the smell", I commented. "Actually mixed with your perfume, it smells good", she smiled. "Really, as in how?" I asked her in surprise. "It's kinda nice, as in manly", she said trying hard to explain. "Is it sexy?" I asked her with a sly grin. Poonam blushed and looked down. She looked up at me again and said, "Kind of." I grinned within now.

Poonam sat down on her chair and I sat next to her. "So how are the preparations for the boards going on?" I asked. "It's good", she answered. "I am sure you will be a topper", I said looking in her eyes. Her big fair asymmetrical nose turned a little pink. "Come on, why everybody says that?" she said breaking into laughter. "Of course, you study so much, you are a teachers' pet, etc. etc.", I chuckled. Poonam tapped me with her knee under the table. I looked at her as she smiled flirtatiously. "It begins with the touch", I thought and tapped her back, with my knee. The tapping game continued till my leg and hers just stayed touching

---

[101] *Fermented Cabbage Pickle.*

each other under the table. "You never had a boyfriend?" I asked her. "Ahem ahem, look who is asking!" she said flirtatiously. "What's wrong with me asking?" I asked dryly. "You are already with Anita", she said with a 'hard to get' smile. "Yes I am, but I am not asking you out. I am just asking if you ever had a boyfriend", I clarified.

Poonam looked at me silently as if she was trying to judge whether or not she should answer my question. "There was this guy I really liked. He is in college but in a different department. Then one day he asked me out, and we went on a date", she narrated. I was happy for her judgment and excited to know her story. "Then what happened?" I asked excitedly. "That's it, we never went on a date again", she concluded with a smile. "Are you that bad that he never met you again?" I chuckled. "Just, I didn't feel anything. So let it be Uday", she said with a straight face. I felt the need to change the topic to avoid any chance of making her uncomfortable. The curiosity to know what happened on her date was still poking my tongue and I blurted out another question, "What do you like in a guy?" She looked at me and tried answering, "Looks are fine. What I really look for is stability." "Stable as in he has a job and all that", I added. "Much more than a job, someone who can take care of stuff", she said confidently. "So you mean someone rich", I added. "Yes kind of", she gave a sly smile. "How rich?" I asked excitedly. "You make me sound like a 'gold digger'", she answered with a confused grin. "It's nothing like that", I quickly added. "It's like most girls want the same things but few are honest enough to admit it. You are an honest person", I completed and just rubbed my leg against hers.

"How is Aunty?" I asked her. "You know your mother is really sweet", I smiled. "She is fine. I guess my mom really likes you", she smiled back. "Really?" I asked astonished. "Yes, she feels you are a little lost but she says you are a nice boy", she explained with admiration. "I remember the last time I met Aunty in college. She was so hilarious", I smiled flirtatiously. "And she also said you should quit smoking", she added sternly. My fingers ran on the blue denims hugging her thighs and I leaned in closer to her and whispered in her ears. "You shouldn't talk to Aunty about guys like me. A good girl doesn't talk about a 'bad boy' to her mother", I said reiterating my point as I openly flirted with Poonam. She looked at me and smiled and looked down again.

The students continued the experiment while Poonam and I sat in the corner of a big granite lab table. Being gorgeous, I guess no one approached her especially after the three years of graduation where she had made the point very clear to all the guys checking her out that she wasn't easy to get. As for me, I had just turned into an outcast with a tarnished reputation for cheating on my girlfriend with my friend's ex-girlfriend, ending up with the definite impression of a scumbag. In short, I had nothing to lose.

Anita looked around as she was done shredding the cabbage and looked back at me hustling with Poonam in the corner. My eyes met hers but I chose to ignore Anita and focused back on Poonam. The teachers asked each one of us to take our flasks and the cabbage sample to begin the experiment. Ratish looked at Poonam and me talking and he rushed in trying to talk to her. My conversation with Poonam was interrupted and I cursed Ratish for poking his nose but my 'guilt' of dating Zaida came back and I left for my table to complete the experiment. Poonam left Ratish and rushed to get her flask while I smiled silently looking at both of them. I guess scoring good grades was still was a higher priority to her, than enjoying my bald and smoking outcast 'bad boy' company, who was silently cuddling up with her to get out her secrets or rather Ratish with his open crush on her. Anita gave me a weird look as she took a seat on her table in the lab. I tried hard to figure out the meaning of her look, which I couldn't. My partner for the experiment was absent and thus I sat alone on my place with my flask and sample.

The experiment started off and I tried doing it on my own till I lost track of the instructions and just passed my time away. I saw pieces of paper which were used to autoclave the pipettes. They were dry and wilted; something I could pretty much relate to – its drained and bored state. I passed that paper over the flames of the burner and it quickly caught fire. I threw the lit paper on the floor and quickly stubbed out the fire. The burning paper did give me a temporary excitement and I felt the urge to repeat the experiment. I guess dry paper and bored people are alike and they are highly inflammable.

I repeated my experiment with another autoclaved paper and it caught a fire of a much wilder nature. To avoid people's attention I threw the burning paper in the dustbin and looked in it. The green plastic dustbin had a lot more autoclaved paper trashed in it and they caught fire. The thought of losing my valuable cabbage sample for the sauerkraut preparation quickly subsided beneath the rising flames in the dustbin. I panicked and threw the cabbage sample I was stirring for the last fifteen minutes in the bin to extinguish out the fire. The fire just continued to spread from paper to paper. I rushed to the sink and filled in water in the flask and quickly splashed it in the dustbin. I repeated it twice till the flames were extinguished and heavy dense fumes were coming out of it, visible to everyone in the lab.

The peon came rushing towards my table while I ensured that the fire is out. "What happened?" he asked me. "There were fumes coming out of the dustbin. I saw and ran quickly to put it out", I hurriedly explained, lying outright about the cause of fire. The teacher in charge for the experiment also rushed in, "What happened here?" she asked in panic. "There were fumes coming out of the dustbin. Guess it caught fire, I was just putting it out", I said re practicing my lie. "How did it begin?" asked the teacher. "I don't know", I said making the utmost innocent face. "Are you sure Uday?" she asked looking at me suspiciously. I guess my reputation was as tarnished with teachers as it was with the students. A majority of students stopped their experiment and huddled around my table like the bored dry pieces of paper desperately waiting for something exciting to happen.

Though the peons took over the melted plastic dustbin and began investigating the cause of fire, Ratish asked me, "Did you set it on fire?" "Of course not fatso", I replied. "Don't lie Uday, I am sure you did it", he chuckled. "Uday leave the lab, you don't realize how serious this is. There are gas cylinders here in the lab. There are beakers containing ninety percent alcohol present on every table. Actually you don't even care to understand how serious this is! There could have been a major fire", screamed the teacher, sure that it was me who had set the fire. "Ma'am but I did not light it. I saw it and I was just putting it out", I said insisting on my innocence but was eventually turned out of the lab as no one was ready to believe me. I waited in the corridors. The peon came outside and called me, "Ragade madam wants to meet you." I felt a sudden fear to face the H.O.D and to prove my innocence to her, when

I was sure that she wasn't going to buy a single word out of my mouth. I entered her cabin, which to me looked more like a den. Mrs. Ragade was an aged lady with graying hair and a sharp face. She had gray eyes and fair skin. I always felt she would have been very 'hot' during her youth and an alter thought makes me realize now that even Tanya would turn out to be like her in the future.

Tiny white whiskers like hair covered the upper lip of Mrs. Ragade as she sat on her chair like a tigress draped in a blue *sari*. A sharp array of white predatory teeth showed up as she asked me, "Why did you set the lab on fire?" I looked surprised and said defensively, "I did not set anything on fire. In fact I was the one who was putting it out." "Come on Uday, you have been caught playing football in the locker room. You have been involved in numerous incidents of sleeping in the classroom and mischief in the lab. You disrespect teachers and all I have always heard about you is complaints. See if you are not serious about this course then go ahead and do something else. But please don't waste our time and resources", she said firmly, completing her long speech about my shortcomings and bad reputation. Her face remained disgusted while her eyes remained cold. I silently listened and thought, "Is it the bald look which is getting me into all this trouble? My mother said that I was looking like a Buddhist but here in the eyes of Mrs. Ragade I am pretty evil!"

"Ma'am I swear I was really putting out the fire. I mean I don't know about the other times but today I was just putting out the fire. I guess that's the irony that the one who puts out the fire is generally accused of setting it up", I completed my justification looking innocent. Mrs. Ragade smiled a minor affectionate smile. "Tell me one thing Uday, you claim to be innocent but why every time wherever a mischief occurs you are always present?" asked Mrs. Ragade with a motherly smile. "I guess it's just a coincidence or my luck is absolutely bad", I said looking at her sheepishly. "Well in that case go, I cannot prove if you caused the fire or not", she said like a predator who didn't get to kill. I thanked her and my stars and left from her cabin.

As soon as I came out the students waited anxiously for me including Ratish and Anita. "Someone amongst the students had set me up", I thought and faced everybody. "What happened in there?" asked an anxious Anita. "Nothing, I am safe", I said with a smile. Anita pulled me by my arm into the corner and asked me, "Did you light the fire?" I stayed silent for a moment and my solemn face broke into a sly grin. I said, "Yes but don't tell anyone. Someone complained and set me up." I held my muffled giggle. Anita looked at me and couldn't help laughing though I signaled her to keep it low.

The next lecture was about to begin in a while and Anita said, "Did you start studying for the boards Uday?" "Not much, I don't know where to start and where to end. It seems like a lot and even my notes aren't in place", I replied in confusion for the massive syllabus. "Come to the lecture, I will tell you how to prepare for it", she instructed and I walked with her. Her sudden concern for me brought me out of my insecurities and somehow all the madness began to make sense.

My crazy erratic behavior finally managed to get me Anita's attention and concerns but I wasn't quite satisfied with that. I was still intrigued with the fact that Poonam talks about me to her mother. "What if Poonam also likes me?" I wondered as I sat next to Anita in the classroom. Poonam entered the class with Gurdeep and sat on the bench just ahead of us.

I said a friendly "Hi", to them as they took their seats. Anita was definitely jealous and she started running me through her notes to keep my attention. I was mesmerized by the neatness of her beautiful handwriting as it often gave me a thought to write like her. But in spite of repeated efforts I could never match her handwriting. I tried to concentrate on the syllabus for the boards but I was easily distracted by Poonam's conversations and laughter. Anita observed my distractions and got angry. "If you don't want to know the syllabus and what to study for the boards then don't waste my time", she said rudely. "What? I am here listening to what you are saying!" I said in surprise. "Yeah right!" exclaimed Anita. "Come on Anita, don't fight with me unnecessarily", I protested. "Why don't you do one thing, ask your Poonam darling to explain you the syllabus", she hissed sarcastically. Her nostrils flared and I was floored watching her egoistic nature. "No Anita, I don't think anyone else can help me", I chuckled, which got her angrier and she punched me in my stomach. I gasped for breath but still laughed. Watching me laugh enraged her further and she gave a hard slap on my shoulders. "Ouch", I shrieked. Poonam and others looked behind at our bench. I smiled while Anita pretended as if nothing happened.

Within a month my bald hair grew back again into a short spiky hairstyle and the realization of being a senior in college slowly dawned. Anita and I began attending lectures together and the coziness grew back again. Though the formal breakup didn't change but Anita's behavior became friendlier. While I kept yearning to touch her in the classroom, at times she gave in and at times she resisted me, occasionally slapping my naughty hands. My concentration always stayed divided between the subjects being taught and my ultimate subject of interest and that was Anita.

It was just another day in college when Anita and I walked out of the lecture when a plump yet cute fair girl walked towards us. She interrupted us and asked me, "Hi are you Uday?" "Yes", I answered. "Hi I am Nutan", she said with a blushing smile. "Hi Nutan, do I know you?" I asked returning the smile. "No, I am your junior. Just wanted a few guidelines with what to do after my boards", she asked still blushing and trying hard to control her erupting smile. "Hey Nutan! Why are you worried about boards? It's a year later for you. I suggest you should have fun right now", I replied cheerfully. Anita walked ahead and turned back and returned a real 'dirty' look. I knew she was angry. Nutan kept blushing and I said, "I gotta go now Nutan, will catch you later." Nutan smiled, shook my hands again and said, "Bye."

I walked towards Anita with a cheerful smile. She wore a blue collared sleeveless with her favorite torn denims. Watching me cheerful and happy triggered a little envy in her. "Let's go", I said. "So did you guide her with the career alternatives after boards?" asked Anita with an obvious sarcasm. "Kind of, I told her to have fun for now. Boards for them is a year later", I answered ignoring her sarcasm. "Yeah right, Uday Singh who doesn't even know the syllabus for the board exams is now helping juniors make career choices", she said with a smug face. "Oh come on Anita, don't be jealous now", I chuckled. "Balls I am jealous of that fatso", she screamed defensively. "As she is fair", I added sarcastically. "Yeah fair and fat. Why don't you go lick her 'down there' in that case", ranted Anita angrily and began to walk faster. I laughed and ran behind her out of the college gate. "No, I can't lick her. It's gross, I am happy licking you", I flirtatiously laughed. My hands reached out to touch Anita again and she shrieked. "Uday it's the road and this touch of yours is very creepy", she said making a disgusting face. "Creepy? How?" I asked, still smirking. "It's like an insect walking on my arm", said Anita sarcastically. I reached out to touch her again. "Yuck Uday it's creepy", she yelled and shrugged. My hands didn't stop from creeping her out and she began to run.

I laughed and I ran behind her till we reached the coffee shop nearby. "You look like a lizard when you run with your bag", I chuckled. "And you look like a *langoor*[102], all the time", she mocked. We laughed together and sat next to each other at a table. "I will go and order a coffee for you", I said getting up. A hard slap hit my ass as I got up. I looked back and it was from Anita. She smiled and said, "You are my bitch!" I looked around at people and felt embarrassed as many people looked at us. I returned midway after checking out my wallet, before I ordered the coffee. "What happened Uday, are we not having coffee?" she asked making the cutest possible face. "Actually Nitu I thought you might like to have *Idli Sambhar*, I asked sheepishly. With the *Idli*[103] dipped in the *Sambhar*!" said Anita already tempted with the *South Indian* cuisine. "Yes, what do you suggest?" I asked her. "Let's go", she said happily. We left the coffee shop and went to the adjacent fast food vegetarian restaurant. Anita ordered for two plates of *Idli Sambhar*. The waiter got two bowls of hot steaming *Idlis* dipped in yellow brown *Sambhar*. Anita quickly started eating and I followed. Anita was a big foodie and she loved to eat anything and everything edible as long as it was served with hygiene and eloquence. I looked at her affectionately, as she hungrily ate her bowl and moved to mine.

"Hey are you going home after this?" I asked her as she continued chewing. "There are lectures to attend", she answered sarcastically. "I guess they will get cancelled. A couple of professors are absent", I said

---

[102] *White fur black face monkey found in the hilly terrains in India.*
[103] *A south Indian steamed cake of rice, usually served with Sambhar.*

positively hoping for the free day. Ratish came excitedly to the restaurant and ordered for his bowl of *Idli Sambhar*. "Fatso, are you not coming for the lectures?" Anita asked Ratish. "The lectures got cancelled", he said enthusiastically. We finished our food and walked to the *tapri* for a smoke. Ratish had a few friends waiting for him and he joined them. "Let's go to your place and study", I asked Anita. "My mother is on leave today. So we cannot go there", she said with unease. "Then in that case, let's go to my place and study there", I suggested. "Don't you think it's too far Uday?" asked Anita. "It will just take forty five minutes by local train Anita", I answered, minimizing the effect of the distance. "Alright, then let's go", she agreed, after thinking for a moment.

We took a cab to the nearest railway station and took the train. After an hour Anita and I stood at my house door ringing the bell. My mother answered the door. "Hey Anita, I am so glad to see you after ages", welcomed my mother as she opened the door. "Hello Aunty", exclaimed Anita and quickly hugged my mother. "So what are you guys planning to do here?" asked my mother. "Nothing much *Ma*, the lectures got cancelled so we thought of studying here", I answered. "Alright, but before that have lunch", said my mother affectionately. "Come Anita, I have prepared some nice chicken, I am sure you will like it", she called serving the food. "Of course Aunty", said Anita cheerfully and we took our places on the dining table to eat.

I felt happy watching my mother and Anita serve the food on the table. I was a little relieved from the trauma of separation watching my tall lean egoistic girlfriend gel up so well with my mother. "*Ma* wasn't wrong about imagining Anita and my kids", I thought as I ate. "Aunty the chicken is so yum!" announced Anita. "Thank you", replied my mother and blushed. Anita and my mother discussed recipes while I ate silently, happily watching them.

"I have to go for a movie with the neighborhood ladies", said my mother as we cleaned the table. "You guys study sincerely", directed my mother and she left after giving me instructions. We sat down at the dining table to study. "Anita, do you want to go inside and study?" I asked. Anita looked at me and I silently walked in. She eventually followed, and sat down on the bed. Anita began arranging my notes while I kept looking at her do it. She meticulously arranged photocopies of papers and books according to the subjects. Along with it she made a master paper in which she wrote topics and weightage in the examinations. I couldn't help falling for her again. My gaze remained stuck on her. She realized in a while that I am immobilized. She looked up at me and I saw a little moisture pool up in her eyes. "Don't look at me like that Uday", she said softly. I saw the same Anita whom I was dating, before that fateful day when I broke her heart. I didn't waste time in talking any further and crawled on the bed towards her face and kissed her. The touch of her lips after so many months surged a different feel. It was like the 'blood' whose taste was longed for ages and has finally come back. Anita grabbed my head and pulled me closer into her face till our teeth clattered against each other. My hands rushed to open up the buttons of her shirt. The evening outside called the clouds to darken our privacy and the latent sun which was slowly setting lost its brilliance. It was gray, providing the privacy in the room as Anita and I wrestled, clutching each other, feeding the 'crave' of the mate.

It's 'insecurity' which pushes two people closer in a physical bond. Anita had her insecurities regarding me and she fiercely kissed me flushing it from her system. My insecurity was still resting in the thoughts of the 'dark dream' where Anita had a different mate. The 'little warrior' too badly needed to feel safe in the realm of isolation. Anita was his only true mate and the insecurity drove the 'little warrior' to his safe cradle which was inside Anita.

She grabbed me, digging her nails mercilessly in my back till I expressed my pain in a loud moan. The frenzy caused by the separation moved the 'little warrior' deep within and I looked into her eyes. It was the same look which had always made me come alive. Suddenly, the look changed and went hollow and sad.

"What happened *Jaan*?" I murmured. "Nothing, just get done with it quickly", she blurted with indifference. Relationships are like beautiful objects of porcelain. To make one it takes a very fine concentrated effort till the clay takes shape from its semi solid form and then it is subjected to fire, which bonds the clay together forever. Then the porcelain vessel of 'love' is colored with various beautiful colors of dreams and fantasies seen together, and like that, a beautiful relationship is made. But at times, fools like me drop the beautiful porcelain relationships down on the harsh floor of perversions. And then, more often they break into small unworthy components. And at times, even if they don't break, they still incur the crack. And the crack continues to remind the sad downfall of the beautiful porcelain of a relationship.

My beautiful love story too, had a crack and Anita's sad empty eyes reminded me of it. I kept thrusting the drive of the insecure and needy 'little warrior', but the look in her eyes made me realize the 'irony'. The 'irony' of the crack – that it will always remain and no matter what I do, it will never heal back to the beautiful, colorful porcelain relationship it used to be.

Alas, the ironies of 'time' can never be reversed, as 'time' gone by shall never return. The 'little warrior' lost to his insecurity by an 'irony' that it shall always remain tainted with disloyalty and indulgence. The fact that the 'little warrior' was no more innocent and no matter how much he tried, he can never prove himself.

"Please say something, I am losing it", I said begging Anita to encourage me in any way. The realization of my deed lit up my conscious and the 'little warrior' retracted. The more he lost, the more the 'dark dream' grew, scaring my innermost core. I rushed in to kiss and like a ray of hope in the 'darkness', Anita sprang back to life clutching me to a faster movement till my 'little warrior' makes it. "Come on fast", she squealed and I took a breath of peace but hers remained empty. The 'little warrior' quenched his thirst but something was missing. I rushed to grab her and cuddle up. Anita stayed silent. "I love you *Jaan*", I whispered sadly.

Tears poured out of Anita's eyes. "What happened *Jaan*, why are you crying?" I pulled her face and wiped her tears. Anita kept crying silently. "Please tell me what happened, did I do something which upset you?" I asked in anguish. The 'little warrior' is cowardly and greedy too, as he rested lifeless hanging on my body.

"You broke my heart Uday. You cheated on me. I did everything for you", cried Anita and she kept on weeping. "I am sorry", I said feeling miserable. "Please forgive me", I mumbled. "I can't", cried Anita. "No matter how much I try, I can't. I would never be able to forgive you for this", she said in a cranky voice and silenced. Tears still trickled down her eyes. I desperately tried looking for the spark of our dreams in her eyes, but I saw nothing in the graying light coming in from the window.

Often painted in the thoughts of Anita, I kept dreaming her dreams wondering what beauty it would be to live them. But in that moment, when I looked inside her eyes I saw none of those dreamy colors, just the gray reflection of the dusky evening in her dark eyes.

The shade of gray often resembles the torn apart colorful dream, as if the 'life' went missing in those colors.

Gray was the color which was becoming my reality or perhaps the reality of everybody in my life. The dreadful color was even settling in the most colorful eyes I had ever seen and they were the mesmerizing brilliant eyes of Anita.

I felt unsettled and desperate, too scared to lose her dreams to my 'darker' ones. "You don't love me anymore?" I asked sadly. Anita remained silent. I was further petrified and desperately looked for an answer. "You hate me right, *Jaan?*" I probed. Anita turned towards me and looked into my eyes. She calmly repeated her dreadful phrase, "Uday, the opposite of love is not hate, it's indifference."

It took a moment for her words to sink in my mind, but the meaning of her phrase stayed for much longer. Perhaps indifference is the only feeling which I can deeply feel towards myself as I drive my car back to my apartment. It's the same feeling which Anita left behind for me and now Tanya has for me. The feeling of indifference, which also can safely be called the gray area of 'love' as there is no feeling in that emotion; representing an absent state between love and hate which neither 'love' nor 'hate' can touch.

Days passed and the emptiness in Anita's eyes still held its shade. Sometimes her eyes would elude me to believe that the love is gone but whenever I got closer to reassure my belief that it's gone, it would resurface again reminding me of the crack. The 'light' of my true love had turned gray forever and as a natural discourse I began to drift towards the dark.

Back in college, I often paved my way towards Poonam. At least having the prized possession was still an aspirable trophy. Poonam remained cordial and friendly in her own mysterious ways. One day, I went to her asking notes for a certain topic which I didn't have. "Hey I got a joke", she smiled. "What is it?" I asked. "Imagine a waterfall", she said with a smile. "Alright, I can imagine a waterfall with crystal clear blue water flowing down", I replied visualizing the falling waters. "Now, on a scale of one to ten, tell me the speed with which the water is falling?" she asked. "Nine", I said immediately. She laughed mildly at my answer and I looked at her with further confusion. "Why are you laughing?" I asked in surprise. She hesitated for a while and showed me the remaining message. It read, "The speed of the falling water is directly proportional to the sexual drive of the person taking the test. I laughed and asked her, "How much did you score?" "Seven", she answered in embarrassment. "Not bad", I grinned a naughty smile checking her out. Poonam looked at me with hesitation and her flirtatious face changed as she said, "I don't think your girlfriend would like it!" "What do you mean?" I asked in confusion. "I mean I don't think Anita likes me talking to you", she said bluntly. I couldn't bitch about Anita to Poonam since they were arch enemies. I accepted her hesitation and went back to my desk. The chance with Poonam was over though the speedy waterfall kept falling in my head making me imagine the forbidden. I looked at Anita who was happily chattering with a few guys from the class while I felt the restriction to communicate personally with any other chick.

The college festival was the last event of the year before the board examinations. A day was dedicated to wearing formals for the kids who always dressed up in casuals throughout the year. On that day Anita wore a red and golden *sari*[104] and heels. I wore my blue formal shirt and trousers. She met me in the corridors as I was always late. I saw her walking towards me and I felt as if my heart is already reaching out for her. "What have I done to deserve this angel?" I thought hard.

---

[104]   *An Indian dress for Women. Damn Hot!*

As if her grace was making me ask these questions to myself. She wore golden ornaments and the simple stud on her nose was replaced by a plain yet glittery golden ring. The dimples of her smile showed up as she recognized me. I felt like the ordinary boy badly looking out for her in the crowd. I also felt nervous watching the surge of affection in her eyes. "I am so scared to give in to her love, for a creepy thought that always says... what if one day she leaves me and I stay doomed in it forever?" I mumbled as I embraced her.

"You look gorgeous", I whispered and Anita stroked my hand and slowly entwined her fingers in mine. My fingers curled around hers like creepers grow into empty structures. "You don't look so bad either", she said slowly pulling me towards the auditorium. "Come, there is an orchestra event where our friends are performing", she said cheerfully. "So what? Let's go somewhere else", I said with lesser concern. "This is the last year of college", she emphasized as she walked towards the auditorium. "All this would end", I mumbled to myself. It was a hard realization seeping in; that my 'time' with Anita in the college is coming to an end. I didn't even know if we would again be studying together. "You smell good", whispered Anita in my ears, as we stood at the entrance gate of the auditorium and witnessed the orchestra perform.

The splendid evening went to a session of photography where like every year, we posed to click a lot of photographs. Anita often readjusted herself to make her unworthy boyfriend look taller in the photographs; like the dreamy version of ourselves, the way we saw it. I looked at her awestruck for this treatment. "Am I worthy of her?" I asked myself again.

'Worth' is a critical thing, like a mirror and often I looked in it trying to see beneath my shallow youthful appearance for the substance to match Anita. My 'little warrior' was also addicted, but had totally lost his innocence.

> *Like 'time', maybe even 'worth' is a gray thing; 'to each his own'.*
> *Like 'good times' and 'bad times', we keep struggling in its various*
> *perceptions trying to distinguish between our black and white...*
> *Even though gray is a single color!*

Anita 'stood out' in the crowd. It wasn't just about her body, it was in her aura. She rarely had an expression of malice: just trust, affection, sincerity and fun... and a little 'dirty love' which she shared with her shady boyfriend. The dirt was just visible to the outer world till I brought it within our relationship. But there is no point in brooding over something which I cannot change.

Love is also as much a part of 'habit', as is winning or losing. The comfort and security which love brings in the lives of people often makes it too comfortable for them to leave. Imagine the comforts of knowing another person in and out and letting yourself be as you are in this dangerous unpredictable world. The loop of love formed between two people keeps the biggest insecurities, guarded and protected. But why did it still feel that the colors in our loop of love are as enchanting as they always were?

I still felt a mild 'hope' that the loop might still not be grayed...

The boards exams commenced and they taught the biggest lesson of my life. 'Worth' and 'habit' go hand in hand, and that was the biggest mismatch with my orientation.

Though in my perception, I was worthy of the scores for the boards but Anita had never seen the hardworking side of mine. She was habituated to my shameless low self-worth. Anita was worth someone much better than me, but I was habituated to her affection. In the month of the board exams I concentrated more in looking good and getting better with every aspect of life other than the notes which could actually give me that. Anita's notes were helpful but I couldn't take much help from them as the help was required somewhere else – it was needed in making me realize my self-worth. Boards ended and on the last day of the examinations, I remember waiting for Anita after the exams. After every exam Anita used to be outside discussing each and every question from the question paper. This was one activity which really annoyed me as it often broke the truth to me that the answers which I wrote could possibly be wrong. After every exam she asked me "How did it go?" to which I could only reply "It was awesome." I guess it was the safest answer.

Post boards, I began spending a major time in the comforts of my home with occasional meetings with Anita. My twenty first birthdays arrived and I was given a marvelous gift of a bike which was a *Royal Enfield Thunderbird*, black and gray in color. The bike gave a new freedom to my life, freeing me of the dependency of public transport. Anita joined in on my birthday to celebrate my new bike. Nikita and two of her friends had also joined in. One was a lean guy called Rizvi and the other one was a muscular handsome chap called Abhijeet.

Other than for Anita, it was strange to have different company on my birthday. Vini had gone to visit his relatives in his hometown, and his presence was being missed only by me. Sanky, Gino and Kirat had distanced since they didn't like Doctor. Moreover, Kirat was finally successful in turning Gino into his follower, claiming his super moronic pseudo Godfather status. Vini and I never gave a fuck about it. But since he was gone, celebrating a birthday with my girlfriend and her stranger friends was a certain new experience.

I took all of them to a nearby smoking parlor to have a *hookah*[105]. The familiarity of Anita with the friends of her friend was alarming in a strange way. I stood out as the birthday boy taking all the best wishes of the world and paying the bill for it.

Anita called up on my birthday night after reaching home. "Hey birthday boy, how are you?" she asked cheerfully. "I am good, just so very excited to ride my bike tomorrow", I answered enthusiastically. "Thanks for the treat", she said softly. "You are most welcome", I replied. "So what did Nikita and her friends say about it?" I asked. "Nothing much; I didn't have a word with them. I left in front of you", she replied with a hint of clarification. "Did Nikita take admission for learning dentistry here in *Navi Mumbai*[106]?" I asked. "Yes, she, Rizvi and Abhijeet are together in the same college. Rizvi and Abhijeet are her seniors", she explained. "Nice, is she seeing someone out of the two guys?" I asked curiously. "I thought so, you would figure it out. Yes, she and Rizvi are going around", she said with minor sarcasm. "Oh nice! But the way she was with Abhijeet, I guess

---

[105] *An oriental tobacco pipe with a long, flexible tube. Must try!*

[106] *Planned township of Mumbai.*

she is seeing him too", I said pointing out my analysis. "Shut up Uday, you are so 'pig brained'", she said angrily. "Sorry, I just said what I felt", I apologized. "So how did they meet?" I asked. "Who?" she asked. "Nikita and Rizvi. Who else?" I remarked. "Nikita bumped into Rizvi in their college fest and got drunk with him on the dance floor and now they are here", she narrated. "They are here as in? Are they sleeping together?" I asked with my usual curiosity. "Yes", said Anita after a little pause. "And what about Abhijeet?" I continued. "Nothing he is a good friend of Rizvi", she continued. "Okay", I replied. "Some days back he called me as he was here, near my area", she added. A minor shudder ran in my heart. "So?" I asked. "So I met him. He was on his bike with a friend of his. We went to the nearby coffee shop to have coffee", she continued. "Nice!" I replied with minor sarcasm. Anita sensed it and remained silent. "Uday, what are you getting at?" she asked alertly. "Nothing, just you and your happy life with your friends", I taunted sarcastically. "See, even if you try to make me feel guilty I won't. Abhijeet is a friend and if he comes by to see me then why shouldn't I meet him?" she protested. "Yes you should, he is so handsome. Why not?" I added with my obvious jealousy. "At least he came to see me, you don't even move your lazy ass out of your home", she taunted back and instantly regretted her words. "Fine, I guess you should date him", I said angrily. "He is definitely better than me", I added, reflecting my own low 'self-worth'. "Look Uday, I am sorry. I didn't mean that", she recuperated quickly. "It's ok, I know what you meant", I mumbled and kept the phone. Anita tried calling me repeatedly but my wounded ego didn't let me answer.

"Why am I so surprised?" I mumbled as I walked out to buy a cigarette. "I cheated on Anita, she is bound to find someone else. Abhijeet is also better looking and well built. What if Anita finds him attractive? He is even making excuses to meet her", I continued talking to myself.

The idea of Anita drifting away was still challenging my security.

'Anger' and 'insecurity' when blended together can make a dangerous combination; something so risky that it can destroy a lot of things. Insecurities are nothing but fear. And ironically, "Fear is the root cause of Anger."

But before I could conclude the anxious night of my birthday, another well-wisher had something left to say. My phone buzzed and when I checked, it appeared to be a familiar number. I answered with a smile for I remembered the caller. "Hi Rita", I said cheerfully. There was silence on the other end. "Hello" I called out to check. "You bastard!" a feminine voice erupted in the silence. "Excuse me!" I muttered in shock. "Yes, Mr. Uday Singh... the biggest bastard on this planet", hissed Rita. "It's my birthday today Rita. At least you can save your abuses for all the other days, just not tonight", I reasoned sadly for being abused by my cheated flame. "You called after such a long time! How are you?" I asked, with glimpses of the moments spent together. And perhaps that's the mistake I did...

"Yes how could I forget you? You left me with such beautiful memories. And the more I think about them, the more I hate you. Why did you lie that you loved me? I so wish, you die a pathetic death", her voice resonated with anguish. "I don't think I did something so bad to you Rita that you are wishing for my death. I am sorry for whatever happened but I really never wanted to hurt you", I pleaded for forgiveness for my uncouth deeds. "If you never wanted to hurt me, then you wouldn't have lied to me, and made me fall in love with you. But you did all that, for that fucking hungry 'little monster' of yours. The only way I can be at peace with you is if you die. Please die Uday!" she cried with her sobs turning hysterical. "Kill me then! What the fuck? It's my birthday today you bitch!" I reprimanded angrily. "Call me whatever! But you actually turned me into a bitch. I can only be at peace when I hear the news of your death. You know, I pray that you die. And I want you to die in pain. I so wish I could see you dying..." she cursed in a painful voice which left eerie sensations on my skin.

I was petrified to see that a false vow of love can cause such a damage that perhaps only the death of the lover can heal it. Maybe it's the degree of vulnerability of one's broken heart which determines the kind of vengeance they seek to mend it.

Though I accepted my wrongdoings but couldn't quite equate my death as its just punishment. Rita continued to cry, turning my twenty first birthday into a gloomy shade of gray.

"Don't worry Rita, one day we all shall die. And I hope that you are there with me when I am dying. At least, I will be happy that your wish came true", I said conforming her wishes for my death. "This is my craziest birthday Rita. Imagine how would it feel, when someone wishes for your death on your birthday", I remarked sadly, as I slowly realized that the worth of my life was also equitable to the worth of myself.

Rita didn't stop there. It wasn't enough to heal her wound. She wanted some more for me... "And I wish that all those who love you, should cry for you when you are dead. And they should know that you would never come back", she cursed like a heartless witch devoid of any kind of empathy. The mention of my loved ones, took me back to the faces of my loving family members and my adorable girlfriend. A strong repercussion surged within, when I imagined their gloomy faces for my loss. "You have gone crazy Rita, stop brain fucking me! If it's about a boyfriend then you will find plenty. But please I am not dying for you! Because, if for no one else, I will still live for my family. So thanks a lot for your birthday wishes but I will go now", I said rudely. "Wait you bastard..." she screamed. "Stupid bitch!" I snapped and hung up. She repeatedly kept calling, but her deliberate attempts to make me feel guilty on my birthday pissed me off. I hesitantly switched off my cellphone and walked back home, thinking about the grayish end to my birthday, which ironically had a brilliant start.

> *Perhaps this is a very common phenomenon in most people's lives. They all usually have a brilliant start, full of 'light' and divine love with which they are born. But sooner or later all of us end up reaching this shade called gray, and when we do – we often wonder, if this is what we really wanted? Whether it's a little bit of white in a lot of black, or a little bit of black in a lot of white – the degree of grayness doesn't matter. I guess this is the closest I could define gray as – the color which occurs when two extremities meet, turning into a hue of a paradoxical moment called 'irony'. Very similar to the 'time' when a death wish for you, was being made on your birthday!*

I realized my adamance and its probable effect on Anita. Rita's death wish strongly brought back the urge to call Anita, as she would never wish something like that for me. I switched on my phone after a while and I recklessly tried calling her at midnight but I guess she had dozed off.

The next day I waited for her call hoping that she would have checked her phone in the morning, but she didn't call. Though my new bike kept me distracted but intermittent thoughts of Anita kept pricking me. Rita's painful curse also knocked on my head. The worse thing about curses is that it's even more ironical if a curse destined for you affects somebody you love.

I wanted to hold on to my arrogance for longer, but with the insecurity eating in I decided to call Anita again. "Hey", she answered happily. I felt relieved to hear her cheerful voice as if I just escaped the curse. "Hi, I am sorry for hanging up last night", I said softly. "It's alright", she said in a good mood. Probably she wasn't as hung up on minor nuances, as much as I was! "Where are you?" I asked. "Just came back home. Nikita and Abhijeet had come over. So went for a coffee with them", she answered nervously. "Oh cool", I said taking control of myself. "Should I say sorry?" she asked doubtfully. "No *Jaan*, you should have friends", I said trying to sound reasonable. Probably curses have a greater significance, as they suddenly make you thankful for what you have, and probably could lose. I was elated for her affection and concern, and without wasting much time I steered the conversation to a romantic note which ended in a sensual *phonegasm*[107].

The next morning I took out my new bike and went riding. Having a new toy was better. While riding I reached Nikita's college. I couldn't help giving her a call. "Hey Uday", she answered. "Hey Nikita, guess where am I?" I asked loudly. "Don't tell me you are at my college", she responded with surprise. "God, you are smart! How did you know that?" I chuckled. "Well I am, but what are you doing here?" she asked. "I was just riding and happened to reached here", I replied casually. "Can you come out?" I asked. "Just wait for five minutes and I will be there", she said and hung up. Nikita joined me in a while. "How's my bike?" I asked her. "It looks sexy I must say", smiled Nikita. "And the rider?" I grinned. "Well, let me guess", she smiled flirtatiously. "Oh come on, you have to guess that now!" I laughed. She began to laugh and finally said, "Yes he is sexy too." "Finally! I am relieved", I said with a breath of pride. Rizvi

---

[107] *Oh, come on!*

and Abhijeet also joined us outside their college and we had a brief discussion on bikes and regular topics.

I rode back home after a while. I called up Anita before anyone else tells her that I met Nikita. I guess for someone who has cheated in a relationship, it better to bring out things pre-emptively before anyone attacks the integrity of the cheater.

"Hey sexy", I said as Anita answered. "Hey *Jaan*, what are you up to?" she asked in her sweet yet husky voice. "Nothing much, I was riding my new bike and I happened to reach Nikita's college. I met Nikita, Abhijeet and Rizvi there", I said enthusiastically. "Oh really! Shit, I live so far away or else I could also be having some fun with you guys", she exclaimed with her usual longing to be with her friends. "You are most welcome to come here anytime and ride with me", I teased. "I want to ride your bike", she said excitedly. "No you can just sit behind me", I firmly replied. "As a pillion?" she asked. "What's a pillion?" I asked dubiously. "You dumb ass, a pillion is the one who sits behind on a bike", laughed Anita. I felt embarrassed by her correction and my limited vocabulary. "For now you can just ride me", I chuckled. "Okay", she replied sarcastically. "Anyways what did Nikita say?" she continued. "Nothing specific, just general stuff, but she said that my bike and its owner look sexy together", I said cheerfully. "I guess you do", she said in her coy way. "You never told me that", I asked in my usual impish demanding tone. "I always wanted to", she said affectionately. "So how are things between you and her?" I asked. "Well good as always. You know recently a very interesting thing happened", she began. "What?" I asked curiously.

"Few days back, Nikita and I were in *Bandra*. And a guy came up to us and asked if we would like to model. We were confused wondering who he was talking to. So Nikita asked him, for what he needed models. Do you know what the 'guy' said?" she narrated. "What?" I asked curiously. "He said that he is asking me and not Nikita for modeling", laughed Anita. I couldn't help laughing along with her. "Then did you say yes?" I asked nervously as the idea of Anita becoming a model, again triggered an insecurity that she would soon become inaccessible. On the contrary, a feeling of pride surged downwards from my head and reached the 'little warrior' considering the fact that Anita is indeed model material.

"No, I didn't say yes. I said I will think about it. But when I reached home and asked my mom, she gave me a piece of her mind", she said with her voice turning low but it simultaneously eased me out of my insecurities.

"How did Nikita take it?" I asked trying to distract her attention. "She was so jealous!" she giggled. Somehow the fact that Nikita got jealous rose a chord in Anita's voice. "She later told me that modeling is for losers and most of the models are sluts", she narrated with minor disappointment for her envious arrogant friend. "Fuck, it pricked bad I guess. Come on it's obvious", I said trying to empathize with Nikita. "Yes of course, but demeaning it also makes it sound like she is just jealous! I understand our parents might never let us choose this as a profession, but it's still a profession. People feed their families through it. So please respect it!" reasoned Anita in a strong voice.

"Of course she is jealous. Plus you cannot generalize it. Even prostitutes feed their families. No matter what your opinion might be about their work, they still take care of their people. But forget all that... you are definitely so very 'hot' *Jaan*", I cuddled affectionately charmed by the rationale of my sexy girlfriend. "But chuck it Uday, she is a good friend", she sighed. "Even in her sister's marriage she was so hell bent on showing her cleavage", she complained. "Really, that's so amazing!" I chuckled enjoying the girl talk. "Then what did you guys do?" I asked curiously. "Nothing we kept telling her to pull up her blouse and reveal lesser of her extra thick cleavage. Even her assets are so huge that you can't do anything, and the dress she was wearing made her look like a big voluptuous buffalo", she chuckled. "I saw the snaps, a glittery blue buffalo I must say", I sniggered sarcastically. "Her hairstyle was also looking weird in the photographs", I added. "Yeah she looked like a..." paused Anita. "Like a slut", I whispered on the phone. "Shut up Uday, she is still my friend", revolted Anita. "But seriously, you look so much better than her", I compensated, trying to stroke my girlfriend's pride. "Aww... Uday. Thank you. Muah", she kissed the words in a sexier tone.

The internal chemistry amongst girls was sexier than it usually appeared and listening to Anita bitch about Nikita gave me a crazy pleasure. "Did you ever discuss 'us' with her?" I asked curiously. "Yeah, at times we do", she replied casually. "Did you discuss our love making part with her?" I asked with a higher curiosity. "Kind of", she said in an embarrassed tone. "Kind of; like how much?" I probed. "Just enough I guess, don't ask me it's too embarrassing Uday", she answered. "So what did she say?" I probed further. "She said that I am too fast", replied Anita after a brief moment of silence. I laughed to her remark and asked, "Why?" "She said that she never expected from me that I would lose my virginity at eighteen", chuckled Anita. The idea of her discussing my 'love making' performance with Nikita turned me on.

A day later I was struggling with a stroke of afternoon boredom as my mother had hid my bike keys since I was too unavailable since the bike had arrived. Separating someone from their new beloved toy could be painful. I tried channelizing my energy to something different but nothing appeased me. I began to mess with my cellphone and I ended up calling Nikita.

"Hey Nikita, how are you?" I greeted as she answered the phone. "I am good Uday", she replied in her husky voice. "You know you sound like you are on cocaine, or you do drugs!" I chuckled. Nikita laughed along. "Like you are the daughter of the *Colombian* drug lord", I laughed. "What happened?" asked Nikita jovially. "Nothing, just getting bored", I sighed. "Why what happened, why aren't you riding your bike?" she asked. "My mother took my bike keys away", I sighed like a baby. "What? Really?" she laughed. "I am getting bored. Let all of us catch up in the evening", I insisted. "Where?" she asked. "Let's go to some place in *Bandra*", I suggested. "Yeah, even Anita can come then", I happily added. "Ok I will ask Rizvi and Abhijeet too", she said. "Yeah that would be nice", I peacefully summed as it would be nice for me to stop being so insecure and let Anita chill.

We disconnected and I happily called Anita. "Let's catch up at *Bandra*. Nikita, Rizvi and Abhijeet are also coming", I said enthusiastically. "You called all of them?" she asked in surprise. "Yes, kind of", I answered. "How come they became such good friends of yours?" she asked in confusion. "I don't know, but it would be nice to have some people around since college has ended", I added. "Let me see", she replied. "Don't see, just come, they are your friends more than mine... so I would be comfortable only if you are around", I cuddled. "But permission...?" mentioned Anita.

"Jaan; I want you to come out to *Bandra* in the evening and that's it. You don't need to travel for hours through crowded local trains. Just go down and take a rickshaw to a place ten minutes from your home. You can leave whenever you want. Please Anita, come out. I haven't seen you for days now", I pleaded. "It's only been a week my tiger", she chuckled. "I so badly wanna see you *Jaan*, please you have to come!" I insisted with all my heart. "Alright, I will come *Jaan*", she said in her best mushy voice. "I love you Nitu", I hushed my love words aggressively. She didn't reply as if the old pain caused by my indulgence suddenly became so fresh as if it happened yesterday. "I miss those words. It feels 'out of this world' when you say it", I said with sadness. "Let's get ready, you will take two hours to come here", she continued in a low voice. "Alright, I will get ready", I sighed with disappointment, for not hearing what I so badly wanted to hear, and then I began to get ready.

Unfortunately, my mother refused to give me the bike keys to go to *Bandra*. I left home angrily because still I was just a tamed kid, with limited options. "Why is she so scared to just let me ride a motorcycle?" I mumbled angrily as I waved for a rickshaw. "But it's ok", I consoled myself thinking about all the traffic and having Anita as pillion won't be as cool as being with her happily in the backseat of Nikita's car. "Finally", I sighed as I walked up the platform of the railway station. The crowd was picking up before an evening train, and it scared my clean shaven self which was wrapped in a nice black shirt, showered with my dad's perfume. The train was visible and people waited to pounce inside. The zombie fight was about to begin to get inside the train and I jumped in. Pretty soon I was stuck holding a side bar behind my head and crammed with people from all sides. There was no possible space to even wriggle. Two short men pushed their heads into my face, in the crowded compartment. Being taller than a few, did make me feel a little good, but the hair on their heads were black and shiny and smelt of country made hair oil. For quite a while I fended the poking heads, till my cellphone began to ring.

The pelves of people crammed up in a *Mumbai* local train become very connected and thus they felt the vibration buzzing through them. People around in the general compartment looked at me. Many smelly heads turned to look at my face. I managed to slither one hand to finally pull out my cellphone and wriggled it back to my ears. "Hello", I answered. "*Jaan*, I won't be able to come", said Anita. "What? Why?" I spoke out loud in the chaos, as it got too noisy in the compartment. She began to sob on the other end. The train passed *Kurla*[108] and a gush of people swarmed in like a bunch of rioters. Space became the matter of survival as I pushed back with the other hand. "Stop crying Anita", I yelled louder. The crowd pushed in cramming me in the corner and my head hit the side bar I was holding. A fit of rage surged up and I quickly pushed my cellphone back in my pocket, and began pushing the crowd with all my might. Two men looked at me in the face with astonished eyes. Astonishment wasn't enough to cool me down and I pushed in more till finally I reached a comfortable corner of the train wagon. People bickered but I just stayed silent and angry that Anita won't be coming to meet me while I will be getting bored as an outcast with her friends.

When I finally got off on a station where I had to change the train for *Bandra*, I called up Anita. She had called a several times before when I was in the train. "Hi", she said in her cranky voice. "What happened *Jaan* why aren't you coming?" I asked affectionately. "Mummy didn't allow", she said with her voice getting feeble. "Didn't you tell her that exams are over?" I protested. "I did", she mumbled. "Then?" I asked. "She said that we haven't spent so much on your education that you go party after the board examinations are over. You should prepare for the next entrance examination", Anita quoted her mother and began sobbing again. I tried consoling her for a while and when nothing helped, I said, "Okay stop crying now, I will go back home and tell Nikita that I won't be able to come." "But you are already more than halfway to *Bandra*", she said affectionately. "Man! It was so crowded", I said wiping the sweat off my brow. "*Jaan*, I so wanna be with you now", she mumbled. "Then come out please", I begged. "I don't even have money. I haven't got my pocket money also", mumbled Anita. "I have money, mummy gave me for not going on the bike", I said enthusiastically. "Just come", I insisted. "No *Jaan*, you go and meet them", she said with disappointment. "You are so sad that I don't feel like going", I said feeling upset. "No, you go and have fun. Please don't go back now, or else I will feel bad. And don't get

---

[108]   *A central suburb in Mumbai which has maximum rush for the local trains; and also the highest number of pickpockets.*

too drunk either", she said forcing herself to sound happy again. I took a breath of relief. "I will feel lonely there, we can never go out like normal couples", I grimaced. "I know, but don't worry *Jaan*, one day we will", she said affectionately. "Sure", I sighed and the train to *Bandra* entered the railway station platform "The train has come, I have to hang up", I said in an urgent voice. "Uday", screamed Anita. "What? Say quickly", I asked. "I love you *Jaan*", she said in her husky voice. My heart melted and everything silenced around me. "I love you too", I gasped and no matter how much ever I wanted to remain stuck on the phone with her, but I had to disconnect. I rushed in the crowded train, unbothered by the many stinking people. I was happy, exuberantly hanging on a railing of the crammed up compartment. She had finally said what I so badly wanted to hear. The smelly people and the lack of breathing space didn't matter. I kept smiling for Anita and I were back.

Perhaps love gives us the strength, to tolerate the shittiest situations of our life, and that too... with a smile!

I reached *Bandra* and Nikita's message popped in, "I am outside the station, come out quickly and give me a call." I walked out and called her. "Hey where are you?" I asked. "Just outside, in front of the rickshaw stand", she answered. I saw her standing next to her car and I waved to her. She recognized me and I rushed to her car and quickly got inside it owing to the increasing traffic.

"Hey", I said as I opened the door of the car and sat inside. Nikita also got in quickly and started the engine. "It's too crowded in here at evenings", I mentioned. Nikita began to drive through the chaotic traffic till the next signal. "What car is this? I missed to check it in the hurry", I asked. "Oh this is a *Fiat Palio*[109]", she smiled. "Nice, is it your car?" I asked. "Yes, now it's my car. Earlier it wasn't", she laughed. "Cool", I exclaimed. "Where are Rizvi and Abhijeet?" I asked. "Oh Rizvi couldn't come and Abhijeet is at *Malad*[110]. He also works in a call center", she answered. "Oh cool, I didn't know that!" I said with dubious thoughts. "So he studies dental and works in the call center as well?" I asked

---

[109] *A Fiat hatchback, with low fuel economy.*

[110] *A western suburb in Mumbai, close by the sea.*

curiously. "Yes!" she exclaimed with a hint of pride. "I spoke to Anita, she wouldn't be able to come either", I said sadly. "Aww why are you so upset?" she purred. "Just, haven't seen her since ages", I sighed. "Wow", she exclaimed. "What happened?" I asked. "Nothing", she smiled. "Even I am missing Anita. Then it's just you and me I guess", sighed Nikita. "I spoke to Anita and she asked me to take care of you", she laughed. "I feel as if I am a little boy", I smiled. "More than that. Anyways where do you wanna go?" she asked. "Anywhere, I don't know much here", I said hesitantly. "Well, let's just go to *Mocha* then", she said and paused as she turned her car into the inner lane of the road. "Okay", I agreed.

Nikita dropped the car keys with the valet and we walked inside the lounge. The lounge had a rustic feel with ethnic artifacts decorating it. The crimson lights in the corners contrasted with the yellow of the chandelier at the center of the lounge. "Let's sit here", she said. I sat watching Nikita move her chair. Her dress was gleaming in the dim crimson lights. She wore a maroon knee length one piece. She sat down on the chair in front. I looked at her forehead, fresh new passion pimples had popped out. She wore a silver nose ring and her dusky skin glowed in the candescence of the lights. When I traveled further down her face I reached a dark shadow where a dangerous curve began to take shape and ended in the glittery maroon of her dress. "Fuck", I mumbled as I noticed her cleavage. "So what would you like to have?" she asked. I looked down at her cleavage and pulled myself up to her eyes, and hurriedly said, "Anything, beer or something like that." "They aren't serving alcohol today, it's a dry day", she pointed. "Its fine", I said as if nothing mattered, as I was too concerned to look good because in some way I was representing Anita. Somehow the line of distance was very clear in the environment considering the threat of being in front of Anita's best friend and what repercussions it could create.

"Can we order a *hookah?*" she smiled. "Ok" I said. "Which flavor?" she asked. "I don't know, anything", I said in a confusion. "Still, tell me", she insisted. "Well honestly, I don't know many flavors of *hookah* as such", I said feebly. "What? Really?" she asked in surprise. "I am not much of a *hookah* smoker. I know I am not all that cool as I don't know all the flavors of *hookah.* It's ok, you order", I smiled sheepishly. "Well I like grape and I like mint too. And double apple is also nice", she said in a happy tone. "Then why don't we go for any of these?" I asked. "Ok then let's call for mint", she decided. The thought of mint and the coldness it will bring to my throat gave a hint of a bad throat coming ahead. "Let's just go for something which is more regular", I suggested. "Okay, double apple is nice then", she said helping me pick my flavor. "Hmmm", I pondered. Watching me confused and pondering over the *Hookah* flavors got Nikita restless. "Okay, let's just call for double apple", she said impatiently while I just nodded.

Nikita placed the order for a *hookah*. The tables around had beautiful women sitting peacefully smoking *hookah* or cigarettes as they laughed and chatted. The lounge had a flirtatious atmosphere. I looked around the table at the others. Many eyes locked with mine, though only for a few moments.

"This place is so posh", I said nervously. "Why? It's just normal", she asked in shock. "Anita, me, our ex-boyfriends, we used to come here so often", added Nikita with a smile. "To do *hookah?*" I asked in astonishment. "No, as in, we used to hang out in *Bandra* a lot", she said and a forlorn nostalgia showed up in her big dark eyes and eventually spread across her face. "Those were such crazy days. It's like you can make sitcoms out of those days", she said with a sad laughter.

The mention of Anita's ex drove the old insecure feelings again. "What if she was closer to him than me? That chap is really cool, way smarter and easy going than me", I thought as I noticed my stiff body language which was making me feel so conscious. "I need to be better than this nervous guy that I am", I mumbled. "Excuse me, did you say something?" asked Nikita. "Nothing, just, at times I talk to myself", I said with embarrassment.

I felt as if Nikita has started to get bored and she began talking about the school days she and Anita spent together with the obvious mention of their boyfriends all the time. It was difficult to explain the pinch which I felt growing on me.

My eyes went red and watery and I felt my face stretch. "I will just go to the washroom and come", I said and got up and left. The loo had an ethnic feel and a candle lit in the corner with a small dim bulb glowing on the top. I washed my face and lightened myself up. I walked out of the washroom with a wet spiked hair redo. Nikita had begun puffing the *hookah* and I took my place again.

"You look fresh", she smiled. "Yeah, kind of", I blushed. Nikita blew a puff of smoke on my face. The double apple flavor smelt good and fresh. The pipe came to me and as I took the first drag, sweet apple favored velvety smoke came out of my mouth, leaving a mild lingering touch of the sweet apples behind. The fragrance of the aromatic smoke loosened my stiff body and soon I felt a different swing. My worries and insecurities about Anita slowly blew up in the smoky atmosphere. People appeared friendlier and I leaned in my couch. I noticed the color of the couch and it was red. The 'Red Couch' fantasy of Anita replayed in my head.

"It's nice", I mumbled happily. "You liked it?" asked Nikita. My eyes dropped down from her eyes to her cleavage. She readjusted her dress and I immediately realized the offense which my insolent eyes had caused. I dragged them up again. She continued talking while I just struggled to keep my eyes on her face. There was something strange about her 'hearts'. Her 'hearts' had such gravity which pulled my eyes down and even after putting conscious efforts, it felt difficult to keep looking up. I smiled and nodded as normally as I could while she continued talking about various things in her life. Her cleavage cleared most of my thoughts and I kept struggling to not to stare at them. Cleavage is also referred as the line of breakage. And Nikita had a thick dark line of breaking; breaking her voluptuous 'hearts'. The brown color of her upper bosom glowed in the dim yellow light falling on it and the maroon of her dress contrasted, making them objects of fantasy.

"Why do I feel this heaviness around my eyes? As if the volume of her 'hearts' is affecting my vision. It's clear in my head that there is no chance with Nikita and I surely know that I am not looking for any either. It's an accident that we all planned to meet and Anita couldn't be out here with us" I thought. "What the fuck are you thinking, Uday?" a counter thought jolted me out. I had to keep looking into her eyes to ensure that my presence doesn't make my girlfriend's best friend uncomfortable. "Nice earrings" I mentioned, looking at her ethnic bronze jewelry. "Thanks", she smiled. "They look really good on you", I added, trying to keep up the conversation and my rebellious eyes. At least, they should look straight ahead while I hardly knew then, that still they will rebel anyways.

"So do you still talk to Kunal?" I asked her about her ex-boyfriend. A sudden anguish crept up in her eyes and she said in a low voice, "Not much." "If you don't mind, how was he as a boyfriend?" I asked. "Why?" she asked inquisitively. "Just like that", I added. "He was nice, strong and very charming", she said with a temporary brilliance replacing the anguish in her eyes till the sadness returned for his absence. "It's ok, you and Anita helped me a lot to get over him", she smiled with sadness. "So, let's not talk about Kunal now", she added with a wry smile. "It's ok, I understand, we just so wanted that you come back to being the lively vivacious Nikita that we know of, and I am glad that you are doing much better", I smiled empathetically. "The Nikita I met in the *Xavier*'s fest. The one who taught me how to *jive* initially", I added, thinking about the hug which she gave me on that day and I looked down at her 'hearts' again.

"Lively and vivacious!" she exclaimed looking into my eyes while she adjusted her dress again. I looked up back into her eyes covering my nervousness with a smile. "A lively and vivacious coke addict!" I chuckled sarcastically. "Yeah right", she said with a smug face. "Really! You sound like you are 'high' all the time", I added enthusiastically. She just blushed silently. "You know, those days I thought you guys were too cool for me", I laughed trying to make her comfortable. "And now?" she asked with a sly smile. "Now too but even I am cool now. Am I not?" I asked seeking her approval. "Oh come on Uday. We found you cute too", she said in revolt. "Really?" I blushed. "Yeah, I mean Uday Singh sounds 'hot' as if the name of some big businessman or politician", she grinned. "Seriously?" I said and just continued blushing. "Oh you are blushing. That's so cute", she chuckled pointing towards my face.

The lounge had its last order and Nikita asked me, "Do you want to have anything else?" "I don't know", I answered thinking the little money which I had and whether blowing it on her was wise or not.

"Let's have a dessert", she suggested. "Okay, which one?" I asked in confusion. "See, I don't frequent this place. So it's best you order", I said looking at the prices of the desserts on the menu card. "You wanna have a chocolate avalanche?" she said interrupting my search for the most affordable or rather the cheapest dessert. "I have heard about this from Anita. She talks about chocolate avalanche all the time", I said thinking about the smile which chocolate and it's by products brought on Anita's face.

"It is yum", said Nikita with a broad smile. "I have never tried it", I said nervously. "Let's have it then", she said energetically. She ordered for a chocolate avalanche. "My god you guys get so excited for desserts", I commented. "Obviously, it's a dessert!" she exclaimed happily. The chocolate avalanche soon arrived on the table. Big dollops of chocolate ice cream covered the brownies and a beautiful decoration of dark brown chocolate syrup lined the dessert.

"It looks good", I said. Nikita nodded while she impatiently dug her spoon in the dessert. "It looks very rich, like full of calories", I couldn't help commenting as I wondered about the destination of the sweetness of the dessert and where it would accumulate. "Would it add up to her 'hearts'?" I wondered as the dessert gave me a perfect alibi to take a proper glimpse of her 'hearts' again. Nikita was too involved in the dessert to care for her cleavage which looked like a deep dark inviting cave.

"It's sinful", she said as she took a bite of chocolate which oozed out from the side of her lips. "It definitely looks like it", I said hiding the surprise caused by the word as I moved my eyes back from her cleavage to the dessert. I took a spoon of the sinful chocolate and looked at her. "There is chocolate on your lips", I pointed. She tried to wipe it but couldn't and so I wiped it out for her.

"It's indeed sinful", I mumbled with my mouth full. "What?" she asked. "The dessert", I said. The chocolate melted in my mouth as the drops of syrup slowly flowed down my throat, sensualizing my already swinging head.

"Smoke and chocolate tastes so good", I said gulping the chocolate in my mouth. My eyes traveled from the dessert to her face only to get stuck again at the glittering gleam on the edge of her cleavage and the dark shadow of the line drawn on her body. I struggle hard to not look at it but my eyes just won't listen to me. I pulled my heavy eyes up again to her face. The surge of intoxication added to the dark line of her cleavage, and I ended up pushing my spoon to grab a bigger bite of the dessert. I chewed on the desert as chocolate oozed out on my lips.

"You eat like an animal", she commented as she dug in the plate for her bite. "Primitive instincts", I mumbled as I scooped the bite out of her spoon. "Hey, that's cheating", she said with a faint laughter. We struggled and fought till we finished the dessert. The waiter got the bill and I panicked looking at the bill of a thousand bucks.

"Hey, let's dutch", I said mustering up all the courage it required to ignore the chivalry of not letting the girl pay. "Ok, sure", she shrugged. We paid the bill and got ready to leave. The last few tables had their customers left in the cloudy smoke which was slowly clearing up.

"Let's go. By the way you still have chocolate on your lips", said Nikita. "Where?" I said and moved my tongue around my lips to suck in the last drops of chocolate. "Is it clean now?" I confirmed. She laughed and wiped the chocolate off the side of my lips. "Where are we going?" I asked.

"I don't know. Should I drop you or what?" she asked. I thought about what to do next. "What's your plan?" she asked again. "I don't know, I am just too bored since the college ended", I answered. "Let's go to *Malad* and meet Abhijeet. What say?" she asked excitedly. "Yeah, why not?" I answered with boredom.

We got into her car and Nikita drove. "So I guess we can also have fun together?" she commented on the evening we had just spent. "Sure why not!" I grinned and asked, "You don't have time restrictions?" "No, I had told my mother that I am with friends and would be coming late.

She has gone to my aunt's house in *Ahmedabad*[111]. So no one is at home. Hence I can go whenever I feel like", she smiled. "That's so cool. I still have to take permission to go out", I sighed.

"Though I know you for almost three years now, but I never asked. What do your parents do?" I continued the conversation. "My dad is a businessman so he keeps moving", she replied promptly. "And your mom?" I asked. "She is a housewife now", she replied. "What did she do earlier?" I asked curiously. "She was an air-hostess", she answered. "Oh wow!" I exclaimed. "So was it an arranged marriage?" I asked curiously. "No, it was a love marriage", she emphasized. "So how did they meet?" my curiosity continued. "They were on the same aircraft and my mother was serving my dad, as he was travelling business class and love happened", she answered. "They aren't the same *caste*[112]?" I asked. "No", she said. "Wow", I said wondering about the lives of people in urban cities. "You guys have a different life altogether, your stories are so different", I said reflecting on my simple background. "I will take that as a compliment", she smiled. "Sure why not?" I smiled back.

I rolled down my window to get some fresh air. The wind blew in and the fragrance of the apple flavored *hookah* returned. "You smell like double apples", I said sniffing the air. "What, seriously?" she asked in surprise. "Wow", I said crashing back in my seat. Nikita laughed as we pulled over on the road near Abhijeet's office. Nikita called him, "Hey", she said. "Come down, we are here", she said excitedly. "Uday and I", she added. "Yeah, he is also with me", she said with her tone sounding a bit sly. She began to laugh on the phone and I felt weird again wondering if they were laughing at me and finally she hung up.

"What happened? Why were you laughing?" I asked. "Nothing", she said as she continued laughing. Abhijeet came down wearing a black t-shirt covering his well-built biceps and a bandana on his head pulling back his long hair. "Seriously, a bandana in office?" I thought. "Maybe his office is pretty cool", I thought again. Nikita got off the car and ran

---

[111] *A city in the state of Gujarat in India.*

[112] *Caste is a form of social stratification. In India we do it on basis of place of birth, language, culture etc. etc. The list is long!*

across the road towards Abhijeet and threw herself in his arms giving him a big hug. She lingered in his arms for a long time while the people around turned to see the romance on the road.

I closed the windows of her car and then locked it and crossed the road. I felt as if I am interrupting the show of public display of affection on the road. "Hey", I said as I shook hands with Abhijeet. "Hey", he smiled. "So what have you guys been up to?" he asked. "We were at *Mocha* and had a *hookah* and chocolate avalanche", said a chirpy Nikita.

Nikita and Abhijeet continued talking while I stood like a silent listener. My cellphone rang, it was Anita calling. "Thank God you called", I said as soon as I answered. "What happened?" she asked in a concerned voice. "Nothing, just getting bored", I mumbled. "Why, thought you were having fun?" she asked casually. "I was, until we came to meet Abhijeet", I answered sounding like a bitch. "Why, what did he do?" she asked. "Well he didn't do anything, it's just that Nikita is pretty fond of him", I said sarcastically. "Why? What did she do now?" asked Anita with the excitement rising in her voice. "She ran across the road leaving the car open and unlocked, just to run into his arms. It looked fucking romantic! Are you sure she and Abhijeet don't have a thing?" I complained. "Obviously not dumbo, she is dating Rizvi", replied Anita defending her friend. "Yeah I thought so but Abhijeet and Nikita have a different chemistry. I wonder if Rizvi knows of it", I added my suspicion. "Of course, he knows they are friends and they hang out", she said casually. "Sure, but is he ok with it?" I asked. "I am sure he is", she replied boldly. "Well, I guess you guys are just too cool for me", I replied sarcastically. "You guys?" she exclaimed in a shocked voice. "I meant Nikita and her boyfriends", I answered correcting myself cautiously.

"Hey I mentioned Kunal in front of her", I added. "Why did you do that?" yelled Anita. "Just accidentally, had nothing to talk about", I replied trying to cool her off. "You know Uday, how depressed she was when he left her? Rizvi is helping her get over him", she said with obvious concerns for her friend. "Did she lose her virginity to Rizvi?" I asked with a sick curiosity. "No", Anita replied hesitantly. "Then to Kunal?" I continued guessing. "Yup, I mean literally but not literally", she said. "As in", I asked in confusion. "I mean he got condoms and all but they didn't do it. He just entered her, I guess", explained Anita. "*Jaan* all this virginity talk is making me horny", I whispered. "Me too", she whispered back. "You should have been here. I realized I am too lonely without you", I said after a pause. "Me too *Jaan*", she replied in her husky voice. "And your friends are nice but nothing like you", I said consoling her. She laughed in a demure manner. "And yes, Nikita is definitely fatter than you. You are the model material!" I said stroking the 'ego' of my 'love'. "Hey Uday, do you wanna play a trick?" she asked in an excited voice. "What trick?" I replied enjoying the adrenaline rush caused by Anita's voice.

"Like go close to Nikita and see if she falls for you but don't end up kissing or making out with her!" she said slowly in a sly voice. "Excuse me?" I exclaimed at the idea of her wicked trick. "You sure you want me to do this?" I asked hesitantly considering my guilty shady past. "Yeah it would be fun. I would love to see her face", she said in minor arrogance. "Yeah it would be fun, but I don't think it's a good idea", I said cautiously. "Just go ahead *Jaan*, don't worry I trust you", she replied confidently. "I am still not sure. Let's see", I answered in a serious tone. "Okay, your wish, I just wanted to see if she would advance on you", she prompted, adding curiosity to my sane self. "Why should she? I am not that 'hot'", I reasoned. "Who said that? You are so fucking 'hot' Uday. I can never be done with you", she giggled in her husky voice. "Yeah right, I mean look at Abhijeet. He has all the looks and the body and everything", I began to argue. "But I love your shoulders and your chest and your jawline. The way you look at me. Nobody has that", interrupted Anita. "Really?" I asked feeling a little shy. "And your 'little warrior' too. You are such a tiger Uday", she said, nailing it! I just chuckled with pride.

"Did you ever share with Nikita about our love life, as in the 'dirty' part?" I asked curiously. "Kinda yes, don't you remember I had told you? You have already asked me this?" she answered in embarrassment. "What are you saying? Oh yes; I remember. Damn she knows that we did it", I replied. "Of course, she is not dumb", she replied. "What did she say?" I asked, calming myself down. "She just laughed a lot and said that I am too fast and then we both laughed", giggled Anita. "Yeah I remember", I sighed. "And what else did you tell her?" I asked sarcastically. "That you are a very good kisser and I can kiss you all the time", she replied adoringly. "Crazy!" I shrieked. Nikita and Abhijeet began to pack up. "Ok we are leaving I guess. I will call you later", I said in haste. "I love you *Jaan*", blurted Anita. "I love you too", I said as Nikita opened the car. I hung up and we left.

Back in the car with Nikita, the challenge reoccurred in my head. "Should I go ahead with her and do as Anita had suggested?" I thought. She is Anita's best friend. The idea is sad and both of us know it. "So where shall I drop you?" asked Nikita. "Anywhere, it's your car madam", I answered playfully. "Shall I drop you at *Bandra?*" she asked. "No Nikita, it's four in the morning, I wonder if the trains have started", I replied. "By what time do the trains start?" she asked.

"Probably by five", I answered. "Ok. Well in that case I shall drop you at *Chunabhatti*[113] station", she suggested. "Yeah ok, but wouldn't it be far for you?" I asked. "No that would be fine", she replied. The highway was relatively empty as she kept driving while I played the songs. All the songs more or less hovered around Anita and so did the number by *Def Leppard*[114].

"I am crazy about you baby, so damn crazy... so crazy, that without you even one night alone seems like a year without you baby, do you have a fuckin heart... of stones and boulders..., So wounded I am that I don't even have your shoulders. Without you, I can't cry alone... I can't stop the hurt inside, when you and I collide", I hummed my extended version of the song as she parked the car in an empty parking lot of the railway station. "Are these the same lyrics as in the song?" she asked in doubt. "No... actually this is my extended version of the song", I answered with a nervous smile. "Oh nice! You really know this song? Huh", exclaimed Nikita. "Yes", I said in a sad voice. "I feel bad for what I have done, as I was selfish. But more than that, I really feel bad for Anita. You know she is my first love", I mumbled loud enough for her to hear. Nikita remained

---

[113] *Chunabhatti (Chuna – lime, bhatti – kiln) a suburb which is also home to the first cotton mill in Mumbai.*

[114] *Def Leppard are an English rock band formed in 1977 in Sheffield as part of the New Wave of British Heavy Metal movement. As one of the world's best-selling music artists, Def Leppard have sold more than 100 million records worldwide.*

silent for a while and then turned to look into my eyes. "You know what Uday? Everybody is selfish and emotional at the same time", she said in a firm voice.

I nodded pondering over her observation of people. "Wow, that's so true. I quite like the way you think. It's like you just showed me a side of people which was so present in front of my eyes and yet I could never see. With every angle, the world looks different. Like watching you from here, you look different, but if I just lie down here on your lap and look, from below you would look totally different", I blabbered. She returned a strange look but smiled. It was an awkward moment of silence. "Should I go ahead or should I leave? I am staring at her. I don't want her anymore! No more creepy thoughts! But what if I check if Anita was right? I anyway don't want anything to do with Nikita", I struggled with my thoughts as Anita's plan made its way back in my head. Though hesitant to experiment, I couldn't ignore my curiosity to check if Nikita responded to my advances.

"And yet all I could say is, you look so different. Like someone else. Like someone much free and not at all that Nikita who was once sad and silent", I said trying to communicate my goodwill to her and slowly rested my head on her lap. I looked into her eyes and it felt very awkward so I closed my eyes and just completed my jabber. "Fine, this is not working. She is indeed a good, loyal friend of Anita", I thought and I was about to get up, as I felt her hands grab my head, stabilizing it in a steady state. Just then, a wetness entered my lips coupled with a mild sour odor. I opened my eyes mildly to see her face immersed in mine and subsequently her tongue pierced in my semi closed mouth.

I got up startled by what had just happened. I sat up in my seat and looked at her. There was no remorse on her face. I breathed heavily accepting the look in her eyes. "Should I give up or should I...." I tried to think hard. I could still smell the smoky flavor of apples on her.

"So you want it?" I hissed to my losing self and before I could think I had already grabbed her. Her kiss was passionate and lusty, and she stroked my tongue with her wet mouth. Her warm yet wet mouth swallowed me as if 'darkness' forced itself on the little bit of 'light' which I was still trying to protect.

In that moment I melted in her assault. The 'guilt' was huge but it was still comfortable. As if the 'darkness' which was always inside me found someone 'ready to sin' with. And as we sinned, Nikita stroked my pride deep within as I strived to demonstrate my superiority.

It all became gray in that moment. I didn't know what was 'good' or what was 'bad'. Or maybe I always knew, but I was just enjoying the 'bad'.

Grabbing her head and kissing her ferociously, my hand went racing to the sleeve wrapping her right shoulder and I pulled it down to reveal her right 'heart'. My left palm curiously grabbed her voluptuous breast while I pulled her wavy dark hair behind to reveal her neck. With a certain different hunger I slithered down her neck to the bare brown nipple of her right breast. Her boobs still smelt of apples and the dual origin of the smoky fragrance enchanted me to have a sinful bite of it. The temptation was finally on my tongue and it was still very difficult for me to believe that it happened.

Nikita ruffled her fingers through my hair. "I am wanted", I thought as I pushed my mouth to gulp her mysterious 'hearts' which kept me involved for such a long time. I couldn't resist licking her cleavage, for its mystery was unveiled and I had it definitely conquered. The element of surprise was still prevalent pertaining to the point that how did it all actually happen. "Fuck, I had no chance of this happening tonight", I thought and a surge of guts propelled me to go even further. My right hand went down pulling the maroon end of her dress ending at her knees. I pulled up her dress and my hands raced between her bare, flabby legs to her 'inner core' which was covered in her wet underwear. "You are wet", I mumbled. I kissed her again while I felt her wetness at the surface of her last piece of cloth. I pushed my tongue in her mouth while she encouraged me with her participation.

"Fuck you are 'hot'!" she gasped. "Am I?" I asked in surprise. I could hear my heart pounding as if I was doing something very wrong. It kept beating harder and harder, pumping my blood. Even my breath became heavier. "I can feel my heart beating out", I gasped. She was exhausted too and drops of sweat shimmered on her brown skin. "You are a very good kisser!" she said breathing heavily. She pulled in her revealed 'heart' beneath the maroon of her dress which mildly gleamed under the dim light of the yellow street light falling inside the car.

"One second, may I?" I asked. "What?" she said. I wrapped my arm around her waist and pulled her dark cleavage to my face. I immersed my face in the darkness of her 'hearts' and then I heard her heart beat. They were beating like drums. I let out a heavy breath. She pulled back after enduring a few more breaths and said, "Uday, let's go." "Can we go to your place?" I said breathing heavily and out of control. "No", she replied. "My watchman would complain to my parents", she added. I insisted but she urged to leave, and eventually, stopping made sense to me as well. The early morning train held only two thoughts; the 'darkness' of Nikita and the morning 'light' of Anita.

When pride mixes with love, it's often pride which wins. I was too proud to conquer Nikita to realize what shit I had done.

My phone rang and it was Nikita calling. "Hey you reached?" she asked. "Yes, what about you? You know, I slept off in the train", I answered. We stayed silent for a few seconds till I interrupted the awkwardness of the 'silence', "What the hell just happened an hour ago?" "I don't know", she said with a faint laughter. "I hope you wouldn't share this with Anita?" I asked holding my breath. "No, I hope you won't", she replied. "Of course not", I added. "Nevertheless, you sleep, thanks", she said. "Yeah, you are welcome", I added. "Really?" she exclaimed and we both laughed a sinful laughter. "But just curious to know, how was it?" I asked her. "It was nice", she said stroking my ego. "Anita told me that you are an amazing kisser. She is not wrong at all", she said in her 'high' voice. "And you are 'hot' and juicy", I said slurping on the glimpses of what happened. "What?" she exclaimed listening to my lustful adjectives. "Like a chocolate avalanche. Dark and sinful", I added cautiously. "Aha", she breathed heavily on the phone. "Alright, you sleep now. See yaa, bye", she breathed reluctantly. "Yeah, my mother would also be up by now. I will also sleep", I answered and dozed off after a tiring unpredictable night.

I woke up at four in the evening to Anita's call. "Hey sexy, what time did you get back home?" she asked in her husky voice "Early morning, I guess I took the first train in the morning and reached", I answered in a sleepy voice. "*Jaan* I missed you so much last night, I so wanted to be with you", she cuddled in her mushy voice. "Me too *Jaan*", I mumbled but couldn't differentiate if the words were for real or just empty. Perhaps in my head, I had already accepted my reality.

"So what else did you guys do?" she probed. One question lead to another and I chose to cease her probing. "That's it, she dropped me at *Chunabhatti* in the morning, and I took the train", I said narrating all the events of the previous night except the little moral detour in the end.

"I so wanted to come today and see you, but *Mummy* and *Papa* are home. So not possible", said Anita with her voice getting sadder. "I so wish you could come", I said, still with mixed feelings, like feelings of love mixed with sinful indulgence. On one hand I could feel the craving to have Anita in my arms but on the flip-side, Nikita's fragrant 'hearts' and wet lips kept adding shades of the unimaginable possibilities.

The 'taste of blood' had induced its cravings and to my horror I didn't know what such bloody 'cravings' were capable of. Well for me, they were already pulling me towards Nikita as I was riding towards her college on the next Monday. She received me at her college gate dressed in a black tee and denims. "Hop on", I said gesturing her to sit behind on my bike. She obeyed with a smile and sat. As she sat on the bike, she clutched my chest and I began to ride. Her 'hearts' stabbed right through my back while her breath danced on my neck. I kept riding for quite a while till we reached the vicinity of a lake. I took a small broken road nearby and continued to ride. Surprisingly, the road traveled through the lake, dividing the lake into two halves. Perhaps it was an artificial lake or some greedy builders had started dumping earth on the lake to use it for development and construction. Somewhere midway, I stopped my bike and we dismounted. We were surrounded by water from both sides. We looked around and the place appeared unusual for the crowded streets of *Mumbai*. No human being was in sight. Probably no one would even take the pain to travel to such a remote extreme, unless and until it's for some accidental forbidden indulgence.

I looked at her and I knew that other than the place, whatever happens next won't be an accident. She looked at me and then looked around. Her sudden silence slowly whispered what she might have never said. I heard her unsaid words and answered her hesitations as I pulled her towards me. Beyond 'red', we meet gray and the curious gray blended, mixing us, as we were soon in each other's arms tasting each other. Though she often shrieked, Nikita was fiercer as if she was compensating for her previous feeble performance. I was more than happy to cooperate as she pushed her tongue much deeper in my mouth. In return I gave her 'hearts' the attention they deserved. The thrill of making out in a forbidden place is like discovering a treasure which mankind was never supposed to find.

"May I ask you something?" I said between the kisses. "What?" she asked. "Are you a virgin?" I asked slyly. She looked down for an instance and looked back in my eyes. A sly smile appeared on her face as she nodded otherwise. "Why? Where did you lose it?" I asked jovially "I did it with Rizvi", she answered after a pause. "How was it?" I was curious. "It's always been *Old Monk*[115] and 'sex'. Plus the thing that I like about it, is when it's completely inside me. I could feel his thing going to my stomach", she explained the gross details. We shared a 'dirty' laugh and continued. "Let's go", I said after a while. "Okay", she answered and I began to take out my bike. "Shit, it happened twice", I said as she clutched me again sitting on the pillion seat of my bike.

"Hey, I am throwing a party for my sister's marriage. You would come right?" she asked. "Of course, why not?" I answered. "Where are you planning on having it?" I asked. "In a lounge in *Andheri*", she answered. "Okay, I would love to join in", I said instantaneously. "Yeah Uday, please come. Everybody would be there", she chirped. I dropped her at a nearby coffee shop next to her college where Abhijeet and Rizvi waited for her. She got off, and had no sign of remorse or guilt on her face as she hugged Rizvi. Maybe the pain caused by Kunal had made her immune to the gray feelings or even worse, it had left her gray forever.

Maybe for me, I still believed that I was innocent since Anita didn't know about the little hanky-panky between Nikita and me. We finally

---

[115] *Friend, philosopher, survivor and guide in a bottle of dark rum.*

met for Nikita's party and Anita was anxiously waiting for me to arrive. Luckily, this time I rode to the venue on my new bike. Anita waited for me with Abhijeet and Rizvi. Watching them standing with her like long lost pals, kicked back the insecurity. I felt a surge of competitiveness to win back Anita's 'awe'. "Hi", she said and gave me a hug. The degree of public display of affection was lower as she was conscious of people. "Was she ever this conscious in college? Is something going on?" I tried hard not to think, as it was directly jarring my body and I was becoming stiff as I walked up the stairs to the lounge door. The big wooden door opened up to a cozy lounge with a small dance floor scantily lit up with blue and red lights. The darkness in the lounge was still apt to show the faces of the guests present for Nikita's party. Nikita's mother was also amongst the people, and Nikita took me along with Anita and the boys to introduce us to her mother. After a courteous smiling nod to her mother I looked at the people present in the party. Nikita pulled Anita to the dance floor with a familiar girlie excitement. I stood with Abhijeet and Rizvi looking at the dance floor where other friends of Nikita were already dancing. She came to us and took Rizvi along, to the dance floor. I stayed and watched. Abhijeet also stepped on the floor dancing to his grooves and soon formed a group with Nikita, Rizvi and Anita. I saw the four of them dance together like a happy family.

"Why can't I be like them, easy and free? Why am I so conscious?" I struggled to find a way to ease myself. Maybe something like dance needs a lot of freedom inside one's own self! I was definitely more imprisoned with all the baggage of my deeds and its incurred shame. Somehow knowing my guilt pushed a miserable insecurity of losing Anita one day. The realization of 'karma' is dreadful, especially when you are on the wrong side of it. It somehow makes you believe that one day it will come back for you. And perhaps I was witnessing the beginning of my worst fear coming to life as Abhijeet grooved with Anita. Thanks to the presence of Nikita's mom, things on the dance floor weren't getting too touchy. Even though I adored the idea of 'dirty' dancing on the dance floor, but watching my girlfriend with someone else was not acceptable to me.

Hot tears were about to swell up in my eyes, reminding me of the memory of staying out of the football team in my boarding school, when there were better players for the game and maybe I just wasn't good enough. Similarly, maybe I was not an awesome dancer to match Anita on the floor which perhaps Abhijeet was. Anita's eyes met mine as she was dancing and a sudden surge of the forbidden appeared. I smiled a weak smile and looked away. I walked towards the balcony of the lounge to have a lonely smoke.

"Hey why aren't you dancing Uday?" asked Anita as she walked into the balcony. "What are you doing here?" she asked. Her long ponytail was still moving around her waist and her black sleeveless made her look sleek like a certain street fighter girl from an anime game. "Can't you see I am smoking?" I said coldly. "What happened *Jaan?*" she asked with affection. The sudden bulge of the teary affection in her eyes melted me down, as if her watery eyes were cooling the envious fire burning my skin. "Nothing", I sighed blowing the smoke out of my mouth. "It's just that, I don't belong here. I am not like any one of these. I mean I can't dance", I said in a low voice. Anita walked towards me and rubbed her palms on my face. The touch of her palms sent cold peaceful warmth through my face while I leaned in her palms. I extended my hand out for her waist and pulled my girl towards me. "I love you", I mumbled staring in her watery eyes. "I love you too *Jaan*", she smiled and leaned forward and kissed me. I gasped as her lips touched mine and I responded with passionate strokes, kissing her in desperation to cool off the fiery insecurities caused by my guilt.

"Ok don't get too lusty now", she pulled back her head. "Nikita's mom is around and if she sees us doing this, it would be very embarrassing", she suggested rubbing my chest. "Yes *Jaan*", I nodded with a smile. "Hey give me a drag, I so feel like smoking", she hushed. I gave her the burnt half cigarette and looked at her. "You look like you are here for a street fight tournament", I remarked looking down at her sport shoes blending in with her blue denims and her black sleeveless tee. "Especially with your ponytail", I said turning her around to face her back and pulled her towards me. "You are looking so 'hot' *Jaan*", I mumbled in her ears as I grabbed her waist from behind and rubbed myself lightly against her. "Although I am not that good a dancer, but I am sure I can grind", I murmured and executed my simple desire. "Uday, you are so 'hard' right now. I can feel it", she exclaimed as we stood crammed against the wall in the corner of the balcony. "Let's go, or they will start searching for us", she giggled and I walked with her to the dance floor. "How do I look, you didn't tell me?" I asked nervously. "You are looking good. Just you could do better if you pulled your shirt out", she chuckled. "Why what's wrong with this?" I asked doubtfully. "I don't know but I find this tucked in attire very avuncular", mocked Anita sarcastically. "Look at Abhijeet, perhaps that might help you", she added. "Yeah right, I am so sorry I am not like him", I hissed with obvious bitterness. "Come on Uday! If you can learn from someone, you must learn... and stop being a bitch now", she scolded authoritatively smacking my bum with a hard slap. The slap lightened me up though I still struggled with the idea of learning from Abhijeet. "I am really a very pathetic dancer", I said nervously while she held my hand pulling me to the dance floor. "You are not that bad, even Nikita thinks that you are flexible", she said as we made our space on the dance floor. "See, you are flexible", she said as she watched me groove with her. "I can't *salsa* or *jive*", I said loudly. "It's ok, you don't need to *salsa* or *jive* to be a good dancer", screamed Anita in the soaring volume of the music. "Dance is all about expression and you have to just openly express yourself", she continued screaming. I wondered if I could ever really express myself openly as I grooved holding her waist.

The song changed to a dance number by *Modjo*[116] and its lyrics filled the dance floor with euphoria.

> *"Lady, love me tonight,*
> *Cause my hunger... is just so right,*
> *As you glance... through my sad eyes,*
> *On your neck... is my love bite!*
> *Lady, I must feel like,*
> *I am so lonely... with my vice,*
> *I feel you... for the first time,*
> *And I know, I am gonna eat you, all through the night!"*

Anita sang along. Her moist eyes were way more excited and I blended in with her excitement singing along and leading her on the dance floor. She tried not to giggle watching my unconventional moves, which just

---

[116] *French house musical duo.*

got better than my previous robotic dancing. "See *Jaan*, we are finally in a discotheque together", she said in my ears and I could just kiss her neck in my heart filled anticipation. "We are dancing together, *Jaan!*" I screamed with the unbelievable feeling of this desire coming to life.

We were still cautious of the spectators and soon Abhijeet, Rizvi and Nikita found us on the dance floor and soon I was a comfortable dancer, dancing with everybody with the blessings of an angel of a girlfriend who set me free of my insecurities. Nikita danced by my side and her glittery blue one piece held her 'hearts' out with temptation. As a natural response I readdressed my new found skills of dance towards her and she happily grooved along. In a sudden realization I looked at Anita who was closing in on the dance floor with Abhijeet and Rizvi, and I quickly danced back to her. "Fuck you Uday", I cursed myself. "You want it all right! But you can't have it all, all the time", I reminded myself and continued dancing with Anita. When the party ended, Nikita and Anita were going home in Nikita's car, and thus they came to see me off. "How are you guys going?" I asked Abhijeet. "Rizvi and I are going to *Malad*, on my bike", he answered. I took a breath of relief knowing that they were all going to different places. I looked at Anita to say goodbye and she walked up and shook my hands. "Shaking my hand?" I thought angrily. I waved a sour yet expressionless goodbye and left. "A cheater in love will always fear being cheated", I mumbled as I rode back empathizing with my paranoia. I couldn't help stopping by and messaging Anita, "You could have hugged me goodbye but I guess that would be too uncool in front of your happening friends." Anita called back several times but I didn't answer, maybe as my way of punishing her for not soothing my insecure ego.

It is strange how a single shade of 'darkness' can darken all the 'light'. I was in a similar color where one minor hesitation from Anita angered me way more than all the love and care she bestowed. I still wanted to win it perhaps, everything on my terms and conditions. The 'darkness' drove me as a few days later I couldn't resist the urge to see Nikita and get my ego stroked again.

I picked her up from her college and we rode back to the lake. "Where is Rizvi?" I asked. "He is absent today", said Nikita. I sat on my bike and she leaned in on me making way for her standing in the space between my legs. Nikita wore a black tee again and her 'hearts' were protruding out on the surface. I grabbed her 'hearts' and stared in her eyes maybe searching for my victory. The spark in her eyes didn't' twinkle, it rather gleamed... Like the dull gleam which often occurs when gray tinds it way between 'dark' and 'light'. It was a 'habit' to her, to hunt and to be hunted... and that's what her eyes were all about. In short, I had found 'red' in the gray...

Nikita had succumbed to her instincts and she leaned in to kiss. But as her wetness touched my mouth, my nostrils smelt a stench of bad breath. In just a moment, Anita's face appeared in a flash before my eyes. "What if she comes to know that I cheated on her with her best friend?" I thought. I could see a very devastated face of Anita before my eyes if she learnt of this. "She could lose hope in both friendship and love at the same time and I cannot do that to her", I thought smelling the foul smell coming out of Nikita's mouth. I pulled back from the lip lock and hurriedly said, "I need to rush back home. I just remembered, my mom had asked me to get something. It's very urgent." Nikita pulled back with disappointment and we left. "As least I am better than that for her bad breath", I consoled myself and my lame excuse, still compensating for leaving Nikita's voluptuous and inviting 'hearts'.

It was naive of me to think that the 'darkness' was just driving me, it was well present in others too, especially the ones touched by me. Soon it was knocking at the door of my fate when Anita and I were breaking up a couple of weeks later.

The way you push my buttons,
The way you unleash,

Don't listen to that bitch,
She pays no heed,

She burns in envy,
All hell fell loose,

A SHADE CALLED GRAY

She competes with you,
For the 'Love' you choose..

I know I am wrong, I know my mistake,
But it's our dreams here,
"Our fuckin stake!"
Left for the World to define its fate,
As the World just enjoys,
When lovers separate...

I still try to recollect the reasons for which we were breaking up that day in the palace of my daily diminishing memories. Well, maybe after some years, the real cause of that incident is diminished or forgotten. Only the glimpses and a few words remain of that gray day when we were standing at the parking lot of a *Mumbai* suburban railway station which was very close to my house. I remember walking furiously towards the station to meet Anita as we were fighting for a couple of days majorly regarding my insecurity towards her friendship with Abhijeet. I saw Anita and Nikita waiting for me at the parking lot. I walked up to them in a furious rage only to be greeted by scorn from Anita. "What is your problem?" I screamed as I reached them. "My problem is you Uday", she screamed back. Nikita stood silently watching us fight. I could hardly see any concern in her mannerism to keep Anita and me together. She stood behind Anita with her arms folded. "Would you stop talking to me like that", I said rudely to Anita. "Nikita, why don't you say something? Why is she fighting with me all the time?" I pleaded loudly.

"Guys I am out of this", said Nikita with her hands off, gesturing her lack of participation in our argument. "Why are you out of it? Don't you remember how we helped you get over Kunal when you were so depressed?" I yelled at her trying to shake her out of her nonchalance. "And what about the way you harass Anita all the time?" she screamed back. "When did I harass her?" I demanded. "And why are you being such a bitch Nikita? I mean, aren't we all friends?" I yelled back. "You cannot talk to my friend like that Uday", Anita screamed pointing her finger towards me. "Please don't get influenced by her. I know she is behind all this", I said pointing towards Nikita. "Stop this bullshit Uday, I cannot be what you want me to be all the time. With your

304

insecurity over anyone and everyone I talk to", screamed Anita. "When am I insecure about anyone and everyone Anita? And anyways, it is a personal matter. Can we walk a little ahead and talk?" I protested. "No, I am not going anywhere with you Uday. Stay here and talk", she demanded. "Yes Anita, don't go anywhere. Talk to him here itself", hissed Nikita from behind. "How dare you speak between me and my girlfriend?" I said scornfully to Nikita. Anita stepped forward towards me and pointed her finger in my face and said, "Uday, it's over between you and me." "Please don't say that *Jaan*", I retorted. Watching me beg in front of Anita, Nikita hid a faint smile which appeared on her face. "Bitch, she is enjoying it", I thought. "Uday, stop begging me to take you back and be your girlfriend... all the time! Get a grip on yourself", ranted Anita bitterly. "I cannot do a day without you Anita. Please don't do this. I love you *Jaan*", I insisted. "See Uday, you don't love me, you are just habituated to me. So you will get over me", she said sharply. She turned back to look at Nikita and she gave her a go ahead gesture, still hiding the bitchy smile on her face. What I could see was perhaps, what Anita couldn't. Although it appeared that Anita didn't find out from Nikita about her advances on me. "I can't even tell her what a bitch Nikita is", I thought helplessly.

"Let's go Anita, there is no point talking to him", commented Nikita. "Yes, let's go", replied Anita abruptly. A few people passed by, cherishing the pleasure of the public display of anger which was no longer affectionate and was full of scorn. "Wait", I interrupted. A fit of rage driven by the caused humiliation triggered me and I slammed a slap across Anita's face. She remained in shock only for a few seconds as she retaliated with a hard slap right across my face. Nikita screamed from behind, "He raised his hand, wait I will call Abhijeet and Rizvi right away", and she took out her cellphone. I looked at Nikita with an unending rage, but maybe God made me turn towards Anita who stood devastated looking at her lover who lost control and raised his hand on her. Drops of tears oozed out of her eyes and she turned towards Nikita. "Chuck it, don't call anyone, let's go", she said in a shaky yet firm voice. "Don't ever show your face to me again", she mumbled amidst tears. They began to walk away and I stood there watching Anita leave. I started walking back while tear drops kept pouring out of my eyes.

"What the fuck did I do?" I said with regret as I lit up a cigarette sitting beneath a tree which was my usual smoking hangout. One after the other, I kept smoking cigarettes but the tears didn't stop. I walked back home with a heavy heart.

Looking back I could never see, which conversation was going where. Everything appeared so black and white. A "yes" is a yes and a "no" is a no; a smile is good and a tear is bad, a hug is friendly and restraint is creepy. But now it just seems like it all got messed up on the way. The blacks and whites of life just mixed themselves making life gray. The irony of 'time' presented itself as I cannot blame anyone for my fate. It were my deeds which brought me here. I couldn't even blame Nikita completely though it was obvious that my breakup was orchestrated by her but somewhere, I had started this mess.

I reached home and was greeted by my happy parents. My father had developed a clue about the troubles between Anita and me. He looked at my upset face and anticipated it with a sad song which he sung cheerfully. "*No woman, no cry*", he sang and looked at me. "I slapped her", I mumbled out loud expressing my guilt. "What? Are you serious?" he yelled at me in disbelief. I nodded, deeply embedded in shame. "Shame on you Uday, how could you raise your hand on a girl and I presume she is your girlfriend?" he yelled again. I stayed silent as perhaps I didn't want to defend myself anymore. "Would you tolerate it if a guy raised his hand on your sister?" he asked angrily. I nodded a silent 'no'. "Shame on you Uday, I don't want to talk to you. She is such a good girl, I feel unsure now as to what kind of a son I have raised", he cursed with spite and walked out.

The shades of gray made me realize that I have walked so deep into the 'dark' that perhaps there is no return. My 'white' will always remain tainted and gray.

A week later the board examination results were out. I had scored a *pass class*[117] which was unbelievable. The exact figure surmounted to a

---

[117] *The formidable students who have just passed and their aggregate scores rest between 35%/40% to 50%.*

point zero seven percent less than fifty. It simply meant that my career ahead was fucked. In the ever competitive *India*, career is a big deal, at least for the average middle class population. Each parent dreams of a bright brilliant future for their child, and education burns a hole in pockets of every middle class family. But the hopes and dreams of my parents for me had lesser chances. The destination of my curious journey of 'red' ended up shading the other vital aspect of my life, also in gray.

But when you accept that you can't change what has happened, and every remaining bit of the sad memories prick you, it's always better to use an anesthetic to ignore the pain. Thus, I finally settle in my couch in my rented apartment in *Pune* re-living the shady memories of those days as I sipped the last peg of dark rum which I had saved from the previous night's party. Probably alcohol serves as an anesthetic which is widely used to deal with the pricking memories of the unchangeable past.

Watching the gray evening turn into a dark night, the clouds began to pour into a heavy rainfall as if they were crying with me. But still, the only thing which the 'little warrior' remembers is the moment when he conquered Nikita... and the consequences it brought, in the 'red' he sought. The deed had added another dent in my 'karma', darkening the 'gray', of the 'time' of my life.

WHEN I FOUND RED IN GRAY

The spark in her eyes didn't' twinkle, it rather gleamed... Like the dull gleam which often occurs when gray finds it way between 'dark' and 'light'. It appeared more like a 'habit'. Perhaps it was a habit to her, to swoop down and embrace me. There was no loss of innocence, guilt or shame in her eyes... Though the 'rouge' didn't leave its place, prominently marking its presence between 'dark' and 'light'. What if love is an accident and lust is a habit? A 'habit' of conquering... And keeping it as spoils. Is it an indication that we lived more?

But then, when I got up and looked at her, there was an undefined stillness in her eyes, still waiting to be channelized as mischief or regret.

I didn't feel it then, as more than Anita's 'light', my 'red' wanted its mark. I pounced back forcefully rubbing my lips on hers. She reciprocated with her wet tongue, fully tasting the span of my lower jaw. I looked again in her eyes. The stillness of the gray, gleamed with excitement. The one we feel when we meet our kind!

I still resented the thought of being conquered. Playing the game by her rules was unacceptable. I had to overreach, to prove that I am a superlative to her shortcomings. I swooped down to her neck and like a vapor of tempestuous sin which fumes through the nostrils of the predator..., the sweet shallow fragrance of the apple flavored smoke reeked from her dark cleavage. Predators are often driven by the smell of 'blood'. It helps them feed, even if they are blind, dumb or deaf. I sneered down to her dusky yet glittery voluptuous 'hearts'.

The moment before the kill is a very promising yet an unpredictable breath. She breathed heavily as she waited for me to devour. I wasn't unsure either, but surprise is the best way to deliver a shock! I pulled the strap of her maroon dress from her shoulder to her forearm, releasing her fleshy treasure out of its clothed prison. I swooped down to one of her 'hearts' and it filled my mouth, the biggest I ever tasted.

Her initial resistance was the little victory, and her long strokes on my scalp were the rewards to encourage me to continue swallowing her 'heart'. Gray is endless, in its gloomy stillness...

The first wound is often intimidation, but the peace of conquering comes with the kill, and gets even better with a prisoner of war. My hands moved downwards to her core most piece of her clothing. The thin wide strap was wet. I intruded with my fingers, but she responded with strength and stopped my advances. I looked back in her eyes... They were dark again.

"Let's go to your place", I said many a times. But she gave one reason or the other. My twinkle failed to impress her. Her 'darkness' was the clear victor. I felt excited again, to find my kind...!

ANSH SETH

JOURNEY OF COLORS

The color of the bodies is fawn,
The spice in the eyes is 'red',
For the dark hollow which all cover,
Oblivious to its existence,
To know it ourselves is what we dread...

But our journey is eventually towards light,
As even buried souls come out to witness,
That even after the world burns down,
The dark ashes too turn gray...

Love hurts but doesn't kill,
For the pursuit of blood is the only thrill,
It will eventually take away a bite of you,
Damaging you, to seek your fill.

In Light you will seek Dark,
And in dark you shall light the Spark,
The Journey of Colors is from Black to White,
The 'Red' remains between dark and light,
So does love and so does life...!

CHAPTER 8
DON'T CURSE ME, MY LOVE...

The gray evening has turned into a dark night. Looking back at the last few days, I just spent them thinking about Anita. Perhaps it was boiling up due to Tanya's coldness towards me, or maybe Anita's exit from my life had already set me on the path of doom. Crying is said to be an activity which really helps lighten up, but maybe I am just too insensitive to cry. I try hard to pour out the anguish which had started to boil up like a volcano inside me, but my eyelids are too stubborn to give away. The leftover rum from the previous night's party got over, leaving me further restless. I felt too drained to leave home and go looking for the dark elixir which brings temporary relief to burning hearts. I furiously searched my metal cupboard, though with negligible hope, for my gang of drunken friends and our common habit of binge drinking. I dug my hands through the cluttered pile of clothes, but my weary forage brought no result of relief. I was about to give up, when in a last attempt of despair I swooped down to the shoe rack of the metal cupboard. I ruffled through old shoes in a hurry and just when I was about to get up, there it shone... a tiny luster of glass. I felt a moment of peace as if I found a treasure of 'hope'. I removed the shoes from the rack and there peeped a bottle of the wise *Old Monk*; the best black rum available in *India.* The drink of wisdom brought a smile of 'hope' on my teary face, as perhaps a little 'hope' was required to survive through the darkness of the cursed night.

Finally, when peace seemed difficult to achieve, I opened up the brand new bottle of my newly discovered black rum which perhaps I had bought some days back. Maybe I had preemptively known, that it might be really required to make it through such a night. I added a few cubes of ice to my next drink. The sip of cold rum had a different heat and as the heat trickled down my throat, it met my anguish, boiling it further, taking me back to last few memories of Anita.

Love stories often have sad hopeless endings, which harbor a lot of pain and often it is better to move on, than to hold on to any memory of it. "I could never move on from Anita", I mumble as I continue to sip my drink and light up a cigarette in an attempt to blow out her memories – which always kept me comparing any girl I ever dated with her. Also, her memories always questioned my 'worth', a question which I had always answered differently with a new gimmick every time. Yet I could never figure out what I am 'worthy' of. The answer to this impossible question was plain and simple – 'love'; an answer which I believe I might never find.

It was the same question which the world had put across when my board results were out. Anita had met me at college, when we all had gathered to receive the mark sheets of our board examinations. The hint of the breakup was immediately replaced by a highly dramatic environment where everybody was either charged up or looked sad because of their results. A few morons, though they had scored relatively better compared to others, still appeared or pretended sad, and obviously were amongst the most hated kids. Anita was one amongst them too.

"Why do you look so sad Anita?" I asked her. "I missed a *first class*[118] by just a percent. I am giving my papers for re-evaluation", she said in a low voice. "You should be happy, at least you scored a *'second class'*[119]", I said in a wry tone. "Why, how much did you score? Sorry, I totally forgot to ask", she replied. "It's better if you don't ask. You don't know how tough these last two weeks were for me, since you broke up", I said accusing her of my misery. "Shut up Uday!" she commanded. "Just bloody hell...! Just tell me how much you scored?" her loud yelling broke down into despair. Her rudeness sounded more like concern.

"Well, I missed the fifty percent benchmark by just point zero seven percent", I said in a dry, hopeless tone. "So did you fail?" she asked in astonishment. "No, I passed in all the subjects, but it's as good as

---

[118]   *More than 60% aggregate score is refereed as first class.*

[119]   *Between 50% to 60% aggregate score is referred as second class.*

failing", I said sadly. "I told you to work hard, but all you could do is bullshit around", she regretted, and then her concern appeared to smirk. Her dimples still mesmerised the innocence of our 'time' and thus returned the horror... That she would go away! All I could see were her dimples through the memory lanes of our recent years. The small even depressions which occurred on her cheeks were so potent that it had perhaps overshadowed all the earlier memories which I had, before I had met her. Maybe the spell of 'love' does that, it helps you forget all that you could remember; of failures and loneliness replaced by the 'fear' of having them back. The mere thought that she would go away, replaced my previous failures with a new fear. I could do nothing but blame her... or everybody around her. But even my blame only ended at me.

"Come on, you left me to my own sensibilities. You broke up with me during the boards. How am I supposed to concentrate when all I could think about was you?" I retaliated. "The thought of losing you kept haunting me all the time. I love you!" and even I broke down to despair. Feeling helpless for losing everything that mattered – past, present or future! My past; which was fading away in 'time', her presence of which I couldn't be devoid off, or my future; which appeared hazy. "Don't blame me for your failure. It's your extra-curricular activities which got you this awesome result", she said sharply. I felt helpless, and a reflection of the forbidden glimpses reoccurred. "It's all my fault, but why am I losing it all?" I wrenched inside. I looked at her with a 'hurt' face knowing that she might be correct.

"Perhaps it is too difficult for you to feel what I am feeling. I guess you are usually not on the same side of examination results like I am", I said with a defeated sore face. "I don't know what I will do ahead. How will I communicate this result to my parents? I don't know if I would even get an admission for master's?" I said, panicking to take the result home. "It's ok, it's my problem now. I will deal with it", I said coldly and began to walk out of the college. "Where are you going?" she asked. "Home, and hope you enjoy your second class", I said bitterly and left for my bike. As I sat on the bike, a fear crept inside me. I was too scared to face my parents and especially my father who had bought me a bike since I had finished graduation. In terms of financial assessment, I then realized that I had become an expensive, non-profitable, non-productive, non-reliable and an emotionally dysfunctional asset. And such an asset is generally called liability!

I reached home in the hot noon where my mother was anxiously waiting for the board examination result. She had called several times but I hadn't answered my cellphone. "How much did you score?" she asked excitedly as she opened the door for me. I took a few pauses till I mustered up the courage to blurt out my result to her. "*Ma*, I got forty nine point nine three percent", I said in a feeble voice. "What! You are joking right?" she asked with a sarcastic smile. I looked at the innocence of my mother who was expecting a respectable result from her moronic son. "No, honestly", I said with a serious face. "What? Don't say that Uday. How did you get such marks?" she asked in shock. "I don't know what went wrong. I was expecting at least a fifty percent plus result", I reasoned. "But I enquired there is a room for re-evaluation of the papers. I will apply for that", I said trying to console her. My mother bickered for a couple of hours but watching me upset she quickly tuned into a much positive mood trying to keep up my spirits. "What will happen when your father comes to know of your result?" she asked with the 'fear' already creeping into her eyes. The 'fear' was just residing in the corner of my eyes too and was already prevailing in my heart.

"What will you do ahead in life with such a result?" screamed my father when he saw my mark sheet. I feared a slap or worse from him for the 'class apart' result which I had scored. Moreover the expensive birthday gift of a bike had already been making me nervous. "Bloody hell, after so much of hard earned money I have put into your education, this is the result you could get! Shame on you Uday, you are such a failure!" he continued screaming. "I did not fail Dad, I passed in all the subjects", I solemnly protested. "This result is as good as failing. Did you even think what would you do ahead with such a result? Who is going to give you an admission? I suggest you go to your uncle, he will teach you his business. At max, I can open a shop for you to run in the future", he yelled sarcastically and every word out of his mouth pricked. "You are being too harsh on him", interfered my mother. "I feel like beating him up. Ask him if he is going out to party? Ask him if he found a new girlfriend? Bloody he doesn't deserve an expensive bike for a birthday gift", he taunted angrily. "Now can you change it? What happened has happened. We can just look ahead", suggested my logical mother. "What ahead now, he will polish people's boots!" added my father. His eyelids fluttered in anger as he looked at me. "Still, give him a chance!" pleaded my mother. My father took a deep breath and said, "You deal with him. But if I see him going out for any party, he will have it from me. Take his bike keys too, he doesn't deserve that bike." I kept silent and listened while I handed out my bike keys and gave it to my father. He was right about everything he said. Everybody had scored better marks. I couldn't compensate myself with the thought that at least I had passed. Examples of those who failed didn't make me happy, as with them I was never competing. Even Anita had scored much better marks than me. "How could I be so foolish?" I thought bitterly and just stood there, listening to my father's angry appreciation.

The worst thing to do is to meet friends and acquaintances after a horrible board examination result, because they just mock the failure. I feared the 'mockery', but in the course of previous events, my fears were coming true. I met a couple of local acquaintances, people whom the world referred to as 'your friends', but to my senses, Doctor was the only friend I had. "Hey Uday, did you get your board results?" asked one of the acquaintances. "Yes buddy", I said in a low voice. "How much did you score? A 'distinction'[120]?" he asked with a sly grin. The look in his eyes and the glint of his yellow teeth had already pinched me deep inside, yet I took a deep breath and answered, "No, just got a fifty percent." Both of them laughed and howled, "Cheers, awesome grades buddy!" I felt like smashing a punch across their faces as I could do to them in football, but that would just make me look childish and vulnerable to more criticism. "So where is the party?" chuckled the other one. Anger flushed up on my face and my nostrils flared and in spite of an attempt to control my tongue I blurted out, "Did your father give you a party when you got your results? Motherfuckers, I will fuck your happiness for good. Don't fuck around with me." They both still laughed and I walked away straight to my home. "Give me the bike keys", I demanded from my mother. "But your father said that you are not supposed to ride the bike anymore", she took her stand. "I have to go to the University to put my papers for revaluation. It is too far, I have to change two trains to

---

[120]   *Above 75% in aggregate score is refereed as distinction.*

reach there. Give me my bike please", I insisted. "You want to go to the University on the bike? Shut up and take the local train", protested my mother angrily. "Very well, then just give me the money to pay for the re-correction of the papers", I said to my mother. "Yes, take it but you have to go by train", she insisted. I nodded and took the money. "I am very tired. I had been in the kitchen since morning, and you and your sister really don't care. I am going to sleep", said my tired mother. "Ok, then I will go", I said and waited for her to sleep. As soon as she slept, I stole the keys from the key rack and rushed for my bike.

Stealing my bike was a crazy experience, it just brought me to an element of 'time' called uncertainty. And it stayed with me throughout the road, as I traveled through highways and unknown turns. Many strangers guided the way, and every place I reached appeared like a surprise. I finally entered the old gates of *Mumbai University.* The lanes inside were paved with greenery on both sides. I rode down watching herds of people turn, pulled to the sound of the thump. I reached the revaluation department, where hordes of students crowded to submit their papers, to have them rechecked. I searched for my college mates, and when I couldn't find any of them, I called up Anita.

The University had a tedious process to give the papers for re-evaluation. Anita instructed me to stand in a line for the submission forms which required the photocopies of my mark sheets. I rode out again on my bike to get them. By the time I reached, Anita was already packing up. She had given her papers for re-evaluation.

"Nitu, where would I get the forms and where do I have to submit it? I asked her. She hesitantly responded to my affectionate redo of her name. "Yes Uday, just ask anybody and you would know. Or wait even Gando is submitting his form, he will help you", she answered with a hint of avoidance. It was pretty unusual of hers to deny me any help, especially of the administrative nature. "Why can't you help?" I asked with a cold stare. "Hey don't mind, I need to leave with Rasika as she will drop me midway. I will take a rickshaw from there..." she answered curtly. "Or just wait, lemme finish. I will drop you on my bike", I looked at her intently, fancying the ride. "No Uday, I will have to leave you... Err now! I need to cover all the colleges in two days. I need to apply in all of them", she answered firmly, ignoring my idea of riding together. "You aren't applying for master's?" she asked with concern. Her innocent question appeared more like an insult. "Why are you mocking me? You know my score. Do you think anybody will give me admission?" I asked in disappointment.

She paused in embarrassment. Rasika passed by calling her to leave. "Never-mind! Just do your best. Okay Uday, I gotta leave" she smiled formally and left. I saw her walk to Rasika's car. She didn't turn back to glance even once. Probably she was just indifferent. As she walked away, I wondered about indifference. Is it where love and hate turn both gray? And then it starts resembling a tensed conflict between 'light' and 'dark'... But when she turned around giggling over a conversation with Rasika, in her eyes I saw no missing spark... Or the gray battle for her 'red', was slowly being won by 'dark'.

Gando helped me fill a form and left. I copied the information in the remaining forms for each paper. And again stood in a long queue to submit the final re-evaluation papers. The submission window was cluttered with students. When I looked inside, stacks of collected cash were kept around the cashier, inspiring ideas of robbing them. After spending a five hundred rupee note on each paper, I restored a little faith, so much so I wasn't far away from the positive day dreams like "What if I suddenly sum up to a first class?"

I struggled out of the hoarding students, and began walking back. I turned around to spot Ratish who had just entered the long queue. I walked up to him. "Hey Ratish", I called. Ratish returned a dry tensed smile. "Since when are you standing here?" I asked. "Quite some time. These motherfuckers have made a very tiring setup for submission!" he cursed the University administration. "How many papers are you submitting for re-evaluation?" I continued. "...All the papers Uday. And you?" he answered, as if he was already anticipating the question. "Even I have given all the papers... What an irony? Though I have passed, but my result is no good to me!" I answered, reminiscing my helplessness. "What happened? How much did you score?" I continued, diverting myself from my misery. His smile became empty and his eyes turned tensed, and words took effort to pour out.

Ratish was the only guy who failed in the entire class. "His year is wasted. He has to appear again unless he passes in the re-evaluation", I thought about is bad luck. It was strange to watch the ever arrogant and tough Ratish mellow down. I wondered if he was too dumb or was he also cursed, perhaps by Zaida?

"Does this re-evaluation help?" I asked him curiously. "I had asked a few friends. They said you usually end up getting the same marks. In fact they will only increase your marks if your total score at least increases by a percent and not just by a single mark", he said with disappointment, perhaps accepting his failure. And then reality slapped me, telling me what I really needed, and that would be anything above a fifty percent.

I reached home only to be greeted by my mother with future career options. "Uday, let's enroll you for master's in your college", she beamed. "With these marks do you think anyone is going to take me?" I asked shamelessly. "We will donate money to college if necessary", suggested my mother. "I am not taking any more money from you guys", I protested. "The money is not your concern. You just go ahead and study", said my kind mother. "I don't know. I thought I will prepare for CAT and go for MBA", I suggested. "Let's see", she added. "Uday, where are the bike keys?" she asked suspiciously. "What do I know, it must be in the key rack", I lied. "Stop lying Uday, I heard your bike when you were parking", she said solemnly. "It's my bike and I can ride it when I want to", I protested in agitation. "Let your father not know about it Uday. He is really mad at you", she said and the humiliation returned. I guess when someone is humiliated for a long time, they become 'thick skinned' and so had I. I walked back into my room with the keys in my pocket.

My college opened admission for the masters' program. In the next couple of days, I had filled the forms of only a few colleges where I hoped that perhaps I had a chance. Though somewhere inside I knew that with the given competition and reservations, my chances of scoring a seat was next to impossible.

The final lists were put up and news arrived. Anita was taken in the final batch for the master's program. I clearly hadn't even qualified in any list. My enthusiastic parents were still not giving up hope as they went to meet my H.O.D – Mrs. Ragade for donations, perhaps to get me through. Though I was totally resilient as paying money for admission badly hit my own self-worth.

My father left home angrily, perhaps knowing that I clearly wouldn't qualify for the seat or maybe he knew that I was a 'worthless' son, too lost in my own odyssey of 'love' and 'blood' to empathize with his pain to raise me.

By evening my heart pounded anxiously, awaiting their return. I saw their car enter the gate at dusk and my parents rang the doorbell as they returned from the parking lot.

"What happened?" I asked nervously. "She rejected the idea of even having you enrolled", said my disappointed mother. "It's ok, not her fault. Our son had been so studious that she cannot afford to keep him. What if he tops again?" added my father sarcastically. I stayed silent and he quietly walked into his room. "I am sorry, I disappointed you guys", I said to my mother in a sad voice. "Don't be sad Uday, we will find something for you. Just promise that you will work hard this time", cheered my mother empathizing with my pain. "I feel bad for *Papa*, was Ragade rude to you?" I asked anxiously. "A little bit, I won't deny that she is a stern lady, but imagine Uday, being at that position you become like that", said my mother. Fumes of anger began to boil inside me. "How dare she?" I mumbled angrily. "Don't get angry Uday. It's not like if she says 'no', we will stop", consoled my mother. "But then what exactly did she say?" I asked curiously. My mother began narrating the meet. "She welcomed us inside her cabin and when she came to know that we are your parents then she looked pretty amused. She said some good things about you but had a lot of complaints against you too. Did you set the lab on fire?" asked my mother sternly. "It happened by mistake", I answered avoiding the incident. "She finally said that if we want to pay donation we can go ahead, but she would prefer a student who is more serious about the subject. Also she said that you are more suited for management studies rather than master's and doctorate", continued my mother. "But then I want you to prove her wrong. You should pursue master's", she encouraged passionately, perhaps with a hint of vengeance. "*Papa* must have been very angry", I asked her. "No he wasn't. He was very cool and calm", she consoled with a smile. "Do you know what he said?" she began to narrate in excitement. "What?" I asked anxiously. "*Papa* said that my son is on the lines of *Einstein.* It's ok, even if he doesn't finish master's, he will make it in life", completed my emotional mother. A tear drop struggled to pool up around my eyelashes but I held it from falling. "Uday you have to do something now, you need to have a good career. Your father still thinks you are capable", reassured my mother with a heavy throat and I nodded silently. "Anyways tomorrow we will enroll you for the MBA coaching", she said and left.

Anita called up at night and I answered, "Hey wassup, what are you doing?" she asked. "I am fine, how are you?" I answered coldly. "I made it for the master's program", she said with mild excitement. "That's nice", I said masking my feeling of loss. "What about you? Did your parents go to meet Mrs. Ragade?" she asked curiously. "Yes, they did", I replied. "What did she say?" she asked.

"Nothing much. Just that she doesn't want me!" I answered. "What exactly did she say?" she asked curiously. "She said that I am not serious for the subject and I should go for MBA. So finally it's simple, she doesn't want me", I replied coldly. "Hey, it's ok you will get admission somewhere else", consoled Anita.

"Where?" I asked in frustration. "Somewhere! God is always there", she said hopefully. "Yup but you know what?" I said getting a bit cranky. "What?" she asked. "My Dad said to Ragade, that my son is of the likes of *Einstein* and the other school drop outs that made it big. If for no one else, I will do something in my life for him. He still believes in me", I said with hot tears mustering in my eyes.

"But Mummy wants to prove her wrong; she wants me to go for master's. And I want to do that too", I laughed thinking of my mother and her 'never give up' spirit. "Maybe Ragade is right", said Anita hesitantly. "Ragade is so cruel, how could she ever be right? And how could you support her?" I snapped. "Maybe because you are not really ready for master's and doctorate in biological sciences", she replied. "Shut up, I can do that easily", I replied arrogantly. "See it's more like all the

320

teachers feel the same way about you. You are more apt for advertising and the marketing side of things. You should do an MBA. It would suit you", she suggested.

In the echoes of her soft voice, Anita just made me feel what I still wanted. 'To be with her' and I felt that all the career mess would automatically sort. Even if it didn't, in the echoes of her soft voice, the importance of my career began fading. "I love you *Jaan*", I mumbled on the phone. Anita took a few uncomfortable pauses and said, "Uday focus on your career right now. You are in a deep mess." "Thanks for reminding me of that, but if you could just love me right now. I am feeling too weak to do anything", I said begging for her 'love'. "That's ok Uday", she said with a sudden coldness.

"Please Anita, hang on. I love you and you love me too, right!" I insisted. "That's not possible Uday", continued Anita. "Please please please", I kept begging in desperation. "Take a grip on yourself Uday, focus on your life", she interrupted my desperate pleading. "*Jaan* please", I mumbled. "Bye Uday", she said coldly and hung up.

In a brief moment of sadness and desperation my eyes opened up to a bigger reality. Directionless and clueless in life, the pain of Anita didn't matter anymore. It was a life crisis scenario. Failing at basics can cause a lot of loneliness and the desire to be with people in such a state can also bring in the feeling of humiliation.

"Anita left me at my weakest", I mumbled choking on a big gulp of anguish in my throat. "It doesn't even matter now, even my family is so disappointed with me", I said in tears. "Please help me God", I begged asking that someone 'above' to open a door for me to fix up all the mess. The next morning the door opened, when my mother took me to get me enrolled in the coaching classes for MBA.

The institute was called 'Time', a dimension of life which will never lie to you. Or perhaps, it's the biggest lie in itself. In these classes then, I hardly knew that I was going to find the one who would lash out my 'time' on my soul, for perhaps the rest of my life. That was where I met Tanya.

The next day I sat amongst really focused kids from all places, everybody buzzed about management colleges and percentiles. The feeling of mismatch came easy, especially when I attempted mathematics. Other than being the passion, biology kept mathematics safely away as it was my weakest subject. A dark bald guy raised his hand to answer a question asked by the language teacher. The teacher praised him, and half of the class looked at him in awe. "He is sure shot going to the *IIM's*[121]", murmured the kid sitting next to me. Well I realized it is going to be a very slim possibility for the kids to say something similar about me.

Once out of the class, I saw Anita's missed call on my cellphone. I called her back and she answered. "Hey wassup?" she asked in her husky voice. "I am good. I am here in the class", I answered. "How is it going?" she continued. "It's fine, just the first day though. How are you?" I replied. "I am good. The master's program has started and we had lectures here since morning. There are new students who have joined in. It seems like a nice batch", she narrated. "Nice, I am happy for you", I said coldly. "Thanks, but it seems like there's something is missing without you", she added hesitantly.

"Thanks for missing me", I said with a hint of nostalgia. "What do you think, what is *CAT* preparation like?" she asked. "It seems difficult, I have no clue", I answered. "Yeah right. Don't act moronic there. Do as much as you can", pointed Anita. "Yeah you don't need to tell me, I will manage", I snapped.

"It sounds like you are blaming me for your state", she chuckled teasing me. "My blaming doesn't matter, I am in this fix and I have to figure my way out from here", I said dryly. "Yeah if you weren't bullshitting with your chicks, you wouldn't have been in this situation", she snapped instantly. She said dragging the syllable 'chi' of 'chicks', with an immense stress, elongating the pronunciation. "Now stop mocking me, shut up and bye", I said and abruptly hung up the phone.

---

[121] *Indian Institute of Management: The best in India, if you do your MBA from here, you are entitled to a lot of dowry.*

When the world around you, especially the ones who make your 'reforence frame' with respect to important things in life like success, love and happiness move on, it often leaves you feeling miserable and lonely. Thanks to my father's daily sarcasm and bickering that staying at home too, became difficult. Well 'peace' had to be searched somewhere outside and it wouldn't be found even with Anita as her mockery of my state, had its own repercussions.

The irony of 'peace' is very lethal in itself. 'Peace' always presented itself to me as something which the world provided, pretty synonymous to my own 'sense of worth'. Much later, I realized that 'worth' is something which has to be achieved within one's own self, and so is 'peace'.

Buzzing in the crowds of the students, I was talking to practically everyone. Maybe that was the only way I saw then, to make peace with my brazen self and my sense of self-worth, as I knew that maybe I am not worthy of love and friendship. I had betrayed my lover and my friends creating a very big mess. People were soon becoming the need for a normal life. The students spoke about their lives and I was living a realm of unending stories. Well, honestly, the world isn't that bad a place to find 'peace'. Even if 'peace' is temporarily unavailable, the world keeps you distracted enough to ignore it.

But in these unending stories I found the glimpses of those memories which overlapped here in my destiny and will continue to do so. The story of the 'search', and the story of the 'curse' overlapping in the life of my 'time'.

Sitting in the classroom again and this time with stranger kids, my eyes still kept wandering. From kid to kid, from boys to girls my eyes kept moving. Sometimes they got stuck on pretty girls and their curls, and sometimes they got stuck on the images of the last three years which changed my life. On one such morning my wandering eyes witnessed the door of the classroom open and I saw her walk in.

She was dressed in a smart black full sleeve V-neck t-shirt and blue denims. She was very fair and had a sharp jawline. Her physique was lean and she swiftly took her seat on the first bench of the class. An old interesting smoker for a lecturer, entered soon after her and an interesting lecture on verbal abilities began. He laid emphasis on non-verbal communication and how effectively it communicated logic, reasons and feelings without even saying a word. I didn't knew then, that in years to come, I would require these abilities to communicate with her.

The new pretty face sat in the corner of the first bench, invisible to my wandering eyes. The lecture ended and I ran out quickly for a smoke along with the lecturer. I guess the non-verbal communication of 'worked-up' brains between smokers is pretty commendable. I returned to the classroom as most of the students left for their daily lives. Going home, those days felt terrible as all I could feel was the bitter disappointment of failure. At least, sitting amongst other students kept me away from the bitter reality of my life.

As I opened the door of the classroom, I saw the fair faced girl still sitting on the first bench and solving sample questions. I felt a strange force pulling me towards her, as I simply stood near her bench and looked at her. She looked up and saw me approaching her. "Hey, hi!" I said with a big smile naturally growing on my face. "I am Uday", I continued. She stood up and the smile reciprocated on her face showing her gums along with her teeth. "Hi, I am Tanya", she introduced herself confidently. I noticed gray hair around her hair roots. "Who has gray hair in such an early age?" I wondered as I closely observed her graying hair. Nevertheless, the graying hair reminded me of a villainess from a popular animated series called *G.I.Joe*[122], and I quickly blurted it out. "Hey you know, your hairstyle resembles a lady villain from an animated cartoon series", I pointed still looking at her gray hair. She smiled suppressing a giggle and asked, "Which one?"

"It was called *G.I.Joe*. Have you ever seen it?" I asked. "Nope, never seen it", she smiled. "You must watch. She was a kick ass villain; a total bad girl", I said enthusiastically. "By the way what did you study for your graduation course?" I asked her. "Well I am a chemical engineer", she answered. "Nice", I smiled. "What about you?" she asked. "Well I am a

---

[122] *American toy soldiers which evolved to comic strips, animations and movies.*

biotechnologist", I answered. "Where was your college?" I asked her trying to keep up the conversation. *"Bandra"*, she answered. "And you live in?" I continued. "Here in *Vashi*[123]", she answered. "So you traveled every day?" I asked her. "Pretty much, yes", she answered. "Nice, so how do you find the *CAT* preparation here?" I asked. "It's good", she smiled again. "I find it so tough", I answered, over exploiting my honesty and as I demonstrated my incapability to compete for the *CAT* entrance examination. Tanya suddenly looked disinterested and started going through her questions again. "Well I guess she is ambitious and standing here for too long would just make me look like a push over", I thought and said, "Hey, I will catch you later. Nice meeting you." "Same here. See you later, bye", she said with a curt smile and I walked back to my last bench to attempt the impossible questions.

The quest for 'love' wasn't over and no matter how hard I tried, I couldn't find it... till the quest found me when an unknown number called. I answered to a sweet voice on the other end.

"Hello, who is this?" I asked. "Is it Uday?" questioned a female on the other end. "Yes this is Uday here, who is this?" I answered. "Guess who am I?" she asked putting me in a curious state. It doesn't happen daily that a sweet feminine voice calls to play a name guessing game with me. Nevertheless I was scared of answering it wrong owing to the females I might have pissed off on the way. "I can't guess, please could you help me?" I asked in the sweetest possible tone I could. "Oh come on Uday, you forgot the nice time we spent together!" she suggested sounding a little raunchy with a direct effect on my 'little warrior'. "I really can't guess, and could you please re-run me through the nice times we spent together?" I asked, suspicious of the caller. It was obvious that it was a revenge call but I still wasn't sure who could it be. The only way to identify the caller was to provoke her to say her name. "Keep guessing sexy", she said seductively on the other end. "Alright maybe this would help, what exactly did we do when we were together?" I asked in a raunchy tone. "Something exciting!" she answered provocatively, trying to play along. "No, you need to be more specific. As in did we reach first base or second base or did I actually use a condom?" I said giggling into a

---

[123]   *Prime residential suburb of Navi Mumbai.*

laughter. "What?" she exclaimed on the other end. "Or if you could tell me the size of your 'hearts', I could take a better guess", I blurted before she could express her embarrassment. "Huh! Hearts?" she exclaimed. "Oh sorry if you don't know 'hearts' then perhaps you could tell me the color of your nipples. I will definitely recognize you", I said in a hornier tone, sure of pissing off my unidentified stalker. "You are disgusting. Wait a minute", she snapped and put the call on hold for a while. I waited for her to resume, laughing silently for my misbehavior. "You bastard", suddenly a familiar feminine voice interrupted the silence. "Who is this?" I asked in surprise. "You bastard, how could you speak to my friend like that?" the other voice demanded angrily. "Wait a minute, is this Rita?" I asked in astonishment. "Yes you bastard, it's me", she screamed, with every word hitting my earlobes like projectiles flying out of a tank. "It was you who orchestrated this entire trick?" I asked in shock. "Uday, why are you such an asshole?" she yelled again. "Excuse me, it's you who made a prank call and tried to harass me", I retaliated in defense. "I wonder how you didn't die till now, I so wished for it", shrieked Rita but this time, strings of anguish strummed in her blaring screams. I wonder what about pain is so sexy that it can create music in the hollow most sounds.

"How dare you curse me to die? You did that on my birthday too, aren't you done with it? It's you who called, and harassed me!" I mumbled angrily. The death wish did prick again since in a normal life people generally live without anyone cursing them to die. At least I thought so; nevertheless I repeated my lines to the only person who curses me to death for breaking her heart. "I don't know why you hate me so much!" I topped her voice but somewhere my guilty anguish poured out in my angry retaliation. Rita stayed silent for a moment and hissed, "You are saying; you harassed me; as if I raped you!" I stayed silent but I could hear a fading chuckle on the other end. "Look I am sorry, but trust me, life on my end is also in a really bad shape. So I guess your 'curse' is somehow working", my voice got sadder as the words poured out, hoping that perhaps my disaster would bring her some peace. "What happened?" she asked curiously. "Well I screwed up my boards, and Anita broke up with me, and here I am", I sighed. Rita began to laugh, and soon her laughter got hysterical. "You are such a bitch", I remarked, sad and annoyed at the same time. "I am sorry", she chuckled still trying to swallow her laughter. "Fuck off", I snapped in annoyance and hung up the phone.

I rushed to buy a cigarette to quench the surging rage. As I was lighting the cigarette she called back again. "What?" I answered in a strong voice. "Listen you bastard! You dare not raise your voice. I just called to ask you to meet. I wanna return a few things which you left with me", she instructed in a rude tone. "It's ok, keep it with you. I don't want it", I said disinterested to collect her trash. "What the fuck?" she shrieked. "You better take it back Uday. I so don't need those gifts of yours", she screamed angrily. "Fine, fuck it", I said giving up. "So you will meet me tomorrow; right?" she asked arrogantly. "Where?" I asked. "*Bandra*", she ordered. "Alright, I will call you when I leave", I said. "Fuck off", she snapped and hung up.

I took a deep breath and got on my bike after stubbing the cigarette. Her words echoed in my head, as I looked at her number. I could never recollect deleting it. In fact, somehow, I always remembered her digits. I felt doomed with a mere thought that someone hates me so much. I looked around at the busy suburban street, which buzzed with people... each at his own pace. But yet they all are running a race, towards or against 'time', and yet again 'time' remains the only master. I didn't want to leave my master. Perhaps that's the best thing about losing, it keeps you humble enough to sincerely try, many more times. And if not for my love, then at least I would try for myself.

I smiled again, ignoring her curses, and kick started my bike. The beginning throttle of a bullet engine sounds like music. The symphony of the thump soothed me and my thoughts. I rode my new bike, through the highway towards my home. The wind couldn't stay away from us for long, and it blew on us. I felt every ounce of her thump throttling between my legs. I raced up, and so did the vibrations. My iron horse throttled, while the wind pulled my hair, and soon I was flying out of despair. A thought of forgiveness occurred, and I preferred keeping it. "Maybe that's the way I pay back for breaking her heart. She's a good soul, and keep her happy God!" I prayed to the winds blowing on my face.

The road turned at the exit, and I left the highway, following it inside to the suburb... I thought about the times spent with Rita, and our encounters on the beach. The 'little warrior' is selective and yet very perceptive; he catches only the things he wants to catch. The throttle of the bike turned him on and he simply casted the lewd fantasies which began to build up.

Maybe with Rita's unexplored 'red', or the airy freedom...
Or with the wind on my face, blowing away my boredom.
I floated back to the ruins of memories, lost in the lanes of 'time',
But the few shady glimpses of her 'red', still make my palaces... So fine!

Maybe the 'taste of blood' never leaves,
I throttled my engine, turned on... By speed.
A couple of girls walking on the sidewalk glanced back... and one of them smiled.
Her curious smirk and her plump 'hearts', couldn't escape my reddened eyes...
Counting a million possibilities of turning her 'red',
From biting her lips to taking her in 'bed'
But all my blood descended down,
And a thought occurred to him,
To the one with a 'hard on'!

Are we free to fall in love again?

Love is a quest we all are meant to find, and even if it goes away... there is a way to forget,
Just don't lose heart, and follow the 'red'...
'Red' brought us here, and it's 'red' for the rescue.

Don't brood too much, without 'red', for long... You much cannot do...!

We will find it again,
In someone's warmth or someone's pain...
Red is around,
Like droplets pouring out in rains,
The damsel from the morning,
Is a little mellow and a lot more vain.
Ignore the jinx... And be smart!
Remember the fresh face from the morning,
Which brought a fresher start.

As I rode, I looked in the rear view mirror, adjusting my new long uncut hair. "This is the longest I have ever let my hair grow", I acknowledged with a 'feel good' smile till I glimpsed back on the road and suddenly a golden sedan appeared around the corner intersecting the lane. I felt a sudden pain in my legs as my bike crammed into the car. I was thrown ahead, almost on the bonnet of the car, and then I went down with my bike. I struggled to get up as people hustled around me. "Shit", I mumbled.

"Who the fuck is this?" screamed the angry driver, coming out of his car. His bulky arms sent a rush of adrenaline in my body, creating a 'fight or flight' syndrome. I had to 'fight' for my bike, but my body signaled towards 'flight' as I felt my legs weaken. "Shit, I am sorry", I said loudly and looked at the face of the owner of the car. I knew that guy as he was a friend of Gino and Kirat. "Hey Nitin", I said recognizing him. "Hey I am so sorry buddy", I apologized as I pulled my bike out of his car. The junction of the right front door of his car had a considerable dent. "Oh shit, oh shit", I repeated in regret looking at the dent. My bike's fender was bent towards the left, along with the bent footrest. "Fuck! It's a new bike", I shrieked in regret. Nitin looked at me in shock and said, "Dude, do you think my car is old? Fuck, I am screaming Uday; but you are riding with your face in the rear view mirror!" He yelled as he flexed his biceps. "Shit I am so sorry dude. How much do I have to pay?" I asked, scared of the idea of going to my parents to ask for money but it appeared to be the only solution. I was just glad that we recognized each other before the collected mob got violent. My defenseless submission to dodge my fault sobered Nitin. "What the fuck Uday?" he said losing interest in the argument. "It's ok; shit happens. I am sorry. Just tell me", I consoled making a sorry face. Nitin was a rich guy and he looked at my new bike. "Fuck it dude, I will claim insurance", he said throwing away the argument. "Thanks buddy, I am really sorry", I apologized again as he got inside the car. "Dude, if there was anyone else here in place of me, he would have really thrashed you. Ride carefully", he remarked arrogantly and started his car. Perhaps he was right too, "Thank God", I said taking a breath of peace but a protective fear for the health of my new bike made me rush to lift up my bike.

I felt guilty as I dragged my broken bike to the nearby service station. The front tyre and the fender rubbed against each other, creating heartbroken sounds of unwanted friction. When I couldn't push ahead for long, I kick started my bike and rode it slowly. "Fuck! Her curse did work!" I mumbled. All way I thought about the possibility of my death, which she had wished for since my birthday. The quest called love had turned scarier, and I thought about all that which went wrong since then - when Rita had bitterly cursed me to die. Her painful voice resonated in my ears. "Please die Uday", her teeth clenching sobs replayed, dulling all my new found 'red' back to the gloomy 'gray'.

I started seeing all that which went wrong since that day. From Anita breaking up, to my boards getting fucked, to the accident... was I slowly moving towards my end?

I wondered about all the funny incidents, happening one after the other. The way things I was so sure of broke apart. How Nikita orchestrated a break up, when Anita and I just started doing fine again. The weird tricky way I got screwed with my board examination result. My new life where folks whom I love the most are troubled because of me... and I don't have a defined path for my career or life ahead. I felt breaking down into paranoia, thinking about all that which could go wrong, all that what I had to lose... To this fucked up curse of hers. Strange worries crowded my head, as I even felt scared to ride the bike again.

Riding back home, broken after the crash,
My new hope of freedom, just turned trash...!

"Was I really free to fall in love again? Or am I blocked by the curse forever?"
I thought as the gloomy clouds waited to rain...

Words colored with pain,
Echoed in verses,
"Either ways My Love...,"
It works with curses,
The 'red' of your deeds,
Is lost forever in gray,
Saddening all your happy moments,
No matter how hard you pray...!

ON A BAD BOY NOTE

Even if you were sad all along,
Or stumbled upon a jovial mood,
Whether you repel the consequences of a good deed,
Or enthralled for a deed not so good,
Doesn't matter in the jinx of curses,
Or for someone misunderstood.

They will find their way through Ironies of 'time',
While you will never know, when it comes alive!

And that's how curses come true...
Pretty much like a drop of tear,
Simple and few,
Though destined for a misfortune,
Curses are gray too...

I stopped only at the service station. The mechanic estimated an expense of a thousand bucks and suggested me to ride safely. The bike was supposed to stay there for a couple of days. As I walked back home through the service road shaded by trees on both ends, I realized the pain building up in my body. My left knee and elbow were bruised. Thanks to the front and rear guard, the bones of my legs didn't fracture. Although I wasn't wearing any helmet, but because of falling on the side, nothing happened to me head. A few internal injuries surfaced up their agony, which earlier I didn't feel. The adrenaline rush had mellowed and so did my thoughts of 'red'.

It was very saddening to acknowledge all that I lost, in its pursuit, and it further worried me for all that I may. The clouds poured, turning into a heavy rainfall as I dragged myself back home. Perhaps even they were waiting for me to slow down. It was slowly dawning on me the consequences of being cursed. I felt doomed, that I cannot change whatever happened. No matter what I do, I couldn't be whatever Rita wanted me to be. Even pretending won't matter. Anita is growing distant day by day. I questioned my 'worth' again, which left me in a spiralling myriad of many unanswered questions... And the most haunting one, kept repeating itself – "Maybe I am not worth love but am I even worthy enough to survive?"

The wind blew along sending chills through my drenched self. My wounds temporarily became numb. The glimpses of my broken yet new bike saddened me the most.

"Broke down my baby, my iron lady, my free bird... or my
Thunderbird", I hummed missing her unavailability.
With a few more steps, some more words condensed as poetry for my wounded love.
"I lost my bike and saved my life,
She stayed with me when Rita cursed or Anita cried...
As she left me, played by that bitch Nikita...
Why did you get yourself hurt, my love...?
Played by that stupid curse of Rita!"

I mellowed down in the stillness of the damp hurtful moment and prayed for my survival. "Please forgive me god! Thank you for keeping me alive! Give me strength, I will fix it all. I promise that I won't fuck up" I cried, to the clouded heavens. Or to the God of Judgment following me, lurking in my shadow..., following me around like her curse! My concerned mother opened the door to let me in, and I narrated her the accident. She nursed my wounds, thanking God for my life.

Whether curses are a bane?
...Or it works like a boon?
Would it stay forever... and follow me...?
Even if I go to the moon...!

Resting on the edge, whether it's 'dark' or 'light',
Keeping us hooked, through joy or plights,
Followed me for long, for days and nights,
Showing up its presence, in both 'black' and 'white',
It occurred to break something away, and yet it set something right.
For I lost my bike, and saved my life,
Left me broken, yet I survived...!

The next day I had to take a crowded train for *Bandra* to get done with Rita. The thousand bucks for repair and the additional scolding from my parents for the accident had already left me in a bitter mood. After an hour plus long haul of struggle in the crowded train, I reached *Bandra* station and waited for her.

I wondered how Rita would look after so many months. I looked around trying to find her face in the crowd which buzzed with people. The degree of the physical beauty of girls as one reaches *Bandra* increases ten folds. The pretty faces made me forget the crass reality of my life as I floated in the view. Suddenly a plump Rita with a lizard like girlfriend of hers came along. She wore an off white knee length top with leg hugging stockings. Her friend wore a white sleeveless shirt and thick spectacles. "Hi", I said making a sad guilty face. "Hey Hi", said Rita in a familiar tone. She appeared quite friendly for her abusive cursing avatar on the phone. "Nice hairstyle", she said pointing out. It felt stupid to have a new hairstyle which won me compliments but also was the culprit who got my bike damaged. "Thanks", I said mustering up a smile. "This is Charmi", she said introducing me to her lizard like friend. "Hey!" I said. "She is the one with whom you spoke yesterday", said Rita rudely. It was an awkward moment. "I am so sorry, I was just trying to find out", I said trying not to feel any word of it. "It's ok", said Charmi with a fake smile.

Suddenly I felt a vibration in my pocket and took out my cellphone. To my worst fear, it was Anita calling, "Oh no Anita, not now, what a timing!" I mumbled to myself and cut her call. I messaged her, "In the class, will call you in sometime." Rita instantly snatched my cellphone and began to check. Guess her friendly state was as fragile as my love for her, especially after the way she had cursed me. I tried to grab back my cellphone, but she was already on the 'received calls' screen. "Oh, she still calls you? I thought she broke up with you" she remarked sarcastically. "Yeah... so she can't call or what? Please give back my phone", I said coldly, reaching out for my handset. But before I could take it, she was already searching for her number in the contacts section. "You don't have my number saved", she yelled in shock. "You are such a bastard!" she said accusingly. "Why are you abusing?" I asked with minor guilt. "Fuck you, you asshole. I can't believe, you don't have my number saved", screamed Rita indicating the beginning of a fight in public. "Oh no, not in public", I pleaded her.

"Hey guys, I have to leave", said Charmi in a hurry. Perhaps she didn't want to be a part of public display of rage. Rita said a hurried 'bye' to her and she left. "But where is my stuff, for which you called me?" I asked Rita. "I have already set it on fire", she answered arrogantly. "So you called me all the way for nothing. How could you be so dumb? I have traveled for an hour in this fucked up train, bunking my *CAT* tutorials just so I can make up for my wrong. I don't think you understand how fucked up I am with respect to my career and life. Why the hell did you call me here?" I yelled. The public display of rage, now had two patrons.

Rita laughed relentlessly. "Yes, I called you here for nothing. I just felt like fucking around with you", she chuckled arrogantly. I felt disappointed for the hatred which she harbored towards me. Well, I shouldn't have expected anything better either. On the contrary, her tiny revenge did bring a little peace to me – for I felt like I paid a small part of my debt for hurting her. "Alright, thank you. I hope you are feeling better now. So you chill and I shall leave" I said extending my palm for a goodbye handshake. "Where do you think you are going? You better walk with me, for you have been such an asshole in my life" she ordered angrily. "Ok then just to make up for it, I will walk you to the bus stop", I quickly retaliated, still burdened with guilt.

We began walking down the foot-over bridge of the railway station towards the nearest bus stop. "You know I couldn't upset Anita", I mumbled. "I always knew you were an asshole. And what the fuck did you say to Charmi. Your 'heart' color, your nipple color!" she screamed, uninterested in my sob story and pinched my belly with her fingers digging mercilessly deep. "It hurts", I tried not to giggle. "By the way, the prank you guys played was so dumb", I said sarcastically. "Shut up", she snapped. "Pants down", I chuckled.

Waiting in the noon at the bus stop, I hovered around Rita as she kept on abusing me with a multitude of hurtful words. Her fair face glowed in the post noon sun and her cream dress swayed in the wind blowing through the bus stop. A fat lady stood on the road near the bus stop.

"Why are you abusing me so much?" I asked, annoyed of feeling guilty. "Because you deserve it", she snapped. "For what?" I asked. "How could you get physical with me when you already had a girlfriend?" yelled Rita. "I am sorry for that but at least be thankful that I didn't do anything extreme", I answered shamelessly. "Yes, you fucking lied and cheated on me... you bastard", she continued cursing me.

"Will you stop abusing me?" I said, cornering her into the edge of the bus stop. "Yes you are a bastard", she hissed. "Why? Because I stole your 'kiss virginity?'" I smirked and my hand touched her belly. "No because you told me a story about a girlfriend which you never had! You are too smart to have moral values. It's good Anita left you, and you fucked up your exam", she ranted her accusations, which I knew were correct. But when life is fucked, public display of 'affection' is better than public display of 'rage' or 'accusations'. "You filthy pig", she screamed out loud but her voice mellowed, as my claws dug in her waist... much like a purr from a steamy cat.

Perhaps feeling too bad for her heart break was lame! It doesn't help much in this bad, BAD world. Especially, when I can't really change anything about it. The world will continue to muster out of some righteous bullshit, and it suddenly made sense to me to derive a certain value for my useless trip.

I nearly escaped death... for I broke her heart,
This curse for a whim called 'love',
Is honestly unfair!
I looked at her and her anger seems breezy,
Is she also craving for 'blood'...?
She nearly got me killed
And still she laughs...!

"You called me all the way till here,
You tasted my 'blood',
Now also taste my heart...!"

So I dived in her eyes, and I said in her ears...

DON'T CURSE ME, MY LOVE...

"I know you don't like it alone,
Thus you keep me coaxed.
So you desire to be taken?
For you like to be forced...!"

My gaze fixed onto hers and the color around her eyes changed from that of anger to the playfulness which had always attracted me to Rita's eyes. I leaned in to her face and in an instance her plump lips gobbled up mine. "The kiss virginity is gone for good", I mumbled while we kissed. "Rapist", she said and pulled back. I clamped a little fat on her belly with my fingers and said, "You have put on, fatso!" "Shut up", she said but before she could complete the words, I was back to taking the remains of the virginity of her kiss. I felt as if I was back in my element, though much lighter than my previous escapades with Rita where I was burdened with guilt.

The fat lady turned behind and gave us a dirty look, cursing us for our 'filth'. Well that day, the filth was just mine. "Old habits die hard", I whispered in her mouth as her bus approached the bus stop. Love is also a function of 'habit' and the bad habit of 'love' is called indulgence. The fat lady and Rita boarded the bus, and though the lady passed some womanly scorn to her, Rita quickly took a window seat and waved a goodbye to me. The hatred with which she had met me had mellowed down into a fiery seductive gaze. I smiled waving her goodbye and walked back to the railway station to take the train home.

She began texting again, and her hatred mellowed to an extent as if it was never there. Probably she felt guilty for cursing me and the subsequent mishaps that happened. Or perhaps she just needed some 'bad' company, flavored with 'dirty' acts. Her struggle to save herself from my lustful advances made her feel righteous. What fun would it be if there is no 'bad'? Then how would she feel good again!

Rita's birthday was near and the continuous texting had made some base for me to surprise her. Though Anita seldom called me..., she was too busy in her life to visit me and thus I focused on Rita. The old proverb which said, "One bird in hand is better than two in the bush" made utmost sense to me.

336

"Hey happy birthday!" I called up Rita at midnight. "Hey... Thank you Uday", she answered playfully. "And this is the difference between you and me. I called to wish you a long happy life on your birthday... other than a few friends I have who probably choose to curse me to death on mine!" I remarked sarcastically. She remained silent for a moment, bringing me to peace for perhaps realizing her mistake. "Don't talk about that. I had my reasons. Do you want me to go back there?" she asked firmly. My false peace lasted only for a moment as I didn't want to go back to my death curse. "Okay, forget it! Where is your birthday party?" I sniggered to distract her. "Come and get it", she chuckled, getting distracted. "Where at your place?" I laughed. "Yes you can come to my place and stay in my balcony", she played along. "Seriously, won't there be any issues?" I asked curiously. "Stupid, don't ever even dream of that. My dad is anyway suspicious of me these days about my outings. He thinks that I am seeing someone", she gossiped. "Who are you seeing?" I asked her sarcastically. "I have a few friends", she said trying hard to sound exclusive. "Good for you. So I guess you would want to be with your friends rather than me", I said coldly. "Uday, I want to meet you", she said in a soft provocative voice. "And do what?" I asked bluntly. "Rape me", she said playfully. Rita's outrageous attempt on humor definitely touched the 'little warrior'. "Rape you huh?" I mumbled. "Yes you rapist. What better can you do?" she laughed. "Well, not a bad idea", and the 'little warrior' spoke. "Shut up Uday", she said. "Pants down Rita", I played. "Don't worry, I am not wearing any", she answered playfully. "Really?" I said with my voice getting huskier. "Hey I guess my mother is up. I have to hang up now", she mumbled and hung up. The 'little warrior' took offence on the sudden interruption in his conversation and I eventually had to pacify him.

The next day I wore a black tee and denims, sprayed a musky perfume form my father's closet, and rode down on my bike to wish her birthday. The previous night's conversation kept re running in my head. I recollected her fantasies of dominance and kept checking my chances, if I had one to dominate her.

> *I floated in her fantasies, smiling to her thoughts.*
> *Soaring on the roads,*
> *Happy perhaps for all that I lost,*

DON'T CURSE ME, MY LOVE...

Her passionate eyes, the way they left me,
The way she cursed,
And her bare fantasies,
I wanted her 'red', while she still wanted my 'blood'.
Awaiting another forbidden encounter,
Thumping on my dirty thoughts.

Rita waited for me at the base of a flyover on the *Western Express Highway*[124] and I halted to pick her up on my bike. "Hey happy birthday!" I grinned extending my arm out to hug her. Rita resisted the hug and said, "Stupid, I can't hug you on the road!" She wore a parrot green *salwar kurta* and her fair cheeks reflected the sunlight. She mounted on the bike with a little difficulty. Once she was seated I began to ride ahead. "Why aren't you wearing a helmet?" she asked speaking in my ears as she held me lightly. "Just didn't feel like", I said. I felt her breath on my neck as she whispered in my ears again, "Uday, your perfume smells so nice." An unexpected compliment is always a very effective mood elevator. "Really?" I asked with a wicked grin. "It's kinda turning me on", she whispered and kept sniffing my neck and with every breath, turned me on. "Where are we going?" I asked her. "Let's go to *Aarey Colony*[125], it's a good place to ride", she said. She grabbed me tightly as I soared up the speed. Her 'hearts' massaged my aching back out of the harsh reality of my life.

We entered *Aarey Colony* and it looked like a jungle. When I asked Rita, she confirmed that it was a part of the jungle present in *Mumbai* but ironically it has residential colonies and occasional incidents of leopards; where the swift feline has attacked and even killed domestic animals and people. Lush greenery was widespread on the curvy roads of *Aarey Colony*. Venturing deep inside the residential area through the jungle, we headed towards a dead end.

---

[124] *The Western Express Highway, is a major north-south 8-10 lane arterial road in Mumbai, stretching from the suburb of Bandra to Dahisar. The 25.33 km highway continues beyond the city limits, as the Mumbai-Delhi National Highway 8.*

[125] *An agricultural area amidst Mumbai surrounded by the jungles of Sanjay Gandhi National Park. Popular for leopard attacks and haunted places.*

"Hey stop Uday!" screamed Rita. "What happened?" I asked. "My stole got stuck in your wheel", she screamed. I stopped immediately and took the bike in the corner. The parrot green piece of synthetic cloth covering Rita had got stuck in the center of the wheel. I tried to pull it out and black grease had already covered the cloth tainting it at different places.

"Let's relax here?" I suggested. "Yeah, this place is fine", she said. The touch of her 'hearts' had instilled back the lost feelings into me as their mush touched something deeper within me. A big tree casted the shade on the hilly slope where we had stopped. Rita dropped her stole and got down revealing her semi bare chest. I parked my heavy bike on the side stand and rushed to help her get her stole back. The piece of cloth was mildly stuck as I tried to pull it out. "Uday be careful, just don't tear it", she said cautiously. "How do you think it matters now? It's already greased and dirty", I said. "Stupid if I go back home with a torn stole covering me, it won't look good", she said laughing. "Why? What would it look like?" I asked. "It would look like as if I got..." she said and took an uncomfortable pause. "You are such a bastard", she giggled. "Yeah, who was talking about it last night?" I smirked.

"Let's sit here", she said. "Alright", I obliged and we sat at the base of the tree leaning our backs against the thick bark. "What if a leopard comes here?" I asked still suspecting a lurking predator watching us in the vicinity. Rita glanced around for a while but appeared calm. "Stupid; I am more scared if a human comes here", she laughed. I took a thought about it and agreed to her. "True, I guess humans would be worse than a leopard at this place", I nodded with seriousness. "Because it's humans who rape and not leopards", she giggled and I laughed along with her.

"Your honor is exposed Rita", I smirked looking shamelessly at her cleavage. "And now I think, even a human is better than you. I don't know if they would rape but you are definitely a rapist", she giggled. I looked back in her eyes and they peeped in mine from beneath the camouflage created by her golden brown colored hair.

I put my hand on her waist and as I touched her a wave of current ran down through my palm to my head igniting many circuits together. The primary 'fear' was of Anita calling at this sinful 'time' when I wasn't really sure of what is going to happen next.

I lit a cigarette and began smoking. I had just had a couple of drags when Rita snatched the cigarette and puffed a drag. Her distraction gave aid as I slyly removed my cellphone from my denim pocket and switched it off. Rita smoked in peace, unaware of my stealth. I kept looking at her and she kept looking up at the leaves of the trees. I rubbed my palms against her waist again. "Can you give me a drag?" I asked in a soft voice. Rita took another drag and offered me the cigarette but I grabbed her head and pulled her lips towards me and swallowed in the smoke which she slowly exhaled.

As our lips parted from the mild embrace, strands of smoke slithered out of my mouth and I stared in Rita's mischievous eyes. They looked in mine challenging me to make the mistake again, thrilling my nerves and stirring up my emotions. The brain knew 'right' and 'wrong' but the heart wants what the heart wants. I pushed myself back in her face, accepting the challenge.

The feel of approaching Rita, somewhere had a taste of stealing innocence. Loaded with my boyish charms, I stormed in her aura. Stepping inside her boundaries with treachery and force, she looked at me with a confused face, with her eyes wanting me, tingling with her mischievous laughter and her body fighting hard to stop me from crossing any lines. While at the same time, she is unable to resist. I grabbed her, mesmerized in her voracity and the landscape of her moon like fair voluptuous 'hearts' oozing out of her parrot green clad semi bare chest. I couldn't resist nestling my face in it, hungrily licking and sucking every bit of everything available within my reach. It felt like grabbing her soul through her body. "Anyways, she always wanted me to take her soul away but she is too weak to experience separation. And I can't be attached because I can't diminish the spark in Anita's eyes", I thought and it mellowed down the thrill which I had briefly enjoyed.

I loosened up my grip on her and reclined backwards on the thick trunk of the tree but just a touch from her was enough to bring back the sinful thrill which I was so devoid of in those tough times. I pulled out a major part of her bosom and dug my teeth into them, chewing and sucking her visible 'hearts'.

The need of the body was slowly becoming the need of the soul. And perhaps so was it for Rita. We were too busy quenching the thirst to realize any guilt. I guess 'abstinence' does that often, whether voluntarily or otherwise.

"Ouch!" shrieked Rita. "What happened?" I looked up at her and asked in surprise. "You bloody rapist. You bit me so hard", she squealed. I looked at the fresh red love bite which I had given her. "The beautiful thing about fair girls is that they turn pink and at times 'red' too", I smirked. "You are so lusty Uday", she said moaning in pain. "Stupid, it's just a remembrance. As long as it will hurt, you will think of me", I nudged. "And when people ask you about it, then you tell them any story which you want to", I chuckled. "Yeah, like the one you told me about your ex-girlfriend who dumped you for a rich guy!" she taunted. "But you know what, it's not that bad a story to believe. Looking at you, anyone will believe that you got dumped for a better guy. Fuck yeah; even I would have done the same... in fact I would have dumped you even for a 'not so rich' guy", she taunted in pain, rubbing her fresh scar. "Ouch that's harsh, but yeah I really don't understand then... Why are you here with me?" I reasoned ignoring her disguised accusations and her openly revealed disgust. "Maybe so that you can still finish our story?" I asked with a smile. "A story with you? Really! After all that you have done? You really have some audacity? Such a filthy pig you are!" she remarked sarcastically. "Well if you like it filthy, then so be it!" I grinned unaffected by her attempts to humiliate me and grabbed her and continued kissing.

Lust is also a function of habit and though circumstances had kept me away from it, but it never changed the 'habit'. The thrill of cheating was soaring the 'lust' in me, but the innocent appearing Rita was the same when it came to lust.

She kissed me back and we continued the heavy exchange of saliva. That day 'filth' found 'filth' as we kissed like animals. On the dead end a human appeared making both of us conscious.

"Let's go", she said hurriedly putting back her greased stole on her semi bare chest. "Ok", I anticipated, considering any unwanted incidents and we got on my bike. I kick started my bike and said, "So did you like smooching on the bus stop?" Rita sniffed my neck again and kissed it. "Hey don't stop, keep doing it", I breathed. Her 'hearts' pressed against my back and touched my soul again as she began to chew on the rear of my neck digging her teeth inside. "Ouch", I shrieked. "How does it feel rapist? Revenge time", she mumbled and continued biting me.

We rode back to her locality. "Hey Uday, can I change and come?" she asked. "Yes of course", I said. "My friends are waiting", she added. "So, should I leave?" I asked dubiously wondering if the day had any more chances left to offer. "You can come to my party if you like", she smiled clearing my doubts. "That would be nice", I mentioned with a grin. "But should I wait here in this lane?" I asked. "No, you go and take a ride and come. It would be suspicious for my neighbors to spot a guy waiting on his bike", she said in panic. "What the fuck? I am riding since long, I will rather wait!" I insisted parking the bike on the side. "It's my birthday..." she whined winning the budding argument. I pleaded again in exasperation, "Please let me wait here, I am too exhausted to ride", I moaned. She disagreed but was to no effect. I waited while she left.

The two extreme ends of the spectrum from 'light' to 'dark' danced in front of my eyes, showing me the gray mirror again. "Why am I even waiting? I feel like her pet! Or should I have just left, after a nice jungle make out?" I reasoned my 'worth' with myself. "Was I so weak that I stayed back just to please her, or so that I can unleash my desires on her?" I wondered.

Desires are crazy; like the desire to explore the unknown enchanting pictures of the future. A future full of possibilities which is shaped up by curiosity, and would continue to haunt till it is achieved.

The thought of "What if..." brings out a myriad of possibilities making one so curious about the different outcomes of their future, and with this bent – 'future' keeps driving one's curiosity to know the unknown and to see the unseen! "What if it happens?" I thought thinking about the possibilities and the beauty of what I wanted to see. Fair and fleshy thoughts began to consume my head and I smoked out the new spark, my spark to explore again.

Rita in traditional green came back as Rita in a black leather jacket with her curves draped in a skimpy black tee. Her new attire made my wait 'worth it' answering my struggling thoughts. "Are you serious, you are wearing leather jacket in *Mumbai?*" I asked in astonishment. "So what?" she said as the mild embarrassment climbed over her face. "Black suits you, it makes you look sexier", I said smoothening out the cynic in me.

"Perhaps that is what Anita hates about me. I really don't know what she likes in me", I thought as I looked around the unknown road I was standing on. "Come let's leave quickly", she said and hopped on my bike. I started my bike with a full thrust kick and Rita grabbed me mimicking her favorite *Bollywood* day dreams. Perhaps it is the best gift I could bestow upon her; a happy memory of a cheater.

Sitting next to Rita at the restaurant table, I kept thinking about the hungry kiss we shared in the jungle. But amongst her friends, I had to keep my desires in control. Charmi too, sat amongst them on the table. Rita brimmed with brilliance with her bubbly conversations. A tall and slightly fat fair guy seemed to look a little straighter than others and he barely smiled. It was easy to guess that he had the 'hots' for Rita. I realized I was the 'bad' one there, the guy who dated Rita and later turned out to be a con of a lover. Somehow when hate is felt for oneself, the world soon appears to be hateful. The 'hate' pouring out of her friends for me did scare me a little showing me the blunt reality of an outcast; the one who wronged, the one who sinned – the one who tasted 'blood'.

But 'blood' remains blood and no matter if it's 'black' or 'red', it still flows, carrying the burning heat of life. Rita looked the 'most alive' after a happy adventurous day. My scared body parts automatically searched for her and soon my palms reached and met her curves under the table. Her fair chubby face darkened with a hue of pink.

On a bad boy note,
She glittered in her eyes,
Waiting curiously,
To unfold the surprise...

And so was I, waiting desperately for a new surprise. The surprise happened after the *CAT* exams where I was still hoping for a miracle out of my modest expectations. A week before the exam, I had bumped into Tanya again. She appeared cold then too, but that's perhaps because she saw me smoking, but fortunately she still gave me her number.

"At least I can say that now", I mumble with a laugh trying to soothe my ignored pride by my latest object of love. I gulp a sip of cold rum and laugh thinking about Tanya's friend from the class. The funny part was that she studied with the ugly brilliant guy who had the highest probability of making it into the *IIM's*. I laugh gulping the glass of rum thinking about the things he would have imagined when he was preparing with Tanya for the *CAT* examination in the classes. I soon laughed at myself thinking about the possibilities with her, which I might have had wondered inside my head during those days.

The 'time' for the arrival of my results turned gloomier, as it was the 'wait' for the unknown. A chance of destiny waited to change my life but the biggest roadblock of reattempting the board exams resurfaced. The delusional love of the pretty faces and smoker friends suddenly went absent from my life leaving me with the only choice of reattempting the boards. "Things which I couldn't study in the classroom for three years and now I have to do it in four months", I often wondered helplessly. Anita tried to reduce the distance which had grown between us as I drifted towards Rita.

It was comfortable to focus on the delusional and vague Rita and I totally left my focus there; on her curvy, fair, bubbly glitter. Some days later, Rita took me out for a movie. Her absolute love for the dreamy *Bollywood* movies kept me intrigued as I infested myself with her childish dreams and perhaps the hope of her curious 'blood'. I flowed with her as a capricious *Kareena Kapoor*[126] left me bedazzled in the innocence of her character. The traces of her character remained in Rita too, as she kissed me voraciously during the intermittent breaks which we kept taking in the darkness of the movie theatre.

Perhaps courtship didn't need words as I chewed her lips bearing her inability to kiss like Anita. "Don't touch my breasts", she whispered in the theatre. "Why?" I gasped. "Bastard, since the last time you bit it in the jungle, it still hurts", she whispered. "You taste like 'blood'", I murmured still pulling her to kiss. The movie left us in a mesmerized state of each other. The 'dark' in me saw 'light' again and this time in Rita; as she left me at my bike with a goodbye kiss. Just this time, the 'light' poured out in her eyes too.

Well the 'irony' of gray is that, in the shades of gray, at times even 'dark' can lead to 'light'. A couple of days later in a candid unusual *Mumbai* shower, Rita accompanied me on a bike ride to the hill top in *Navi Mumbai*. I lost the way to the desired hill and we happened to reach a *Gurudwara*[127] on another hill nearby. In the 'light' of Gods, I hardly knew that my 'darkness' still awaited me.

"My house is empty. Let's go there!" I said to Rita. "I am hungry and all soaked up", she whined. "I will cook pasta for you", I smothered her with a romantic bribe. "Where are your parents?" she asked after a helpless thought. "My dad is on a work tour, my mother has gone to *Colaba*[128] and my sister is in school", I answered 'word by word' very clearly. "Ok, let's go then", she said excitedly and hopped on my bike. As we started riding down the hill, the short rain drizzle gained intensity.

I rode back as quickly as I could, trying to time my opportunity to be with Rita in the space crunch of a city like *Mumbai*. I reached my home and quickly collected the keys from the watchman. I opened the door and welcomed Rita in. "Nice house Uday", she said looking at my father's art collection hanging on the wall. "May I have some water?" she asked.

---

[126] *An Indian actress – You can trip on her!*
[127] *A Sikh place of worship.*
[128] *Timeless heritage of Mumbai.*

"Sure", I said and helped her quench her thirst. "Would you like to change?" I asked politely. "No it's okay. Can you just give me a towel?" she asked courteously in her drenched clothes.

Like a good host, I quickly rushed in to get her a towel. Once she dried up her hair, she looked at me and said, "What next?" My idea of things that should happen 'next' were exciting and I said, "Come you should see my house." "May I use the washroom?" she asked. "Yes sure. Please go ahead", I said and I guided her to the washroom.

While she was inside, my brains kept rattling the possibilities which could happen once she is out. The only entity which enjoyed all the possibilities thoroughly was my 'little warrior'. As soon as Rita was out of the washroom, I grabbed her hands and pulled her to the bed. She gained momentum and landed on the bed with a thud. "Uday you bastard!" she shrieked and before she could complete her curse my lips were already on hers. I kept kissing her with ounces of increasing force on her lips. There was a strange resistance in her body. I could feel her body 'turned on', but a strange question danced in her eyes. The glitter was missing, and she looked at me with doubt. When I look back now, I feel that perhaps I was to be doubted. After all the chaos which I had created amongst the lives of my beautiful girls, with my selves of 'love' and 'lust', this was bound to happen.

Maybe 'light' was no more an option for me. All I could do was to seduce Rita to a level where she succumbs to her own 'darkness'. "Uday, stop it", she said weakly. "Take off your top", I said in my desperate voice. "No", she gasped. "Come on Rita, shirt up now", I growled. "No, you rapist", she chuckled, still resisting me. My hands found their way inside her top spanning the scope of her voracity. I inserted my tongue in her mouth and she obediently sucked on to it. The 'taste of blood' is never satisfied, it just increases the 'craving' even further. My hands rushed to unbutton her denims while she quickly clasped my wrist and exerted all her strength to stop me from reaching her secrets. When I couldn't undress her with the entire struggle, I finally gave up and rested beside her.

Watching my sullen face of that of a loser, Rita whispered, "Uday, can you give me a massage?" I looked at her with a suddenly developed 'bad' taste. Maybe my 'darkness' couldn't find its way, and like a puppy who just seeks a little love, I succumbed to her request. Rita laid on her belly, while I sat on her hips and massaged her shoulders. "Ooh Uday, you are good!" she said in an orgasmic tone. "Thank you, I regularly massage my father's feet when he returns from work. I guess it's just practice", I bragged, enjoying her orgasmic sounds of relaxation and comfort.

The state of reality and alter reality meet each other in such moments. So in spite of having a real 'hot' girlfriend, why the fuck do I have to serve Rita. "I miss you Anita, I can imagine you every moment", I mumbled in my epiglottis. The vivid glimpses of Anita returned, haunting me with her brown skin, and the innocence drowning in her deep eyes. Bells rung in my ears coupling with the wind chimes reminding me of dimples which guarded her smile. Her relationship status didn't matter, she was always mine – at least that's what I believed all the time.

My hands stop massaging and barely touched her back or the satin of her shirt. I looked around the room, and muffled wind blew in through the windows, marking its presence on the metallic wind chimes, perhaps as if the universe is ringing a bell. "Go back Uday", a thought echoed in my head. "The 'dark dream' is just an imagination, an imagination of your own sickness", it continued, suddenly making the flames of my bloodlust wither away in the cool wind on an unexpected rainy day. "Let's go Uday. Anyways *Ma* would be home soon", a lighter thought appeared clearing the 'darkness' in my head.

I looked at her fleshy back again where her black shirt had masked all her unexplored curves. The glimpses of the gone empty days reoccurred and my fingers dug back in her covered flesh. "What about the 'blood', what about the successful hunt?" another thought nudged as the 'little warrior' extended his heat on her cushy hips. The 'taste of blood' had met my demons, and it's all about victory. "Can you take off your shirt?" I requested as I massaged. "No", mumbled Rita softly. "Why did you stop?" she asked amidst her relaxed moaning. "See buddy, I am not able to get a grasp of you. My hands are slipping on your shirt", I said losing interest in the moment and just before withdrawing my palms I nudged into the sides of her neck. My palms took a wide grip of her fair fleshy shoulder muscles and squeezed the misery out of them. Very similar to the way Anita squeezed the mystery out of me with her palms.

I relaxed back, sitting on Rita's hips and took a deep breath. The glimpses of 'first love' are too enchanting to leave the clutter of daily memories. "It's ok Uday, take off my top", she said in a shy muffled voice with her face dug in the pillow. The 'little warrior' called me back to the surprising words which I least expected in those moments. I was still unsure of what I heard and my wounded pride didn't allow me to pounce on her again.

"No, you remove it yourself. It feels too desperate, I don't like it anymore", I snubbed. Rita turned around and looked at me while I sat expressionless in a silent blank moment which generally awaits a disaster. 'Darkness' presented its gift to me and Rita stretched her hands behind pulling away her black satin shirt. As the dark cloth left her body uncovering every inch of her light skin; my eyes stretched themselves in disbelief of wishes coming true. Rita's 'light' was the gift of my 'darkness', and its last remains held Rita in the form of her black bra strap.

For the 'taste of blood', 'darkness' devoured 'light', fiercely gobbling the view in my sight. Burning with the thought to corrupt the delusion of 'love', but the more I saw of Rita's bare light, the more intrigued it left me. I continued massaging her as I promised feeling her touch on my bare palms. Between 'light' and 'dark', it's tough to make a choice, but I chose 'darkness' as I removed my t-shirt, pouncing again to unstrap her out of her darkness only to immerse in mine. I traveled the serenity of her body wrapped in her forbidden innocence, grasping everything which all of my senses could devour.

"You are so wild and hungry Uday", murmured Rita. I looked in her eyes and kissed her. "You are 'hot'", I whispered in her mouth. A faint drone of a vehicle made its way to my ears. In a thought of caution I left Rita and rushed to the window to have a quick look and to my surprise 'light' hadn't left the war yet. It was my mother getting out of a rickshaw and would soon be ringing the bell of my house. "Rita my mother is here, get dressed quickly", I shrieked in panic. Rita rushed with her clothes into the washroom while I quickly wore my tee.

I waited for my mother to ring the bell and Rita quickly joined in as the bell rang. We sat together on the couch in the living room appearing like innocent kids as the bell rang. "Hi *Ma*, meet Rita", I said cheerfully. Rita brimmed with a big smile and greeted my mother. "*Ma*, do you have something to eat? We didn't get food outside and Rita has to leave", I said hurriedly to avoid any suspicious gestures from my mother. Rita and my mother continued a friendly chat while I regretted the timing of my mother. The 'blood' thirsty 'little warrior' demanded peace and I left to pacify him.

When I came out of the washroom, Rita and my mother were sharing a meal of rice and curry. "Get a plate and eat some", instructed my mother. I obeyed as I was hungry and soon we wrapped up, as Rita had to go before my mother asks any awkward questions. "*Ma* I will drop Rita and come", I said. "How are you going?" asked my mother. "By train", answered Rita. "Where do you live?" asked my mother. "Aunty, I live in *Malad*", she replied. "Oh my god, *Malad* is very far from here", said my concerned mother. "*Ma* I will go drop her on my bike", I suggested. "In this rainy day, no way", protested my mother. I felt a surge of regret for confessing my plan of action as my mother happily killed my style. "Do one thing, take the car and go", she said generously. "Alright", I smiled and took the car keys. "Let's go", I said to Rita. "Aunty, may I give you a hug as a token of thanks?" she said abruptly. I looked at her in a panicky surprise while my mother smiled a mild embarrassed 'yes'. Rita gave my mother a happy cuddly hug and left with me, leaving my mother with a broad smile for her gesture of gratitude.

As I drove on the drenched highway to drop Rita, I kept thinking about her gesture. "Is she marriage material?" I wondered. "What about Anita?" I thought again. The gift of 'light' brought creepy uncertainties along. The confusion of choosing a person and the parameters we decide to compare. I realized that the gift of 'darkness' had just corrupted my own delusion of love.

"Hey Uday, tell me something", asked Rita as her face had turned pink since she the time she had left my home. "Yes?" I asked giving her a glance and then looked back on the road. "Do you still love Anita?" she asked. I hesitated to look back in her eyes as much as I hesitated to think the answer to this question. "Yes I do of course, even if she doesn't care for me", I said coldly. "Drop me here near the park", said Rita in an abrupt annoyance. "Are you angry because I love her?" I said feeling a little sorry for my honesty. "Nothing like that. It's just that I am a muse to you, right?" exclaimed Rita. "You know what Rita, I am really sorry that I lied to you. But the fact that the more I know you, the more I fall for you", I said feeling a little 'shame' admitting it. "But then can I ever be your girlfriend?" she asked. "I don't know about that, but I don't even know if Anita wants me or not", I said, not sure if Anita would have been calling all day with my cellphone switched off. "You are beautiful Rita, and so are your 'hearts'", I smirked and leaned in to kiss her as I parked the car on the corner of the road. The evening had turned into night and Rita obliged me with the kiss. She wrapped her arms around my shoulders and I could hear a faint sob roaring like soft music in my ears. I pulled her face back to look at her. A few drops of tears trickled down her eyes and Rita said the words of 'light', dooming me forever. "I love you Uday", she said looking deep into my eyes scaring me with the intensity of her 'love'. "I can't break your heart Rita", I mustered up the courage to mumble, as I knew I couldn't do it again. "But I love you too", I said helplessly as the words stumbled out showing its presence. Rita kissed her passion out in the brief moment on a *Mumbai* suburban road, while I fretted the fears of bothering people and cops. The way she kissed was intense, way fiercer than her regular moments of expressing affection. I remained surprised by her new found passion. I returned her kisses with equal ferocity, mesmerized in the beauty of her tears which had poured out just for me. She left with a monosyllabic "Bye." Neither did she ask any question on when are we meeting next. I left, still looking at Rita and too consumed in wondering about the possibilities ahead with her, to realize that it was the last time I was meeting her as mine.

On the way back, I switched on my cellphone and a message popped in. It was from Anita and it read, "I was trying to reach you for the whole day. Where have you been?" "Holy fuck", I gasped thinking about the path that I would have to take to lie to her again and the complex fragile road of lies where one lie leads to the next and eventually breaks into tiny piercing pieces of plain words which never meant anything, just illusions.

After a night of empty lies which I kept telling Anita, still wondering if she really cares or it's just her bruised ego. "Why are you telling me all this?" Anita often asked during the conversation while I kept reiterating my cautiously thought lies so that no wire crosses each other this time, to cause my doom again. A baggage was incurred with each lie, shoving every bit of my remaining 'light' into darkness.

I still wonder, "Why did I keep lying to her?" Maybe deep down I could never make her feel any lesser. She still rules my blood, and I always wanted her back. Perhaps it was a 'dark' deed done then, only in the hope of 'light'. But no matter how much I still want to believe that I was gray, I had begun to drift towards 'darkness'... even in my own conscience.

Slowly and slowly I became darker and darker. Till one day 'guilt' showed up, I knew then that God has arrived. And it happened the very next day. "Go fucking die with your bitch", a message from Anita popped. "I never want to see your face again", was the message waiting from Rita. I woke up and rubbed my sleepy eyes to the hateful words.

I rushed to a panicky start trying to save the last few dreams which had caught the 'fire' of my heat. Anita was unavailable and not answering my calls. It was Rita again as my savior who explained how God showed up in my colorful 'darkness'. Rita had posted a snap of mine and hers from her birthday on the social network. I hurriedly checked her album and saw her and me sitting beneath the tree of *Aarey Colony*. Rita looked pink in it as she had just finished with me. But when I clicked on the comments, there was only one comment which appeared 'red' with rage. It was from Anita and she had written, "Nice snap, you should start a course called – 'how to steal someone's boyfriend?'" Though it felt good momentarily, being referred by Anita as her boyfriend, but Rita's cries immediately diluted that feeling back to 'guilt'.

I heard her sobbing on the phone. "Why are you crying?" I asked, reminiscing her tears of the previous night. "I wanna complain to your mom", she sobbed. "Why, what did I do?" I reasoned. "How could you, I am so mad at you", cried Rita. "But you always knew that Anita and I were seeing each other. You should have never posted that picture online", I argued. "I know, it just feels like my fault. You were right, it's just me who fell in love with you", she cried helplessly. "I am sorry", I mumbled in shame as that is what 'guilt' often brings. My perfect arguments and reasons might help me win in talking but it can't win me my bliss. I will always carry the weight of a broken heart as her sobs still echo in my ears. "Uday just remember one thing. You will never find love, and when you do, it will leave you at your worst. Because that is where I am, at my worst", sobbed Rita as her words stormed my ears and again flowed to my soul like cursed waters.

Don't curse me my love,
As I feel helpless too.
Don't curse me my love,
As I have lived your dreams through.
Don't curse me my love,
As your words are gonna stay,
Dooming my life,
In misery and dismay....

I rushed to my college to find Anita as she wasn't responding to my calls anymore. I reached college on my bike and parked it. A strange fear kept gripping me, the fear of losing Anita forever. I never knew that the two words of "What if" can cause this unbearable feeling of doom. But still, I felt a compelling need to face it. A funny thought also occurred, "What if she forgives me and comes back running into my arms?" I walked up to her department feeling a little low as I was no more a student in the college. The hordes of students were leaving, and some were previous batch mates. They greeted me reminding me of my sense of belonging. Poonam was amongst them and she smiled at me, "Hi Uday." "Hi Poonam", I said with a bland face. "What happened? Are you alright?" she asked. It was surprising to see her sensitivity to my state. "Nothing, just", was all I could muster. "Have you seen Anita?" I asked her. "Yes she was in the lecture", said Poonam. "Alright, thanks",

I smiled to her pretty nose. "Hey Uday, don't worry, everything will be fine", she smiled as she turned to leave. "Thanks, but I feel that 'fine' happens to good people", I said with a wry smile. "Who said you are bad?" asked Poonam with her innocent smile. "Trust me, I am", I said looking in her eyes and felt like a strange weight falling off my breath as that was the relief of acceptance. "Why expect good when I am not?" I said to her still smiling to her pretty face. "My mother says that you are a good boy, just a little misguided. And I think so too", she said, beaming my hope for forgiveness with her 'light'. "Really?" I said feeling a strange surprise. "Yes", she said and paused. "You go now Uday, or you will miss Anita", she said and walked down the spiral wooden staircase of the college.

I looked down at the strange feeling with which she left me. I ran upstairs to find Anita and the hordes of students decreased sending a skip to my heart. "What if she has left? What if she never answers my phone? What if she never meets me again?" the thoughts kept questioning me. With every step I took on the curved balcony of the *French* architecture of the college building, a little more of the end revealed to me. And there I saw Anita in her blue striped white t-shirt standing in the corridors. She was lost looking at the buildings which surrounded the college. I tiptoed to her waiting for her to explode. "Anita", I mentioned her name softly and she turned to give a startled look. I could see her sadness and her usual brilliant skin looked pale while thick dark circles surrounded her eyes. I expected her to slam a slap across my face but the look she had in her eyes was that of disappointment. "Why is she disappointed with me? She was supposed to be angry!" I wondered in surprise.

"Anita", I said. She looked at me and walked right away with her nostrils flaring in anger. I chased her while she ignored me and kept walking away. "Please hear me once", I begged. She didn't pay any heed and I was too scared to touch her. I kept chasing her from the top floor of college to the coffee shop. "Please listen once Anita, I am surprised why are you so pissed at me when you really didn't care?" I accused. "That's what Uday! Why are you fucking chasing me then? I really don't care, not anymore", she said in her grumpy voice. "Please I am sorry, just let's have a coffee and then you can leave", I pleaded trying to make a truce. I chased her to the nearby café. Anita looked at me and when she realized that I am not going to let her go, she angrily agreed and threw her bag on the coffee table. I lit up a cigarette while Anita went to the washroom. I looked at her new cellphone kept on the table. I curiously opened its flap and read through her messages.

Both these women hated my guts and wanted to destroy me. When I saw through the chat conversation on Anita's cellphone, I read both of them cursing me together, wishing bad for me, wanting to cut off my 'little warrior' and beat me black and blue. Amidst all this misery, they wanted to defame me and isolate me from any happiness coming my way while taking away any, which I might have been left with. But watching all this I realized and saw something which was astonishing. Both these women initially hated each other like their worst adversaries. They hated their names, their mention, even a possible strand of each other's hair if they had found, but now they don't hate each other anymore, they just hate me.

Sometimes life doesn't need a big hero to bring people together, but it needs a much bigger villain to do the same. I am the villain, perhaps their worst experience, which they would say and maybe feel otherwise.

Here I am, standing against a million curses being hurled by the women I loved and cared for. Nevertheless, at least I found them some friends, friends of common 'love' and common 'hate'. Somewhat like this, 'light' won that day, because like in every dark cloud there is a silver lining, and I could see mine in my own distorted way.

Anita returned and saw me reading through her cellphone. She snatched her cellphone and screamed, "How dare you touch my phone?" "So you really hate me so much?" I asked with disappointment. "I can't believe you have the guts to ask this", she said with wide angry eyes. "Stop it Anita! You never cared for me. You were never bothered", I continued to accuse her. "Yeah because you are such a cheat and a liar", she screamed back. "Yeah right, you couldn't stand by my side when my results got screwed", I tried to argue, only to be demolished by her fiery oration. "Uday maybe you didn't deserve it. Just accept it, maybe it's a very difficult subject for you that your results turned out to be so miserable", she said with cruel sarcasm. "Yes I guess I never deserved anything. The subjects, you, or love, or my life or rather anything", I said in despair. "I am breaking up with you Uday. Forever and final", said Anita firmly. "Please don't do that", I begged, feeling the doom coming true as I had imagined. "I love you Anita, I am just so sorry", I said, although my deeds made my words sound empty. Watching me in despair triggered the disappointment back again in her eyes. "I cannot do without you *Jaan*", I said, gasping a heavy breath of air and going a bit hysterical. Anita held my arm tightly as her nails dug in my forearms. She chewed her lips and clenched her sharp nails, even further in my body. "Aah!" I shrieked in the piercing pain, but still a smile appeared as I saw her face struggling to injure me. That was her love, and I guess I still smile thinking of it. I laughed mildly in the pain, confusing her and then enraging her further. "But I am glad, at least you called me your boyfriend on the internet. I love you", I smiled at her, smitten by her basic instincts and her angry face. She returned a mild smile but remained silent.

Suddenly she relaxed, and calmed down. "I don't love you Uday", she said with her anger, desperately trying to cool down. "I know you hate me", I said blowing out a breath of air. "I don't hate you either Uday", she said calmly. "The opposite of love is not hate, it is indifference", she repeated her infamous words again with cold eyes. Somehow I couldn't believe and accept the sudden surge of coldness in her eyes. She looked different than what I knew of her. "Please don't say that Nitu, I really can't do without you", I mumbled again. "Get over me Uday. You know what; you don't love me, it's just a habit", she said with her enforced coldness. Gray had won her reds of 'love' or 'hate'. No matter how much I wanted either of them, but probably my actions had done otherwise. Finally, I just ended up making her what I was, and then I felt miserable... to find my kind!

> *Even for 'love', gluttony is a sin;*
> *For I lost it all, in the glory of my wins.*
> *The saint called 'Love' needed just one, and not a 'few'*
> *But when they lose all their glory,*
> *Sinners turn holy too...!*

Arguing further was pointless as the argument itself was brought upon by me, putting the 'dark dream' as the excuse and perhaps paving its way to come true. Anita got up and began to walk away. I chased her for a while but something about her last lines repelled my efforts. She continued walking away, ignoring my pleas, and I finally gave up. The 'guilt' made it easier to give up and residues of her 'love' made it difficult to cry. I left for home riding my bike, trying to unburden myself with the speed, thinking of my directionless life and all those moments which brought me to where I was.

In my attempt to describe the nature of 'love', and the curiosity to explore the various colors it brought along. The simplified look of the vivid rainbow of unexplored dreams just brought me to the two sides, the ends of 'light' and 'darkness' divided amongst people. Being alive is just the journey between these two ends and most people keep traveling in between for a major part of life.

On a bad boy note,
'Light' is dark's antidote,
And to light, 'dark' wrote,

On a bad boy note,
As it is here, it all ends,
It brings along your destiny's bend,
But to my naked light,
'Darkness' still pretends,
As there is 'light' in 'dark',
And that's how it extends.

On a bad boy note,
Here it begins,
The age of life,
Burdened with wins.
The smile it brought,
Peacefully laced with sins.
And the spark it casted,
Touched the kins,
Of dark's vastness...

ON A BAD BOY NOTE

On a bad boy note...
With smoke and rum,
It's just another day boy,
You lose some,
And you win some...

On a bad boy note...
To all you pretty girls,
Bewitched by your charms,
And lost in your curls...
You still have my heart,
I tried to keep it,
But I just lost it,
To your love so judgmental,
Please Smile girl,
As in your eyes,
I am still going mental...!
Cheer up girl,
You are and always will be my angel.

My only angel...
And with only three words,
I caged the hope,
Of my lovey dovey bird,
As with you, my heart robed,

To find another angel,
To have my resurrection,
As again in this wide world,
I shall never find this devotion...

On A Bad Boy Note,
I guess, too much I wrote...

The focus was clear; it was career and winning back the respect which I had lost. Suddenly academics turned to be the most important priority as the ugly face of my bitter reality had shown up in my life. The *CAT* exam had passed and I couldn't redo what had already happened. I had clearly broken Anita's heart and somehow everything else about my detrimental situation helped me accept the basic fact that it was over between Anita and me and now I shall face the doom for breaking her heart. "Even if I made it through *CAT*, how would I ever give the boards again?" I often thought to myself wondering doubtfully about my capability to have a secure career.

The mystery slowly unfolded and I had been shortlisted in only two colleges for my formidable *CAT* score where Anita had again beaten me. The clarity of my bleakness when it came to the real challenges in the correct directions of my life was thrown in front of me, constantly challenging my confidence and revealing a simple fact that I really couldn't have made it through the graduation years without her. I often regretted the simple point of not concentrating on my career with her support and help.

My foolishness added up to the curses and I continued cursing myself, often trying to decipher the 'darkness' which intrigued me so much, that it began to corrupt my innocence. The 'taste of blood' caused this change, but neither could I deny that I wanted it so much.

I guess it's the nature of 'dark', insinuating and intriguing, spreading the 'light' in our selves about our own creepy realities, wants and fantasies. The 'taste of blood' did induce the instincts to survive; pushing the new found and yet treasured 'darkness'. The 'darkness' which brings a strange desire to survive, and to grow ahead in life; to pursue one's passions and interests. Perhaps a life... beyond the doom of the most precious dreams.

The interview was lined up in the coming week and Vini and I left on my bike for the management college in *Pune*. Despite the strict restriction by my mother to ride up a hundred and twenty kilometers to *Pune*, my father had agreed to let me go. Perhaps he was a bit happier at the appearance of an opportunity for his hopeless prodigal son, and his bitterness towards my useless self, had relatively reduced. Despite the bleak chances, I had cracked the interview and had secured a place for myself in the MBA batch.

Anita was pretty surprised that I got selected, even though words of praise didn't come from her, other than a mere "Congratulations." I could never understand her sadness on my selection; whether she was sad for my future after my horrible deeds, or was she sad because she knew that I would soon leave her life.

The only mammoth task which still remained to be accomplished was the fifty percent score in my re-attempt of the board examination. I still kept trying to call Rita to have a word with her. The way she had left and her last glimpses did keep me haunted with the possibilities I was forbidden to imagine. The amalgamation of Rita's innocence and her wits often painted endless pictures of new possibilities with her. Somehow, it also began with the 'blood' which the 'little warrior' wanted to taste. The 'little warrior' is also stupid and delusional; he craves the 'dark' and then wanders off searching the 'light' often brimming with the idea of a delusional yet fulfilling love. The cursed words of "What if...?" often popped in my head as I kept fidgeting with my phone, day and night trying to reach her.

The news of my recent selection for MBA had reached Doctor as he called one evening when I was busy fidgeting with my phone. "Hey Uday, congratulations. I heard you got through MBA in *Pune*. I heard it from Aunty", he said cheerfully. "Thanks buddy", I said. "When are you joining?" he asked. "Forget joining. I still have to attempt the boards again. It's like I have to climb *Mount Everest*", I stressed. "Is that the only thing remaining?" he asked coolly. "Fuck, if I couldn't do it in three years, how would I do it in one and a half months?" I said expressing my fear to attempt the board examinations again. Doctor listened to me patiently and pondered for a while. "I don't know how will you do it but you have everything in place in spite of having such slim chances. So I guess you should just gather yourself and start studying. If you need company then I can study my medical books along with you", he said, trying to restore my spirit.

When all doors shut down, a new door opens up. Doctor opened the door of hope and the door opened to courage. "I guess you are right", I said thoughtfully trying to step out of the panic. "The only critical thing which you should be careful about now... is that you don't waste any time on your extracurricular activities", he said with obvious sarcasm. I guess I understood that he was referring to my mess ups with the opposite gender. I chuckled on the phone. "No, you moron if you don't clear the boards", he said and paused with a sudden serious change in his voice. "If you waste one more moment on talking to or messaging any chick then you are for sure the biggest moron on this planet and I don't think you will pass the board examinations", he said to me with blunt practicality which was slightly drawn towards rudeness. Doctor added the garnish of a challenge to the difficult to live cocktail of complicated situations. At the same time he stepped along as an ally in my battle. In the end friendship came to my rescue, the rescue from the doom of the curse of 'love'. I nodded humbly accepting the ally and the challenge. It was a war to fight, a war for survival.

As the loser reddened, for all that he lost,
Riches, love or desires... that he so badly sought,

Disheartened by a hope of 'light', while his 'red' wouldn't leave,
When he totally accepted, no trick left up his sleeve.

But why a smile parted up on his lips?
Would he ever have life, back in his grip?

Like a predator, hooked to the smell of 'red',
Kept grinning the wretched, as he barely said,

"So much I have failed, that I lost even my insecurities,
When I had nothing left to lose, I just weighed my abilities....
Fighting my curses, incurred by my deeds",
Love adulterated with lust, gluttony or greed.

"What have I done so 'bad'?
Just didn't want a life called drab"
He solemnly cried,
As that's what he tried...!

But when you lose it all, it's victory you are left with,
And since that doomed moment, his good mood became a myth...!

ON A BAD BOY NOTE

The battle for survival,
Is a singular fight.
Strongly suggested his failure,
"Don't be deceived by 'light'!"

He sided with 'black',
For an end not so tragic,
As that's what we all do... to live for long,
For survival is nothing but a dark logic...

Only cracking the board re-examinations made significance sense ahead, and with that I sat down to study in the suburban library of *Vashi* with Doctor and Ratish. Ratish had joined in as he had failed too, and the mere fact of pride which I had of doing better than him didn't make much sense. In fact it was way more humorous in my case where I had cleared the boards and yet was re attempting it for a mere point seven percent, just to be eligible to do an MBA. Ratish was often easily distracted by any idea of intoxication, or useless conversations. Though he still kept fooling around like a dumb child unwilling to learn from life's fuck-ups, Doctor and I kept giving him occasional nudges to keep his focus on the incoming re-attempt of the board exams. Watching him I often wondered, "If not for his juvenile emotions, what if he had cursed me too? What if he really fell for Zaida?" Helping Ratish had turned into a way of redeeming me from the 'guilt' of messing with Zaida as we prepared for an impossible exam.

My mother granted me an allowance of a hundred rupees a day, to help with the preparation for the board examinations. The money was blown on only feul and cigarettes. The 'dirty talking' at nights was replaced by activities like finishing notes till mornings. Anita often called but I kept my distance from her, partially angry with her for leaving me at my bleakest and partially guilty for breaking her heart. Somehow the focus on survival had taken over the dreams, and day and night I just brimmed with it. I re-created my own notes from the text books, and practised to remember diagrams and molecular structures in my photographic memory. As the exam dates drew closer, softer feelings like 'love' and 'lust' were kicked out by the core need of survival. While I still remained unsure of what I might reap, hardly aware that the result of my efforts would just leave me bewildered... much beyond what I had ever imagined! Survival is indeed a dark logic, and when threatened it kicks out all the feelings of 'red', just plain 'darkness' prevails.

In the battle of 'light' and 'dark', neither could ever kill each other, so much so that they just keep changing proportions. When although 'light' is at its strongest and most powerful, the smaller proportion of 'dark' hides somewhere deep inside 'light' and it appears as if 'dark' is the core of 'light'.

Drinking the black rum till midnight,
Trying to wash my sins of their plight,
I met your curse my lost love,
Who said I cannot write...?

Maybe that's what curses do to you,
Making you forget your significant achievement for a brighter tomorrow,
to the unchangeable wrongs of the past.

So Don't Curse Me My Love,
Even the deep dark makes the 'light' gray,
And yet for the mirrored darkness,
... It cries and says,
That the mighty Sun shines the brightest in dark and day,
"Oh you moonlit starry heavens!"
How dark would be inside the Sun, with which it breathes away...?

On A Bad Boy Note,
Can't you see...?
That even light breathes darkness' glory,
In the strange mysteries of life,
It's usually a long, LONG story...

CHAPTER 9

GOODBYE MY LOVER

"Beauty is something which is found within", said the pretty magician as she unveiled her real beauty from the disguise of an old hunched crone. And as she did that she cursed the arrogant prince who had disapproved of giving shelter to her on a stormy chilly night. The handsome yet arrogant prince had refused to let someone ugly or unworthy come in his vicinity. In short he had refused the wilted disguise of the gorgeous witch and fell for her pretty trap, failing her test of 'worthiness'. The moment he realized his mistake as he saw her 'real' beauty, he wished for otherwise. The pretty witch didn't have room for a second chance and as judgment, she cursed him.

The curse worked its magic and the handsome prince turned into a hideous beast. The only way out for him from his rotten appearance and to turn back to himself, was by finding true love. To find someone who loves him for his ugly self, and he needs to find her before the sand clock runs out of sand, or else he shall remain the monstrous beast forever.

I took a drag of smoke as Anita and I saw the animated movie of "Beauty and the Beast" on my television. Two weeks remained for the results of my board examination reattempt and despite the distances between Anita and me, she had agreed to come down to meet me. My parents and my sister had gone out of station for a family wedding. The movie was slowly growing on me when Anita interrupted, "Hey Uday, can you get me more booze?" "Sure, what do you want?" I asked. "The thing which we just finished", she said with a mild drunk smile. "What was it anyways?" she asked. "I don't know exactly, but I took a little bit of all the opened bottles and mixed it with sprite", I winked. "And thus I don't get caught when I steal from my father's bar", I chuckled. "Whatever it was, it was nice. So get me some more and also pass me the cigarette", she said and I obliged.

I went to the refrigerator to begin preparing my accidental genius of a cocktail. Appreciated by my lady who makes me believe that the 'crave' of the 'taste of blood' can bring out the best in people. I paused to laugh for a second, and wondered, "What am I doing?" "How was I when I joined college and what am I now?" I chuckled watching myself moving bottles, making the cocktail. I marveled at my dexterity as no bottle clashed with the other one, not a single drop of the spirit wasted. The color of the cranberry vodka added its hint of pink in the transparent fluidic amalgamation of a cocktail. "What should I call it?" I wondered. The 'pink' played with the spirits casting it's hue on the 'high' of the potion. "Love potion", I said as the words popped out of my mouth.

"So how were the boards?" asked Anita as I entered the room with my freshly prepared 'love potion'. "Boards were fine. Don't know what will happen. Would I pass or score above fifty percent? Let's see", I said passing the drink to Anita. "But you worked hard. You kept your phone switched off!" she said coldly but yet I could see the little sarcasm in her eyes. She took a sip of the 'love potion' and said, "Hmm, it's nice." "You know what, I got a name for this drink", I said. "What is it?" she asked. "I call it the 'love potion'", I smiled cheerfully. She laughed a little and repeated the words, "love potion!"

"So this is what you gave them?" asked Anita sarcastically. "Them?" I exclaimed. "Chuck it", she snapped shutting me up.

I realized my need to apologize again and said, "Look I am sorry. I never wanted to hurt you but I guess I was stupid. Please forgive me Nitu." She gave me a solemn look and her face turned a little viscous as she said, "You know what Uday, relationships are like a beautiful vase in which we keep the orchids. But if it falls down, it breaks." "But we are not broken Nitu", I said trying to re-emphasize my 'guilt'. "Even if it doesn't break, it will always carry the crack", she asserted with a grave look. I remained silent and continued sipping the 'love potion'. It felt like the 'pink tinge' of the cocktail called 'love potion' touched me and the all the heaviness of my 'guilt' which I bore.

"Let it be, it's just that you will never forget or forgive me, and I can't get rid of the bad memories for you", I said with a heavy breath. The loss of a perfect love story is something like this, like a cracked yet beautiful piece of porcelain used to keep beautiful dreamy flowers.

"But I am glad it's all over", she remarked with indifference. "It's ok, enjoy the drink", I said trying to change her focus. She took a sip and said, "But why did you do whatever you did?" I lit a cigarette trying hard to avoid the uncomfortable questions being posed at me. "I guess I was driven too much by curiosity", I said blowing the smoke out. "So what was it like?" she asked coldly. "What?" I asked. "Your muses", she taunted. "I don't wanna talk about them", I said with mild annoyance for her constant coaxing me to talk about 'my feelings' for the other girls, with her. "Why are you asking? And... anyways, you left me at my bleakest! I don't know how I studied all that. It's my second attempt at the stupid boards, and I am still nervous that whether I would pass or not", I said rudely. Anita's eyelids shot up in retaliation for my accusing remark. "Don't blame me again. You are such a bitch", she said with a mild drunk shriek. I laughed at being called a 'bitch'. "I never knew that the 'love potion' could bring so much hate", I giggled. "You remember saying this", I added. "What?" said an annoyed Anita. "You are my bitch", I winked at her. A familiar look returned to her face and I smiled. "You know what, I wished they were as curvy as you", I smirked and looked in her eyes. I passed the cigarette to her and said, "Hey did you get your hard disk? I wanted some movies" "'Hard' disk!" she repeated the word sarcastically. I smiled slyly and nodded.

"You wanna eat *Maggi*[129]?" I asked. "*Maggi*, yeah!" she said excitedly. "I have pasta too, by the way", I added. "Oh even pasta is yum", she slurped. "Let's make it", I said happily as she forgot the annoying topic. "Ok I will start while you can transfer data", I added. "Fuck I am swaying, this drink was amazing", I mumbled walking out to the kitchen to get

---

[129] *Another popular term for Instant Noodles in India. Recently discovered with traces of lead making it into a popular recipe for suicide!*

started. "Yeah it's nice. Your father has a nice taste", she smiled. "Thank you. Can you please copy the movie folder on my computer?" I smiled back.

The 'love potion' knocked on the roof of my head, and 'bloody' thoughts echoed within my skull. The pink amalgamation reddened darker shades and heavier feelings like 'hate' and 'envy', and in its tide, she got reddened too.

As I was pouring the contents of the instant pasta in the steel vessel when a guitar whiff played out in the kitchen. Anita walked out changed in a pair of shorts and my tee. "You changed?" I asked her. "Yes I took your t-shirt, I hope you don't mind", she said with a coy face. "No not at all", I replied courteously. "Hey which song is this?" I asked. "It's 'Maria Maria[130]' by 'Carlos Santana[131]'", she said. "It's a nice song", I smiled.

"Hey it smells nice", she said and walked towards the stove. As she stood next to me, the emptiness of my home became emptier. It's strange that even when guilty, the 'little warrior' doesn't care.

"Yeah it does", I said sniffing the vapors of the boiling pasta. "Nitu, can you check on the pasta?" I said trying to avoid the command of the 'little warrior'. The warrior had starved a big battle of abstinence during the boards but I chose the little respect which the hardships had taught. But as I turned, my leg touched her bare legs.

A familiar heavy breath poured out of my lungs and I held Anita by the waist, sliding her to the other side. She turned facing me, breathing into me. "It's like I really don't want to mess up anymore, but my body doesn't wanna leave yours", I ended up saying.

---

[130] *At the 2000 Grammy Awards, this song won the Grammy for Best Pop Performance by a Duo or Group with Vocal.*

[131] *Carlos Santana is a Mexican and American musician, whose band Santana pioneered fusion of rock and Latin American music. With blues –based guitar lines set against Latin and African rhythms featuring percussion instruments and popular vocalists, Carlos Santana and his works are an enigma.*

My hands stayed on her waist clenching it a little more. But I removed my hand and turned slightly. I couldn't resist giving another glance in her dreamy eyes. She leaned a little forward towards me and took another breath. I stepped in and locked my lips on hers. The body might forget the touch of flesh, but the soul never forgets the touch of the mate. We began to kiss ferociously as if we were venting out the anguish we held against each other for all that while. So much so that soon we were on the kitchen floor. The clothes were not important; nothing was, but just the look in the eyes of the mate as we kissed.

Sharing the drunken kiss which reeked of 'love',
Red, hot and fiery,
Setting our blood on a stove.

As the bodies soiled the toil,
The 'love potion' brought us to boil...
For the heat to moist, and rage to wet,
The blurred visions of the pink,
You can never forget...

There is a word for such a phenomenon,
When something is marked Crimson,
As silent kisses narrated the anguish of separation,
When bodies mark the souls... it's called Rubrication.

So was the 'pink',
What she called as 'Love Potion',
I swear I never prepared it,
With such a dirty notion...!

And as the strings played the riffs,
Unearthed the flesh in a reddened whiff,
Lost were the cloaks which covered the gold,
As we burn our bodies, back to coal...

And In her eyes, I saw the ceiling of stars,
Celestial bodies on fire, glowing away so far,

GOODBYE MY LOVER

Like the wishes we make on a starry night,
Hoping the 'light' would might our fight...

And the 'love potion' tuned back the scars,
Played again by Santana's guitar...

"Nice song, by the way", I smiled still looking in her eyes. "Let's go to bed", I added. "Shit! The pasta is still boiling", mentioned Anita and quickly put it off. "Oh shit", I laughed. Anita walked in with me to my parent's room and switched on the yellow lights on the large mirror. I hurried behind to pull off her clothes thirsting for the lust of my mate.

She stopped me with her hands pressing against my chest and I quickly took off my t-shirt. She pushed me behind on the bed and walked upon the bed and stood in front of me. I reached her waist and held hers but the look in her eyes had changed.

She again pushed me back and confused me further. I looked at her more intensely as she began to dance and groove to the guitar of *Carlos Santana*. Though the song kept talking about a certain damsel called Maria, who grew up in a Spanish Harlem and yet for her forsaken circumstances, she finds 'love' or something like that. But in my ears all I heard was Anita, as she sang along... but I didn't know if she had really found 'love'. And then the best lines of the song played and whether Maria ever heard it or not, Anita did.

"Anita you know you are my lover
As you breathe me like a feather,
And how much ever I touch you,
I can never be done with your leather..."

She dressed down to her lingerie and grooved along. I was limited only to 'touch' while she danced to the entire song swaying her long black shiny hair.

"Black suits you", I murmured. "You look like *Salma Hayek*[132] from *Dusk till Dawn*[133]. You just need a python wrapped around your body", I said still slurping on the view. "You just get to see today", she grinned. "Don't do that. You are teasing me", I protested weakly. "You deserve it", she said smiling with cruelty. "Please don't", I smirked. I lowered my head towards her legs and tasted my way to her sweet spot. "Don't Uday, you just get to see today", she gasped digging her claws in my hair. "As if I care", I said as the 'little warrior' was back for his 'blood'.

"'Sex' is like *'Salsa'*", said Anita. "With you, yes! Otherwise I don't know *'Salsa'*", I remarked. "Fuck, you are so 'hot' *Jaan*", I mumbled. "Keep moving *Jaan*, don't stop", she breathed, kissing the words. "You and I alone can never stay normal", I laughed. "Fuck you are so sexy Uday, and after these board examinations you feel even 'hotter'", she said passionately. "I worked out in the free time", I said, kissing her slender neck. "Your shoulders are so amazing", she moaned. "I love your legs. They are so curvy like a belly dancer", I said grabbing her fleshy bottom. "Even your thing has grown big I guess", she remarked. "Really?" I chuckled. "Yeah it feels different. Like harder and thicker than before", she adored as she dug her long nails in my back. "Gosh I can never forget this performance *Jaan*", I mumbled kissing her again. "Uday faster", she shrieked. "Your nails hurt *Jaan*", I moaned in pain. "Oh yes Uday, I am coming *Jaan*", she screamed. "Come *Jaan*, I want you to come", I gasped.

Lying in her arms peacefully I looked at her in the dim yellow light. "I feel like staying inside you all the time", I said touching her sweaty face. "It feels nice though", she cajoled. "I don't know how I would do in MBA", I pondered over the forthcoming uncertainties. "Yeah you should think about that", she smirked. "Listen", she said waving her hands softly over my face. "Now that you are going away for MBA, leaving everybody behind... then I want to see you making it big, like on the cover page of a business magazine, at least within ten years from now", she said brimming with 'light' which slowly faded in the 'darkness' of her sad

---

[132] *Salma Hayek is a Mexican/ American actress and if you don't know her, then probably you don't know the epitome of feminine beauty.*

[133] *"From Dusk Till Dawn" is a simple example of the madness locked within the very unpredictable Quentin Tarantino, of course seasoned with his umpteen fetishes.*

scarred eyes. "I will try my best. Can't believe that one day you and I would actually be separating", I remarked with soaring sadness. "Don't talk about it now", she willfully ignored my words.

"And once I am rich, then I will buy a *BMW* or rather... a sports bike", I immediately added to distract her from the morose conversation. "Oh yeah, that's a nice car", she smiled. "It's a very sexy car!" I exclaimed. "Why cars and bikes are always referred to as sexy?" she asked innocently. "Probably because it's fun to ride, and fast cars and bikes end up giving an orgasm", I chuckled. She giggled along and silenced, lost in her own thoughts.

"I am 'hard' *Jaan*", I said and then she couldn't ignore further. Anita smiled back playfully. "As if you listen to what I say. Do as you like", she smiled in defeat. "You know, if you were a car, then you would be nothing less than a *Ferrari*", I said looking in her eyes. "Then ride me. I am sure I will give you an orgasm" she said softly.

I silently stared back at her. Perhaps words didn't matter as the eyes spoke everything. I went looking for 'beauty' everywhere when it was just lying in my arms. No matter how much platonic first 'love' might turn, it always keeps the spark safe within the many folds of the mysteries of how humans bond and mate for the first 'time'. It didn't take much for me to find the spark I had for Anita and I ended up looking deep into her eyes as she had just wished for something too big for me. Something which I was too scared to even imagine for myself and the spark said the words to her, "You know *Jaan*; I can 'make love' to you like a slave, like my wife and like my queen!" The only word which remained to be said amidst the *'Salsa'* of the Spanish guitar whiffs and the *'Salsa'* dancer was just one word called 'love'. I still wonder what stopped both of us then. Perhaps they were the bruises which we carried from the scars of our togetherness.

The scars of relationships are the marks which remind of the unpleasantness which people go through when they are in 'love'. Sadly, even I couldn't see the beauty of the scars, the beauty of the fact that 'love' once reigned over it. Though still mesmerized in her eyes and losing the sight of those scars, my victory over the pain of 'worthlessness' brought back something which today I really wish I didn't have.

And that is the nature of the 'Love Potion',
Which keeps our daily life rocking in motion,
Too many spirits to figure out the blend,
And sipping through its 'Pink', one day life will end...!

Though Anita had bestowed her best wishes for me to make it to some cover page of a fancy business magazine, I remained dubious for my result. Though I was aware of the efforts I had put in for the re-attempt of the stupid board examination, but 'karma' kept me in fear of my deeds. "All the curses bestowed on me, must have a purpose", I often thought those days awaiting the results which defined what my career ahead had in store for me.

Finally the most awaited day arrived, when I received a message from an acquaintance, which read, "The results are being declared today." I anxiously waited throughout the day to know my fate. The board examination website remained slow for the web traffic composed of many like me. My parents joined in the anxiety, and waited with me. The doorbell rang, and Vini joined us, cheering for the results. Finally the results popped at midnight and Doctor and I sat together to check it out on the internet. With trembling hands I clicked on my roll number, praying for a mere 'second class'. Neither did my calculation add up to anything else. The result clicked open and surprisingly, I had scored a 'first class'.

My parents rejoiced and people who mattered were happier as the news spread. I remained surprised for my judgement was spared. My mother thanked the Gods, to whom she had prayed to, throughout my exile. I thanked them too, especially "The God of Judgement!"

And then it was 'time' to announce the result of my capability, especially to the ones, who thoroughly believed that I could never make it. But I spared the ones who ridiculed me, for I am a subject of so much interest to them that they would eventually figure it out. My phone kept ringing continuously and many turned silent when they heard of my 'first class'.

Maybe it was 'pride' or maybe the never found confidence that I could do it by myself; as I called up Anita to inform about my newly discovered 'self-worth'.

"Hey I scored a 'first class'", I said cheerfully. "Yeah Gando had messaged me. You scored more than me. Even I could just make a 'second class'", she said with sadness. "Why are you sounding sad? It's like you are not happy that I scored?" I said with my excitement dampening.

"Nothing like that, it's good that you got a 'first class'. It's just; I wish I had a 'first class' too", she said, still sounding morose. "The best part, I did it without you", I chuckled. "Good for you", she said bluntly. The rude memories of Anita were what the results brought back. The lonely days spent in humiliation from family, classmates, friends and acquaintances was the slow burning poison I was living with for an entire year. And all she did was 'not care'.... The sadness of the thought of losing her kept boiling into 'paranoia'. A 'paranoia' that had become my life, as everything I thought I wanted always felt incomplete without her. Till now when all I consume fills everything inside me other than the 'emptiness'. An 'emptiness' caused by her absence.

But why stay lost in the fright,
For a future not so bright,

Where moments tremble with fear,
And for a dreadful end, of which I am so near...

So much for a 'Habit' called 'Love',
A lifetime of 'Worth' is its cost,

As the Wisdom of a failure so rough,
Slapped my face, boiling in wrath,

Don't fall in 'love' with the dreams,
Maybe it's better to lose, than to be lost...

ON A BAD BOY NOTE

"I think I should end this"
To let you know,
It's only you,
How much I sought..?
"And what if you leave....?"
All the while I thought....
But then,
Why live such a life... suffocated in load,
When I can write so many stories,
In my Bad Boy note.

"You know what Anita, I have found someone on the internet", I said. "Someone as in?" she asked in a suspicious tone. "Someone I would perhaps like to 'date'", I said mustering the vicious memories of humiliation to spit the harsh words out, which carried my victory over the relationship. "Oh, ok", she said, masking her astonishment. There was a brief silence on the phone and I was glad to not do this in front of her. At times, 'silence' works as a mirror, and in that moment it was just reflecting on the lie which although I had made up to win, but then it made me wonder, what damage it might have caused? "Listen, I will be moving to *Pune* and moreover it will be good. I mean I don't know what happens ahead", I said in a shameless yet cautious voice. But my unsure callous words were quickly interceded by a rapid Anita who said, "It was anyways over Uday, you are free to go." The sudden grant of freedom did surprise me as I had expected a teary pleading Anita asking me not to leave. I tried to contain the fact but sometimes in the knack of winning, one often loses the desired outcome... and also the eventual consequences! I was briefly happy for the freedom granted by her. Not like I hadn't done enough to get it, while I tried imagining the golden possibilities ahead at MBA.

Whatever happened ahead in my MBA and after that, is over... but nothing feels remotely close to what I felt with Anita.

For a lifetime of Glory, the moment 'alive' is lost,
Like a Pearl so dear, floating in the Ocean of thoughts.

GOODBYE MY LOVER

As 'Good' surprised you, happening to the 'Bad' and gory,
But 'Karma' watched it silently, in this Bad BAD Story...

When you have it all, and nothing you pleasure,
In such moments your 'Trash' turns 'Treasure'...!

"I miss you Anita", I mumbled to her photographs on my computer screen. Back in my empty room, and in my empty life, the best way to communicate to her is by talking to her photographs. "I chose my freedom over you *Jaan*. For what, this fucked up life?" I mumble finishing the left over rum in my glass. The rum is making my movements sluggish and even my thoughts.

The stormy rain after my gray evening of 'acceptance' had subsided, leaving the weather outside in pin drop silence. The 'silence' appears spooky, and so are the thoughts of Anita which have kept playing and replaying in my head for all these years.

The 'Silence' is very haunting as if something Supernatural
is asking me to confess my wrong...
My drunken stature is getting too paranoid, and I play the songs,
Which she left with me, and with them, the last memories of Anita played along...

I could remember Anita's husky voice sing to me in the bus as we traveled to my home from college. After two days I had to join my new college and our old college was no more a priority for her. She would never say it, but given a choice to choose between me and anything else, she would have probably chosen me. I had formally broken up with her, staying in mixed feelings of 'guilt' and 'freedom'. It was a very weird feeling where every free breath was burdened with 'guilt'. Maybe this is the outcome when someone tries to escape the redemption of their wrong doings.

Anita sang a song amidst the murmuring drone of the bus as it became the background of her heart breaking solo.

"Did you write this?" I asked but she kept singing. Maybe answering my question was not as important as telling the one who leaves that how much you're gonna miss them. "It's beautiful", I added. Anita entwined her fingers in mine while her clasping palms grasped my soul. "It's a song by *James blunt*[134]", she said. "What is it called?" I asked curiously. She returned a glance, and when I looked at her, her eyes silently questioned me. "Goodbye my lover", she smiled with sadness.

A gift called Goodbye,
And that's what you wanna give me...
No matter how much I try,
You still manage to prick me...

You are such a child with enthusiasm,
Especially the way, you always manage to ignore my sarcasm,
But I still have to tell you something as you go,
My soul and body belong to you, yet some gifts I shall bestow...

The fluffy turtle and the garden basking with flowers...
Think about them when you take a lonely shower,
As they will teach you to be smart,
And yet help you to think from the heart...

But I know, one day you shall return,
Till then, only for you, I will burn...
As you are the bliss with whom I shine,
Don't worry about me, I shall be fine.

Such are the gifts I wanna give you my love,
For you gave me a gift called Goodbye,
So take my gifts with you my love...
Adorned with the wisdom of 'time',
The fluffy turtle and the garden basking with flowers,
I so want them to be the last gifts of mine...

We reached my home and were greeted by my mother. Sitting in my room, I was preparing to pack for my further education. "I got you

---

[134]   *Impeccable vocals along with meaningful lyrics.*

something Uday", she said. "What?" I asked in astonishment since any gift was uncalled for.

Anita opened the zip of her sling bag and took out a little green fluffy turtle. "What is this?" I said in astonishment. "It's for you", she smiled and gave me the soft toy. I looked at the turtle and wondered what could be the reason for her to get me this. "Why did you get me a turtle?" I smiled in askance. "It might bring you some wisdom", she replied with a coy smile. I wondered what could be the missing wisdom which Anita wanted to fulfill in me. Perhaps after all these years it appears to me very clearly what piece of wisdom I had, which I had foolishly ignored.

"And here is another small gift for you Uday", she said as she took out a magnetic sticker. The cute porcelain sticker had a freckled girl made on it which looked like *'Olive Oyl*[135]*'*, the girlfriend of *'Popeye*[136]*'*. It read, "If I planted a flower every time I thought of you, my garden would bloom forever." I looked at the message as I stuck it to the iron cupboard in my room. "Why did you get me this?" I asked her with a sad feeling creeping inside. "It's because I will always think of you", though she smiled but the 'sadness' had crept into the corners of her brilliant eyes. But when the 'sadness' of a breaking heart battles with the brilliance of pretty eyes, it's usually 'sadness' which wins. And then her 'sadness' conquered my eyes too, inflicting 'guilt' inside me which stuck on to me like the magnetic sticker.

My mother came into the room. "Hey *Ma*, look Anita bought me these awesome gifts", I said cheerfully. She looked down with her shy demeanor while my mother checked out the gifts. "Very beautiful", she said positively and Anita continued to blush. "Uday, I am going for a movie with the neighborhood women", said my mother. "Alright *Ma*. In the meanwhile I will pack", I suggested. "Anita can you help him pack?"

---

[135] *A popular comic strip character, extremely thin and lizard like, but she was quite a reason for all the battles of Popeye.*

[136] *'Popeye the Sailor Man' is a very popular cartoon character distinctly known for his very broad forearms and his smoking pipe. The funny part is that, he used to put spinach in his pipe and smoke. I wonder, was it really spinach?*

asked my mother. "Sure Aunty, don't worry. You enjoy the movie", she replied with a reassuring smile.

I looked at her with a strange feeling of what to do next since the old habit reoccurred. Anita was always right. "Love is a function of 'habit'", the thought was mutual, as she looked at me with a similar glance. In a few minutes we were naked on top of each other, lustily trying to absorb each other to the fullest. Once at peace, she got up and walked naked to the computer and played a song. I kept lying down and watched her move gracefully.

"Let's go take a shower Uday", she smiled. I nodded and followed her to the bathroom and we were soon under the shower in the bath tub. "You look so 'hot' when you are wet", I said as the dim yellow light reflected the water drops on her brown skin. "Let's do it here", she said in mild excitement. The enchanting self of Anita was very persuasive to make me forget that we had broken up. In the moment of the wet heat, the 'guilt' and the 'decision' were washed away as we made 'love' under the sprinkling cold water drops.

On the contrary, the tub was filled with warm water and Anita massaged my shoulders as she sat behind me while I leaned on her. I looked at the mirror and saw her looking into my eyes. The peace required to listen to the song which she had played was finally achieved and she sang along. As she kept humming the song, I realized that each word of the lyrics was directed at me.

What is love all about...?
How much ever you have of it, it will never suffice...
Drenched I am all over in your Love,
I just cried out a river, I can never be dry...

If 'love' is all about getting accepted,
Then I had accepted you long ago,
If 'love' is all about getting wasted,
Then I have done nothing but wasted my life on you...

So are the tub and the water,
Like what is love all about..,
One is wet and the other is dry,
It's nothing but a chance, only if we try...

Whether it happens or not,
You will miss it and cry....
What is love all about?
I felt it all along...,
But it's just a lie...!

So much so that you will never believe,
It was a moment which just passed by,
If this is love all about...
Then a fool I am... I shouldn't have tried...!

What is love all about?
No matter how much you have of it, it will never suffice,
Drenched I am all over in your Love,
I just cried out a river, I can never be dry...

"Which song is this Nitu?" I asked partially in pride for the ambitious child and partially guilty for making her wait for me. "It's nothing, just something I wrote", she said hesitantly. But you listen to this song called *Vienna*, by *Billy Joel*. Every word in this song is written for you", she said rubbing my chest still looking in the mirror. "We look nice as a couple", she said with admiration, in a shy voice. I nodded with a lot more guilt. "*Jaan*", she mumbled in my ears. "Hmm", I nodded. "Can we like...?" she said and paused. "Can we like, what?" I asked her to complete. "Can we like, get back again?" she asked hesitantly but her eyes were very sure of what they were asking as they brimmed with love looking at me. "I don't know", I said, feeling like a coward. Anita patted my back and kissed me. "Watch this movie called '*The Notebook*[137]'. It is the story of our lives", she said with saddened eyes. I nodded again as even my

---

[137] *A timeless love story narrated by an old man to a nurse about lovers lost in old wrinkled pages.*

words were afraid of coming out of my mouth. This is the power of 'true love'; at times, when it leaves the ambitious cowards speechless.

My mother was about to return and we quickly got ready. My ambiguous answer wasn't so misleading after all, as Anita remained sad and silent with a dim sweet smile on her face. The doorbell rang and I opened the door. My mother looked at her sad face and then looked at me. "Are you done with your packing?" she asked me. "A little left", I answered in a sad voice. "I am leaving Aunty", she said with a wide smile. In spite of her cheerful smile, her eyes held on to the sadness. "I will drop her and come", I said to my mother. "Uday can you come in here once?" asked my mother as she walked inside. I followed her to the room. "Uday don't break her heart. She looks so sad", said my mother in a concerned voice. "I am not doing any such thing *Ma*", I said hesitantly, trying to leave. "When someone loves you, you shouldn't break their heart Uday", said my mother in a very serious tone. I nodded and quickly left.

I dropped Anita at the railway station, and again watched her go. She stood at the door of the train, hanging out bravely watching my face. I couldn't take my eyes off her and the train began to move. I saw her go away and she went on diminishing slowly and slowly till she looked like a dot and then vanished in the air as the train chugged off. With a heavy heart I walked back just thinking about the amazing moments we shared.

"Let's get hopeless tonight", I mumble wishing the rum to not to get over. I too wish if Anita had stayed back that day and then the night. And then for all the other days and nights coming forward till this lonely night which evolved from the gray evening.

Maybe it's just 'sex' or the 'blood lust', but I miss it so much that it still sounds like 'love'.

Just the day before I was leaving for *Pune*, Anita came to pay me a last visit. It was again a gray day as the clouds overcast the blue skies. I was in a hangover due to a night long drinking session with Doctor where we celebrated the hardships we went through for my victory. Anita plugged in her hard disk into my computer and played her recent favorite number. "Which song is this", I asked her, again trying to brush up my little knowledge about trendy music. "It's *'Turn the page*[138]*'*, by *'Metallica*[139]*'*", she said with a dry smile. The song continued with its heavy guitar riffs till it came to a mellow point. "Listen to this Uday, these are my favorite lines in the song", she said. I paused to listen and the lyrics went saying the words.

"What she said!" cried Anita as she sang along. I looked at her sad face which appeared as if she is at the brim of crying. "Uday, I made something for you", she said. "What is it now?" I replied, a little annoyed with her constant gifts. "Check this out", she said clicking on a file which opened into a slideshow. It was titled, "To Us: A Celebrated Replay." The slideshow played, showing old photographs of Anita and me together. It was an emotional moment reliving the celebrated replay of 'love'; the love story of Anita and Uday. I couldn't keep holding on to my 'coldness' and kissed Anita. She kissed me back with tears and soon we were venting out the needs of our 'habit' on each other.

When you felt me with your eyes,
And then I felt tensed, as if I lied,

For you looked at me for so long,
And to let you know, I sing this song,

When the tiny brushes of your hair,
Color your face,
And in your lost eyes, I see this disgrace,

For I embraced you in my thoughts, from dusk till dawn,
A night just passed away, and I am still enchanted and forlorn,

Please excuse me for my style so vile,
As I am already happy with you, forever in exile...

---

[138]   *Pretty much of a highway song originally written by Bob Seger.*
[139]   *A very popular American heavy metal band formed in Los Angeles, California.*

And like this, I dreamt a lot about you,
Perhaps just for a few moments,
But still, it all seems so true...

As we look so good together,
Like birds flying... covered with feathers,
When the sky encompasses everything that flies,
So are our desires - fleetly and free,
And so is me and thus is thee...

If What All You Dreamt, Came True...
I wish you had dreamt about me...
If What All You Dreamt, Came True...
I wish you had dreamt, just you and me...

As I laid comfortably in the bed while Anita stroked my 'little warrior', her eyes met mine. A strange twitch occurred on her face and she said the dreaded words which still echo in my ears. "I want to tell you something", she said coldly. "Mr. Uday Singh, always remember, you will miss your *Ferrari*[140]", she said with a hint of anger.

"Don't say that Anita", I said sadly. "I will always love you, it's just that I am so 'guilty' that I might never see myself clean again", I mumbled. "When I won't be there Uday, you will miss me", she said sadly and a couple of drops of tears poured out from the corners of her big beautiful eyes. I couldn't believe it then that such a day would actually come where I would keep missing her. Missing her day and night and compare anyone and everyone who is even remotely seductive, with her. Maybe that's the price to be paid for taking 'love' for granted. She was ready to do anything to please me, to win me back. But like I had chosen, nothing else but I would win, and so I did. Ironically for all these years since she left, I feel that my ego had won but I lost. I wanted to write about the beautiful things which 'love' showers on us, but here I am just watching the ugliness which 'love' can bring into our lives.

---

[140] *Though there might be many fast cars, but the red Ferrari is a symbol of speed, luxury and wealth. The riders of this dream vehicle say that its 'high' is a definite orgasm on the wheels.*

The rum is almost about to get over and so are the memories of Anita. But re-living the end of both is very painful. She went to the washroom while I went through her hard disk and saw a folder full of images of heart breaks, loneliness, depression and suicide. I never knew then that 'first love' can leave a scar for a lifetime.

It's always fun to hunt, but difficult must be the kill,
Swifter or mightier, Predators serve the thrill...
I can't trust this damned world!
So, just... shut up and drink my fill.

I know you 'Crave', the touch of 'Red',
The breath called life, heated to glaze,
And that's what I found, nested with you,
Hanging in your arms, and flowing through...
The flame in your eye... Lost in its candescence,
Bubbling through your effervescence,
Bloody 'time' passed by...

It's 'Blood' you need,
And 'Blood' you are...
Please don't go away,
Leaving me behind, so far...

And That's What You Are...

A tigress so wild and blood is your thrill,
As you smile by life, innocently chasing the kill.

My Lady tiger, I burn in this icy fire,
As 'time' ticks by, yet nothing flows...
Many years from then, and old we grow,
And cold I rot, in this frozen 'time'...

I know you well; you can make it through...
It's a thought I fear, of losing you,
The 'light' ain't bright on the grayish face,
Haunted by ghouls, world is a scary place...!

ON A BAD BOY NOTE

Still I will miss, your touch so warm,
The bodies I met, had souls too calm,
Frozen I am, please melt me down...
If I was a star then you are the sun,
Please give me your fire, or else I will burn...

My life is bland, and you are the spice,
I have many vices, and that's your vice...

I still fancy the incomplete sixty-nine,
Summers or winters, it's all so divine,
The way you groove, with your moves so feline,
Enchanted in your madness... Your dreams are mine.

I left with Anita on a drive to eventually drop her home. She looked broken and lost, devoid of the brilliance with which she always brimmed. All I could see was sadness and that's what I carry as I keep missing my *Ferrari*; the red beautiful super-fast car, which gives nothing else but an orgasmic thrill to its rider. "What is it that you want in a girl that I don't have?" she asked bitterly as she rested herself in the seat of the car. "I don't know", I mumbled with words that were barely audible to me. "It's okay Uday. Don't answer. But you know, I pray that you find someone whom you really adore. Someone fair and cute and perhaps shorter than you", she giggled, with tears pouring out of her eyes.

Oh my God, What have I done? How could I break the person who loved me the most? What have I done? Would I ever be able to get over this? My only pursuit since my beginning was the purest devoted 'love'. She was kind to give me much more than I deserved, completing me in every sense of my being.

Alas, I broke her heart and her faith in 'love' and its honesty. I left my worst fear in her that we all get diluted in the 'darkness'. And in my 'paranoia', I just filled 'darkness' in myself and eventually in her. I couldn't stand clean with her, with my head held high, restoring her faith that what I felt for her was true. I don't know what idealism I wanted to achieve that ignored the simplicity of 'love'. The pomp and the glory starts fading away, it's empty now, hollow in its every bit.

I wished badly that she was here cheering for me, celebrating and embracing my success which she so badly wished for.

But there is something beautiful even about the painful memories that with 'time' only the good glimpses of them occur. At least they occur to me and again I live through the memories with the last drops of alcohol. There is no point in blaming the 'dark dream', it was my own 'guilt' which was shown to me by my 'conscience', and my own 'insecurities' drove me to make it come true. "I so miss my *Ferrari, Jaan*", I say and dive down the memory lane of my treasures.

The surge to live life,
The urge to make love,
And we wandered through the streets,
With little money,
But hand in hand,
The only companion we both knew,
Was just each other...

Wherever we roamed,
You saved a souvenir,
Tickets of bus rides and cinema halls,
And your kisses so severe,

But when I look back in the memories of those days,
Only for your happiness and nothing else can I pray,
For you nurtured a demon so insincere,
And I will still miss you even when my death is near...

This is how you turn my 'Trash' into 'Treasure',
Your tears of love still flow like a river,
In the ruins of my memories,
You added love to lifeless papers...

Forgive Me... for I still see your teary eyes!
And no matter how much I try,
I can never forget the 'Story of Our Lives'...

The song is still playing on my playlist and I hum it to the memories of Anita. "How can I undo my wrong for breaking your heart?" I mumble to her photographs. Maybe getting it even is the only solution and perhaps I have to love this 'cold bitch' of a girlfriend called Tanya to an extent that she falls in 'love' with me. Perhaps loving someone obnoxious is the only redemption for breaking a heart.

I rose up in frenzy and took out my crayons and began painting the picture of a biker with bloody teary trickling down his eyes, and the cold beauty whose heart is a puzzle. And as I colored, I hummed last few words of the heartbreaking song.

The song ends in howls which I repeatedly keep singing, "I am so hollow baby, and I am so hollow..." The painful melody of a hollow self was too haunting, and it does remind me of the emptiness within. Perhaps so empty, that I can sing songs for her, forever.

I write the title of the painting, "PLZ BRK IT", hoping that perhaps Tanya would break my heart and redeem me of my sins. That maybe her pain would fill the hollow which I had left inside Anita. The morning sun is beginning to show up as the first rays lighten up the dark night to a clear sky. And like 'light' gave me another chance, a message popped in my cellphone. It was Tanya texting me early morning and it read, "Hey Uday, can we catch up today? I have managed to cancel my family appointment. Should I take the bus and travel to *Pune?* Or are you coming here? Reply whenever you read this message." I smiled with a drop of tear and crashed down to a peaceful sleep.

The 'Time' gone by, remains at halt,
Take it with pleasure, or with a pinch of salt,
A moment to treasure, and a lifetime lost,
Bloody verses of 'Love', reddened at what cost,

If Love is God and God is Blood,
Such is the irony, of this damned Curse...
What has flowed cannot return,
And this is how Destiny churns...

GOODBYE MY LOVER

When deeds buried deep, are unearthed from the grave,
And they tell stories, of a long forgotten 'crave',

The 'blood' earned it, flowing only in the brave,
Left behind a broken heart, is that what it gave...?

Perhaps there is no God, only 'Time' is supreme,
"What you sowed, one day you will reap!"
How could you be forgiven?
'Karma' awaits, even in your dreams...

LET'S GET HOPELESS TONIGHT

Let's Get Hopeless Tonight,
As I am not sure,
If I would see the daylight...

Ploughing with hope,
To free from the rope,
Of the emptiness which I caused within...

So Don't Curse Me My Love,
For the wrong which I had done,
It will follow me till my grave,
No matter how much I run...

The curse of 'love',
And I am still longing for it,
For being prodigal, indulgent,
And full of shit...!

Forgive me my love,
For breaking your heart,
As I still dwell in your memories,
And for 'love', with you it starts...

And yet to my surprise,
Your curse serves as my only light,
With the wish to be with you again,
As they say that if you miss someone so much,
Then the universe puts you back, to keep you sane...!

So let's get hopeless tonight,
To our jam in the 'Salsa',
To your eyes so bright,
Where I can dive in your lava.

ANSH SETH

Let's get hopeless tonight,
For my 'darkness' which feeds on your 'light',
As I see a lesser hope in tomorrow,
Because till then, I am all full of sorrow...

Let's raise a toast for the broken dreams,
For once they glittered with a starry gleam,
So let's get hopeless tonight,
As often a beast is born out of such plight...

EPILOGUE

On a dark windy monsoon night in *Pune*, I sit in the balcony of my short hostel building. Almost a year has passed since my MBA had started. After the initial three months in my new college, life was back to boring. Being single hasn't turned out as rewarding as I had thought. Every passing day, glimpses of Anita regularly appeared in the ruins of my memories. And each time, her kind adorable face turned sad, it questioned me for my unruly decision. With the onset of monsoons, the frequency of her memories has increased.

The light murmur of the scanty rain accompanies me as I sip the cheap yet very precious black rum which I had saved from my alcoholic batch mate and friend, 'Drunkard'.

Sleepless souls need tired bodies. My thoughts always dwelled in the excitement of not knowing what the next moment would hold... even in boredom. Friends to drink with and we all dwell in fantasies of a hopeful day when life would change.

The absence of 'blood' has perhaps caused it. When blood leaves... what remains is dead. So dead... that perhaps it's better to immerse it in rum and burn it to life again. If not in reality, then at least 'hope so' in thoughts. The charm of love also withers off, like rusted leaves falling off in winters. Life in all forms tend to hibernate... But what remains are the memories and they never part, just bubbles out in the black rum.

I guess I am yearning for alcohol even more, perhaps because of her absence... or because of the temporary lack of her replacements.

Still, like 'blood' often finds its way to the 'addicted'; in one way or the other and so does the 'dream' to me. Getting too drunk was required to ignore the hues of her absence. The new dark 'blood' is present in my glass and tonight I need to feel fine unaccompanied, without any conversation. But still why... all I see in the blur glimpses of my thoughts are the dreams we shared.

The thrill in her eyes, the charm of her soul. Her touch and her vulnerabilities. Some experiences in life are so thrilling, that exceeding them is the only way to make peace with it. And that's why I miss her... because I still crave for her. Like a predator in a cage misses its 'blood'... knowing that it will never have it again.

And all that remains is 'silence'. Even the scanty rainfall makes me feel its presence. Like the emptiness within with which the predator dwells, amongst the crowds who come to witness it daily.

It's horrible to be burdened by regret, for the choices I made, for the people I left. And still... everything around me is so silent. Silence is deep, and sometimes very creepy when all thoughts echo in its presence. And all I could do is wish for her.

My phone rings and it is Anita calling. Maybe the so called universe heard my cries, and brought her closer to me. I still want to live, I still hoped that one day she will call and we will be together again. If not, I wish to hear her at least once. She was someone to whom I can really express who I am. And what a miracle... she called!

"Hey Uday", she said in a low yet straight voice. "Hey *Jaan*", I mumble. "I miss you so much *Jaan*", I gasp, exhilarated as she broke the void forming around me day by day and surprised the daily rotting self of mine.

Anita remains silent. *"Jaan!"* I call out for her. "Uday!" she says with her husky voice, after a long pause. "I got my VISA", she blurts and goes back to being mute. 'Silences' get creepy, so much so that just any sound is good enough for ears which have longed for the voice so beloved. "To where", I mumble, feeling a shudder in my heart. "United States", she answers.

I gulp the remaining rum in my glass in a panicking hurry. "What are you saying?" I gasp in shock. "Yes", she said curtly. "How can you leave me and go *Jaan?*" I say, almost breaking into a shattering shock. "I have to go Uday", she said with a hint of hesitation.

"It's like a sudden withdrawal of hope from my life", I mumble as a stranger appeared on the corner of my eye. A tear oozed and rested on my eyelashes. "Fuck", I gasp, realizing that I have cried for the first time since I left *Mumbai.*

"Don't go *Jaan*, I miss you a lot", I say as my voice gets heavy. "You can't imagine how much I miss you", I repeat, trying to swallow the choke in my throat. "I promise I will get a good job after my MBA and then you can marry me and live with me", I mumble, but my last words were muffled by my choking throat. The bulge inside my throat maybe didn't want me to make any more promises.

"Stop Uday!" she said. "Why?" I cried. "Don't make promises", she hissed and went back to silence. Perhaps it wasn't just my choking throat which was stopping me from making 'promises', which even my system knew that I was unworthy of. Suffocated by guilt, I weep, trying to be as silent as I can.

The little future which I still see in the glimpses of my drunk hallucinations echoed back. "I never felt that you went away Nitu, you always stayed with me. I always see these visions of you and me together", I mumble softly.

"Words said in love are so pleasing that you never wanna leave them. I can't rely on you Uday, your 'love' is false and your words are deceptive. I have to go", she said with hesitation. "Please don't go", I pleaded. Anita remains silent and I continue to weep and my sobs soon turn a little louder. "I love you *Jaan*, I am sorry. I feel very lonely without you. I don't care what happened, I still wanna be with you", I cried.

"Uday", she whispers in an anxious tone. "What?" I gasp. I could hear her hesitation to speak. "What is it *Jaan?*" I muttered hurriedly as I want to listen to her so badly. "Uday", she says again and her breath races up sounding like a mild cry remotely arising in her soul. "Tell me *Jaan*, I am getting worried", I mutter. The silences in her hesitation felt like an implosion about to happen.

"I slept with someone", she blurts the words out and in her voice, the remote cry became closer. I remain stunned and my 'laments' exploded. 'Silence' returned but brought a miserable friend along with the murmuring rain. It were her cries as she continues to weep.

"As in...? With whom?" I manage to spit the words out. "An old friend", she says in a while. "When?" I ask with my choking throat. "Two days back", she continues weeping.

No words could come out of my mouth. No wits shone their glory in my head. "What if it came back?" I say to myself thinking about the long forgotten dream.

"What's his name?" I ask coldly. Anita continues to cry. "Tell me", I mumble as I feel that even my heart is resonating with her tears. "I can't", she wails out. "Did you guys do it?" I ask holding my certain anguish. I waited for her answer and silence killed both of us there. She wailed louder, and it resonated on both ends. We cried together as tears smeared our thoughts, hearts and faces with regret.

"Why?" I cry with her. "How did it happen?" I sob along, asking my most dreaded question. "We got drunk with friends in a bar and I happened to go to his house along with him", she says in a frail voice. My heart pounds louder anticipating the moment of 'doom'. "And then?" I said with the last bit of courage left in me. "We were on the sofa and talking and...." she continues crying. "Say it!" I yell at her, wanting to hear my punishment. "Say it Nitu, say it *Jaan*. Please stop crying!" I beg but she just wouldn't stop.

That moment felt like an earthquake crumbling down all our dreams. The colorful fantasies just got engulfed in a dark cloud, recreating those dreadful ripples of my dark dream. I take a gulp of my neat dark rum, straight from the bottle, hoping to pacify the shock. "But then, why am I shocked? It had to happen!" a thought steamed inside my heart, perhaps because of the hellish fire of the undiluted black alcohol.

I silently listen to her cry and she continues to weep. I felt enraged, on her and everybody, and most of all on the God of Judgment. But when broken dreams of love reek of fiery drunken thoughts, even rage turns cold. "Did you 'cum'?" I ask coldly with the choking throat which has begun to hurt me as I talk. She hesitates to speak. "Answer Anita", I gagged angrily. "Yes", she cries and begins wailing. Her cries slice my conscious, accusing me for all my sins, leaving behind scars of ghastly consequences. And then she mumbles something amidst tears. I tried hard to hear her clearly. She said, "I took your name..."

"What?" I gasp in shock. Anita continued to sob, while her last words left me bleeding with love. Our 'red' wasn't a lie, and it yet again brought back the love. "It wasn't her fault. She always loved me, it's me who made her do this", I murmured regretting all my deeds.

"What have I done?" I sighed, listening to her final words. "I am sorry *Jaan*", she wails and cries. "It's not your fault *Jaan*. Don't cry please, it's my fault. I drove you to this!" I mumble listening to her breaking down. "I love you *Jaan*, I love you a lot", I howled. "I love you too Uday", she cried out her last few broken words.

"I am sorry *Jaan*", I sob along the drops of guilt and regret which boiled inside, "I am sorry *Jaan*, I am so sorry", and I cry pouring them out.

"Don't ever curse me *Jaan*, because then I will always curse myself. In fact, I am still living it. The curse of your absence", I sob my tears as I hear her voice break down in the murmuring scanty rainfall.

In many such horrendous ways My Love,
That Nightmare keeps fucking with my 'hope',
As this is how the gift of Karma works,
It took you away,
And your love stayed back like a curse...

ANSH SETH

If I have a way to get you back,
Make you forget my deeds,
And plaster the crack...

For I still dwell with you,
In lurking sobs of my hidden views,
Of the painting you made on my soul,
Are glimpses of 'us', written only for you...

The beauty of our destiny,
Is tainted with my crime,
Like the wind which hums,
Many such wind chimes...
Only for love in the mystery of 'time',
Returned the 'God of Judgment',
What always remained mine!

As fate returns the deeds I owed,
Killing me with silence,
And Choking my throat,
I will always love you...
On A Bad Boy Note...

Why am I so scared,
To reap the fruits of what I sowed,
As that's the law of Karma,
Pleading forgiveness...
and with that I wrote,
For being such a fucking moron,
And FUCK THIS BAD BOY NOTE...

Printed in the United States
By Bookmasters